Impressively original, inherently fascinating, imaginatively thought provoking, and a fun and compelling read from start to finish, (and all the more impressive considering that this is her debut as a novelist), author Susan L. Davis' *63 Hours in Hell* from Abundance Books deftly combines a Christian themed and epic fantasy with a wealth of surprising quest style action/adventure plot twists and turns. One of those unusual and unique novels that will linger in the mind and memory of the reader long after the book is finished and set back upon the shelf, *63 Hours in Hell* is especially and unreservedly recommended for personal reading lists, as well as community and college/university library Literary Fiction and Christian Fantasy collections.

Midwest Book Review

The biblical narrative has been preserved for us in the form of story, inviting us to use our imaginations, to seek to understand its truths from the inside out. Susan L. Davis's *63 Hours in Hell* is a genre-bending, far-reaching exploration, leading us in this use of our sacred imaginations, taking us on a quest to more profoundly comprehend the gift of redemption, now and in the age to come.

—**David J. Marsh**, author of the award-winning novels
*The Confessions of Adam and Waterborne:
Chronicle of the Clan of Noah*

Susan L. Davis draws the reader into a dark world of demons, sinners, and unlikely saints in this unique tale of what may have happened between the crucifixion and Jesus' ascension into Heaven. Rich in imagery, drama, and action, *63 Hours in Hell* is a journey fraught with twists and turns as the characters embark on an unprecedented quest that captivates from beginning to end.

> —**Susan Miura**, author of the award-winning *Healer* series and *Signs in the Dark*.

Enthralled! That's how you'll feel as you read the pages of *63 Hours in Hell*. Susan L. Davis masterfully weaves biblical characters and historical settings into a tale so gripping, you'll let your to-do list gather dust just to see what's next. More than just a story, it's a journey of faith, love, and redemption. Like a rich cup of coffee, it lingers long after the last page.

> —**Robyn Dykstra**, national Christian speaker and author of the bestseller, *The Widow Wore Pink*

Gripping from the very first page, *63 Hours in Hell* pulled me into Davis's descriptive depiction of the spiritual world. Woven with scripture and biblical references, the narrative takes the reader on a fascinating journey, not holding back on Satan's wickedness or Christ's miraculous power, Davis makes the spiritual world come to life, reminding us the devil is alive and active, but so is our Great God. After reading it, I have a renewed appreciation for my faith. I'm so glad I'm on team Jesus.

> —**Jenna Brooke Carlson**, author of *Falling Flat*

Captivating and powerful, *63 Hours in Hell* by Susan L. Davis takes readers on a profound journey through darkness and redemption. With a rich blend of scripture and imagination, Davis vividly portrays the battle between good and evil, leading us to a deeper reflection on Christ's victory and the cost of our salvation.

—**Amber Weigand-Buckley**, multi-award-winning author and founding editor of Leading Hearts magazine

Step into an unforgettable journey where faith collides with darkness, and redemption battles against the forces of evil. In *63 Hours in Hell*, Susan L. Davis reimagines the spiritual realms during the three days between the crucifixion and resurrection. With richly drawn characters and vivid, immersive storytelling, this tale of love, sacrifice, and the ultimate battle for souls will captivate and challenge your understanding of divine grace. Will the light of hope endure, even in the heart of hell?!

—**Kathryn Dare**, *Chicago Book Review*

A fascinating read. You'll be enthralled before you turn even the second page! What a world to explore here. Of course, there's plenty of talk of "heavenly tourism" where people come back from heaven to tell their stories, but this one is from the other side. I dare you to read the first chapter and see if you can walk away.

—**Brad McDaniel**, author of *The Secret to Hearing God's Voice*

63 Hours in Hell

BY SUSAN L. DAVIS

63 Hours in Hell
Copyright © 2025 by Susan L. Davis.

ISBN: 978-1-963377-23-1 (print)
ISBN: 978-1-963377-35-4 (ePub)
ISBN: 978-1-963377-37-8 (audio)

Published by: Abundance Books, LLC
Kalamazoo, Michigan

The information contained in this book is the intellectual property of Susan L. Davis and is governed by United States and International copyright laws. All rights reserved. No part of this publication, either text or image, may be used for any purpose other than personal use. Therefore, reproduction, modification, storage in a retrieval system, or retransmission, in any form or by any means, electronic, mechanical, or otherwise, for reasons other than personal use, except for brief quotations for reviews or articles and promotions, is strictly prohibited without prior written permission by the publisher.

This is a work of fiction. Names, characters, businesses, places, events, locales, and incidents are either the products of the author's imagination or used in a fictitious manner. Any resemblance to actual persons, living or dead, or actual events is purely coincidental.

Scripture quotations marked ESV are taken from The Holy Bible, English Standard Version® (ESV®). Copyright © 2001 by Crossway Bibles, a publishing ministry of Good News Publishers. All rights reserved.

Scripture quotations marked HCSB are taken from the Holman Christian Standard Bible. Copyright © 1999, 2000, 2002, 2003, 2009 by Holman Bible Publishers, Nashville Tennessee. All rights reserved.

Scriptures marked NLT are taken from the HOLY BIBLE, NEW LIVING TRANSLATION (NLT), Copyright© 1996, 2004, 2007 by Tyndale House Foundation. Used by permission of Tyndale House Publishers, Inc., Carol Stream, Illinois 60188. All rights reserved. Used by permission.

10 9 8 7 6 5 4 3 2 1

Printed in the United States of America

63 Hours in Hell

by Susan L. Davis

Susan L Davis

Abundance Books

In loving memory of Ginger Kolbaba (1967-2022), my mentor and editor — the spark behind this story. Our writing journey concludes, but your heartfelt tales endure. Countless authors, shaped by your guidance, will bear your legacy, inspiring generations to come.

Contents

Prologue	i
Chapter 1	1
Chapter 2	7
Chapter 3	13
Chapter 4	19
Chapter 5	35
Chapter 6	49
Chapter 7	61
Chapter 8	73
Chapter 9	79
Chapter 10	89
Chapter 11	103
Chapter 12	113
Chapter 13	121
Chapter 14	131
Chapter 15	135
Chapter 16	147
Chapter 17	153
Chapter 18	167
Chapter 19	179
Chapter 20	197
Chapter 21	199
Chapter 22	209
Chapter 23	217

Chapter 24	227
Chapter 25	229
Chapter 26	237
Chapter 27	243
Chapter 28	251
Chapter 29	253
Chapter 30	263
Chapter 31	271
Chapter 32	275
Chapter 33	283
Chapter 34	289
Chapter 35	293
Chapter 36	299
Chapter 37	303
Chapter 38	309
Chapter 39	313
Author's Note	317
APPENDIX A	318
APPENDIX B	320
Cast of Characters	327
Discussion Questions	328
Acknowledgements	330
About the Author	334

Prologue

I will put hostility between you and the woman,
and between your seed and her seed.
He will strike your head,
and you will strike his heel.
—Genesis 3:15 (HCSB)

Outside the Garden of Eden,
4000 BC

Last night was the first time Adam hadn't mentioned her role in their downfall. It's his fault, too.

Adam had sat next to Eve when the devil tricked her. He could have stopped her from biting into the fruit. But as with every other time they discussed their sin, Adam reminded her about the perfection in the garden and how everything was ruined now. Eve fumed as hot tears slipped through her lashes. How dare he make her feel unworthy. God should have protected us from the serpent. "If a place is named Paradise," she had questioned, "why would God allow evil to enter?"

When Eve accused God of their predicament, Adam's handsome face turned rigid, and he'd bite his plump lower lip as he retreated out the door away from her — from them. Then, the unbearable silence stretched for days. Eve couldn't even talk to the animals now. How she missed confiding in Chaber. God had taken away her lion friend, too. But last night, Eve made an amazing discovery: a delicious meal had ended the silent treatment.

After dinner, Adam surprised her with a wooden cradle. Eve grinned as she remembered her husband's joyful expression over his creation. She patted her enlarged stomach and trudged to the grove, twig basket in hand. Tonight, she would create another mouth-watering dish, desiring to extend his pleasant mood. By the time the baby arrived, she hoped to restore their former love, before their enemy had ruined everything.

Eve forced herself to walk past the apple grove to get to the cherry trees. She kicked a rotten apple core lying on the ground. Adam would not appreciate that fruit in any form. Finally, she reached the trees full of ripe cherries, and soon, her twig basket overflowed with the sweet fruit.

A sharp pain stabbed Eve's back, radiating down her thighs. She groaned. The extra baby weight was taking its toll on her once slim and curvy body. As she gingerly placed the basket on the ground, she saw the nearby grass blades sway.

A forked tongue flicked above the weeds.

Eve froze.

The snake raised its hooded head and glared at her before it slithered in the opposite direction.

The hair on Eve's neck stood on end. She recognized that snake. "I hate you, Devil!" she shouted.

An icy breeze whispered back, "I hate you more."

A strong gust of cold air lifted her twig basket and slammed it back to the ground, scattering the berries.

She hadn't seen the serpent since that dreadful moment in the garden. Why was he back? *Can it be the child I carry?*

Eve recalled the prophecy God had delivered to her and her husband after they ate the forbidden fruit. He'd said their offspring would crush the devil's head. Eve's baby kicked in her womb as though he knew he had a part to play in the inevitable battle between Good and Evil.

"That's right, Baby." She caressed her stomach. "You will right what your parents have wronged."

The second part of God's message brought fear, though: "But

he will bruise your heel." The devil wanted to hurt her child. What did God mean by "bruise?" Maybe it wouldn't be fatal? Eve didn't care. She vowed to see the entire prophecy fulfilled — no matter the cost.

Eve glanced at her overturned basket — the cherries smashed in the grass like bursts of blood. She sighed. Her long walk and efforts were wasted. Why do I keep making bad decisions? Now, she'd have to hurry to have Adam's dinner ready. Every day, he came home famished from toiling in that godforsaken field of thorns. The shortcut past the Garden of Eden was not an option: a cherub still guarded the entrance with a flaming sword. Their lovely paradise was now a prison, complete with iron bars constructed by the angels, all designed to keep them out.

Soon, Chaber would be on the prowl, looking to devour his next meal. She'd strayed too far from home. Not home, she reminded herself. Never like Paradise.

In the garden, everything had been at their fingertips — no hunger, no sickness, and no sadness. The animals cuddled with her and Adam instead of hunting them. She and Adam laughed instead of arguing. And God. Every evening, he walked and talked with them. If she tried, sometimes she could still hear Him, but his voice faded with each passing day.

Eve kept a watchful eye over her shoulder until she reached the safety of their hut. Why couldn't Adam forgive her? Should she admit everything was her fault? Would that appease him? No. Adam had been right next to her when that snake had offered the fruit. And what about God allowing the snake into the garden in the first place?

Eve sighed again. Enough. She had to stop rehearsing the hurts of the past if she wanted a future.

She peeked into her basket. A few smashed cherries floated in blood-red juice at the bottom. There might be enough to make a delectable sauce. Eve debated telling Adam about her latest run-in with the enemy. She didn't want to worry him. He seemed concerned about the childbirth process. Her hands trembled as she touched her protruding stomach. God had warned them giving birth would be painful. She decided to remain silent until their baby entered the world. Then, she would inform Adam of the devil's plan to harm their child.

Tonight, she'd focus on making Adam happy. She would be the perfect helpmate.

1

On the whole world there pressed a most fearful darkness.

—Thallus, as quoted in
Ante-Nicene Christian Library Volume IX

Jerusalem, Nissan AD 33
Thursday, near the ninth hour, 3:00 p.m.

"I'll never forgive Father for what he's done." Hannah slid a silk pillow under Old Scribe's wrinkled head. His long silvery beard speckled with droplets spilled to the white marble floor.

"Pontius Pilate sentenced the false prophet to die. Not Father." Her fifteen-year-old brother knelt beside the elderly man's lower body on the marble bench built into the ivory wall.

"No, Benjamin. Father helped arrest Jesus. Our father along with all the members of the Sanhedrin court are executioners cloaked in self-righteousness." Last night's Passover lamb and bitter herbs clawed at Hannah's throat. She swallowed the sharp taste of dandelion leaves; how could they condemn an innocent man to death?

"We don't know if he's dead." Benjamin stood. "I refuse to nurse this drunkard while Father and the servants—even Mother—are all at the Skull. I'm going."

"Not alone." Hannah snatched her sandals and wrapped the leather straps around her ankles. "I believe Jesus is alive. Maybe he escaped. He disappeared like mist in a crowd before."

Benjamin snuffed out the oil lamps. "This will be a death adventure. For being so learned, you know nothing."

Hannah glared at her brother and placed a blanket over Old

Scribe. "How can you say such a thing after Pontius Pilate placed a curse on our generation?"

"We have nothing to fear. Jesus is the false prophet. He's the one destined for death today. Not us."

"When did you stop believing?" Hannah demanded. "I know you felt power radiating from Jesus when he prayed over you. You were a mere child, and Jesus stood up for you that day when his disciples tried swatting you away like a fly."

His acorn eyes flashed. "I became a man and stopped believing in childish fables." He waved Hannah away like an annoying child instead of a twenty-one-year-old woman.

"A man? Yesterday I saw you climb a tree—when you should have been memorizing Torah," scolded Hannah.

"Stop spying on me and look for your husband."

Hannah tensed. She pulled a cloth from her robe pocket and walked toward Old Scribe. "I'm not leaving him alone in this state."

Benjamin opened the front door. "Pitch black in the middle of the day."

The little hairs stood up on the back of Hannah's neck. Her ears rang, and her stomach swirled like the sea before a storm, just like the day Seth had disappeared.

Hannah dabbed the cloth on Old Scribe's forehead. His eyes opened, making her squeak in surprise.

The man's eyes were bloodshot, and he shoved her hand away. Old Scribe's voice wavered but gained strength with each word, "The day Amos spoke of has arrived, 'I will make the sun go down at noon; I will darken the land in the daytime. I will turn your feasts into mourning, like mourning for an only son, and its outcome like a bitter day.'" With a sigh, he tossed the towel over his eyes. His heavy breathing transformed into a sputtering snore.

Hannah dropped into a nearby chair, convinced by his words that something horrible would happen if they left the house.

"This isn't right. I promised Mother we'd stay home and pray for Jesus."

Benjamin spun around, eyes flashing. "How dare you tell me what to do? Since Father's gone, I am the head of the household!"

Every day he acted more and more like Father, ordering her and Mother around like sheep. If Seth hadn't disappeared, they'd be together and not stuck in her father's home.

He'll come back for me. Hannah twisted and played with her wedding band, her only soul link to Seth. Seven years had made her fingers thin, compared to when he had placed the ring on her hand. Should she obey her mother and stay home or see if they'd crucified Jesus?

Not Jesus. Fresh tears welled, stinging her dry eyes. *Not Jesus.*

Her ring slipped off, clinking on the tile, and rolling toward her brother.

Benjamin snatched her prized possession and raced through the entryway. "I'll give it back at the Skull," he taunted.

Hannah leapt and rushed out the door, gathering her violet robe in one hand, rushed out the door chasing her brother, yelling, "I'm going to get you," Her finger felt naked without her ring.

Benjamin's long legs carried him across the darkened courtyard in no time.

Hannah's sandals click-clacked on the mosaic tile in pursuit. The side gate stood closed. Benjamin tinkered with the latch. Maybe God's blessing rested on her. Soon, the ring would be back on her finger where it belonged.

A gust of wind forced open the gate, and her brother breezed through the gap. In only a few steps, Benjamin would reach the stone road.

Hannah panted, trying to catch up. She had to get her ring

back. He could drop it on the way to the Skull, and it would be lost forever.

Just then, a powerful force barreled into her, followed by guttural neighing. She collapsed to the street, her neck and head bearing the brunt of her fall. She covered her face as horses' hooves stomped her thighs and stomach, crushed her ribs, and stepped on her shoulder, which flipped Hannah onto her stomach just before the cold iron wheels of the Roman chariot rolled over her back.

"Prohibere! Prohibere!" a Roman yelled.

Waves of pain crashed over her. More neighing came closer, and Hannah assumed there might be two chariots.

No! Where was Benjamin? Why wasn't he coming to rescue her? *Did he get hit, too?* Over the horses' squeals, she tried to call out his name but could only groan.

Lord, help me. Forgive me for everything I said and thought about my father. Forgive me for breaking the commandment to honor him. Lord, if you let me live, I will be perfect. No, that would be a lie. She couldn't follow those rules—nobody could. *Cover me with the Passover lamb. Isn't that enough or, Lord, are you just like my father?*

More pain shot through her body, ending her pathetic bargaining. Why should he spare her?

Where is Benjamin?

"Stupid boy darted into the road. The woman followed. I never saw them in the dark," a thick Roman accent barked in broken Aramaic.

The nerve of the barbarian to blame her! *He* had run her down like a stray dog.

"My beasts and chariot are splattered with blood," the voice said again. "Who is the boy's father? He is going to pay to clean this mess."

Hannah forced herself to lift her head. The darkness was too thick to see anything.

"You plebeian Romans sprinting down the streets!" Hannah recognized the gruff voice of the Old Scribe. "Did you think you were back in the Maximus competing in the chariot circus? You swerved and killed that boy."

Benjamin's dead? No. No. No! He can't be dead. She tried to turn her head again to see her brother, but the pain wouldn't let her move her neck. *Old Scribe got it wrong*, she tried to convince herself.

"You saw nothing, old man. You're drunk. That boy and woman ran into the road. It's all their fault."

Oh, Benjamin, why did I chase you like a foolish child? I should have stayed home where it was safe. Hannah began to shake uncontrollably. Her teeth chattered. Hot blood gushed inside her mouth.

Something wrinkly touched her hand. *Old Scribe*. He reeked of his favorite wine and old scrolls, reminding her of all the times she had spent reading to him.

She tried squeezing his hand but managed to move only her pinky.

"Fight. Hannah, you can make it," Old Scribe slurred.

In that moment, she realized she was going to die, not of old age or in childbirth, but lying undignified and alone on this dirty road. Images of her mother, father, brother, and Seth flashed before her.

"Though I walk through the valley of the shadow of death, I will fear no evil," she forced her lips to move. "For you are with me; your rod and your staff, they comfort me." Fear covered her like an icy blanket. *This can't be the end.*

The ground vibrated under Hannah.

Everything went black.

2

At the sixth hour [i.e., noon] that excelled every other before it, turning the day into such darkness of night that the stars could be seen in heaven, turned and the earth moved in Bithynia, toppling many buildings of the city of Nicaea.

—Phlegon of Tralles, as quoted in The Chronography of George Synkellos

Golgotha, outside the walls of Jerusalem
Almost the fifth hour, 11:00 a.m.

A raven flew overhead. Soon, the bird would peck at Dismas' rotting flesh. *I'll be a skull at the Skull.* Golgotha had always creeped him out—the ghoulish cave eyes and rounded mouth formed a giant skull imprinted on the hillside.

Dismas tried accepting his fate. If only his body would stop fighting. He sealed his lips, trying to speed up the dying process by holding his breath. His chest rose instinctively, and a tiny puff of air escaped one nostril. *No.* Dismas' flesh became his enemy, death his new friend.

His raw back scraped the rough wood, and a splinter jabbed him. *Agony!* Cruel how a splinter could bother him even as three rusty nails pierced through his wrists and feet held him in place, displayed like a grotesque piece of art created by twenty years of lousy decisions and miserable circumstances.

Dismas wasn't alone in this torture. Hanging on a second cross to his left was Jesus, a man who claimed to be the Anointed One. *God's Son—whoever heard of such a crazy thing.* On Jesus' other side, Gestas dangled from the third cross. Now Gestas—that murderer—deserved to die, but not Dismas.

He had the urge to curse God's name and shock all these holy men gathered to gloat over Jesus. Let them add blasphemy to Dismas' list of crimes. *What do rules matter now?*

The full sun scorched his naked flesh. Beads of sweat rolled down his back. The faces of the mob blurred, and Dismas clamped down on his cracked lip until blood oozed. No, he would not faint like a feeble woman. He heard incessant ringing in his ears. *Relax, it's the bells of the high priest's robe clamoring around Jesus like a lion going in for the kill.*

Above the noise of the crowd, Caiaphas, the high priest, demanded, "If you are the Son of God, come off that cross! Perform a miracle that we might believe you."

Anger flared. *Miracles.* Their God handed out misery, not miracles.

Dismas despised all priests since the day they had torched his childhood home. Wasn't it enough they had banished his father to the leper colony? Did the priests have to make him and his mother homeless, too?

Despite the pain, Dismas pressed down on his mangled feet to lift himself up enough to breathe. He drew in air and said in a throaty voice, "Yes! If you are God's Son, the Christ, descend from that cross so we may see and believe."

"If you're the Messiah, prove it by saving yourself and us," hissed Gestas, his voice a croak of seething hatred.

Jesus remained silent.

Rocks pelted Dismas on the cheek. "Yes! Got him right on that ugly scar," a boy jeered.

Another young boy yelled, "Easy target. You couldn't miss that red mark." The wicked horde erupted in laughter.

Dismas hated the mark stretching from his left eye to his chin and the man who had inflicted it. Barabbas, his so-called stepfather, the drunk who had raised him and taught him how to steal. By age thirteen, to Dismas' relief, his new coarse beard had started to conceal a portion of his wound. But he couldn't cover it all. What did his mother see in such a man?

Maybe he possessed an unknown magical power. Earlier, Pontius Pilate had presented a choice to the crowd: free Barabbas or Jesus. They voted to free Barabbas. *Barabbas.* If there was a God—*if*—he sure had a cruel sense of humor. Barabbas being released seemed the harshest joke of all. The barbarian boasted of being a dagger-wielding assassin, mimicking the mighty Sicarii assassins. Some witnesses had informed the Romans that Barabbas was nothing more than a thief, robbing spice caravans. Had Barabbas's murder victim been able to speak, there would have been a fourth cross.

The one useful skill Barabbas had taught Dismas was the art of weaponry. How Dismas now longed to feel a cold dagger in his hand and fight his way out of here. A stone slammed against his cheek, interrupting his thoughts. He tried puckering his mouth to spit on the wicked boy clutching rocks.

"Ignore them, they don't know the pain the scar caused you. It wasn't your fault," Jesus whispered with compassion.

Dismas bowed his head in shame. A single tear escaped his eye. Jesus couldn't have known what had happened all those years ago.

Boys cry; men get revenge. Barabbas's words echoed in Dismas' head.

Dismas hadn't shed a tear in years. *Death must be near,* he reasoned. Why else would a few kind words from Jesus twist him up inside and cause him to act like a woman?

"Father," Jesus raised his voice. "Forgive them, for they don't know what they do."

I'm not forgiving anyone, especially not Barabbas.

The boy dropped the rocks and darted back to the safety of his mother at the edge of the crowd.

"If you are the King of the Jews, come down off that cross and save me." Gestas continued to harass Jesus.

Dismas stole another breath and forced his lips to move. "Leave Jesus alone. Barabbas is the only one getting saved today."

"By now, Barabbas is drunk, celebrating his freedom." Gestas gasped. "But you won't be there to protect your mother from his fists." The fool's signature cackle turned into cries of pain.

"Shut your filthy mouth," wheezed Dismas, sorry he had wasted his breath. He had never understood why his mother stayed with Barabbas. *Couldn't Pontius Pilate have picked me to be released instead of Barabbas? Then, Mother and I both would be free.*

Out of the corner of his eye, Dismas saw someone waving as though trying to get his attention. The man resembled his father, before the leprosy had eaten his face into a bizarre honeycomb pattern of lumps and bumps.

Impossible.

It couldn't be his father. This man's face was smooth and pock-free. The wine and gall he had sucked off a sponge to ease his pain must be making him see things. Dismas blinked, watching the man try to elbow his way through the priests and Roman guards. They didn't budge.

Now the persistent man jumped and yelled. "Dismas, it's me! Your father." He pointed to his face in an exaggerated manner and smiled tenderly. "Jesus healed me from leprosy!"

Dismas' heart froze and his blood rushed in his ears. *Jesus healed my father. This man next to me did that for my father? Then—he really is the Son of God.* He turned his face toward Jesus and pressed down on his feet. He paused and gulped trying to fill his lungs with air to speak. "I deserve to die, but you've done nothing wrong. Lord, remember me when you enter into your kingdom."

Compassion mixed with pain flooded Jesus' eyes. "Today, you shall be with me in Paradise."

Dismas murmured in thankful agreement as another spasm tore through his ankles. He continued to stare at his father, still a good distance away. He would try holding on to Jesus' promise of Paradise in the middle of this torment.

***

The sixth hour, 12:00 p.m.

The wind roared, lashing invisible whips across Dismas' raw wounds. In the sky, a black veil descended and blotted out the sun. *How can this be?* The unnatural darkness fooled the stars into shining hours too early.

People scattered, toppling baskets, crushing broken pieces of unleavened bread under their sandals. The holy men stared agape at the black sky.

A priest in a white linen robe observed, "The texture of the black layer concealing the sun looks like goat hair, a sackcloth."

"The sun appears in mourning," another shaky voice added.

A few Roman guards broke rank as they muttered something about Zeus being angry. Once darkness covered everything, the temple guards and Roman soldiers clutched torches and formed a wide circle around the crosses, prohibiting anyone from getting closer. In the chaos of the engulfing darkness, Dismas lost track of his father.

He welcomed the night sky since it covered his nakedness, kept him cool from the relentless sun, and silenced the spectators' cruel mouths.

***

The ninth hour, 3:00 p.m.

Dismas heard Jesus gasp for air, his breath like a death rattle.

"Father," he cried out, "into your hands, I commit my spirit. It—is—" he took in another breath and shouted, "Finished!" Jesus' head fell forward, and Dismas knew he had died.

A Roman guard pierced his spear into Jesus' side. Water and blood gushed to the ground around the cross.

The earth trembled violently, shaking the crosses and causing the nails to rip through Dismas' body. *Agony!*

"Earthquake!" a priest shrieked as rocks fell and the crowd scrambled away.

A halo of light rose from within Jesus, hovering above his lifeless body. The glow eased Dismas' pain, allowing him to steal a shallow breath. But when the strange radiance blasted toward the city, Dismas' pain returned with a vengeance, spreading like wildfire throughout his body. *Lord, please end this pain—take me to Paradise!*

The ground rumbled again. A lone figure ran toward the crosses despite the swaying land.

"Wait!" the man cried. It was Dismas' father. Now that he was closer, Dismas could see he truly was healed. "Is your mother alive?" he said, face etched with determination.

Dismas tried separating his parched, cracked lips but lacked the strength to answer. Yet, he found some comfort—he wouldn't die alone.

A Roman guard wielding a club stumbled toward Dismas. "You are taking too long to die. These good people want to celebrate their holy day." The earthquake ended, and the Roman guard swung the club, shattering his kneecaps—the death blow. Dismas collapsed, unable to inhale. He closed his eyes as the anguish mercifully left his body.

3

The curtain had embroidered upon it all that was mystical in the Heavens … representing the living creatures.

—Flavius Josephus, War of the Jews Book V

Immediately after the sixth hour

The temple priest's shofar woke Dismas. He recognized the high-pitched blasts, announcing the evening sacrifice. Each blare from the ram's horn blew away his brain fog as images flashed through his thoughts. *Cross. Agony. My father healed of leprosy. Jesus.*

Dismas braced for the next torrent of pain to rush his body. Nothing.

He realized his arms were free, not nailed to a cross, and he wore a crisp linen robe. No longer naked. *Who dressed me? Am I dead?*

Dismas stared at his feet, clad in white leather sandals. He stood on a wide stone beam approximately three stories above a dimly lit room. Suspended beneath the beam hung a solid gold rod adorned with thick golden rings, holding an extravagant blue, purple, and red veil plunging to the floor. Dismas' brown hair skimmed the shimmery ceiling. Lilies and palm trees were engraved into the pure gold ceiling. A would-be thieves' paradise. *Peculiar. What is this place?*

Dismas exhaled, surprised he could. Nothing made any sense. Either he should be suffering on the cross or dead. Not wearing an unfamiliar white robe marred with black spots, perched on a beam above an unknown room.

As he inhaled, he smelled sweet incense. The flicker of flames caught his attention. He pivoted to find a second room. *The altar of incense. The table of showbread. The golden candlestick.* Dismas sneezed—the incense failed to conceal the roasting meat intermingled with the foul smells of live animals. He recognized that nauseating yet familiar stench.

He gasped in recognition. *No, it can't be.* In the courtyard, the priest slaughtered the beasts and then sacrificed the offerings over the brazen altar. Next to the altar was the cleansing laver where the priests purified themselves from the blood-splattered sacrifices. That meant this room was . . .

"The holy of holies," he whispered in awe.

Fear flooded Dismas. Somehow, he had been taken from the Skull to Herod's Temple. He stood on the curtain separating the holy of holies and the holy place, as if the two rooms couldn't gaze upon each other. A thief like him would never be worthy to stand here. Only the high priest had permission to enter the holy of holies once a year.

I'm dead. How else could I be in such a place?

If he weren't dead, the priests would kill him for such blasphemy. Dismas gazed back at the holy of holies. His father had told him the inner sanctuary was the center of the universe—the place where God, heaven, and earth intersected. Dismas' eyes adjusted to the dim light from the seven lamps of the golden candlestick. The holy of holies stood barren.

The ark of the covenant had disappeared long ago when the Babylonians sacked the city, carting off every piece of gold and silver, and leveling Solomon's Temple. In place of the ark was the gray foundation stone. Supposedly, God had created Adam, the first human, on that rock.

Balancing himself, Dismas leaned over to get a better look. Drops of crusty blood stained the middle of the gray rock where the high priest sprinkled the blood of bulls, begging forgiveness for Israel's sins, hoping and praying God would show them mercy in the coming year. After the priest's pleading, God would make an appearance in a cloud from the mercy seat, with a hand-delivered verdict of blessing or cursing.

Dismas remembered when his father developed leprosy—the cursed year when the high priest didn't make it out alive. The other priests had fished out the corpse with ropes since they couldn't leave a decaying body inside the room nor were they allowed to enter the holy of holies.

Dismas' legs wobbled, dizzy from the overpowering aroma of incense. *This can't be Paradise. How am I going to get down?* Maybe he could grab the thick curtain and climb down. His thin frame couldn't rip the indestructible fabric—his father had told him it took over three hundred priests to remove the veil.

A whiff of smoke rose from the cracks on the blood-stained stone, then billowed into a cloud, rapidly filling the room. Dismas felt a weighty presence as the room started to shake and spin. The gold walls seemed to melt, forming into two oversized angelic figures. Their expanding wings filled the chamber, touching the opposite walls, and a second set of gold wings concealed their bodies. One cherub had the face of a lion and the other had the face of an ox.

Now hovering above the center of the foundation stone, the cloud started to flash and crackle like small strikes of lightning. The gold walls, ceiling, floor, and statues gleamed from the light. Then, the cloud disappeared, leaving behind the ark of the covenant. On top of the ark were two smaller cherubs, one with a man's face and the other with an eagle's face. Their wings met and formed a canopy, covering the ark's lid—the mercy seat.

This can't be real! Am I a prophet seeing visions? The ark, the cherubim, the cloud. I'm dead, and it's Judgment Day. God is going to judge my life for the wrongs I've committed and all the charitable deeds I neglected—both long lists.

Dismas looked back at the ark. He knew the tablets of the Ten Commandments were inside. Throughout his life, he had broken the eighth commandment: Do not steal. He was certain

God kept track of every rule he'd broken. *Calm down. Breathe.*

A warm wind blew through the windowless room, and the ark began to sway. With each sway, it gained momentum—rocking back and forth, faster and faster, like a rowboat in a storm. The cherubim looked as though they would take flight. The large statues seemed to stand still, though Dismas swore the lion winked at him and the ox smirked.

The wind ceased and the ark stopped its wild dance. The honey-colored mercy seat slid open. A man's fist emerged and slowly began opening, stretching, and shaking as if working out a cramp. On the palm was inscribed a multitude of names—somehow, Dismas spied his own name, and his eyes widened. *The hand of God!*

The hand soared toward him. Waves of fear washed through Dismas' body. God's hand of judgment was coming for him. Now the hand hovered one inch from his face. Dismas braced himself for a slap. But instead, the hand caressed the scar on his face like a mother's touch. Dismas jerked backward, which caused his foot to slip. He stumbled and lost his balance. But two hands grabbed him from behind while the hand of God held his chest. The three hands helped him regain his footing on the beam. He pivoted to see who was behind him.

Jesus.

He flashed a reassuring smile, though his face was bruised and his wrists wounded from the nails. Jesus wore a heavy black robe and black sandals.

"Don't be afraid," Jesus said, but Dismas' hands shook and his thoughts swirled like leaves caught in a tempest. He wanted to question Jesus but didn't dare speak.

God's hand dropped below Dismas' foot and clutched the top of the curtain. Jesus knelt on the beam and placed his hand next to his Father's. Together, they tore the enormous veil from top to bottom. The ripping of the veil echoed throughout the tomb-like quietness of the temple.

Why would they destroy the sacred curtain?

Within moments, priests rushed into the holy room, their sandals pounding against the purple-veined, white marble floor. Horrified, half the priests covered their eyes. While some dove to the ground, others scurried away in fear.

"Impossible!" one priest said, his face as white as his priestly garment. "H-How did it rip?"

"It's a ghost!" A priest fell to his knees and begged God for forgiveness.

The pious priests have no idea what is going on.

Another holy man waved his arms. "Quick, get some thread before anyone sees."

Dismas watched the hand of God as it flew out from the bottom of the curtain, past the candlestick room, and headed for the front of the temple. Then, the palm pressed open the massive brass doors and disappeared.

Jesus flashed Dismas a triumphant smile as he stood at the bottom of the split curtain. "No longer will we be contained to this room."

Peculiar. What can that mean?

The holy of holies was now empty, its splendor gone. The foundation rock stood alone.

Dismas rubbed his forehead. *Am I stuck hanging on top of this curtain?*

He turned back to Jesus, who was now kneeling at the bottom of the tattered curtain. The ground thundered and the temple shook violently. Dismas swayed. The priests not already on their faces fell to their knees.

The floor under the veil became a large crevasse and swallowed Jesus whole. The ground moved again, and the stone beam snapped in half, knocking Dismas down. The curtain rod whacked him in the stomach as it caught him.

The remaining priests rushed away from the widening split in the floor.

The earth rumbled again.

Dismas slid from the rod and tumbled headfirst toward the opening, yet he managed to grip the curtain. He slid halfway down until his hands slipped and his body twisted. He fell backward into the abyss.

Dismas fell deeper and deeper, descending into the belly of the earth. Something swiped at Dismas' ankle. Chills raced down his arms. He landed with a soft thud. The dank dirt pressed to his skin. Suffocating darkness surrounded him, but he couldn't tell if his eyes were closed or open.

4

There are Demon-haunted worlds, regions of utter darkness. Whoever in life denies the Spirit falls into that darkness of death.

—The Isa Upanishad #3, The Upanishads

The first hour in hell

Hannah gasped spiraling weightlessly down a dark abyss. *Where am I?* Her heavy breathing echoed like a panting dog in the vast nothingness.

Her stomach lurched, and she attempted to pinch her sensitive nose against the dank, earthy stench, intense downward force rendered her fingers unbendable.

Images leapt to Hannah's mind: She saw herself on Passover in her family's foyer, behind a column, eavesdropping. Three priests and ten members of the Sanhedrin court had banged on their door right before dawn. They had already arrested Jesus. Now the holy men and Father plotted the quickest method to execute him. At that precise moment, her love for her father had turned to hate.

The image shifted to the moment after the gang of holy men had rushed out. Her father hummed a psalm as he knotted his sash over his blue woolen outer robe, preparing to assemble his precious Sanhedrin court to accuse Jesus of blasphemy.

"How could you?" Mother hissed as she entered the foyer, her lips quivering and her hands shaking.

Hannah didn't want to be reminded of this horrid conversation, but the vision persisted.

Her father crossed his arms. "I decide what is best for my family, my temple, and my nation."

"Condemning an innocent man is not the Sanhedrin way."

"I can't oppose Annas and Caiaphas. They'll destroy my business. The temple is the biggest buyer of my spices and oil."

I must be losing my mind. Maybe this is all a nightmare. Hannah blinked. Nope. Still wide awake, plunging into darkness.

Mother jabbed her index finger toward Father. "You are the one who desires the status, the power and privilege—not me."

Father snatched Mother's hand and yanked her close, towering over her. "You enjoy the fruit of my labor—this spacious house, your fine robes, the endless gatherings with the best wine poured by servants. Do you want Benjamin begging on the street? Your savior may try to reassure you, claiming God will make garments and footwear appear like wildflowers in the field." Father scoffed. "You're a fool to believe such nonsense."

Father always twisted the beautiful words of Jesus.

"My lord," pleaded Mother, "you don't have to be part of condemning Jesus. Walk away. Let's wake our children and flee Jerusalem."

Father released her hand and reached for his Sanhedrin headpiece, prominently displayed on the cabinet. Baring his teeth in a semblance of a smile, he positioned it over his dark locks. With the headpiece in place he glared at his wife "No. You've been mesmerized by the miracles. I should have locked up both you and Hannah instead of allowing you to hear that man speak, hoping one of you would see Jesus is the devil's son."

"My heart tells me he's Messiah, God's Son."

"What else does your heart tell you about Jesus? The way you fall at his feet and worship—"

"Unbelievable," Mother interrupted. "You're conspiring to kill an innocent man because you're jealous."

"Jesus will die today and end this unpleasantness between

us." Father slammed the door.

Mother sobbed.

Hannah fought back tears. Now, she'd never see her mother again. She was all alone—no husband, mother, brother, or father.

Father. She rationalized hearing her parent's voices and seeing these images was a reprimand from God for her actions.

And then the images continued: She saw herself emerge from her hiding place after Father had stormed out. "Father should be the one to die, not Jesus."

"How dare you curse your own father, and sin against God, too. You've broken the fifth commandment: You shall honor your father and mother and you will have a long life." Then Mother spewed more hateful words, "After Seth signed the marriage contract, he never came back for you, because a disobedient daughter makes a rebellious wife. Married but not, stuck in your father's home for seven long years." She huffed. "You're nothing but a bad luck amulet bringing shame on our family."

Mother's awful words wounded her heart, but Hannah should have never spoken against her father. As punishment, her life had been cut short. And now she was plummeting into Sheol.

Benjamin. What happened to him? It's my fault he's dead. Hannah had promised Mother she'd watch him. But she had chased him into the street over her meaningless wedding ring. *I broke another commandment: You shall not murder.*

The heavy darkness pressed around her as she continued to fall. "Benjamin," she kept whispering in a panic.

Hannah heard a faint reply. She forced herself to still her thoughts and listen. Weeping? She heard soft crying and another muffled sound, like someone gnashing their teeth.

She winced. These were the sounds of Hades.

A blast of hot air hit her neck, confirming her worst fear. The sensation of plummeting changed into a dragging motion. Hannah's body took a hard left into a dark gray tunnel. She crinkled her nose at the overpowering smell of rotten eggs. Her family's spice business had made her nose exceptionally sensitive. As she moved through the tunnel, she noticed a patch of green. *Land?* Hannah tumbled out of the tunnel, landing face first onto soft grass.

Something swiped at her knee.

"Get off my leg!" said Benjamin.

Relief flooded through her. She slid off Benjamin's leg and reached for his hand. He squeezed back.

What happened to my purple robe? Now she wore a white robe covered in ugly black stains. It must have gotten dirty in the tunnel. Benjamin wore a similar robe, but his was dirtier.

"Wh-Where are we?" Benjamin stammered, a hint of fear betraying his usually strong voice.

"Life after death. It exists," Hannah declared.. Her mother's Pharisee family believed in life after death, while her Sadducee father didn't. Benjamin furrowed his eyebrows into a frown. Guilt tugged at her stomach, yet the satisfaction of being right overshadowed any regret over her words. A black stain appeared on her robe, as if the fabric itself agreed with her.

Benjamin dropped her hand and stood. "I wouldn't be so smug," he said. "Look at the price you had to pay to be right. We're dead—our lives squashed by a stupid chariot."

"I'm sorry for chasing you over my ring." Hannah's hand still felt naked. *Seth might be down here, too. Maybe I'll finally discover what happened to him.* Thick blades of grass brushed against her ankles, providing a soft bed for her back in her prone position. They had landed in a small grassy area surrounded by a circle of thick, towering hedges. She shifted her attention to the tunnel from where they'd fallen. It extended far into the deathly gray sky, through thin black clouds resembling iron bars.

The passage above them swayed. With a gasp, the tunnel

belched out a man. He landed with a thud, nearly on Hannah's foot. She rolled away just in time. He also wore a white robe, spotted like a leopard. She noticed a jagged scar on his cheek.

The mysterious man leapt to his feet. He backed away from the entrance and peered up as if expecting someone.

The tunnel trembled again and out came Jesus, who landed on his feet.

Hannah's heart clenched. *Jesus is dead?*

He wore a black, oversized robe, hunched under the weight of it. It reminded Hannah of the pagan Roman figure, Atlas, who held the entire weight of the world on his shoulders.

"I thought—" Hannah paused. "I thought somehow you would have escaped being crucified."

"I was born to die," Jesus said quietly.

What an odd thing to say. Hannah couldn't believe he'd perished. Tears pooled, and she swallowed hard. How could the priests, the Sanhedrin court, and the Romans kill someone as perfect as Jesus?

Jesus extended his hand to Hannah and helped her to her feet. She noticed the wounds on his wrists and pondered why her and Benjamin's wounds were healed, but his weren't.

"Who are you?" Benjamin asked the man with the scar.

Jesus flashed a radiant smile, and his brown eyes twinkled. "Benjamin and Hannah, meet Dismas, my newest disciple. You can say we hung around the crucifixion together."

Jesus seemed so relaxed, even making jokes when they all had just died.

"Is he a criminal? We heard you were crucified with vile thieves." Benjamin's eyes narrowed at the newcomer.

Hannah elbowed her brother as joy and surprise filled her. "You remember us?"

"I prayed for Benjamin the day my disciples pushed him away, and I've seen you listening to me preach. I prayed for you too, Hannah, daughter of Reuben, and Susanna, wife of Seth."

"Is Seth in Paradise?"

"No." Jesus' eyes filled with compassion.

Hannah hugged herself. *Seth's alive. So it's true—he did abandon me.*

"What is this place?" Dismas asked.

"Do you remember what I promised at the cross?"

Dismas' voice wavered, "Paradise?"

Benjamin pointed at the bleak sky. "Does your version include bars?"

Hannah squinted. Her brother was right—they were bars, not clouds.

Benjamin marched forward and tugged at the lush hedge.

"You don't want to do that," Jesus cautioned, his tone turning serious.

"Are you hiding something?" accused Benjamin.

Branches snapped as Benjamin yanked two hedges apart, creating an opening. A scorching gust of wind burst through, wilting a few of the leaves. The searing heat stung her face causing her eyes to widen at the utter desolation.

Beyond the branches, a colossal iron fence stretched along a rocky beach, separating the shiny, blackened sand from the obsidian sea. Past the vast sea lay a shadowy land filled with massive, gray-black, erupting volcanoes. Crimson rivers of lava raced down and circled the mountains like pools of blood. The choppy black sea continuously swallowed the lava and vomited out steam.

Her breath quickened, waves of dread gathered in the pit of her stomach. *I am a prisoner in hell.*

Hannah spotted a simple stone bridge spanning the sea, from the land of volcanoes to, presumably, Paradise. In the middle of the bridge, something moved. Hannah squinted. Dark figures with horns. *Demons!* One of them spun around and his blood-red eyes bore into hers. Beads of sweat broke out on her forehead and her hands shook.

Benjamin must have seen them, too. He recoiled, releasing the branch and hiding behind the foliage.

"D-Demons," he said, turning five shades lighter than a grain of salt. Benjamin pivoted to face Jesus. "I don't deserve to be in hell! I have obeyed every law of Moses."

Hannah noticed ten new black spots appear on Benjamin's robe.

"Actually, we are in Paradise, which is surrounded by hell," Jesus replied. "As you can see, there is a great gulf separating the two areas. Unfortunately, Lucifer built the bridge over the Sea of Despair, connecting the land of utter darkness to Paradise." Jesus strolled to the opposite side of the clearing and waved his hand. A soft breeze parted the hedges. "This is the Paradise side."

A refreshing breeze swept across Hannah's cheek as Jesus held back the branches. On this side were thousands and thousands of people of every tribe, nation, and tongue—too many to count. Both men and women engaged in conversation, and the men didn't appear to be ordering the women around like Hannah was accustomed to back in Jerusalem. She relaxed and soaked in the surroundings.

Paradise held a variety of trees—the branches of majestic oaks intertwined with pistachio trees and massive sycamores. Towering lemon-scented eucalyptus trees grew near shaggy-topped palms. Watchmen stood on wooden platforms at the treetops, peering into the gray sky above. *What were they watching for?*

The grass throughout Paradise appeared thick like a luxury emerald carpet. Some people slept on the lush grass under the towering trees. But Hannah noticed huge sections of grass were blackened, as though deliberately set on fire. A few trees also appeared scorched. *Trouble exists in Paradise.*

Roses, lilies, and gladioli lined the grass along with fields of wildflowers she'd never seen before. The aromas from fruit trees and flowers blended, reminding her of Father's spice business. No sulfur smell here.

Hannah rubbed her eyes and stared again at the vast expanse of beauty. The brilliant shades of reds, pinks, violets, and yellows didn't exist in her old world. But what struck her the most were the golden trumpet flowers illuminating the landscape. Their streams of light shined like sun rays, and their brightness faded into the drab sky, reminiscent of unceasing shooting stars.

A massive iron fence and a beach surrounded Paradise like a fortress. The vertical fence bars extended far into the sky, and horizontal bars crossed overhead, forming one large prison cell. She could still see the volcanos looming in the distance and hear the weeping, gnashing of teeth, and crashing waves, but the fiery volcanoes shielded her view of the land of utter darkness.

Jesus walked through the open hedge and beckoned them to join. "Come on, you three, don't be shy."

Benjamin stepped through the shrubbery first, followed by Hannah, then Dismas.

"Hannah! Benjamin!" A woman sprinted toward them.

She had the same acorn-brown eyes as her brother. Odd. The vaguely familiar person clutched Hannah's and Benjamin's hands staring back and forth at them. "I'm your grandmother, Abigail! You never met me. I took my last breath on earth giving birth to your father."

Hannah's body went rigid. Her father's mother. She couldn't believe it! Whenever Abigail's name was mentioned, her father had looked away or left the room.

"One of the prophets told me you two were coming today," Grandmother continued. "I didn't believe it. Your parents must be heartbroken, and you must miss them as well! It's been strange down here. Recently, some of the dead have been raised back to life. One man, Lazarus, was here for four days before returning to the surface. Maybe you and your brother will be sent back, too."

Hannah pointed to Jesus. "He's the man who raised people from the dead. Now that he's here, there is no hope for us."

"There's always hope," said Jesus.

"I'm thrilled I can know my grandchildren," Grandmother Abigail said, smiling kindly. "We can be a family." She twirled toward one of the tree platforms. "Ebenezer! Look who has arrived."

A man scurried down the trunk. Hannah remembered her grandfather, but this man looked younger than her father. Hannah realized she didn't see any old people. Everyone looked about twenty years old, except Benjamin. Would he finish growing here?

"Our grandchildren are here!" Ebenezer looked around. "Reuben, too? Is he here?"

"No, just Benjamin and Hannah."

She saw a flash of disappointment cross her grandfather's face. Hannah knew that look well—she had seen it in her father's eyes. After he became a member of the Sanhedrin court, he had begun to measure his family against the purity laws, and found them all lacking.

"Wait a minute ... I recognize that scar." Ebenezer stared at Dismas. "You were the last person I saw as I lay on the ground dying. You were part of those murderous robbers!"

Hannah glared at Dismas, her heart racing as she realized the truth. Maybe if her grandfather's life hadn't been cut short, her father wouldn't have demanded so much from her and Benjamin.

Dismas' face turned beet red, and he studied his sandals.

Benjamin's nostrils flared. "I told you he was a criminal, just like Jesus."

Jesus didn't defend himself.

Hannah studied Dismas. *He looks about my age.* Her grandfather had died long ago, which would have made Dismas a mere child at the time.

Dismas shrugged apologetically. "Barabbas killed you and stole your spices and money. Not me. I was seven."

Ebenezer waved his fist in front of Dismas. "What kind of child pickpockets a dying man?" Sadness flowed over Hannah as she watched her grandfather blame a helpless child for his death.

Dismas lifted his hands slightly, as though offering himself. "I didn't have a choice. Barabbas made me. I didn't want to."

Barabbas? Hannah remembered her mother's friend, Salome, had spoken of Pontius Pilate releasing a man named Barabbas instead of Jesus. Hannah's mind reeled. Dismas had played a part in her grandfather's death, and maybe he was connected to *the* Barabbas.

Grandfather Ebenezer scoffed. "Everyone has a choice to do what's right."

"Give the young man a break," Grandmother Abigail said, smiling at Dismas. He must have done something right to land here."

"Dismas is a changed man," agreed Jesus.

Dismas hung his head.

"Ebenezer, remember you are still working on unforgiveness," Grandmother Abigail said. She leaned toward Hannah and whispered, "It's a rumor around here that you can't be transferred to heaven unless you're perfect."

Jesus opened his mouth to speak, but Grandfather Ebenezer cut him off, "After your grandmother died, I became a mean drunk, blaming your father for her death. I made such a mess of things when I was alive."

The winds picked up, carrying with them the smell of sulfur.

The watchmen in the trees yelled, "Hide! Incoming."

The Paradise people scattered, smashing flowers and snapping twigs as they ran for cover. Some jumped into the river, while others sprinted behind rocks and trees.

Grandmother Abigail grabbed Hannah's hand and dragged her behind a boulder. Hannah peeked out and tried to locate Grandfather and Benjamin but couldn't. Then, she saw Jesus climbing to the top of a large square rock in the middle of Paradise.

Dismas edged toward the stone platform.

"No need to hide today," Jesus calmly stated. "No need to hide today."

Hannah saw a few people point at Jesus. Some started running toward him.

She tried to lift herself to join, but her grandmother pushed her back down.

"Duck and shield your head," Grandmother Abigail ordered. "If one of those arrows hits you, horrible thoughts and fears will be planted inside your mind like poison." Grandmother Abigail pointed to a disheveled man withering on a patch of burnt grass. "Look at poor Ichabod. An arrow struck him yesterday."

"I will be a prisoner of Lucifer's forever," Ichabod muttered, his eyes wild with fear. "The Lord hates me. He has forgotten me, left me helpless in hell." A charred, broken arrow lay next to him.

A woman behind another bush huffed in disgust. "Takes at least three days for the poisonous thoughts to leave your body."

Hannah thought being alive on earth had its challenges. But now that she was dead, there were still problems.

Arrows whizzed overhead, their fiery trails cutting across the gray sky. A gust of hot wind blew the sizzling darts over the Sea of Despair, hurtling straight toward them.

"No need to cower in fear," reassured Jesus. "Prisoners of Paradise, your hiding days are over." His voice exuded authority. He made a formidable figure standing on the rock—his black robe billowed behind him, like a regal banner declaring victory.

A few more people crawled out of their hiding places and joined the crowd gathering around him.

Again, Hannah began to join the others, but her grandmother held a tight grip on her shoulder. "You need to stay right here where it's safe."

She yearned to join the crowd.

The fiery arrows reached the top of Paradise's iron bars, and Jesus held up his arm. "Return to the evil from which you came."

Immediately, the arrows obeyed, reversing direction and streaking back to hell.

Dismas' jaw dropped as his eyes shifted between Jesus and the fiery shafts falling into the Sea of Despair.

Abigail released her grip. She whispered to Hannah, "We've just witnessed a miracle. Nobody has ever stopped the arrows before."

Hannah grinned. Jesus would shake up hell just like he did on earth.

The people cheered and rushed from their hiding spots. Everyone swarmed around Jesus and asked over and over, "Who are you?"

"My Father sent me to preach the good news and to proclaim freedom to all the Paradise prisoners," Jesus said.

A few people cheered, but many shook their heads in disbelief.

The multitude fell silent as a regal-looking man and woman walked up to Dismas and embraced him. Dismas broke free of the man's bear hug.

"Welcome," the man said in a comforting voice. "I am Abraham, your grandfather. This is your grandmother, Sarah."

Sarah laughed. "Abraham, you have to add a couple hundred 'greats' in front of grandfather."

Abraham chuckled and motioned for Hannah and Benjamin to come forward. "I greet everyone who enters Paradise." Abraham hugged Hannah and Benjamin.

"You are Abraham?" How Hannah wished her parents could see this! They wouldn't believe she had just hugged the father of their people.

Jesus effortlessly jumped from the rock and stood in front of Abraham. "Do I get a welcoming hug?"

Abraham hugged Jesus and sighed. "Jesus, some have been waiting so long for you, and others will refuse to believe you are the One who will rescue us."

Sarah kissed Jesus' cheek. "We have heard so much about you."

"Who has been talking about me?" asked Jesus.

Sarah pointed to a burly man donned in a white robe with a few smudges near his feet. *John the Baptist.* Hannah recognized him from when he had baptized her in the river Jordan.

"Now I know why I had to die before you," John told Jesus. "So I could tell everyone the Son of God would be coming to Paradise very soon." They embraced.

Hannah stared at John's head and neck, looking for some evidence of the horrific way he had died—beheaded. But she saw none.

Another man and woman stood behind a fig tree and frowned at Jesus. The woman's green eyes flashed. "How do we really know you're the Son of God?" The stunning woman had long, flowing black hair, but wore such an ugly, tattered, black robe. There was just a small patch of white over her heart.

The handsome man beside her wore an identical robe. "Look at Jesus' robe. It's all black. Not a speck of white. If he is truly God's Son, wouldn't he be dressed in white? Have any of you seen an all-black robe like his? Jesus must be the biggest sinner of all." The man seemed the tallest in Paradise, and his arm muscles bulged under his robe. He had flawless, white teeth, a strong chiseled jaw, high cheekbones, a straight nose, and perfectly shaped, dirt-brown eyes.

"No, Adam, I haven't committed any sins," Jesus said without a hint of condemnation. "My robe is black because I am carrying the sins of the entire world—past, present, and future."

Hannah figured if that was Adam, the woman touching his arm had to be Eve.

The crowd screamed at Jesus' words, but Hannah couldn't tell if the cries were of joy or disgust.

"I get it now," Benjamin whispered. "These stains represent the sins we have committed."

"I have fewer marks than you," she whispered back. As soon as the words left her mouth, she regretted saying such a mean thing. The word "pride" appeared on her sleeve, then blurred into a black stain. Hannah's cheeks flushed.

"Keep talking, Hannah," Benjamin teased. "In no time, you will catch up to me."

Eve stuck out her chin defiantly. "Adam, you're right. When we walked in the garden with God, his robe was pure white like the sun."

"I am burying your sin in hell so that nothing will separate you from my Father anymore," Jesus said. "You will finally be able to walk with him again."

About one hundred men with long hair and flowing beards rushed toward Jesus, pushing others out of the way. Hannah couldn't understand a word they said, their voices loud and overlapping.

Adam snickered. "Oh great, the talking prophets have arrived."

"Order, order!" A dark brunette leaned against a palm tree and waved her hand like a gavel.

Everyone grew quiet and looked to her. *I bet that's Deborah,* Hannah thought, *Israel's first woman judge and prophetess.*

"Isaiah, you prophesied about the Messiah extensively. You can go first," the prophetess declared.

"Jesus is here to open the prison doors to all of us who have been bound by Lucifer," Isaiah announced.

Jesus nodded. "Yes, that's true. Each of you will have the opportunity to leave this realm, move to heaven, and live with my Father for all eternity."

The prophets cheered.

Adam gave an ear-splitting whistle to get everyone's attention.

Hannah covered her ears.

Adam didn't stop whistling until everyone's attention turned to him. He paused. "How is that going to happen?"

"It's simple," Jesus said. "If you believe in your heart that I'm God's Son, and confess it with your mouth, you will be freed from hell and enter heaven." Jesus' declaration was met by silence, as though each person searched their hearts to see what they believed.

"Nice words," Eve said, "but what proof do you have?"

Hannah narrowed her eyes at Eve, biting back the word troublemaker.

A man with sea-blue eyes and a gray, whale-shaped pendant on his necklace pushed his way through the prophets. "As I was in the whale's belly for three days and nights, Jesus will be below the earth for three days and three nights."

"Jonah." Adam rolled his eyes. "How many times do we have to hear you tell that old fish story? You were the one who got away."

Eve crossed her arms over her chest. "What if we don't believe?"

Jesus pointed across the gulf. "Then there is your new home."

The multitude became dead silent. They could hear the

screams floating over the Sea of Despair.

Benjamin elbowed her and murmured, "He's a lunatic claiming to be God's Son above and below earth."

Hannah swallowed hard. Benjamin didn't believe in Jesus. *He's going to end up in hell. But I'm safe.* She believed Jesus was God's son. But doubts crept in like unwelcome spiders. *Why did Jesus descend into hell, shrouded in black? He said he carries our sins. Is it true?* Her mind churned like the sea. Another black mark appeared, this one wrapping around her sleeve like a snake and reading "unbelief." Chills raced down her spine. She quickly folded the sleeve to conceal the black spot, just in case the letters didn't disappear this time. The weight of uncertainty of their future clung to her like lingering cobwebs.

"Warning!" a watchman in an apple tree cried out. "Lucifer's headed straight for us."

Hannah glanced at the bridge. *They're getting closer.* She shivered as she remembered the devil's evil eyes upon her. Terror tightened its grip on Hannah, as though someone had punched her in the stomach—repeatedly. *Breathe.*

Would Lucifer drag her by her ankle through the bars of Paradise, straight to the pits of hell?

5

The Nephilim were on the earth both in those days and afterward, when the sons of God came to the daughters of mankind, who bore children to them. They were the powerful men of old, the famous men.

—Genesis 6:4 (HSCB)

The shores of Paradise
The third hour in hell

Mahway pursed his lips. *Don't gnash your teeth, not in front of Lucifer and his fallen angels.* He sideswiped a wave pouring over the ancient bridge. He hadn't been this close to the shore of Paradise since he had built the structure, carrying one heavy white stone after another. Mahway rubbed his six-fingered hand along the grimy wall.

White stones—a poor choice between the hellfire and the lava. Everything wore a layer of soot. Mahway speculated the fallen angels desired to recreate the heaven they'd been cast out of—not that he'd ever gain access there.

As the child of a watcher angel and a human woman, Mahway hailed from the mighty giants known as Nephilim. They had ruled the earth before Noah's flood, before God had grown displeased with a race he hadn't created. And then he had spitefully swept away Mahway and his entire world like garbage. When Mahway drowned, he found himself in hell, transformed into a demon. He retained his physical body in hell. But when Lucifer sent him to earth on assignments, he became a spirit, a ghost who could possess humans and pursue his desires like guzzling alcohol and driving people insane—whatever Lucifer plotted.

Four fallen angels hammered Lucifer with questions as they stormed the gates of Paradise. Each question was a variation of "Why is Jesus in hell?"

"One question at a time." Lucifer hissed as he stomped his goat hoof directly into a tiny wave racing over the bridge.

Mahway stood to his full height, towering over Lucifer and double the size of that fool Goliath. *What an utter embarrassment to the race of giants.* He admired the antler-like horns that twisted out from Lucifer's head, surprised he didn't topple from the sheer weight of them. *That must be because of the spiked tail balancing his rear end.*

"You led us to believe that when we killed Jesus," Beelzebub buzzed in his fly-like voice, red bulging eyes flashing hatred, "he would return to the Uncreated One." Two black antenna horns protruded from his forehead and transparent wings opened and closed in eerie harmony whenever he spoke.

For once, Mahway agreed with old Lord of the Flies, Lucifer's second-in-command. In life, he'd believed the two were one in the same, until he'd woken in hell and found them both barking orders at him.

Beelzebub pointed his claw toward Jesus. "Yet there he stands in the middle of Paradise, preaching right where he left off."

Mahway heard a muffled buzzing from the side of Beelzebub's loose hooded robe. Three of his "pets," one-winged hairy flies the size of a man's thumbnail, crawled out from behind Beelzebub's pointy ear. He popped one in his mouth.

Lucifer stopped in his tracks and growled. The flies scurried for cover inside Beelzebub's ear. "I never said that. Does anyone remember me saying that?" He eyed each of them.

Silence.

Nobody contradicted Lucifer without severe consequences. Mahway remembered Lucifer's triumphant announcement at their last meeting: once they'd crucified Jesus, they'd never see him again. Sounded delightful to Mahway, who longed to go back to possessing a human without Jesus casting him out. Demons could not be cast out until Jesus had arrived on earth.

Dagon opened his fish mouth rimmed with sharp teeth. "Jesus was an ordinary man, so he'd have to follow the same death procedure as a man." Hell's scaly scholar spent his time poring over the Hebrew texts, discerning the prophecies. It was wretched work, reading the Word of God, but someone had to do it. Mahway detested Dagon's superiority complex. It didn't help that the gullible multitude worshiped him as their fish god.

The fallen angels relished the sick competition among themselves, trying to fool and ensnare the confused people of Earth to revere them over the Uncreated One. Mahway would rather possess a person so he could feel the pleasures of being human again without the pain. But the fallen angels received immense satisfaction from stealing worship away from God. If it hadn't been for Jesus casting him out of that man at the Gergesenes cemetery and into those grimy pigs, Mahway would still be roaming the earth instead of stuck in hell taking orders from Lucifer.

Moloch, with a wide bull face, snorted. "Jesus is fully God and fully man."

Mahway gnashed his teeth so loudly causing several others to stare at him. He didn't care. It was wrong. Mahway, a hybrid of an angel and a human, was cast into hell while Jesus, a combination of the Spirit and a man, danced into Paradise.

"Jesus is not an unclean spirit like Mahway," Old Fly Face taunted.

Rage erupted inside Mahway like a volcano. Beelzebub was God's reject too, yet Lucifer had placed him in charge of the Nephilim. *Unfair.*

"I earned my right here," Mahway growled, shoving Beelzebub.

Old Fly Face staggered nearly over the edge of the bridge,

but his horn caught against Mahway's robe, keeping him from tumbling over the side. A small cloud of flies buzzed around them.

Lucifer intervened ripping away Beelzebub, tearing a hole in Mahway's robe.

Enraged, Beelzebub swung at Mahway, but Baal wedged between them.

"Attacking your commanding officer," Beelzebub said. "Your punishment will be brutal."

Lucifer red eyes flared like burning embers at Paradise. "Under normal circumstances, this fight would amuse me. But not today. We have a common enemy, and it's time to see what his game is."

Baal spoke up, "My squad leader reported the fiery arrows returned from Paradise and fell directly into the sea at the exact time Jesus showed up." His eyes bulged and he snorted. "Why is he down here? And what does he want? This is *our* region." He rubbed one of his curved horns, reminiscent of the thousands of statues, paintings, and earthenware bearing his image.

Moloch froze on the bridge, gazing at his reflection in the sea. "Is our time up? Are we going to be thrown into the Lake of Fire?"

If the Lake of Fire reflected like a mirror, Moloch might kiss himself into oblivion.

"Shut up or I will throw you in that lake myself!" Lucifer snarled, thrusting Moloch along the bridge toward the craggy shoreline of Paradise.

Mahway treaded the rocky black beach, the rocks giving way to gravelly ash-colored pebbles. They were in the gray zone, where hell's midnight black collided with the gray-yellow light of Paradise, not far from the ancient gate. He doubted Jesus would swing open the gate and invite them to dinner. And fallen angels or Nephilim couldn't penetrate those thick bars no matter how hard they tried. And they tried often.

"Come out, Jesus! We want to talk to you," Lucifer called. To those closest to him, he added quietly, "Look at the fool. Jesus is stuck in Paradise like all my other prisoners."

Beads of sweat rolled down Mahway's back. He surveyed the ragtag Paradise prisoners surrounding Jesus, freely walking around and carrying on conversation. Unlike their unfortunate counterparts across the abyss confined to cramped pens, and tormented by relentless demons, who seized every opportunity to harass them.

Where is she? Mahway thought, desperately scanning the area for a glimpse of his Cecilia. He was afraid he might see his wife, yet terrified he wouldn't.

Jesus effortlessly walked through the solid bars. The Paradise people erupted in a great roar and didn't stop until Jesus motioned them to be quiet.

Lucifer gaped, showing yellow, pointy teeth.

Jesus marched up to Lucifer. "It is finished." His authority boomed loud enough for everyone on both sides to hear. "Your reign of terror is over. The legal rights you have stolen have been terminated. I have fulfilled every requirement of the law of Moses. This is your notice. In three days, I am taking my Paradise saints with me to heaven where they belong."

A cheer rose from Paradise, drowning out the furious growls erupting from the Nephilim, demons, and fallen angels throughout hell.

"Get out now!" Lucifer shrieked. "Why wait three days?" His blood-colored lips matched his red pupils in the middle of black irises. He charged the gate with horns spinning and tail dragging on the ground, but he couldn't pass the invisible barrier.

Mahway winced in embarrassment for the poor fool.

Yet Lucifer wasn't deterred. "Jesus is lying to you!" he screeched at the people secure on the other side. "He has no authority to release any of you—not in three days. You will be my prisoners *forever*!"

Jesus spoke with authority. "Your reign of terror has ended." He calmly extended his hand, palm up. "Hand over the keys to hell and death."

Lucifer pivoted away and held out his claw. Two items appeared: a broken lump of iron resembling half a skull with one ruby eye, and a substantial, ornate iron key with flecks of gold.

Something isn't right with one of the keys, Mahway realized.

Lucifer's eyes gleamed with mischief as he jittered on his hooves, biting his thin lips in anticipation.

Jesus' eyes flashed in anger. "Your deed of destroying hell's key will not go unpunished."

Lucifer smirked and took a step toward Jesus. "It's our intimate dance. You create, and I destroy what you create."

Jesus scrutinized the unbroken gold-speckled key. "The key to death has not been tampered with." He gingerly placed it in his pocket, then crossed his arms and stared at each of the fallen angels. His eyes lingered on Mahway.

Mahway met his gaze briefly, but looked away.

"You are aware when this is all over, each of you will bow to me?" Jesus said without a trace of malice.

"Never," replied Mahway. Yet he felt his knee begin to wobble involuntarily. He willed his leg to stand. As his knee continued to shake, he bent and steadied it with his hand. Anger boiled within. *Lucifer and Beelzebub can't see this display of weakness.*

"Take it easy, Jesus," Lucifer said. "Free will and all that. I know you had a rough day, with me arranging your excruciating death. My demons sounded like they'd swallowed thorns after whispering so many lies into the humans' ears."

"Enough stalling, Lucifer. Surrender the second key immediately." Jesus held out his hand. He bore a deep, purple puncture wound on his wrist.

"I admit this key is ... slightly damaged. With a smirk, Lucifer scraped his overgrown, jagged talon encrusted with Hell's soot along the edges of the broken key. "Every time I came close to achieving a major conquest, the Creator cheated and stole the victory from me. The first time it happened, I flew into a rage and broke off a piece of the key. It made me feel better. So I continued to hide fragments wherever the Creator wrecked my plan."

Jesus laughed, the sound echoing throughout the land. "The words you are looking for are defeated, outwitted, outplayed, and lost."

"You know I enjoy playing games," Lucifer bragged. "If you want the individual pieces to hell's key, you'll have to fetch them in time. Unfortunately, since the Creator clipped my wings, I am unable to go back in time with you. Pity. It would have been such fun."

The fallen angels broke out in manic fits of laughter, Beelzebub the loudest with his annoying, high-pitched, hyena cackle.

Mahway kicked a pebble. *Why is this the first time I am hearing about the key? Beelzebub, Moloch, Dagon, and Baal all seem to know about it.*

Jesus secured both keys in his pocket. "You've lost countless times to my Father, which would mean the pieces could be everywhere and anywhere. The key is large, not colossal. I am here for sixty-three hours only."

Lucifer waved Jesus off like an annoying fly. "It's a shame the one you believe is your Father; he paints me as the bad guy while human blood pours from his hands. Three days and three nights ... sounds like you are on a tight schedule. You'd better leave now."

Jesus stood his ground. "Your tricks won't work on me. I am preaching to the Paradise prisoners so each one can be transferred to heaven."

"You will fail. Your words will fall on deaf ears. My captives won't believe you unless you're holding the completed key. Aside from that, you need it to open the gate."

Jesus nodded. "I accept your challenge."

An infuriating, condescending smile broke across Lucifer's face.

Jesus continued, "However, I am not going to retrieve the key."

Lucifer stomped his hoof. "That's not fair!"

"You never specified it had to be me." Jesus turned and faced the Paradise saints. "Who would like to help me by retrieving pieces of the key?"

Most of the people stepped away from the gate.

Mahway sneered. *Not so brave when you have to act.*

A man with an ugly scar on his face stepped forward. "I will go."

A pretty woman with long raven hair raised her hand. "I believe in you, Jesus. I will go, too."

Jesus smiled. "Thank you for your bravery and assistance."

A sour-faced boy, arms crossed, glared at the girl who had just volunteered. "Hannah, there is no way you are going anywhere with that murdering criminal."

"I don't have to listen to you anymore." Hannah put her hands on her hips.

"You aren't thinking clearly." The boy tightened his jaw. "Why would you do anything for Jesus? He claims he is God's Son, yet he and his Father stand by and do nothing while innocent people like us die. Our grandmother died young, and our grandfather was murdered before his time. Most of the people trapped in here were cut down too soon." The boy pointed through the thick bars at Jesus. "If you're so good, why did I have to die?"

Mahway rubbed his hands together in glee. Bitter, unforgiving people were the easiest to possess.

"Good question, Benjamin," Lucifer's crimson eyes twisted with joy. "If God is so wonderful, why does he kill little babies?" He scoffed. "And people call *me* the evil one." Lucifer shook his head sadly.

Hypocrite. Mahway side-eyed Lucifer. He was the one who relished killing people and blaming God.

"My Father refuses to violate a person's free will," Jesus said. "Unlike Lucifer, we don't want puppets." He turned to Benjamin. "I must warn you, if you are staying in Paradise, your questions will be answered, but you are going to hear the longest sermon of your life. For three days and nights, I am going to preach to hell's captives and explain how I fulfilled the law and describe all the places where my Father has hidden me in the Scriptures. We will go through the Torah line by line."

All the lunatic, long-haired prophets cheered.

Did Lucifer know about Jesus preaching in hell? Sounded like torture to Mahway.

Benjamin yawned. "No problem. I can take a nap."

"Besides, if you judged Dismas to be such a horrible person, shouldn't you accompany your sister?" Jesus said. "After all, you did promise your mother you would protect her."

Mahway glared at the siblings. They were opposites: the suspicious boy and the gullible girl. *But what do I care? I can't possess dead people.*

"Fine. I will go," Benjamin said, elbowing his sister.

"Are you kidding me?" Lucifer scoffed. "Three losers? A nobody thief whose father deserted him, an ugly girl whose husband never stuck around to consummate the marriage, and a foolish boy who never met his father's approval. Pathetic."

Mahway relished the joy of someone else succumbing to Lucifer's poking at weak spots, making them feel like they were nothing.

"Don't listen to his lies," Jesus said to the three volunteers. "I believe in you."

Lucifer examined his long fingernails. "These three will never find the pieces. Not much of a competition. Almost as easy as getting Adam and Eve to eat an apple."

Beelzebub, Moloch, Dagon, and Baal all laughed, so Mahway forced himself to join in. He wearied of the creation story. Lucifer retold the tale nearly every day.

Lucifer searched the crowd gathered at the bars of Paradise. He found his target and pointed. "There's Adam! The first loser the Creator made. But you helped me by biting into the fruit and turning the world into my playground."

Adam's cheeks flushed and he looked at the ground as Eve discreetly maneuvered behind a fig tree.

"Adam, my Father never makes mistakes," Jesus said. "He called you good when he created you, and you are still good today."

Lucifer spat. "Ugh, I am sick to death of hearing how your God created the first man by breathing his Spirit into a lump of dirt."

Beelzebub sneered. "More like a pile of dung."

"You rebel angels were always jealous of God's children," Jesus said. "You even attempted to make your own children."

"My offspring!" Lucifer said, puffing out his chest. "My mighty giants were far superior to man."

"I always wondered the origin of the giants," the boy whispered to his sister.

Mahway smiled bitterly. *He tries to whisper as though we have weak hearing like humans.*

"Boy, you desire the knowledge of how I created my children?" Lucifer snapped his knife-like talons and an image of a beautiful young maiden appeared over their heads. "This is the story of my offspring."

Mahway had never seen a visual reenactment of the story before. Lucifer is showing off.

"Is this like a dream? Who's the girl?" Hannah asked.

The nerve. She doesn't realize her place.

"Shut up, sit back, and enjoy the show," Lucifer said sharply.

The girl in Lucifer's vision tossed a rock into a river, unaware of the man who crept behind her. He placed one hand over her mouth and a knife to her throat. The girl bit his finger and screamed, "Help, Father!"

An arrow flew from the woman's left side and struck the man between his eyes. The assailant released the girl and fell backward into the muddy bank. But the girl also lost her footing and fell, knocking her head on a jagged boulder, and landing in the shallow stream.

"Naamah! No!" cried the girl's father.

The father dropped his bow, kneeled by his daughter, and placed his ear over her heart. "You will live," he said, relieved.

The dead man oozed blood from his head wound. It mixed with the slow-moving flow of water.

"Who would dare try to kidnap the daughter of Lamech?" Lamech turned over the dead man. Tattooed on the man's forehead were the words "Me, Myself, and I." "Oh no!" Lamech wailed. "What have I done? I killed Cain."

A seven-foot-tall angel appeared as bright as the sun.

Lucifer clapped his hand claws, and the action froze. "Don't I look handsome? One of my favorite things to do is masquerade as an angel of light." After another clap, the image resumed.

"Please forgive me," Lamech said. "I was protecting my daughter. Cain tried to kidnap her! I did not see the mark."

"It doesn't matter the circumstances," said Lucifer in the vision. "You killed Cain, a man under your God's protection. Cain's family will avenge the murder of their father, and they will torture and kill your two wives and your children while you watch them die. I am the only one who can save you. I can protect you and your family."

Lamech's eyes filled with tears. "Please help me. I will do anything."

Lucifer patted Lamech's arm. "I will kill any member of Cain's family who comes near you, but you must obey my commands. Do we have a deal?"

Without hesitation, Lamech said, "Yes."

"Let's seal our contract." Lucifer snatched Lamech's hand, brought the pinkie finger to his lips, and crunched down. With every chomp, Lucifer transformed back into his hideous self—horns and all—while his victim shrieked in agony and terror. As Lamech's blood dripped at the corners of Lucifer's mouth, Lucifer flicked his tongue to wipe it up.

"What have I done?" Lamech wailed. "I made a pact with the devil!" He ripped off the sleeve of his shirt and wrapped what was left of his finger.

Lucifer flashed a malevolent smile. "You mean *do*. What will you *do* for me." His fingers moved like a magician's, conjuring a silver coin into existence. Etched into the surface was Lucifer's image on one side, and on the other, a serpent twisted around an apple. "Once I combine a few secret ingredients that you will fetch for me," he gestured to Lamech with the coin, "you will forge these coins that I will use to change the world as you know it. With your help, earth-watching angels will take on human form to mate with the daughters of men and produce a new race. They will be giants. The Nephilim."

"You're crazy. No!"

Lucifer laughed again. "I own you now. And if you don't follow my orders, remember, I will kill your family members one by one. I will start with your two wives who will burn in a fire. Jabal and Jubal will drown, and your precious daughter lying over there will be eaten alive by wolves. I will spare Tubal-Cain because he already obeys me."

Lamech slumped in defeat. "What do I have to do?"

"It just so happens the first ingredient on the list is Cain's blood."

Lamech fisted his good hand. "You set me up!"

"Take it easy. You will be rich and powerful, and the watcher angels will share their ancient secrets with you. The earth is going to advance rapidly as my watcher angels change the face of the earth with their knowledge. You won't even recognize this place. Your Creator has made you live in such primitive conditions."

"I always dreamed of being rich and powerful," Lamech said, as though rationalizing his decision.

"You deserve an abundant life," Lucifer said. "The first step to being rich and powerful is to retrieve Cain's blood while it is still fresh. Don't spill one drop. I have two hundred angels waiting to take human form. They already have their wives picked out."

The vision lingered like a cloud. Mahway gritted his teeth. In some twisted way, Lucifer was his creator. Mahway's father was one of those two hundred.

Lucifer snapped his claws, and the vision disappeared.

"My Father had to cleanse the earth of Lucifer's spawn," Jesus said. "Enough of your theatrics. Tell us where we can find the first piece so I can send my representatives."

"Not so fast." Lucifer flicked his spiked tail. "We need to establish some ground rules. What if your three losers cheat and lie to gather the key parts? Why, the game wouldn't be fair, would it?"

"You are the author of lies," Jesus said. "Whatever you're scheming, it's bound to fail. So I grant you permission to choose someone on your side to go on the quest."

"Ramel!" Lucifer shouted gleefully.

The fallen angels gasped, and Mahway's heart thumped at a

name he hadn't heard since the day of the great flood. Rumor said Jesus and Ramel had been close friends until Ramel had switched sides. No way was Jesus powerful enough to pardon the former watcher angel. What was Lucifer plotting?

If Lucifer's game is to challenge Jesus with a watcher angel from the depths of hell, why couldn't he release my father Barakel?

Mahway again scanned the Paradise prisoners for a glimpse of Cecilia. He balled his fists until his sharp fingernails bore into his palms. *Where is she?*

6

For if God didn't spare the angels who sinned but threw them down into Tartarus and delivered them to be kept in chains of darkness until judgment.

—2 Peter 2:4 (HCSB)

The fifth hour in hell

Hannah strained to see Jesus between the bars of Paradise, but her eyes drifted toward Lucifer, who pranced among his demons. The beast had exposed her lack of intimacy with her husband. She blushed at the memory of her shame. Her grandmother's hand shook. *Maybe I'm the one trembling.*

Benjamin stood close to her side, still glowering after being drafted for the key quest.

Dismas stood by himself.

The familiar appearances of Baal, Beelzebub, Moloch, and Dagon shocked Hannah. She had no idea the pagan statues were based on actual evil beings. A giant towered over Lucifer. His harsh features seemed chiseled out of stone, green eyes glowing yet lifeless, and arms as thick as tree limbs ending in hands that branched out into six fingers.

He looks miserable. Wonder what his story is. Hannah's stomach knotted with dread. *What am I thinking? Volunteering to find those key pieces! Me, up against the devil and his monsters.*

Lucifer folded his hands, a sly smile played across his red lips. "Do you have to beg your Daddy to break Ramel out of Tartarus?"

Who or what is a Ramel? She remembered from the *Book of the Giants*, disobedient angels were chained in Tartarus.

"If he even is your Father," Lucifer continued to taunt. "What kind of Father would leave his Son to die on a cross like a typical sinner?"

Hannah hated that she agreed with Lucifer, but she just couldn't understand why God had allowed his Son to die. She braced herself for another black mark to blemish her robe, but none appeared.

"Don't question my authority or my relationship with my Father," Jesus said. "If you desperately need Ramel in your deluded game, I will release him."

Lucifer smirked like a spoiled child with a double portion of honeycomb. He jabbed his claw toward Hannah and the others. "Bring me those three, the siblings and the thief."

The knot in Hannah's stomach doubled. Her thoughts jumbled. Calm down.

"Why?" Jesus asked.

"It's so impersonal to converse between the bars. While you are in Tartarus, I will go over the rules with the participants. You mentioned being pressed for time before you fail. At least it's not that drawn-out forty days again."

Sweat rolled off Hannah's forehead and dripped onto her nose. Would Jesus abandon them to that fiend?

Jesus nodded. "Hannah, Benjamin, Dismas, please walk to the gate."

As Hannah began to walk, her grandmother stepped in front of her and Benjamin. "No, my grandchildren will not leave the safety of Paradise! It's not right."

True, staying is safer. Besides, she'd like to get to know her grandmother.

Benjamin brushed away Abigail's hand. "Woman, I'm not a child. I have a commitment to honor."

Lucifer will eat us alive. The only reason Hannah had volunteered was to save her brother from condemnation. Maybe through locating the key pieces, he'd believe Jesus is God's Son. The word "liar" appeared along the bottom of her robe and then blurred into another stain. She shuffled her feet, and silently confessed she sought a reward. If she succeeded, maybe Jesus would tell her what had happened to Seth.

Meanwhile, Dismas was almost at the entrance. He paused and looked back at them.

"I promise to protect them," Jesus reassured Abigail as he waved Hannah toward him.

Hannah didn't feel safe. Her feet crushed the trumpet flowers, darkening her path with each step. *Will I pass through the bars like Jesus did?*

Jesus turned his back on Lucifer and approached the gate, humming and carefree. He reached through the bars. "Link hands," he instructed.

Benjamin frowned at Dismas. "I'm not touching you." He reached for Jesus and Hannah.

Hannah grabbed Dismas' hand, which felt like cracked, old leather. When they formed a small, tight circle, Jesus raised his hands and flashed a mischievous smile.

Lucifer growled. "Leave them with us," he said. "They're too weak to enter Tartarus."

"No matter what happens, don't let go." Jesus lowered his arms.

In the blink of an eye, the four were flying toward a massive, ash-gray mountain, its peak on the black, hardened ground. *An upside-down mountain?*

"Our destination," Jesus said, "the farthest place on earth from my Father. This is where Ramel is imprisoned."

Hannah's jaw dropped. *What stops the mountain from collapsing? And how are we soaring like doves with no wings?* Hannah squeezed Benjamin's and Jesus' hands.

"Is Ramel chained to the beneath the summit?" whispered Dismas.

"Brace yourselves," instructed Jesus, closing his eyes.

Hannah heard Jesus praying to his heavenly Father. She tried offering up a prayer, but the words stuck in her throat. Her eyes widened at the otherworldly formation looming before them. As they neared the peak, she realized Jesus intended to crash into the rocky surface. *But I'm dead, I can't feel pain.*

Jesus quickly rotated their circle so that he would take the brunt of the impending impact.

"No!" Benjamin yelled, gripping Hannah's hand so hard her fingers ached.

"Relax. You're under my protection," Jesus said calmly.

How can he be at peace?

Hannah expected a splat upon impact, but with a whoosh, they plowed through the rock layer and slid to a stop. With wobbly legs, she stood on a slab floor before the bars of a jail cell with a lock as big as her head. Torches hung on the walls, bouncing shadows off the walls. Prison cells stretched down the hall in both directions. She moved closer to her brother but dropped his hand. *I can't lean on my little brother.*

"Keep your voices down," Jesus whispered. "We don't want to wake anyone. It's tragic what they've reduced themselves to by disobeying my Father. What a waste." Jesus advance slowly his way down the hall, pausing at each cage for a moment and peering in.

Hannah held in a sneeze, covering her mouth and nose. All at once, she felt a hard shove toward the cage in front of her. "Stop pushing me," she whispered.

"I'm not." Benjamin lifted his hands.

Goosebumps raced down Hannah's arms.

Smack!

Her cheek struck the prison bars as her big toe smashed

against the bottom of the cage. She flinched. *Ouch! So, I can feel physical pain here.*

The torchlight flickered, casting light into the cage. Hannah gasped. A black-winged creature, wrapped in cobwebs like a cocoon, filled the prison cell. A flickering serpent tongue sliced through the cobwebs as more webbing fell on the floor and its spiked tail uncoiled toward her—fast. The tail wrapped around her ankle, its spikes ripping into skin as it tried to pull her thin body through the bars. Hannah struggled against the bars, tearing her robe as Benjamin and Dismas grabbed her upper arms. One of the creature's yellow eyes opened. Its pointed tongue flickered against black lips.

"Samyaza, go back to your sleep state," Jesus commanded.

Instantly, the creature closed its eyes and released Hannah.

Benjamin and Dismas crashed into the bars.

Hannah crawled up from the floor, limping. Jesus touched her ankle, and she felt heat radiating from his fingers to her leg. Immediately, the pain vanished. Even her robe restored itself—black spots and all.

"How can I feel pain when I'm dead?" Hannah asked rotating her ankle, amazed it was healed.

"Outside of Paradise, you can feel physical pain," Jesus said.

The creature in the cage snored contentedly.

"What is that thing?" asked Hannah.

Jesus continued walking down the hall and signaled them to follow. "It's Samyaza, the leader of the watcher angels. They are bound here until the final judgment so they will never be able to mate with humans again."

Hannah stayed away from the cell doors and close to Jesus. *Ramel had better be friendlier than Samyaza.*

Jesus stopped at a corner cell. Another cobwebbed cocoon was held in place by numerous chains. Jesus waved his hand, and the prison door clanged open. "Awaken, Ramel. Be unbound."

The chains clanged to the ground. Out of the cocoon emerged a black-robed creature.

Ramel stumbled toward Jesus and knelt. "I deserve your judgment," he said, face lowered. "I'm prepared to go into the Lake of Fire."

Ramel's facial features were human, with high cheekbones, a pointy chin, and an ashen complexion. His eyes were black and glossy like granite. A set of mangled, broken wings poked from under his black, tattered robe.

"No need for dramatics, Ramel." Jesus touched Ramel's shoulder. "Let's get out of here at once." Jesus also offered his arm to Hannah, Benjamin, and Dismas.

As soon as everyone touched his arm, they were back in front of Lucifer.

Ramel lay on the ground, snoring.

Hannah eyed him suspiciously.

Lucifer grabbed Ramel by his tattered wing. "Ramel! Get up!"

Ramel briefly opened his eyes. "Ugh, Lucifer, you ugly serpent. Get out of my nightmare!" He closed his eyes and made a sputtering, whistling snore.

Beelzebub snarled. "Sleeping is the watcher's punishment. Your Father is unbelievable!"

"He is merciful and just." Jesus touched Ramel's eyes. "No more sleep."

Ramel opened his eyes and rubbed them. "Jesus, is it really you?"

Lucifer winked and nudged Ramel. "You haven't forgotten me, have you? We didn't get to say proper goodbyes before those angels hauled you off to Tartarus."

"I should have never taken matters into my own hands," Ramel said. Springing to his feet, he took a swing at Lucifer. "It's your fault I'm bound like an animal."

Hannah noticed Ramel punched with a fist, not claws. *What is this creature?* The idea of traveling with such a being made her shudder.

"It's time to let go of that grudge," Lucifer said. "It's been more than two thousand years. I swear I didn't know Jesus' Father would lock you up for leaving your watcher post. Honestly, he's a killjoy, always ruining our fun."

"Please," Ramel said. "You know nothing about loyalty. I deserve my punishment. I'm ready for the Lake of Fire." Ramel held out his gray hands.

Moloch held his claws over his ears. "Stop with the Lake of Fire talk!"

Ramel gave a singsong taunt, "Lake of Fire, Lake of Fire, Lake of Fire!" Yet his voice sounded angelic to Hannah.

"The time of judgment is not now," Jesus said. "Only my Father knows the time. I am here to bring momentous change. In three days, you won't recognize the place."

"Why did you release me?" Ramel asked, yawning. "Why am I here?"

"Lucifer broke the key to hell and scattered the pieces throughout history," Jesus said. "He chose you to help retrieve the pieces. I need the key whole so the Paradise saints will see and believe in me."

"Ramel," Lucifer said. "I need you to make sure Jesus isn't cheating."

Ramel looked back and forth from Jesus to Lucifer. "I don't understand. Jesus doesn't cheat, Lucifer. *You* are the cheater." He stretched his body and yawned again. "I'm out. I refuse to be collateral damage in your war between good and evil. Once was enough."

Lucifer laughed bitterly. "Then I'll have Jesus send you back to prison."

"I don't take orders from you." Jesus crossed his arms. "You have no authority over me. Not down here, on earth, or anywhere."

Lucifer snarled. "Ramel don't let our misunderstanding cloud your judgment. Don't betray me like Jesus' earthly friends."

"Many remain faithful to me. When I rise from the dead, many more will follow me. You can't stop my Father's plan," Jesus said.

"Your disciples let you down. And these three losers"—Lucifer jerked a thumb at Hannah, Benjamin, and Dismas—"will fail you, too."

"My Father will work everything for his glory."

Lucifer spat. "You always pick losers. Peter denied you. Judas betrayed you."

Compassion flickered in Ramel's black eyes. "I will go."

Benjamin tapped his foot, arms crossed. "Can we get started already?"

Lucifer laughed. "Boy, you're impatient like me. The locations will be hidden in riddles."

"What if we can't answer the riddles?" Dismas asked, looking at Jesus.

"If you lack the wits to solve the riddles, you won't retrieve the pieces. Fail, and you'll forfeit the game losing any chance to recover the key." Lucifer unfurled his wings the intricate patterns of the tattered feathers casting a spider-web shadow over Hannah face. He met Hannah's eyes. "Ready?"

She looked at the others and then at Jesus.

He nodded and gave her an encouraging smile.

"Yes." It came out as a squeak.

"Once stood a pristine forest," Lucifer whispered. "Weeds invaded the mighty *seed* with a great *speed*. The wood *sunk*, except eight branches on a tree *trunk*."

"What gibberish," Benjamin said.

Think Hannah. Don't let Lucifer win.

Dismas rubbed his head. "I barely heard you. Can you say it again, this time slower?"

"No repeating is allowed," Lucifer said, baring pointy teeth in a wolfish smile.

Hannah glanced at Dismas. He looked away. Hannah gulped and stilled her mind. Figuring out these riddles was all on her. *Weeds mean evil. Evil infested something pure.*

Baal snorted in contempt. "These humans are too stupid to figure it out."

Hannah's head hurt trying to decipher the next part. *Turn it around—something sank with great speed. Maybe water, dirt, or sand caused something to sink. With a great speed, which could be a flood, tidal wave, or earthquake.*

Beelzebub raised seven gnarled claws. "Seven seconds left."

"Six," Mahway said, holding up one hand.

"You are not allowed to count with us, Mahway." Beelzebub swatted the giant's hand.

So odd, six fingers on one hand. Mahway. An unusual name, yet vaguely familiar. Have I heard it somewhere before? Hannah rubbed her forehead. *Wait a minute. Mahway's name is in the Book of the Giants. Mahway existed during the flood of Noah. Noah's family members were the only ones who survived. That's it! The eight branches.*

"Five." Lucifer lowered a claw. "Time's wasting away."

"It's Noah and the flood!" Hannah shouted.

Lucifer's black eyes turned to slits and his red lips twisted into a snarl as he let out a deafening roar. His fists clenched at his sides, veins bulging in his arms as he struggled to contain his fury, forcing Hannah to take a step back toward Jesus. "That's"—his jaw clenched—"right."

Benjamin scratched his head. "I don't get it."

"Boys named Benjamin are so stupid," Moloch muttered, rolling his molten eyes. .

"I don't get it either." Dagon thought he was whispering to Baal, but Hannah heard him.

She bit back a smile and explained, "The trees represent humans. The weeds are the bloodthirsty giants destroying humanity. God sent the great flood and saved Noah's family—the eight branches."

"How did you figure that out?" Lucifer asked, looking at her suspiciously.

"The giant helped me. He showed me his six-fingered hand."

Mahway's face reddened hiding his fingers behind his back.

Beelzebub kicked Mahway, making Hannah almost feel sorry for mentioning him. Almost.

"The giants corrupted humanity," Jesus said. "Noah, his wife, sons, and daughters-in-law were the last of pure Adamic blood."

Lucifer sighed. "I was only eight souls away from corrupting all mankind until the great flood washed away everything I worked so hard to build."

"I don't understand," said Dismas.

"I could be born only through Adam's line and through a pure woman like Mary," Jesus said. "Lucifer sought to corrupt the entire human bloodline so I could not be born. My Father was forced to start over with Noah and his family."

"Lucifer's scheme is always to corrupt mankind, even the animals," Ramel jutted his chin and spoke in a defiant tone.

Lucifer hissed. "You are supposed to be on my side, remember?"

"How will we get to the time of Noah?" Benjamin asked.

Jesus whistled. "Galgal, come forth!"

Hannah gasped. *Galgal, —the whirlwind.*

"Ugh, anything but them." Lucifer closed his eyes and covered his ears.

Winds whipped around, and Hannah felt something she hadn't since landing in hell.

Hope.

7

When the creatures moved, the wheels moved; when the creatures stood still, the wheels stood still; and when the creatures rose from the earth, the wheels rose alongside them, for the spirit of the living creatures was in the wheels.

—Ezekiel 1:21 (HCSB)

The seventh hour in hell

A swirling, golden whirlwind appeared in the distance, igniting over the top of hell's volcanos. As the dazzling twister raced above the Sea of Despair, it whipped up tumultuous waves that pounded against the bridge. Gale force winds howled throughout hell, toppling boulders to reveal red-eyed demons scurrying away like bugs.

Hannah's long hair lashed about her face. She twisted her hair and shoved it under her robe collar.

The whirlwind aimed straight for them.

Hannah tensed and gripped her brother's arm. *It'll throw me right into Lucifer!* She shook her head. *Jesus is here. He called these winds.*

The gusts tossed small rocks high in the air, then pelted them down on Lucifer and his five underlings. He flinched as the stones struck, but did not move. Beelzebub's flies buzzed for cover inside his robe. Ramel merely yawned and stretched his arms.

Roaring flames erupted at the bottom of the whirlwind. Hannah gasped at the sight of four fiery figures moving in the twister. She tilted forward to see more.

Dismas pointed. "In the flames, the creatures' heads. A man, a lion, an ox, and an eagle."

I am undone! They must be angels. Hannah trembled at their powerful presence.

The figures had gold human legs with calves' hooves for feet that sparkled like new brass. Each angel had three sets of wings: a stationary pair from hips to torso like a tunic, a small pair at their ankles, and a third set at the shoulder blades. These remarkable upper wings linked the creatures to each other in a circle and formed one powerful wing, beating in unison, fast as a hummingbird.

With muscular arms, the angels grasped four enormous overlapping golden wheels. A fire burned within the smaller inner wheel. Countless eyeballs of every imaginable color lined the light-yellow wheel rims. A gilded carriage sat on top of the wheels with a large throne shining like the sun.

Hannah blinked and winced at the brightness. Her heart skipped a beat. *I know who these four are!* She recognized them as the creatures and chariot described by the prophet Ezekiel.

The chariot accelerated, approaching them. Hannah ducked as it descended. Benjamin dropped to the ground. Dismas rushed toward Paradise's iron bars. Ramel didn't move. Jesus' eyes shone as he smiled in anticipation.

"They have no legal right to come," muttered Lucifer.

In unison, the creatures lowered their wings as their hooves touched Paradise's rocky ground. Immediately, the flames extinguished. Smoke billowed from the wheels' spokes like a wispy cloud and covered the chariot. Hannah sniffed the sweet, woodsy frankincense mixed with the earthiness of myrrh. *That smells heavenly.* The angels escorted the chariot the rest of the way. Keeping their posts by the wheels, the creatures nodded at Jesus and bowed.

"At ease," ordered Jesus.

Breaking rank, the creatures bolted toward him.

"Victory!" snorted the ox and lifted Jesus off the ground.

"Together again!" squawked the eagle.

"I missed you," the man said in a deep voice, patting Jesus on the back.

The lion tousled Jesus' hair. "Do you remember me? I mean, all of us?"

"I remember the day I created you!" Jesus petted the lion's flowing mane. "As I grew up on earth, gradually I remembered. But as I went through hell's tunnel, everything returned with crystal clarity."

Four puddles formed by the chariot's wheels.

"Here comes the waterfall!" The bull sidestepped a stream of tears gushing from the eyes of the wheels.

"Ayin, I missed you." Jesus touched the rims.

The eyes raced around the rims, making it rock back and forth.

Hannah felt dizzy watching the circular movement. *Even this being has a name! What an amazing Creator!*

Lucifer began a slow clap. "Enough. Take your sob show and get out of hell."

"Traitor!" the lion roared.

"You all have to obey the Creator while I am free to do what I want," Lucifer taunted.

"Rebel." The ox stomped his hoof.

"Can't any of you let go of the past?" Lucifer sighed. "I am just trying to enlighten humanity and free them from the shackles of the Uncreated One."

"Liar!" The ox raised a fist. "You want humans to worship you instead of their Father who created them."

"You are the one who enslaves, Lucifer," said the man. "God is your Creator, too. Show some respect." He shook his head. "Only God knows why he fashioned you and the rest of your insurgents." His eyes flashed directly into Lucifer's.

"I'm warning you," Lucifer growled as he shielded his eyes. "Leave my home."

The eagle turned his head in a full rotation. "It's a real dung hole."

Jesus held his hand between the eagle and the devil. "Let's not waste our precious time arguing with Lucifer. I called you to escort Dismas, Hannah, Benjamin, and Ramel to the time of Noah."

"We obey," the four replied in unison, clicking their hooves together.

"Let me introduce you properly." Jesus turned to Hannah and the others. "Gonael, the eagle, controls the north winds."

Gonael bobbed his head. "I will gladly watch over you."

Jesus pointed to the man. "Jachniel governs the south winds."

"At your service." Jachniel bowed.

"That big guy is Padel, ruler of the west winds." Jesus tilted his head toward the ox.

"I will guard you with my life." Padel placed his hand over his chest.

Hannah felt no warmth from Padel. *Do angels have hearts?*

"Dormel, our lion, guides the winds from the east."

"I will take you wherever you want to go." Dormel winked at Dismas.

"I saw you earlier," blurted Dismas. "All of you. You're the golden statues, in the holy of holies, guarding the ark of the covenant. You've come to life. Isn't that right, Jesus?"

Hannah's eyes widened in understanding. *Dismas is right. They do match Solomon's cherub descriptions.*

Jesus nodded at Dismas. Then, he approached the wheels and gently rocked its rim. "This is Ayin." The eyes blinked at Jesus like twinkling stars.

Hannah sensed the divinity and compassion of the unusual creature. *Maybe they're not so creepy after all.*

Jesus touched Hannah's shoulder.

Butterflies fluttered in her stomach at the reassuring gesture. *How is all this going to work out?*

"Get going already!" Lucifer bellowed.

"Hannah, you will need this for your journey." Jesus held out the broken key, shaped like half a skull with one ruby eye. "Keep it safe. Some of the Paradise prisoners might not believe they can leave this place and live in heaven until they see this key made whole."

She stared at the multitude behind the bars. Hannah gulped. *I hope I won't fail them.*

"Trusting a foolish woman. Is that wise?" questioned Lucifer.

"I will not let you down," Hannah declared, but her fingers trembled when she took the key from Jesus, slipping it into her pocket.

Jesus looked straight into her eyes. "I believe in you, Hannah." He clutched her right hand. "Father, thank you for protecting your daughter. Give her wisdom to find the key pieces and help her return on the third day."

Lucifer growled.

Warmth and encouragement flooded Hannah. The thumb of her hand in Jesus' grip tingled as if held over a flame. She prayed she would be good enough. As she approached the chariot, one of the wheels spun loose and transformed into a golden staircase with Ayin's eyes rolling around the steps. Hannah carefully avoided the eyeballs as each flitted away from her foot. The throne became two butter yellow seats facing each other. She sat and touched its gold armrest.

Benjamin bounded up the two steps at a time and plopped in

beside her. "I'm not sitting next to whatever Ramel is. And we already know the type of person Dismas is. If I sit across from him, I still have to look at his hideous scar."

Hannah's face flushed. No sense in displaying a separatist attitude when they all had to work together. She watched Lucifer give Ramel a parting kiss on the cheek and whisper something in his ear. Ramel nodded discreetly. He placed one sandal on the bottom step.

Padel charged in front of him, blocking his path. "No way in heaven you're sitting up there, traitor." He shook his horns.

"Still all brawn and no brains." Ramel eyed Padel's neck. "Where's your yoke?"

"You forget who I am."

"Let him board," Jesus commanded.

Padel fumed as Ramel brushed past him.

"We need to watch him," Benjamin murmured in his sister's ear.

Ramel slid into the seat across from Benjamin and stretched out his legs, tattered wings pressed against the back of the seat. He nodded at Hannah, but she turned her gaze to the glass floor of the chariot.

Dismas hesitated at the steps. "I can't. I'm not worthy to sit in God's chariot. I have done horrible things."

Jesus took his arm guiding him to the first step, "The old Dismas died on that cross today, Your past is forgotten. Now, walk into your future by visiting the past."

Dismas plodded up the steps and nodded to Hannah before sitting next to Ramel. The staircase reverted to a wheel. The four living creatures gathered around Jesus and spoke in hushed tones.

Based on their posture, Hannah wondered, *Do angels pray?* She offered her own prayer, *Lord, guide us each step of the way. Protect us and keep us safe.*

"How I hate long goodbyes ... so boring," Lucifer said. "Goodbye, fools! Bad luck on your journey." He touched the giant's arm and commanded, "To the strategy room." Then he vanished with Mahway, and the rest of the fallen angels disappeared one by one.

The Paradise prisoners cheered. Some of them began prayers of protection. Hannah's confidence blossomed.

Jachniel, Gonael, Padel, and Dormel hoisted the massive wheels over their heads. They stretched out their wings and shouted in unison, "Fire, wind, ignite!"

The flames reignited in the inner wheels as the living creatures connected their wings and began pumping them. The chariot lifted. Glass rose over the sides and top, creating a crystal cube.

Benjamin pounded on the new glass with his fist. "It's solid."

Probably for our protection. It's guaranteed to be a bumpy ride.

As the chariot rose over Paradise, Grandmother Abigail blew a kiss toward them.

Hannah waved back.

Leaning against a fig tree, Adam and Eve scrutinized the chariot and scowled.

What's their deal? Hannah wondered. A thought to ponder another time.

The chariot aimed for the tunnel where Hannah and Benjamin had entered earlier. Soil splattered against the glass as the chariot rushed up the tunnel and through the earth's surface. The wheels' flames provided light in the night sky.

Hannah peered at flat-roofed houses lining the streets. She elbowed her brother and pointed. "Our house."

She could almost hear her mother's mournful sobs. How she wished she could be asleep in her bed, not bearing the weight of a divine quest. Tears sprang at the corners of her eyes, and she discreetly wiped them away with the sleeve of her robe.

The chariot soared higher into the sky as the constellations came out to play. The living creatures furiously pumped their wings, shedding feathers all over the glass. Hannah remembered David's psalm: "He will cover you with his feathers; you will take refuge under his wings. His faithfulness will be a protective shield."

"That's right, Hannah. Hold onto those words."

She looked around for the source of the voice. The living creatures' faces appeared immovable. But Jachniel nodded at her. *Can he hear my thoughts?* She hoped not. *Keep it together. You're just nervous.*

"The earth is round like a ball," Benjamin said, peering through the floor.

"A blue ball covered in water," Dismas said, holding his stomach. His face had turned green, even his scar. "How much farther?"

Hannah's chest ached with worry. *I can't swim.* Panic rose within her. She longed to ask the creatures when this would be over. She opened her mouth but closed it again. What if she distracted them? Instead, Hannah turned her gaze to Ramel. His head had slumped onto his chest, and he snored. Hannah whispered to her brother, "How can he sleep when we're hurling across the sky?"

Benjamin kicked Ramel's shin.

Ramel's eyes bulged open, and he grabbed Benjamin's foot. "What do you want?"

"Sorry for bothering you, but could you tell us where we are?" Hannah asked. "I know we are headed to Noah's time, but how?"

Ramel's eyes softened, and Hannah noticed flecks of azure in them. "There are three heavens. The first heaven is where earth's birds fly and the mountains touch the sky. Presently, we're approaching the second heaven. The angels call it spatium—space. The sun, moon, and stars live here. The fallen angels try to rule the second heaven. Lucifer even built a foothold." Ramel pointed below and far to the left. "See that white blob over there? That is Pergamon, Lucifer's throne room. He had everything built in white stone." Ramel leaned back in his seat.

"But Pergamon is a city. Doesn't Lucifer live in hell?" Hannah asked. Old Scribe had once told her Pergamon was a pagan place excelling at wickedness.

"Lucifer always wanted to be like God, so he needed his own throne room, too. Unless times have changed, Lucifer still has legal rights to the third heaven. He'll barge into God's throne room to accuse God's people."

"How does he get access to the third heaven?" Dismas asked, easing his grip on his stomach.

"In the beginning, God allowed all angels access to all the heavens. But when Lucifer rebelled, God banished him from the third heaven along with one third of the angels. But God always honors his laws, and the fallen angels still have legal access. Of course, there is fierce opposition from the Lord's army. Most battles occur in the second heaven." Ramel gazed out the window. "Look closely at the North Star. See those flashes? They are the swords of the angels standing guard at one of the entrances to the third heaven."

Hannah looked closely, but it was no different from when she peered at the North Star for an extended time and saw dancing, elongated flashes. Was Ramel just teasing? She peeked over her shoulder, expecting to see Lucifer flying by with his fallen angel army.

"I see streaks," Benjamin said excitedly. "Shooting stars from earth zooming straight into the third heaven."

Ramel shook his head. "No, those aren't shooting stars. They're prayers flying to the throne room and filling the golden bowls of heaven. I can still remember the sweet aroma of incense."

Hannah's heart raced. *Can this all be true?*

The chariot climbed higher and higher as it took them farther into space.

"I don't understand. Is Noah's time concealed up here?" Dismas asked.

Ramel stood, and twisted around, almost poking Hannah's eye with his tattered wing. He peered into the skies and pointed over Hannah's head. "See that gray mass? Now look in the middle where it's pitch black. Beyond that blackhole is the time of Noah."

Black was an understatement. It was the blackest of black, completely devoid of light, despite being surrounded by the moon and stars.

"It's spinning like a top," said Dismas.

"Brace yourselves!" shouted the four living creatures.

The chariot accelerated toward the swirling hole. Flames shot out from all four interior wheels. Then, the chariot darted forward, dumping Hannah to the floor. Black smoke rose from the wheels and Ayin's eyes raced. Despite the glass, the burning smell filled her nostrils. Slowly, she lifted her head and found the others clinging to the armrests. Hannah hoisted herself back into her seat and seized her armrest in a death grip. Her brother's eyes were wild with fear, and he squirmed in his seat. Dismas' hand shook, wiping beads of sweat off his forehead. Ramel released a loud yawn.

"It a trap!" yelled Benjamin. "The creatures are working for Lucifer. They're going to kill us!"

Hannah craned her neck again, searching for Lucifer.

"Quit yammering, kid," Ramel said. "Those creatures and this chariot are straight from the throne room of God." He blinked slowly, and his eyes closed again. His snore sounded like a cross between a lion's roar and elephant's trumpeting.

No way can he sleep through this. Maybe he just didn't want to answer any more questions.

From the corner of Hannah's eye, a rock the size of a large platter whizzed by the chariot and nearly hit them. Soon, more jagged rocks and massive boulders flew around them. Hannah peered through the glass floor at the creatures who were now flapping all their wings. They remained undeterred when a storm of pebbles pelted their legs and faces. A pointy stone banged on the chariot's glass wall and Hannah flinched. Surely, the glass of God's very own chariot would hold. Another psalm came to mind, "He makes the clouds his chariot; he rides on the wings of the wind."

Just then, a larger boulder crunched against the glass.

Oh no!

Cracks spread like a spiderweb on Hannah's side. The chariot approached a layer of the gray mass. It covered them like fog. The creatures steered them toward the spinning blackhole as the crack extended over her head. She prayed the glass would hold as the blackhole loomed before them.

"Then He will also say to those on the left, 'Depart from Me, you who are cursed, into the eternal fire prepared for the Devil and his angels!'"

—Matthew 25:41 (HCSB)

Lucifer's strategy room
The ninth hour in hell

Mahway paused at the oversized ebony door. He gagged at the stench of death within the hardened volcano. If the obsidian walls could talk, they would tell tales of snares, traps, stolen souls, plots, devious one-sided deals, and the devil only knew what else.

Lucifer had brought the others here after the quest send-off. They took their places at the round table in the middle of the room. Lucifer marched to his polished ebony desk. A primitive distressed oak chest sat in a corner and candles flickered from sconces on the walls.

Mahway sat in one of the black iron chairs, beating Beelzebub to the coveted seat under one of the five points of the pentagram burnt into the tabletop. To remain cautious, he resisted the excitement of finally being invited to Lucifer's strategy room. He couldn't afford to lose another piece of his soul to this wretched room.

"Can't believe one chariot can kick up so much sulfur." Moloch sneezed repeatedly. "There's no getting used to it."

"Do you think I care about an abundance of sulfur?" With a growl, Lucifer lunged for the table and flipped it with ease.

Mahway shoved back his chair just in time to dodge the attack. *Another bad mood.* Then again, none of them had expected Jesus' three-day weekend in hell. To prove his loyalty, he planned to stay on Lucifer's good side. He'd weigh his words before he spoke, avoiding being a spark or a target for Lucifer's wrath.

"This turn of events is beyond disturbing," growled Baal. "Are we really going to lose all our prisoners in Paradise?"

"What is this game about a key? And why wasn't I notified?" Moloch's eyes narrowed.

Mahway rolled his eyes. *Shut up, Moloch. Who cares about a key? We need to focus on the main problem.*

"I knew all about the key," Beelzebub preened. "But why did you send Ramel? And how will we ensure they won't find the pieces?"

"Enough questions. I need answers!" Lucifer screamed, his thin lips curling and face purpling. "Does anyone have reports from the demons on the ground?"

Beelzebub picked his teeth, with his sharpened fingernail, dislodging a decaying fly wing. "One of my informants told me Jesus told the humans to fear hell since it has the power to destroy both the body and soul."

Mahway used the opportunity. "I heard Jesus tell a person, 'If your arm or leg causes you to sin, it's better for you to cut it off than to have your entire body go to hell.'"

"There are plenty of one-armed and one-legged people in hell." Lucifer waved away the comment.

The fallen angels jeered at Mahway.

He hated them all.

"Wait a minute," Dagon stood, "the only place in hell that can kill both the body and soul is the Lake of Fire."

"Ugh, you too, dredging up the Lake of Fire." Moloch shivered.

Dagon walked to the oak chest, engraved with illegible words of the angelic language, pulled a key from his necklace, and opened the rusty lock. After rooting around, Dagon eased out a scroll. He scrunched his face in displeasure at the item, then snapped at his comrades. "Table."

Beelzebub and Baal leapt up, snatched the table legs, and righted it.

"It was something that insufferable David said," Dagon explained as he spread the scroll on the table.

Mahway skimmed the words. The Book of Psalms. David had written most of them. *What a singing fool.*

Dagon paused and tapped the page. He cleared his throat and snarled as he read, "'For you will not abandon my soul to hell, or let your holy one see corruption.'" A savage smile turned to his colleagues. "David's psalm confirms it. Jesus has a soul since he's a man. If that's true, we can destroy his soul along with his body by throwing him in the Lake of Fire."

The room erupted: Lucifer squealed in delight. Moloch gasped. Baal stood, toppling his chair. But Mahway crossed his arms, deep in thought. Dagon rolled up the scroll and tossed it into the chest.

"I solved our problem." Dagon leaned back in the chair, claws behind his head.

Beelzebub pounded on the table. "Jesus is vulnerable. His God spirit is contained in a weak human vessel."

"With no Jesus, we have only his Father and his Holy Spirit remaining." Giddy, Lucifer stood and raised his claw. "We can mount a counterattack against heaven. This time, we will be victorious!"

An eternal optimist. Mahway smirked in admiration.

"When one door slams shut, we force open another." Beelzebub popped a fly into his mouth.

"No way would Jesus put one toe into the Lake of Fire. He's no fool." Baal drummed his claws on the table.

"What if we bring the Lake of Fire to Jesus? Burn him along with their precious Paradise," suggested Moloch.

"If we kill Jesus, none of our prisoners will ever see their mansions in heaven." Beelzebub curled his treacherous lips in a grin; a fly squirmed between his sharp teeth, its wings struggling to escape

Dagon's face lit up. "The Lake of Fire would spread like wildfire through all the grass, trees, and bushes. Everything would go up in smoke."

"Lucifer, this crazy idea might just work." Baal leaned back in his chair. "The element of surprise is crucial."

"It's ingenious, and of course, I thought of it." Lucifer puffed out his chest, and strutted behind his ebony desk.

"Wait a minute, it's a brilliant idea because I thought of it." Dagon furrowed his brow.

Lucifer always takes the credit. Until things went wrong, then it was never his idea.

Lucifer banged open drawers and clawed through the contents. "Where's my map?"

"Where was the last place you put it?" asked Moloch.

Lucifer rolled his eyes and checked another drawer. "Yes!" He held up the map scroll, brought it to the table, and unrolled it. It curled up again. "A little help here," Lucifer huffed.

Baal retrieved two knives from a pocket and stabbed them into opposite corners of the map.

The map displayed the locations of the twelve gates of hell, and the portals and tunnels between earth and hell. Mahway eyed the tar pits and ocean caverns, making sure Lucifer didn't hold back any of these sacred spots. They were the only places where he could maintain his physical form.

At the bottom right was Mount Nevermost, and the Lake of Fire covered a generous portion of the left side of the map, represented by red-orange flames. Mahway had never been to the vast lake.

Lucifer placed his claw tip on the icon of prison bars in the middle of the map. "There it is, the Lake of Fire, west of Paradise."

Baal shook his head. "Impossible! We have only three days. Besides, how can you divert the lake?"

Lucifer pointed to a segment of the lake which ran diagonally above Paradise. "We build a tunnel here and divert a portion of the lake right over Jesus' head. Of course, we will widen the tunnel enough to burn down the whole place."

Another construction project. Mahway leaned back in his chair. Now he knew why he was here. *Quick, say something to deflect this risky mission, showing you want no part of it without exactly saying no.* He coughed lightly and chuckled as he shook his head. "Who would be foolish enough to volunteer to move it?" *That should do it.*

Lucifer rubbed his horns and then smiled, showing his teeth and the malice about to lace his words. "But Mahway, you were the lead in the Baalbek project. You completed it in record time, and that's why I have selected you to manage the Lake of Fire project. Congratulations!"

"How I loved the city of Baalbek," Baal sighed. "Cain built that as tribute to me before the flood. Ah, the good old days."

Mahway remembered it differently: Cain had built the city to hide from God's wrath after killing his brother, Abel. Somehow, Baal had seduced the entire city to worship him. His back began to throb at the memory of lifting those elephantine stones. He should have declined coming to this meeting—he'd known they'd make him do their dirty work. "I'm honored you asked me, but there is risk involved. One false move and the flames of that lake blot you out for all eternity."

"What if I make you an offer?" Lucifer leaned back and rubbed his horn. "While Paradise is burning down, you might be able to rescue Cecilia. It's a shame how she slipped through the cracks." He shrugged. "Who would have thought the Uncreated One would lower his standards by allowing her into

Paradise?"

Rescue Cecilia and return her to me? Mahway's heart leapt and he forced an even tone. "I accept. I will lead the project. But I am going to need help."

"What about the twins, Ohya and Hahya?" Beelzebub suggested. "Didn't they train with you?"

Mahway shot Beelzebub a deadly stare. *Of course he'd suggest the gruesome twosome.*

"It's settled," Lucifer said. "The Lake of Fire construction project will begin immediately. Any Nephilim who aren't working on the project will ascend to Jerusalem to spread doubt and rumors about Jesus. If all else fails, fall back on our standard operating procedure—steal, kill, and destroy."

The fallen angels joined the chant, "Steal, kill, and destroy!"

As they celebrated, the ground shook. The map of hell rolled off the table.

"What's happening?" Dagon struggled to stand.

Lucifer mimicked praying hands with his claws. "The chariot broke through the time barrier. I certainly hope and pray they weren't crushed."

The fallen angels cackled like hyenas.

Mahway didn't join the revelry—the joke was just deflecting that Lucifer couldn't travel back in time. He focused instead on the task at hand. Construct a tunnel, fill it with flames, divert the lake into Paradise—without touching it—and free his Cecilia.

Even if he couldn't free his beloved, maybe it would be enough just to grab her and explain his side of the story. He owed her that much.

9

Their judges and rulers went to the daughters of men and took their wives by force from their husbands according to their choice, and the sons of men in those days took from the cattle of the earth, the beasts of the field and the fowls of the air, and taught the mixture of animals of one species with the other, in order therewith to provoke the Lord; and God saw the whole Earth and it was corrupt, for all flesh had corrupted its ways upon earth, all men and all animals.

—The Book of Jasher 4:18

Northern Mesopotamia, 2378 BC
The tenth hour in hell

Hannah exhaled. The window held together, at least for now.

Cutting through the gray mist, the chariot barreled toward the looming black abyss. Light fragments danced outside the white rim. *Stunning, but where will this perilous ride end?* Her leg began to twitch at the unsettling thought.

"Prepare for impact," commanded the creatures.

All she could do was grip the seat's arm tighter.

Ayin closed his eyes and the creatures shouted orders to one another in a language Hannah didn't understand.

As they exited the gray area, the living creatures folded all their wings and leapt inside the wheels, standing on the bottom rung of the outer wheel spokes and gripping the higher ones.

"Oh, that can't be good," Ramel said.

No longer guided by the angels, the chariot flipped on its

right side and the blackhole sucked it in, like a storm swallowing an anchorless vessel.

Hannah's legs slipped from under her and a sandal flew off. Her little toe rammed into something hard. She guessed it was Ramel's hoof. She winced and teared up at the pain. As she tried rearranging herself in the seat, she recalled a partial verse from Moses's first book: "I am with you and will watch over you wherever you go." *This place certainly qualifies as "wherever."*

The chariot plummeted relentlessly, spinning through the blackhole. Hannah spotted thousands of shimmering lights, resembling a colossal shattered mirror showering from the white rim. The chariot's flames sputtered into nothingness. Even the voices of the creatures seemed muted, overshadowed by the lights bursting through the blackness. Then, the chariot began to bounce. It felt like being tossed and shaped on a potter's wheel. Hannah screamed, no longer able to contain her fright.

Shortly, Dismas and Benjamin joined her with high-pitched screeches, like a dissonant pair of windchimes.

Lights continued to gather outside the white rim, a twinkling and twirling avalanche around the blackhole. Hannah shut her eyes, but white dancing dots still appeared through her eyelids. Finally, the chariot jolted to a stop in midair. The sudden motion sent Hannah forward, banging her head against Dismas'.

"Sorry," Dismas rubbed his forehead.

At least it's stopped. Maybe the chariot is stuck? It remained suspended in the air, but Hannah still felt the whirling sensation. Clasping her hands behind her neck, she bent over to regain control.

Ramel mumbled something about rings.

How does he know my ears are ringing?

"Amazing," Benjamin whispered.

Please be quiet, she silently begged her brother. She certainly didn't want to throw up all over God's chariot.

"Rings of fire!" Dismas gasped.

Smoke burned her nostrils. *What now?* Hannah lifted her head, expecting a fiery inferno. Instead, thousands of blazing halos spiraled around the chariot creating a tunnel of fire. Through the cracked glass, twisting red, orange, blue, yellow, and white flames paraded around the chariot. Soon, the colors and patterns had soothed Hannah's wooziness and her breathing steadied. Then, the magnificent display vanished —like everything precious in her life the fire rings dissipated, the shadowy black returned.

The chariot wheels banged on something hard. *Ground?* Hannah peeked through the glass floor to find rocky terrain under the chariot. Brown granite walls glistening with moisture encircled them like a tomb. Sunlight filtered through an opening ahead. *A cave?*

The four creatures emerged from their holds and rested against the oversized wheels.

Ayin opened his eyes but remained motionless.

Hannah touched her pocket to ensure the key's safety. But the pocket, her entire robe, had been replaced. She now wore an odd set of black pants and a zebra-patterned top. "Where's the key?" Had she lost it in all that spinning and whirling?

"Try your pants pocket at your hip," Jachniel suggested.

Hannah reached below a black leather belt, held by several loops around the waist of the pants. She touched the jagged metal key and sighed. Gazing at her companions, she noticed they all still wore black, but the design of the outfits had changed, like hers. Benjamin and Dismas wore similar black pants, but their black-and-white striped shirts had different patterns. Ramel's clothes remained the same, his black robe and wings still tattered. She slipped her sandal back on her foot. *At least my shoes didn't change.*

Hannah touched the smooth, flat stones down the front of her shirt.

"Don't tell me you've never seen buttons before?" Ramel rolled his eyes.

Hannah's cheeks flushed and her eyes dropped. She noticed the blackened nail on her right thumb.

"Our clothes and thumbs have black spots," Benjamin said. He and Dismas held up their hands.

We still can't leave our sins behind, even while traveling through time.

"The mark on your thumb does not represent one of your sins," explained Jachniel. "Jesus presented you with a time marker. The color of your nail will track the amount of time you have before your return to hell with or without the completed key."

Benjamin said, "Before we left Paradise, when Jesus prayed over us, I did feel a burning on my thumb. It's like a reverse sundial."

Hannah drew a deep trembling breath, her glaze fixated on the sliver of white gradually appearing at the edge of her nail, like the first light at dawn. She concealed her thumb under her other fingers. *What if we fail?* Yet a gentle smile spread across her lips, marveling at the power Jesus had to measure time through her hand.

Dismas tugged at his shirt. "How did you change our clothes?"

"We have our ways," Padel said gruffly. "Keep your eyes on the tunnel walls. We'd like to show you a vision."

Hannah's reflection stared back at her through the chariot's cracked glass. She frowned at her long, braided hair, piled high on top of her head, fastened by two blue beads on sticks. *I have never worn my hair like this.* She touched it, amazed at her transformation.

Dismas rubbed his elbow on the glass, wrinkling the sleeve of his pristine top. "I can barely see through the cracks."

Gonael waved his arm and screeched, "Goodbye, glass."

The glass faded, revealing a room with floor-to-ceiling shelves, a tall, thin, wooden door in the middle. Over the door, a sign read, *Lucifer's Apothēca.*

"Lucifer's storehouse," Hannah translated. *We escaped hell only to meet Lucifer again.* She narrowed her eyes and continued her perusal. Amid the bookcases leaned an oversized mirror trimmed in gold. One shelf behind a red ladder was filled with chalice-sized brown bottles. Hannah translated some labels large enough to read: lizard king teeth, unicorn horns. *What's a unicorn?* The other labels were either too small to read, or words she didn't recognize.

Upside-down candles hung in glass clusters over a dark pentagram-shaped table where a red-robed Lucifer occupied a regal chair. He had no horns, but tarnished blond locks cascading to his masculine chin. Instead of claws, long thin fingers flipped through a neat stack of white papers. Beyond the chiseled complexion, his gleaming black eyes with red pupils gave away his true nature. Hannah shivered and the hairs on her arms rose.

The bell over the store's entrance chimed as a white-cloaked figure darted inside, glittering wings brushing through the doorway. An oversized hood concealed the figure's face. Lucifer locked the door and steered the new arrival to the table. The figure sat gingerly in one of the chairs, wings draping over the back. The angel shifted nervously. Lucifer returned to his chair and rubbed his hands together.

"You better have made the changes or no deal." The male voice of the mysterious figure resonated sunshine.

Lucifer snatched a slim file from a pile and withdrew a paper with an emblem of a snake encircling an apple. With authority, he read, "Item number one: The undersigned agrees to immediately abandon his position at the first estate known as the watch—"

"That clause hasn't changed. Don't waste my time." The figure dropped his hood, allowing long, golden hair to spill down onto the table.

A watcher angel! This vision continued the story they'd been shown before they left hell.

"This is the start of your new life," Lucifer growled, slamming the paper to the table. "If you don't leave your post, then nothing happens." With a sigh, Lucifer smoothed back his hair. His tone became sickly sweet. "I hate this fighting. We used to be such good friends."

"Humph. Even when you fooled us into believing you were a good cherub, I never liked you. Over the last five hundred years, you've corrupted the earth. I will no longer remain idle while you destroy those I vowed to watch." The watcher angel shoved the table, sending a stack of papers fluttering to the floor.

Hannah strained to see the angel's face, but it was no use—his back was to them.

"That's not all you watched," Lucifer hissed. He searched his papers again. "Ahh, there. Item two, the undersigned—that's you—will marry Nava."

"Did you include the section I requested about Samyaza?" asked the watcher angel.

Samyaza! He tried to drag me away at Mount Nevermore. Hannah's head throbbed trying to make sense of this vision.

"See for yourself." Lucifer slid the paper over to the angel.

He picked it up and read, "Samyaza will terminate his plan to impregnate Nava and will cease harassing her family effective immediately upon your signature." The watcher angel's hand shook, but his voice remained calm.

"Does the rewording meet your specifications?" Lucifer asked.

The angel nodded.

Nava must be someone important.

"In conclusion," Lucifer paced the length of the table, hands behind his back, "the undersigned agrees to immediately abandon his post and be transferred into the kingdom of darkness, where Lucifer will be his master." His forked tongue darted over his thin upper lip.

"I have already agreed to that condition." Now, the angel's voice shook.

"It bears repeating since the words please me." A silver coin materialized in Lucifer's hands, and he rolled it between his fingers. "Number two hundred, the last of its kind."

Hannah's mind flashed back to the pivotal moment in Lucifer's vision of Lamech when she had witnessed the coin materialize for the first time. *Lucifer used the coins to turn watcher angels into men primed for procreating.* She squinted, noticing the coin had Lucifer's ugly profile etched on one side, and the image of the serpent wrapped around an apple on the other. *Same as on the papers.*

"Let's get this over with." The watcher angel turned to the last page. He glided his finger across it, leaving behind a golden signature.

The lights exploded. Then came the sound of fumbling, and a candle flickered in Lucifer's hands.

"Catch." Lucifer sneered and tossed the coin to the watcher angel.

As soon as the angel caught the coin, thunder echoed throughout the room. He fell, writhing in pain. His robe turned black, and his wings vanished. A few minutes passed before he stumbled to the mirror. Hannah gasped at his reflection. He was a tall man with violet eyes, short dark hair, and a trimmed beard. He wiggled his toes. "Feet instead of hooves." His voice no longer sounded divine, but ordinary.

Hannah balled her fists. *I hope Nava is worth it.*

"You will need a new identity," Lucifer declared. "Item fifty-seven of the contract states that I am the one who chooses your name because I own you." He leaned back in his chair and rubbed his pointed chin. "What about Liraz? It means 'my secret.'"

"It's—fine," the former angel answered, clearing his gravelly throat.

"Your human voice will get easier with time. If you want to be a singer, I could make you rich and famous"—Lucifer snapped—"just like that."

"Thanks, but I'd better keep a low profile." Liraz looked in the mirror, studying himself.

"You will do whatever I tell you." Lucifer surged toward Liraz and grabbed him by the back of his neck, then shoved his face into the mirror. The mirror shattered the jagged pieces hitting the floor. "You've been remade," Lucifer pointed to the door. "Now, go make me proud and enjoy yourself."

Liraz continued to peer into the broken mirror. "All these years of watching mankind, now I am one of them."

Lucifer returned to the table and carefully gathered the contract. "Remember, the coin must always touch your skin, otherwise you will return to your spirit state. Well," he chuckled cruelly, "to your new fallen angel state. Don't lose that coin, understood?"

"When can I see Nava?" Liraz's face lit up and he smiled with perfect white teeth.

Hannah wanted to cry at the exchange. *Liraz gave up everything for Nava. Seth never came back for me after he signed our marriage contract.* She shook her head. Stop getting wrapped up in Liraz and Nava. *I know how it ends—horribly. Everyone dies. Focus on locating the key piece.*

"I've arranged for you to meet Nava tonight," Lucifer said. "The sooner you get her pregnant, the better. Ah, I can't wait until Noah meets his giant freak grandchild. Maybe it will eat the entire family." He cackled.

Hannah's mouth dropped open. *Nava is Noah's daughter.*

Liraz's eyes flamed. "The contract states you can't hurt Nava's family."

"I won't touch them. But accidents happen every day in this world."

"Do you think Nava will fall for me?" Liraz checked his

reflection one more time.

"We'll do whatever it takes for her to lust after you. We always have the love enchantments available at our disposal."

"Yes, um … I'm looking forward to starting a family with her," Liraz murmured. His eyes shifted to his feet.

The vision faded, leaving Hannah confused. Liraz had been a human for only a short time and already learned how to lie. But why?

10

And the sister of Tubal Cain was Naamah. R. Abba b. Kahana said: Naamah was Noah's wife and why called Naamah? Because her deeds were pleasing (ne'imim).

—Bereshit Rabbah 23:3

The eleventh hour in hell

The creatures rolled the chariot to the cave entrance. Growing just outside the cave, long, smelly fern branches obstructed any view of the outside world.

"We delivered you successfully," said Dormel. "Now it's time for you to find the key piece."

Hannah froze in her seat. *But they told Jesus they would protect us.* She and her brother exchanged uneasy glances.

The wheel rims converted to a staircase again, and the group disembarked.

"Where are we?" asked Dismas. He, Benjamin, and Ramel moved toward the ledge to investigate.

Hannah maneuvered around the stinky leaves to catch up. When she lifted her head, she gasped. *Noah's ark!* The enormous vessel dominated the flat hill. The elevation rose above a green forest valley. Behind the ark loomed a walled city—its lofty buildings stretched into the sky. The blue line of ocean reached the horizon beyond the city.

"This city could be the eighth wonder," said Benjamin. "The towering buildings seem so thin and frail, they should topple. And those walls of glass should break. How can this be?"

As Hannah observed the valley, a low roar rumbled above their heads. *Is that Dormel?* But a peek over her shoulder revealed the creatures speaking in hushed tones near the chariot. The creatures and Ramel weren't disturbed by the racket in the sky.

"What is that?" yelled Dismas over the rumble.

"There." Hannah pointed to a strange white bird gliding through the sky. *No face, no feathers, windows, two motionless wings. How does it stay in the sky?*

Dismas and Benjamin craned their necks to watch the object glide across the muted blue sky. Shortly, it left their vision, leaving a trail of white streaks that dissipated into the sky.

"What is that thing?" asked Benjamin.

"No rapid travel machines in your time?" mocked Ramel rolling his eyes. He sauntered to the edge of the ledge and frowned at the ark.

A commotion broke out near the chariot. Jachniel attempted to restrain Padel by the waist. Breaking free, Padel charged from the cave, wings shaking as he glowered at Ramel. He lowered his head and butted Ramel on the left side. Ramel wobbled and fell on his back, nearly tumbling off the ledge. Pebbles scattered below. Padel pumped his fist in the air, ready to strike Ramel like a cobra. "How dare you! It's because of you those things are in the sky. Giving our sacred knowledge to mankind resulted in the earth being wiped out."

The three creatures surrounded Padel with mummers of "Resist evil," and "Wait on the Lord."

"Don't you think I've been punished enough?" Ramel brushed himself off. "And I'm not talking about Tartarus."

"You don't know the half of it." Padel lowered his fist and spun away. He brushed past his companions and stood before Hannah and her brother, face flushed.

Hannah's stomach tightened as she steeled herself for Padel's boiling wrath.

The heavenly scent of frankincense wafted from his gesture as he waved Dismas closer. "Hurry and retrieve the key piece," he said curtly. "The sooner the key's completed, the faster I can return Ramel to Tartarus."

Ramel stood and shook fern leaves from his robe. "Can't one of you perfect beings muzzle Padel's big fat snout, so we don't have to hear his grating voice? Better yet, grab a yoke and I'll wrap it around the old ox's stubborn neck and force him to return me to Tartarus. I won't have to see any of you ever again except in my nightmares."

Padel stomped back to the chariot.

"Find Noah and he will direct you to the key piece," Gonael advised and returned to the cave with Dormel and Jachniel following.

"How are we going to get off the cliff, across the valley, and climb up to the ark?" asked Dismas.

"Ramel knows the way." Gonael's his feathers rousted softly as he gilded between the wheels.

Hannah looked at Ramel. He remained at the edge of the cliff with his fists clenched by his sides. She certainly didn't want to follow him anywhere.

"You can't change a thing, Ramel," Padel taunted. He slid inside the wheel. A burst of fire sparked within.

"You can't change anything either," Ramel shot back.

What on earth is this feud about? They reminded Hannah of bickering siblings.

"Call us when you have located the piece," the living creatures said in unison. And with a bright flash, the chariot and creatures disappeared.

"How dare they leave us with a traitor as our guide." Benjamin kicked a pebble off the cliff.

Hannah watched it drop. It was a long way down. As her eyes moved across the land, she spotted a small river encircling the forest. How would they cross it to get to the boat? *Don't cry.* Remembering Scripture would bolster her thinking. *Be strong and courageous. Do not be discouraged, for the Lord your God will be with you wherever you go.* She wiped away a tear and straightened her shoulders.

Ramel groaned. "Let's get something straight. Jesus rescued me from Tartarus to go on this quest, and I will help, but on one condition: the three of you must stop looking at me as if I will throw you off this cliff and eat you."

"Aren't you on Lucifer's side?" questioned Benjamin.

"Make those two conditions: I don't answer to you," Ramel snapped.

Hannah resigned. *I guess a fallen angel is better than no angel at all.*

"Fine. Lead the way," Dismas said flatly.

"Thief, you don't speak for me or my sister," Benjamin sneered. "Stay in front of us, so I can keep an eye on you. One of us might end up dead like our grandfather."

"Enough!" shouted Ramel. He stretched out his arms and launched himself off the cliff.

Hannah raced to the edge and leaned over. Benjamin and Dismas followed at her heels. She expected to see Ramel in a crumpled mess at the bottom of the hill. But to her relief, Ramel was fine. His tattered, flittering wings held him aloft, while his hooves found footing on the boulders. Ramel leapt to the grass and winked at Hannah.

"Sure, it's easy for mountain goat hooves and wings," muttered Benjamin. "We don't have either."

"I'll instruct you on where to find the hand and footholds," Ramel suggested. "Dismas, you first."

Dismas glared at Benjamin before he scrambled over the side.

Ramel skillfully guided him to the ground.

Dismas brushed off his sleeves and looked up at them with a shrug that seemed to say it had been easy.

"Hannah's next," Ramel yelled.

Hannah's heart thumped. *Dismas did it. Maybe it won't be so bad.* She crawled to the edge, but already couldn't find a handhold. Benjamin grabbed her hands for support. She gingerly dangled her leg, fishing for a foothold. Pants afforded much more freedom than constantly tucking her burdensome robe into her belt.

"That's it, Hannah," Ramel encouraged. Then he cleared his throat and a more impatient tone came out. "Hurry. Put your foot to the left on the rock that resembles a piece of bread."

Hannah tried to concentrate, but Jesus' warning popped into her head. They could injure themselves outside of Paradise. *If I die again, would I plummet back to hell?* She couldn't return without the completed key, so she slowly trekked down the hill one rock at a time.

"The rocks are slippery," warned Ramel.

A fine mist greeted Hannah as she landed on solid ground.

"You're next, Benjamin," Ramel said.

Benjamin bounded off the final boulder and sent droplets of water flying in all directions—right into Hannah's face. She scowled her displeasure at him, but had no time to be upset. The four trudged along until they reached the river. Hannah sighed in relief—the water she had spotted above was only knee-high.

"Why do the trees look like they're floating?" Dismas pointed to the partially submerged forest in the middle of the river.

"No floating forests in your time?" asked Ramel as he sloshed through the stream. "It's called an island."

When the water rose past Hannah's knees, her heart thudded. If there was a drop-off, she'd drown and never find the key piece. A tiny fish brushed against her calf and the bright green moss tickled the tops of her feet. A soft honking grew steadily.

A flock of silver geese filled the sky. The birds reminded her of home. But as the honking approached, the sound was more like a warning. *Something's not right.*

From behind the misty cloud cover came a shrill wail. Hannah covered her ears, scanned the sky, and spotted an enormous orange bird as it swooped from the mist.

"How does it fly? It's as big as a rhinoceros!" Benjamin exclaimed.

"Looks like a cross between a bird and a lizard," Dismas observed as he approached the island.

The fowl scattered, but the orange bird scooped ten geese into its bright orange beak. It delivered an ear-splitting screech, then flapped its wings, and aimed directly for Hannah and her companions.

"Run," whispered Ramel. He and Dismas struggled through the ferns and vines, finally lifting themselves onto the island and hiding behind a coarse tree trunk.

Hannah tried to run, but couldn't lift her sandals, mired in mud. The bird pounded its jumbo wings, sights set on her. *Killed by a chariot and eaten by an overgrown bird. What are the odds.* The bird's bright green gaze drilled into Hannah. The thing had overgrown talons with nails like sharpened knives. Hannah's slim frame could easily fit in the bird's clutches. She struggled against the mud holding her in place. Unable to budge, she closed her eyes.

Something hard shoved her back.

"Hurry!" Benjamin cried. He yanked her arm so hard, she feared it would pop out of its socket.

Hannah didn't dare look behind her as the screeching intensified. She ran as fast as the muck allowed. Dismas peeked out from behind a tree, eyes widening. *Not good.* Hannah and Benjamin almost reached the island, but the vines tangled around Hannah's ankles. Benjamin released her hand. Frantically, they both tried to free themselves from the plants. Dismas and Ramel rushed out to help. Hannah prayed, *Please, God, let this ugly bird go after the geese. Spare us.*

Renewed honking came from Hannah's right. More geese filled the sky.

She glanced back and watched the bird-beast veer toward its new target. She breathed a sigh of relief and freed herself from the greenery. When she ascended to the grassy shore, she felt the ticklish blades against her bare feet. *Ugh. I lost my sandals.* "What was that creature?" she asked, rubbing her feet against soft peat moss to remove the mud. *Barefoot is the worst.* Before Ramel could answer, she added, "And no, we don't have those things in our time."

"It was known as an orange-crested lizard-bird," Ramel explained. "God drowned them in the flood with the rest of the monsters."

Dismas' eyes grew wide. "Monsters?"

"I'll tell you all about the man-eating beasts on the way to Noah's ark." Ramel skirted around two oversized fern bushes and stepped onto an overgrown stone path.

As she stepped on the wet stone, Hannah wondered if a monster would leap out from the foliage.

Ramel continued his lecture, "The Nephilim were the offspring of watcher angels and human women. The first generation had impressive strength. But when the Nephilim mated with each other, each successive generation became even more vicious and wicked. Their long lifespans and ferocious appetites soon depleted earth's resources. Then they started eating humans."

"That's horrible!" Hannah scrunched her face.

"Dreadful," agreed Ramel. "The earth-bound watchers and the fallen angels developed an unusual plan by creating behemoth animals to kill off the man-eating Nephilim."

"Create how?" asked Benjamin, raising an eyebrow.

"Through their genetic makeup."

"Ge-ne-what?" said Dismas.

"I keep forgetting how primitive you all are. Do they even have fire or wheels where you come from?" Ramel asked.

Benjamin stomped his foot. "You don't have to insult us for asking simple questions."

"Yes, you are quite simple." Ramel crossed his arms and peered down his nose at the humans.

The snap of a twig startled Hannah. A bunny the size of a small dog darted through the underbrush. With a hand to her chest, she sighed. "Well, did the plan work?" she asked.

"After much death and destruction, the Nephilim signed a treaty to stop eating people. Most of the monsters were hunted and killed, but thousands still roamed the earth."

They fell silent as they trekked through the marshy forest.

"The air here is amazing," Dismas said. "With each breath, I feel invigorated."

Hannah breathed in deeply. *He's right. After climbing off the ledge, running for my life, and all this walking, I'm not tired at all.*

"The air was purer before the flood. In your time, what is the lifespan of your people?" asked Ramel.

What a strange question, thought Hannah.

"Not very long," Benjamin said bitterly. "I made it to fifteen and Hannah twenty-one."

"I was murdered at twenty," Dismas added quietly.

"You mean you finally paid the consequences for your crimes." Benjamin shoved aside an overgrown tree branch that blocked their path.

"After the flood, God limited a person's lifespan to 120 years," Hannah said. "Only Moses lived that long. Many people never see their fortieth birthday. A few live to their nineties, but that's rare. Why do you ask?"

Ramel pointed up. "That milky white sky is a protective barrier—one of the reasons men lived so long, and why you have so much energy. Until God punched a hole in it ..." his voice trailed off.

The path ended at another stream bridged by a haphazard mound of rotting plants and rope.

"The gate's over there." Ramel pointed across the water.

Dismas and Benjamin dashed across the rickety bridge and waited.

Hannah's pulse quickened when the bridge creaked under her weight. It bobbed with each additional step. Benjamin held out his hand, but she refused, making the final leap off the bridge herself. Her joy waned, however, at the height of the gate. There were no gaps or loose bars, only claw marks scratched in the fence, more signs of those monstrous animals. *What do we do now?*

Benjamin kicked the bottom of the fence "We came too far to be overcome by a gate."

Dismas looked at Ramel expectantly.

"My tattered wings are useless," Ramel said. "Won't get us over the fence. Ah, but I have another idea." His black eyes twinkled. "Griffonflies, come." He repeated the phrase and watched the sky.

Never heard of a griffonfly either. Must be wondrous to be a supernatural creature with the wisdom of the ages.

Ramel smiled as the sound of rattling dice filled the air. "It still works." His wings fluttered in excitement.

Who is this version of Ramel? He seems almost human.

"There they are!" Ramel pointed to the ferns.

Hannah saw long, blue, shimmery bodies rising above the plants. The creatures' gossamer wings spanned two cubits. *Giant dragonflies.*

"You can't be serious," said Dismas. "How will those bugs carry us over the wall?"

I hope they don't have teeth. After the orange bird, Hannah didn't delight in an animal carrying her anywhere.

"Griffonflies, take us over the fence," ordered Ramel.

Hannah tensed. *But how?*

The griffonflies swarmed around them. One seized her at the back of her collar, two more tugged on her sleeves, and one on each leg. Hannah's body lurched vertically for a moment and then horizontally, her face toward the ground. They carried her to the top of the fence, then glided over. She caught a glimpse of the ark on the hill's summit surrounded by woods. The griffonflies descended and released her onto a peat moss cushion.

Hannah patted the head of one insect. "Thanks."

In quick succession, the griffonflies dropped off Benjamin, Ramel, and Dismas in the same manner.

Ramel pointed between two stone markers. "We want to reach the ark before nightfall." He took the lead on another wet, muddy trail in the side of the hill. Hannah trudged behind him. Complaining of sore legs, Benjamin struggled to keep up. Dismas lagged. After a quarter of an hour, Ramel stopped and put a finger to his lips. He motioned for the group to hide behind a thicket of blackberry bushes.

At the sound of voices, Hannah adjusted some greenery to get a peek at the speakers. She spied two raven haired women about twenty cubits away, maneuvering around tree stumps. Based on their similar features, they were related. One seemed about a generation older. *Mother and daughter?* Hannah pondered.

"But Nava, I thought you and Liraz couldn't conceive?" The mother's face twisted in disbelief.

So, Liraz did *marry Nava.* Hannah's mind reeled, making connections.

"Naamah, I believe I having twins, any day now." Nava's face beamed as she rubbed her belly. "Once I started taking Grandfather Lamech's special medicine, I got pregnant right away. I admit, Liraz appeared to be happy when I told him, but I could tell he was lying. Once he sees the babies, he'll fall in love with them."

"I'm your mother, don't call me by my first name." Naamah wrung her hands. "I've warned you to stay away from Lamech, especially his evil potions."

"Grandfather's the only one who has stood by me, the only family member who came to my wedding. Since you refused to witness my ceremony, you've lost the privilege of being called my mother."

Tears fell from Naamah's eyes. "Let's not bring up the past. The reason I begged you to meet me is because the flood is coming tomorrow. You must—"

"Here we go again." Nava rolled her eyes. "You and my brothers believe everything Father says. The end of the world, water from the sky. Liraz is a watcher angel masquerading as a man, and my children will be monsters." Nava paused. "Everyone thinks Father is an old fool. Do you know what it feels like to walk into a room and have everyone stop talking because of your lunatic family?"

Hannah knew how it felt to be an outcast—after Seth disappeared, people had called her cursed and avoided her.

"I must admit, I too had a tough time believing your father until the miracles started." Naamah sat on a tree stump.

"Miracles?" Nava raised an eyebrow.

"I wish you could have been with us when all the animals arrived." Naamah paused, lost in thought.

"Animals were always showing up at the vineyard," Nava said. "Father had a special bond with the four-legged beasts. You got anything else?"

"Well, this might sound crazy."

"You know it *all* sounds crazy when we're talking about Father." Nava gave a bitter laugh.

"God showed us rain when all eight of us had trouble visualizing it. You should have seen it—drops of water fell from the sky." Naamah's voice became urgent. "God said it would rain for forty days and nights, washing everything away."

"Nonsense. I'm sick of hearing about the end of the world. That's been my entire life! I am going to have an amazing life—with Liraz and my twins." Nava crossed her arms and glared at her mother.

"I don't want to fight anymore. Go home. Tell Liraz what I told you. Pack enough food and water for forty days and get on Liraz's boat. Maybe as a favor to your father, God will show mercy on you and your babies." Naamah paused. "I can't bear the thought of never seeing you again."

Hannah held back a sob. She'd never see her mother again either.

"Don't be so dramatic. Next time we meet in secret, I will bring the twins so you can see for yourself they are normal babies and not six-fingered giants."

"I hope you're right." Naamah bit her lip.

"I'm right and my perfect babies will prove Father wrong." Nava scoffed. "Water from the sky. Father has lost his mind." It started to drizzle, and Nava held out her hand. "Tears from above?" The rain stopped. She wiped the droplets from her nose. "Not rain. The mist is clumping together and sputtering from the trees."

"Your father says the flood is going to start tomorrow morning when the sun rises," Naamah raised her voice. "Tonight is your only chance to prepare for survival."

"I don't believe it." Nava placed her hands on her hips.

Naamah rushed to Nava, embracing her as close as her daughter's pregnant belly allowed.

Tomorrow. We have to find the key piece tonight and flee before the flood starts.

"Go, Nava. Tell Liraz. He might figure out a way to save you. I know he loves you."

Nava held her stomach as she tried to walk as fast a full-term pregnant woman could.

Naamah rushed away, disappearing among the trees.

"Follow the mother because she will lead—" Benjamin's words cut off when he fell to the ground.

Powerful hands tightened around Hannah's bony wrists.

11

"You are also to bring into the ark two of all the living creatures, male and female, to keep them alive with you."

—Genesis 6:19 (HSCB)

The seventeenth hour in hell

Hannah strained her neck to locate Benjamin and trembled to see her brother on the ground, a dark-haired assailant crouching over him, pressing a knee into his back. Benjamin thrashed about in the grass, but his efforts were futile against the barbarian. With a wince, she peered up at the burly man restraining her. Thick, wavy raven hair fell to his shoulders while a bushy beard adorned his cheeks and chin. His forehead glistened with sweat, which trickled down his temples. A pungent stench of cedar and wet fur filled Hannah's nostrils, but his firm grip prevented her from retreating. He offered a reassuring smile, but she didn't feel reassured at all.

Why are they doing this to us?

"Stop struggling, shorty," said the beefy assailant, pulling a rope from his chest pocket as he stood over her brother. The stranger plucked Benjamin from the ground and forced him to stand. Wet grass and dirt stuck to her brother's face. The man wrapped twine around Benjamin's wrists and allowed the rope to extend two cubits.

"My brother's a boy, not an animal." Hannah's anger flared. She aimed her kick at her captor, but her foot smashed air. *Useless.*

"Fool. I'm going to teach you a lesson!" shouted Dismas,

fighting the third aggressor and landing three quick punches on the man's stomach. The man staggered, gasping for air.

Hannah's captor laughed cruelly, cutting through the air like a bitter gust of wind.

Despite her current predicament, the fight between the two men presented a rather ridiculous sight. Dismas was at least fifty pounds lighter and at least a cubit shorter than his brawny opponent. Every time the bully tried grabbing Dismas, the thief eluded him, bobbing and weaving just out of his reach. Dismas' red-faced aggressor's veins stuck out from his neck, looking poised to explode.

"Ham, are you going to let that scrawny rat beat you up?" said the brute, yanking Benjamin toward the man battling Dismas.

Ham? That's Noah's son. The other two must be Shem and Japheth. Oh please, God, let them take us straight to Noah.

"Enough, scar face!" bellowed Ham as he pounced on Dismas, swiftly tripping him. Ham slammed his boot against Dismas' chest, pulled a hammer dangling from a loop on his pants, and brought it close to Dismas' face.

He froze.

"Move and I'll scar the other half of your ugly face. Japheth, tie up this guy and I'll hold your prisoner."

The man holding Benjamin moved toward his brother. Hannah relaxed slightly. *Shem was Noah's favored son.* Maybe he was the least cruel.

"Are you spies or stowaways?" Ham demanded, taking Benjamin's tethered rope from Japheth.

"Neither," Benjamin replied in a flat tone.

Japheth tied up Dismas.

"Let's tie them to that tree and let the orange birds feast on them," Ham snarled, tugging Benjamin's lead.

"No!" shouted Hannah. She never wanted to lay eyes on that

vile bird again.

"The girl's right. Let's not waste our valuable time tying them to the tree. They will be dead by tomorrow anyway, along with the rest of this pitiful world." Japheth stared at the ground.

"We get to survive," bragged Ham.

"We haven't survived anything yet," said Shem. "Remember, Father said if we find anyone roaming our lands tonight, we are to bring them directly to him."

Hannah grabbed that glimmer of hope. *Yes! Take us to Noah.*

Shem released her. "You don't look like the type to run off and leave your friends behind."

"I won't run away," promised Hannah.

"No shoes?" Shem pointed to her bare feet. "That won't do. The ground is littered with rocks, nails, and scraps of wood. Do you mind if I pull you in this cart?" Shem wheeled out a small wooden cart containing a basket of blackberries.

"Please," Hannah said.

They walked along an upward path, giving Hannah time to gather her thoughts. "How do you know the flood will start tomorrow?" she asked.

"It's a wild story. My father claims he heard from God. For years he told us. God would cause rain to fall for forty days and nights, wiping out every living creature on the earth. Shem's voice dropped to a whisper. "I still had my doubts after Father's announcement, even though I labored over this ark for more than seventy years. But all my concerns were wiped away after the miracle." His brown eyes sparkled.

"What miracle?" Hannah leaned forward to hear better.

"Two weeks ago, the ground quivered, and then wild animal noises exploded throughout the air. The eight of us were inside the ark, so we raced to the deck and saw every type of animal lined up for miles, trudging up the hill, two by two. I thought of how God brought the animals to Adam to name them—only now it's our responsibility to save them."

Thank you for saving the animals, Lord. They didn't cause the earth's wickedness. "How do you know the rain will start tomorrow?" Hannah persisted.

"Six days ago, Father said the flood would begin on the seventh day. I have no reason to doubt him."

She frowned. "Why did you leave the ark tonight?"

"You are inquisitive," Shem replied. "An hour ago, Father had a strange look in his eyes. He sent me and my brothers into the woods for a farewell-to-earth walk and said if we stumbled onto three people, we were to bring them to him immediately. Father told me to take this cart—that I might need it, which I did. Sorry about tying up your companions, but obviously we can't take any chances." Then Shem pointed, "The ark is just beyond the line of pine trees." He picked up the pace and pulled the cart between a small gap in the trees.

A branch brushed Hannah's hair. She pushed it away and gazed toward the setting sun. Lingering crimson rays glowed across the ark, giving it the appearance of amber-red glass. In the center of the side of the vessel stood an open doorway. A ramp led from the ground to the door, supported by beams.

Hannah clutched the sides of the cart, its unsteadiness making her remember the fate of the ark. *God really did wipe out the previous world.* She swallowed hard at the thought.

Benjamin and Dismas paused next to Shem. They wore the same disbelieving stares.

"Move it along. We don't have all night," Ham said harshly. He jerked Benjamin's rope.

Hannah's brows furrowed with concern.

As Shem rolled her across the flat summit, the air filled with myriad sounds of humming, grunting, and braying inside the ark. By the time they reached the ramp, only the stars lit their way.

"What is the shiny reddish gloss all over the boat?" Benjamin asked. "It still shines even in the dark."

"A special pitch we made to make the ark waterproof," said Japheth.

"Took us six months to apply it," Ham said. "My hands were stained red for over a year. Tonight, I'm adding another coat on some entry areas to ensure not one drop of water will get inside our vessel."

Hannah stared at the doorway as she stepped onto the smooth ramp. *Shouldn't they be working on closing the massive door? Especially if the flood will begin tomorrow?*

"No worries about your bare feet stepping on anything," Shem told her. "Father runs an immaculate ship." He grabbed a glass lantern from a railing.

She pictured the elephants, sheep, cows, and even ants trudging across this same ramp.

"Last time walking up the ramp," Japheth said. "God knows how many times I've lugged food, water, lumber, or anything else Father wanted up this ramp." He rubbed his back.

Hannah hoped Noah had the piece. As she plodded up the incline, questions swirled in her head. *Will Noah hand over the key piece? Why did the living creatures leave and where is Ramel?*

"Watch your step," Shem told her. "I've tripped over it countless times."

Hannah watched where she placed her feet as she stepped through the ark's open doorway.

"Father's workshop is on the right. The light is on, so he's there."

Only faint starlight streamed in from a large skylight above to illuminate the interior. Doors lined the hallway to Hannah's right. As she passed them, she wondered, *Anything could be behind them. Water, food, seeds ... poisonous snakes.*

Finally, Shem stopped in front of a door and rapped. "Father, we have something to show you."

"Enter," replied a deep, kind voice.

Hannah's heart skipped a beat. *Calm down, he's only one of the patriarchs of the Torah.*

Shem opened the door and led the group inside. Tools lined the walls of Noah's workshop, all safely secured to the wall with leather straps. The man himself sat behind a simple workbench hammering nails into a small wooden box. Next to him sat an untouched platter of fruits and nuts. Noah's disheveled hair and beard flowed down to his elbows. Muscles bulged under his garment, the product of years of manual labor. His gray-white robe was covered in stray animal hairs.

"We found these spies lurking about." Ham tugged the rope tied to Benjamin. "They might be trying to sneak onto the boat."

Noah's bloodshot eyes bore into Hannah's. Something like disbelief passed through his gaze. His weathered hands shook and dropped the nails, which pinged on the smooth wood floor. "They are not stowaways or spies. They are signs from God. Untie them at once."

Hope rose in Hannah. Since he was expecting them, the section of the key would be easy to obtain.

"Are you sure about that?" Ham arched an eyebrow, but slowly untied Benjamin.

"Don't question me," Noah said sternly.

Benjamin rubbed his freed wrists. Hannah sighed in relief at his and Dismas' freedom.

Ham clenched his jaw. "I'm going to see if anyone else is lurking about."

"Don't leave the premises, that's an order."

"I'm bored. For six days, there has been not a single drop of water from the sky."

"If you have nothing to do, clean out some cages or comfort the women."

"Shovel dung or a torrent of tears. Tough decision." Ham

tapped his foot.

"Show some compassion. All their loved ones will be corpses, our civilization gone." Noah gave all three sons a stern look. "Change out of your overalls and into your robes. I told you to throw those garments overboard. We can't bring previous tools and materials into our new world."

"Are you sure you want to be alone with these strangers?" asked Japheth.

"I can guard the door," offered Shem.

"Go," Noah commanded. "They will not give me any trouble. I will explain later."

Shem and Japheth nodded to Hannah as they left the room.

"I'll be outside." Ham's statement sounded like a threat. He slammed the door on his way out.

Noah rose from his bench and stared at the visitors.

Hannah blushed under his intense gaze.

Finally, Noah smiled. "I'm relieved to meet you, Dismas, Benjamin, and Hannah."

"You know our names?" Hannah squeaked.

"God told me that the night before the flood, I would be visited by two males and a female from the future. God said they would be a personal sign to me, confirmation that the ark and everything aboard will survive." Noah paused, deep in thought. "Are there lizard kings roaming the earth where you're from?"

Dismas rubbed his scar. "Not sure. What do they look like?"

"Monsters that will rip you apart with sharp teeth the size of your hand. God forbade anything made by the evil angels to board the ark."

"Definitely no man-eating monsters like that," said Dismas.

"That's wonderful news. Are there any man-eating giants?"

"Well, there was Goliath. He was a giant," said Benjamin.

Hannah jabbed her brother's side. "He was just extremely

tall, not a man-eater." Not a wise story to tell the man concerned about the threat of Nephilim, on the eve of the flood that destroyed them.

"Then all this was not in vain." Noah's shoulders relaxed.

Hannah remembered why they were there. "Did God tell you to give us something?"

"Yes, he did." Noah shifted toward the cupboard. "Now where is it? I ran across it just the other day. Oh, I remember." He reached up and released a wooden stick holding two doors closed.

Hannah stood on tiptoe to peer into the tall cabinet. *Ha, Lucifer, we found the first key fragment.* Next, they would have to summon the creatures and leave the ark before one raindrop fell on their heads.

Noah rooted inside the cupboard. "Yes, right where I put them."

Them?

Noah pulled out a pair of sandals, dropping them next to Hannah's feet. "Now you won't have to walk around barefoot."

"No." Hannah resisted the urge to punt the footwear across the room. Disappointment slumped her shoulders as she clutched the key in her pocket.

Benjamin slapped his head, and Dismas slumped against the tool wall.

"No?" repeated Noah in disbelief. "God informed me the girl would need a pair of shoes. He's never wrong."

Dismas snorted.

Hannah calmed herself and slipped her feet into the soft leather shoes, a perfect fit. "Thank you, Noah. I don't mean to sound ungrateful, but we're looking for a piece to complete this key." She pulled hell's key out of her pants pocket. "Have you run across something like this?"

"Put that away! It reminds me of death. Let me think a moment." Noah rubbed his forehead. "I've been through every room and alcove of this ship. There is nothing here like that key."

"Now what?" Dismas shrugged.

"We've come so far." Benjamin dug his toe into the wooden floor.

"I will seek God about your key," Noah promised. "You three wait here while I make the rounds and talk with God while I walk."

Hannah looked at the floor but nodded. "What choice do we have?"

Noah waved his arm toward the neglected tray of food and pointed to some chairs tied together in the corner of the room. "It's not fancy, but it's adequate. When you hear the shofar, meet me on the upper deck and hopefully we will find the key piece."

Benjamin and Dismas untied the chairs and munched apples from the tray while Hannah's stomach churned. *How can they think of eating at a time like this?* In a few hours, everything would be destroyed except Noah, his family, and the animals.

"Eat." Dismas extended a pomegranate toward Hannah.

"No, thanks." The seeds reminded her of blood droplets. Her meal would be the salt from her tears. She peered at her new sandals and rubbed the soft, luxurious leather. *Is God guiding my steps with these shoes? Or was Noah exaggerating?*

A lion roared rumbled in the distance. Her thoughts turned to Ham, *Did he secure the cages?* She tapped her foot, hoping Noah would soon arrive with the key.

I will destroy the climate which could support life on earth by interfering with the sun's orbit and rearranging it from the beginning of the deluge for the entire future. ... This accounts for the lifespan of man having been drastically reduced after the deluge.

—Rabbi Ovadiah ben Jacob S'forno, Torah commentary on Genesis 6:13

The twenty-sixth hour in hell

Long blasts from the ram's horn jerked Hannah awake. *Seth! He's come home!* But as she looked around at the dark wood walls and the bed of hay, she remembered today was the day God would drown the earth. She must have dozed off while waiting for Noah to hear from God. Hannah shook away thoughts of her wayward husband and focused on the task at hand. Her eyes darted to her thumbnail, and her heart skipped a beat as she observed the white overtaking the darkness like the expanding morning sky. They had to find the key piece soon.

Dismas leapt to his feet, knocking the remaining fruit platter to the ground. He mumbled something about hearing it inside the holy of holies. His hand trembled picking up the scattered fruit.

What does he mean about being in the temple? No way would priests allow him allowed him access. Probably just one of his thievery dreams.

"What's with all the clatter?" asked a groggy Benjamin. As he came to, fear crossed his eyes.

Hannah's empty stomach twisted. *Will Noah deliver a message from God? And where are Ramel and the living creatures? Lord, protect us today. We're going to need it.*

"Noah told us to meet him on the top deck when we heard the shofar," Dismas said.

The three of them raced into the hall. They found the staircases in the middle leading to the upper levels. Sunlight streamed in from the open balconies and skylight. The stairs looked wide enough to move the animals around the ark. The stench of hundreds of animals overpowered the woodsy lumber scent of the walls and floor. Hannah's calves burned trying to keep up with Benjamin and Dismas. At the top, she paused, mesmerized by the city of magnificent buildings reaching the sky. *They'll all be gone soon.* Her heart ached.

Noah faced the muted sun rising behind the milky-white cloud covering. When the group approached, he turned to them. "God did give me a word for you."

"Please tell us," Hannah said.

"This is what God told me, 'The key will be revealed when you see the seven crowns. Don't worry; you will not drown. Victory will be found.'" Noah lifted his eyes to the sky. "It's settled. I won't have to be concerned about you three anymore."

Hannah sighed. *Another riddle.*

Benjamin scratched his head. "That's all?"

"Are there any crowns on this ship?" Dismas asked, voice tight.

Noah shrugged. "The Lord didn't provide an explanation."

The wind whipped through the trees, snapping branches and sending them flying across the hillside. Hannah took a deep breath of moist earth. *Rain is coming, but still no key piece.*

Then, a screech filled the sky.

Her heart clenched at the thought of another orange bird, but the sound had come from directly overhead. The clouds began to part as if invisible hands tore a piece of parchment, exposing a sapphire sky and glorious sunlight. Despite the warmth of the sun, everyone began to shiver at the sudden drop in temperature. Then, water gushed from the crack, and a cold droplet hit Hannah's face.

"A drop in temperature—that's impossible." Noah squinted at the sky. "The canopy is broken."

"The angels have arrived," Benjamin said, pointing up.

Thousands of winged beings wielding flaming swords swooped through the split in the sky. The beating of their wings sounded like peals of thunder. Each being had immeasurable height, and a rainbow adorned each head. Their faces shone like the sun, and their limbs appeared as fiery pillars. As they streamed through, the crack widened, and more water unloaded onto the earth.

"Woe to the wicked inhabitants of earth," cried the heavenly messengers. "Woe to your cities." Their booming voices repeated the ominous message.

Hannah scanned the skies, hoping to see the living creatures. No sign of them. Inhabitants from the city below poured out from their buildings like ants onto the streets and rooftops.

The angel army divided—half of them flew toward the ocean while the other half spread across the sky.

"Woe to the sky," roared the army in the air. They punched the remaining cloud canopy with fiery fists. Waterfalls gushed from above, drenching everyone and everything. Hannah looked down at the puddles forming on the deck, quickly losing dry places to stand.

"Woe to the water," shouted the angels over the ocean. With flaming swords, they pierced the depths, causing the waves to twist in spiraling cyclones, giving birth to towering waterspouts reaching far into the sky. The earth trembled beneath their continuous mighty strikes and numerous fountains shot forth, propelling water high into the air before crashing back down.

The angels scattered, flying in different directions—north, southeast, and west. Probably off to destroy the rest of the earth. The combination of the rushing water from both the sea and sky raised the water level at an alarming rate.

Hannah recalled her Torah studies: "All the fountains of the great deep burst forth, and the windows of the heavens were opened. And rain fell upon the earth forty days and forty nights."

The remainder of the milky, hazy layer of sky dissipated like smoke. For a brief moment, the more familiar azure shone through, but black clouds quickly hid it.

Thunder echoed across the valley. Lightning split the sky with fury. The giant trees became uprooted by the bolts. Torrential rain poured from the angry heavens. On the horizon, an enormous wave barreled toward the city. All the waters combined into a roar, muting all other sounds.

"Down," mouthed Noah, pointing to the staircase. His face wrinkled with worry and fear.

Hannah took one last look at the doomed city, a giant wave looming closer and closer. *It's all too sad. Poor Nava.* She descended into the safety of the ark.

Japheth and Ham, now in their robes, helped Noah close the deck's hatch. Shem held a small bucket and liberally brushed pitch under the deck door, sealing the flap.

"It's the beginning of the end—now, you three get off my vessel," barked Noah.

Hannah's mouth dropped open.

"You can't be serious!" Benjamin yelled above the howling winds. "We'll drown out there!"

"You're not on the list. Only eight humans are allowed on this ship," Noah commanded. "Japheth and Ham, show them out."

Ham grabbed Hannah's elbow and escorted her down the stairs. She stepped into a pile of pitch, ruining her new sandals.

How dare Noah toss us out like yesterday's fish. The excess pitch stuck to the bottom of her shoes, leaving a sticky trail behind her.

"Hold on to what God revealed," Noah called. "You're not going to drown."

Easy for him to say, sheltered from the deluge. Hannah reached the ark door. The ramp was still there, disappearing rapidly under the rising water. "How are you going to close the door?" she screamed above the raging storm.

"Father said God would do it," Japheth said. "So far, he's been right about everything."

She stepped on to the ramp, and froze. Benjamin knocked into her. And Dismas stood a bit behind them.

"Don't get any ideas of stowing away." Ham pulled out a knife and pointed it toward them. He stood guard at the doorway while Japheth retreated into the belly of the ark.

Dismas pointed at the ramp. "In no time, the water will rise over our heads. Don't leave us like this!"

"I hope you are good swimmers," Ham yelled.

Hannah trembled and clutched the drenched railing as the ramp swayed. She could no longer see the gigantic wave approaching the city. *I can't swim!*

"Help! Help!" Dismas hollered.

"Jachniel, Dormel, Gonael, Padel, Ayin! Anybody!" Hannah joined in. An incoming wave roared like thousands of angry lions. The water rose almost to the door. Frigid water washed over her ankles and her heart raced.

"Look!" said Benjamin.

Hannah pivoted and saw a bright light about the size of a man's hand. As it approached, it grew. She breathed a sigh of relief. It had to be the creatures.

"The hand of God," said Dismas in awe. A look of recognition flickered across his face.

God's hand flew to their feet, flipped the ark's massive door shut, and dislodged the ramp from the boat. The three tumbled to the plank flooring as water rushed over them, and Noah's ark began to float.

Hannah's hand slipped on the waterlogged railing.

"Don't let go!" Benjamin screamed.

Hannah clung to the railing with both hands. She gagged and spat out salty water, then clamped her lips shut. The ramp spun wildly in the currents and submerged. Hannah tensed as the freezing water washed over her. She gripped the railing and held on to Noah's assurance that they'd survive and be victorious. *But how?*

The ramp popped above the surface, bouncing as it rode the wave's crest. Gale-force winds tossed them. The waved gobbled everything in its wake while they soared on the tiny ramp. Finally, the wave subsided, Benjamin still hunkered beside her, and Dismas squatted opposite, both clinging to the railing as a lifeline. Hannah's teeth chattered, her wet clothes clinging like ice. A broken fern rammed them hard on the right, launching them back toward the ark. *No!* Part of the floating tree island rushed toward them. Thunder boomed and lightning crinkled again. Hannah spotted a pair of glowing yellow eyes with huge black pupils staring at her from behind another fern. A bright green lizard rose on two hind legs and its short arms pointed at them. *At least it can't swim with those tiny limbs.*

"The lizard king," Dismas shouted.

A series of choppy waves drove the ramp closer to the island. The lizard king locked eyes on them and trotted closer. Dismas grabbed a branch floating in the water and tried rowing away. The lizard king growled, exposing triangular teeth. Dismas paddled frantically, but another wave pushed them even closer to the giant monster. Now closer to a death kiss from the ugly beast, it flicked its tongue over its lips. The earth shook again and another wave crashed over the ramp.

Hannah dipped below the surface and swallowed a mouthful of water. It burned her throat, making her heave the water from her mouth and nostrils, and stinging her eyes. Dismas and Benjamin also coughed up water. She could no longer see the lizard king and the island. But now they were closer to the ark. *Oh God, please don't let the massive ark run us over.* Movement caught Hannah's eye. She blinked to clear her vision. Two people clung to a tree trunk. One appeared to be yelling toward the ark. Hannah gasped. *That's Nava and Liraz.* But bitterness soured her thoughts. *Don't waste your energy asking your father to allow you inside. Noah won't allow it. Only eight on God's guest list.*

Nava's face contorted with pain.

Oh no! Nava must be in labor.

"What's that?" Benjamin tilted his head at a different area.

The water swirled in a circular motion, forming a whirlpool. The force of the churning black water pulled their tiny ramp and the tree carrying the expectant couple. A rising odor of sulfur overpowered the salt in the air. A shudder passed through Hannah at the reminder of hell. From the swirling vortex emerged a dragon head. Its orange eyes locked onto Hannah with pure hatred.

13

"We even saw the Nephilim there—the descendants of Anak come from the Nephilim! To ourselves we seemed like grasshoppers, and we must have seemed the same to them."

—Numbers 13:33 (HCSB)

The twenty-eighth hour in hell

Six more heads surfaced. The seven-headed beast beat its powerful wings and hovered above the tumultuous waves.

What is this thing? Hannah swallowed hard, eyes widening with terror.

The heads spread out, each on top of its own neck, like the temple's seven-branched lampstand. A spiked horn protruded from each head, topped with a golden crown. Tattoos of Latin words adorned each head. Hannah read them: Lies was on the middle, largest head. Pride, Murder, and Wicked Imaginations were to its left. Evil, Gossip, and Strife were to its right. Shame rose in Hannah's cheeks. The words brought condemnation, but she didn't know why. The Proverbs stated the Lord hated those seven things. *Could this beast be from hell? Or maybe a judgment from heaven?* But the beast's armored belly, outstretched talons, and long thorny tail couldn't belong to heaven. It reeked of sulfur and death.

The hideous beast smacked its pointed tail on the water, creating large, choppy waves. Hannah gripped the ramp's slippery railing, but her icy fingers were numb. She couldn't hold on much longer. She glanced at Nava and Liraz, still desperately clinging to a tree trunk. Liraz placed his hand over his wife's lips to silence her. Nava buried her head under a branch. But the flying serpent didn't seem interested in them. Again, it turned its glowing, hate-filled, orange-red eyes on Hannah. The thing could easily crush all of them in its giant bear claws.

"I am Leviathan," roared all seven mouths.

Hannah tried to recall anything she had read about Leviathan. *It extinguishes all hope. It's impossible to overcome, and terrifying to behold. Yes, I'm certainly terrified!* A glance at her companions showed Dismas' face paler than a whitewashed tomb and Benjamin not much better.

All seven of the beast's mouths opened, exposing double rows of sharp teeth and a double set of lion's fangs. Flames darted from within and smoke billowed from fourteen nostrils like a pot boiling over. Noah had said that they wouldn't drown, but what about being devoured? *Wait. Noah's prophecy. This creature has seven crowns on its heads. The key piece is nearby.* Hope and fear mixed within her. All seven of Leviathan's heads shrieked as it flapped its powerful wings against the battering storm and plunged straight at them. Hannah squeezed her eyes shut tight, waiting for the teeth to rip her apart.

"It's after Liraz!" yelled Dismas.

Hannah peeked and saw Leviathan in all its horrifying glory perched over Liraz. Continuous lightning cracked all around.

"Nava, do you want to know who the real father of your children is?" snarled Lies. Leviathan's talons swiped at Liraz and ripped a chain from his throat, leaving a nasty wound.

Hannah glimpsed a shiny silver coin as it rolled off the chain and into the turbulent sea. In the same moment, Liraz transformed into a fallen angel with black tattered wings. *What?* Hannah blinked and looked again. *Liraz is Ramel?* She thought back to the apothecary shop where the angel had signed the contract. The mysterious watcher angel is Ramel? Hannah felt bile rise in her throat.

Nava's face contorted in agony. "Our entire life was a lie. I hate you!" She let go of the log and sank like a millstone under a wave. Hannah closed her eyes and forced back a sob remembering how she had longed to die when Seth had vanished. Breaking a vow of love was the worst kind of betrayal.

"Nava!" Ramel yelled, weeping while blood oozed from his throat.

"Love never wins," hissed Leviathan. It dove into the ocean heads first.

When the beast did not reemerge, Hannah breathed a sigh of relief.

"Liraz is Ramel?" Dismas shook his head in disbelief.

"This is so confusing," said Benjamin.

Hannah's mind spun from all that had happened.

Light burst forth, and two dazzling angels appeared, carrying black chains. They plucked Ramel from the tree and began wrapping him in the chains.

The waves began to circle again. *Oh no, not the beast again.*

Leviathan reemerged. Dangling from the mouth of Murder was Nava.

"Leave her alone," begged Ramel. He struggled against his restraints.

One angel pulled out a black padlock and locked the ends of the chains together. Both angels grabbed their prisoner and dragged him down into the water.

There must be a portal to hell somewhere down there.

"Enjoy your forever stay, Tartarus, loser," Evil rasped, his voice dripping with malice.

Poor Ramel. No wonder he was acting so strange and knew how to help us.

Leviathan flew to the ark. Six of the seven heads banged their spikes on the door, each knock so powerful the ark swayed. Murder gripped Nava in his lips like a trophy mouse.

What a horrible end for Nava. She should have been safe inside the ark with her family.

"Knock, knock, anybody home?" sneered Gossip.

"Not up for visitors today?" snickered Strife.

"Since you won't open up, I'm dragging your daughter back to hell where she belongs," boasted Wicked Imaginations.

"Don't worry, we'll be back when you land. We'll give you time to settle in your new place," scoffed Lies.

Pride spat out something metal, which struck the door like a knife.

Another lightning bolt lit up the sky. Hannah jolted with a gasp, heart racing. But in the flash of light, she looked closer at the metal object. *The key piece!*

Leviathan vanished into the sea.

"How will we reach the ark?" Dismas shook his head. "No way can I row against this storm, and the ark is getting farther away. Besides, the key is lodged so high up!"

"Need a lift?" Jachniel's comforting voice floated to their ears. The four glorious living creatures were inside the wheels, hovering above the waves.

"Protect our friends against the rain," commanded Gonael.

At the command, Hannah, Benjamin, and Dismas sat on soft leather cushions inside the warm chariot. All three marveled at their dry clothes. The chariot glass no longer covered them, yet somehow no rain or waves touched them. Another surprise— Ramel occupied the seat across from Benjamin. Hannah felt the strangest urge to hug him, but she simply nodded a greeting. Ramel ignored her, focused on the spot where Leviathan had disappeared with Nava.

The chariot sped toward the ark. Hannah dropped her eyes, conflicted. She shouldn't sympathize with Ramel because he had disobeyed God. But she knew the pain of losing a spouse. The chariot rose and hovered, now eye level with where the rainbow-colored piece stuck in the door like a splinter.

"What are you waiting for? Grab it," ordered Padel.

Benjamin stretched out his arm as far as he could and grunted. "It's out of reach. Can't you maneuver closer?" He strained further, face contorting, still unable to touch the colored fragment.

"No!" roared Dormel.

Hannah huffed. *Not another one of their annoying rules where they won't help us.* Then guilt washed over her. *They are helping us, probably more than we realize.*

"We can't take any chances," squawked Gonael. "The flames in the wheels might set the ark on fire."

"You try, Dismas," said Benjamin. "Your arms are longer than mine."

Dismas could touch the piece, but his fingers kept slipping. "I can't grab it. I need something dry to snatch it with."

"Maybe a piece of cloth!" Benjamin tore at his shirt.

Hannah stood to see if there were any other materials. Her foot stuck to the floor. *Ugh, will I never be free of that sticky pitch?* She gasped. *That's it!* "Use my shoe! It has Noah's special pitch on it." Hannah quickly untied the straps and handed her sandal to Dismas.

"It might work." Dismas took hold of the long leather straps. He snapped the sandal toward the door. With a splat, the pitch stuck to the key piece. "Got it!" Dismas reeled it in like a fish and handed the sandal back to Hannah.

She scraped the piece from the bottom of her sandal. It was in the shape of a circular rainbow. She removed hell's key from her pocket. With supernatural force, the piece leapt from her hand and affixed itself around the half-faced skeleton and formed a handle. She held it up in triumph.

"Woohoo!" Benjamin shouted and smiled. "We found the first piece of the key."

Dismas clapped.

"Show some respect," snapped Ramel. "Everything's gone."

Hannah's countenance fell.

"Let's leave this tomb," Jachniel said.

They soared over Noah's ark, and the flames ignited. The chariot sped toward spatium. "Suspend," called out the living creatures in unison. The chariot hovered over the destruction of the earth. The living creatures emerged from the wheels and flitted around the chariot. Their jittery movements belied agitation.

"Would you like to see what happened to Nava?" Dormel held something round like a cat's eye in his hand.

"Is that … one of Ayin's eyes?" Benjamin asked.

"Yes."

Hannah shuddered.

"You should have never left your watcher position," Padel said softly.

Dormel lifted Ayin's eye, and it grew to the size of a watermelon. Within the oval, a picture formed. Leviathan carried Nava in Murder's mouth through an underwater cave. He set Nava's body on the rocky floor. All seven heads took turns listening to the young woman's belly.

"The babies are still alive," Evil growled.

With a razor-sharp talon, Leviathan ripped open Nava's pregnant stomach.

Hannah squeezed her eyes shut. But she couldn't blot out the sound of tearing skin. *Why does it want Nava's babies?*

"You can open your eyes." Dormel placed a warm hand on Hannah's shoulder.

She resumed watching.

On the ground next to Nava's discarded body lay two babies. Wicked Imaginations and Strife blew air into the newborns' faces. Helpless cries pierced the air.

"Transform ad Lucifer," said Leviathan.

"Transform back to Lucifer," Hannah translated. *Wait, Levia-*

than is Lucifer?

Leviathan's seven heads and horns merged into one head with two horns and only one crooked crown remained. Leviathan's talons transformed into goat hooves.

"Well, I had fun." Lucifer stretched his arms and shook out his wings.

Leviathan is Lucifer, and Liraz is Ramel? Hannah blinked. What a strange journey.

Beelzebub entered the cave, flies and all. He strolled to the infants, picked them up individually, and wrapped them in black cloth. "They are perfect," he said. "Twelve fingers and toes and two nubs on their heads. Soon they will have double rows of teeth, like all the other giants." He swatted at the flies buzzing around the babies, making them cry more. "A boy and a girl, just like we planned. Giving those special potions to Nava paid off."

Ramel released a guttural cry.

"Be quiet, Ramel," demanded Padel. "Listen carefully."

Can't he have a drop of compassion for how much pain Ramel is in?

"The Uncreated One has his eight survivors to carry on his race, and I have Anak and Zamzummim, my very own Adam and Eve. They will marry and repopulate the earth. All thanks to Ramel and Nava. When the time is right, our beautiful offspring will resurface right next to the children of the Uncreated One."

"It's a shame Noah didn't meet these beautiful grandchildren." Beelzebub shrugged his wings, the babies' vulnerable heads flopping limply in his arms.

"Well, his descendants will meet our giants. They won't be able to miss them." Lucifer smirked.

Baal rushed into the cavern waving his hands. "God wiping out all the people is a total win for us! Hell is filled to the brim with unclean Nephilim spirits, and we have new humans to torture!"

"What were our casualties? Any make it over to Paradise?" asked Lucifer.

"Minimal. Our wickedness and evil ways infiltrated all areas of their society. The humans are fools." Baal snorted.

"Go rouse Nava," Lucifer ordered. "Since she's our prisoner in hell, we can torture her by forcing her to raise her children."

"She's disappeared!" Baal's voice held rage.

Hannah saw only a puddle of blood where Nava had lain.

"What?" Lucifer stomped his hoof and whined. "It's not fair! I loathe how the Creator bests us with mercy."

The image vanished and Ayin's eye shrank back to regular size.

Padel grabbed Ramel by the neck. "Was it worth leaving your post and impregnating that woman? It's all because of you that the Nephilim reentered the world."

"Nava made it to Paradise, and I'd do it all over again," Ramel said in a hollow tone.

"You are so selfish. You don't know all the wars and deaths your offspring have caused. God had to kill off those wicked giants, making him seem inhumane—while it's all your fault."

"Let him go," commanded Jachniel.

"After I do this." Padel snapped his fingers and a silver coin materialized in the air. It bore Lucifer's image. He shoved it far into Ramel's skin.

Ramel writhed and transformed into Liraz.

"Because of what you have done, you don't deserve to be an angel, good or bad," said Padel. He waved his hand over Liraz's fresh wound, and new skin covered the coin. "The coin is limited and its power ceases in hell and heaven. For the duration of this trip, you are bound to your wretched human existence, and your name shall be called Liraz!" Padel's voice roared with authority.

Liraz's body shook violently, and his eyes fluttered closed.

"Padel, something's wrong with him," Hannah placed her trembling hand on Liraz's shoulder but snatched her fingers away, the intense heat felt like touching a burning candle. He felt feverish.

Liraz opened his eyes and grabbed her arm.

The demonic black and red eyes of Lucifer met Hannah's.

She screamed.

14

The dead do not live;
departed spirits do not rise up.
Indeed, You have visited and destroyed them;
You have wiped out all memory of them.

—Isaiah 26:14 (HSCB)

A tunnel under Paradise
The thirtieth hour in hell

Peering at the hardened black lava wall, Mahway mulled over his scheme. Currently, thirty-three giants excavated a tunnel at the mouth of the Lake of Fire while Mahway and his two underlings toiled away in secret near Paradise. Soon, the two tunnels would intersect, forming a single path of destruction carrying the soul-burning flames directly over Jesus.

Blow it all up, like a fiery inferno. Everything depended on the impending explosion. *Penetrate Paradise's walls and take back Cecilia.*

"When is Lucifer going to send reinforcements?" Ohya grumbled.

Mahway kept staring at the wall, attempting to find the weak spot aside from his slothful workers.

Hahya slammed his chisel on the smooth black ground and clasped his pudgy hands behind his gargantuan back. "This is tedious." The twins looked like pigs with their pushed-in noses and reddish, oversized faces.

"How much farther?" Ohya whined as he mopped sweat off his triangular ear with his sleeve.

All they do is complain. Mahway rubbed his temples against the mounting headache. He grabbed an axe in each hand, and pounded the lava wall, pretending he was smashing Ohya's and Hahya's nasty faces. Success. The lava barrier crumbled. Jagged boulders cascaded off the wall. The black dust rose into Mahway's nose, causing him to sneeze. As the dust settled, he saw they had finally found a break. He grunted in relief.

"Look ahead," grumbled Hahya. "Another lava wall."

"Probably fifty more walls after that," griped Ohya.

Surprise, surprise—they still aren't happy. Mahway reminded himself not to get irritated since the nature of demons was never to be content or thankful for anything. He complained frequently, but he loathed listening to others' complaints.

Ohya continued, "This new wall is worse than—"

A raised hand from Mahway silenced him. He leaned toward the new opening and listened closely. *Who could be speaking all the way down here?* He stepped closer. *Maybe it's some new workers finally. Or just Lucifer playing tricks.* He scoffed. *Wouldn't be the first time.*

The brothers began to moan and groan again, as if the interruption hadn't happened.

"Shut up! I hear something." Mahway cocked his ear toward the lava ceiling. "Don't you hear it?" His enhanced Nephilim hearing never failed him.

"Strange." Hahya laid his ear against the wall. "I hear something, too."

The voice became clearer. "I know many of you have trust issues with my Father."

"That's Jesus," Mahway blurted as his insides twisted. He could never forget the voice that had cast him out of his human in the Gergesenes cemetery. *How can this be? We're still one hundred thousand cubits from Paradise. We shouldn't be able to hear him.*

"Maybe it's Lucifer?" Hahya suggested. "Sometimes he likes to play those kinds of tricks."

"Nah, he would never call the Uncreated One 'Father.' Never," said Ohya, rubbing his foot. "It's Jesus."

They stopped talking and listened closely.

"Who hasn't pondered how a loving Father could destroy everything except for Noah's family?" Jesus continued. "Remember, the watchers and fallen angels polluted the entire planet. Ask Noah and Nava for the details. My Father had to wipe out the unclean Nephilim and their offspring to save the world. I would have never been able to come to earth through a virgin because of the corruption in the bloodline."

Ohya shifted, and Mahway glared at him to be still.

"The ark had one entrance to save Noah and his family," Jesus continued. "Now, I am the one door to heaven. If anyone wants to leave Paradise and live with my Father for eternity, you must go through me."

"I've heard enough." Mahway crushed a rock between his twelve fingers, drowning out Jesus. There would never be redemption for him or any Nephilim. They would always be an abomination to God.

"How dare Jesus call us unclean?It's not our fault if our fathers were watcher angels and our mothers were human. We didn't ask to be born!" Ohay made a vile guttural noise launching a wad of phlegm toward the ceiling aiming at Jesus' condemning words.

Mahway swiftly sidestepped avoiding the falling green substance and for once, he agreed with Ohya. Mahway's mother had died in childbirth. All of the Nephilim births had caused the deaths of their human mothers.

"At least Lucifer gave us a place to live and jobs," Hahya said. "I'd still be on earth if Jesus hadn't cast me out of that boy, the one I liked to play with in the fires. Nearly drove his parents crazy with fear." Hahya chortled, eyes gleaming at the memory.

Ohya started whistling in a low, somber tone to block the words of Jesus.

But Mahway fumed over the persecution of his entire race. "Enough talking. Get back to work and stop fooling around." He stepped over the boulders to get to the next wall. *I'll make them pay. I'll do whatever it takes to burn Paradise and everyone in it. Except Cecilia.*

15

[Jesus] replied to them, "The one who has two shirts must share with someone who has none, and the one who has food must do the same."

—Luke 3:11 (HCSB)

The thirty-second hour in hell

Dismas leaned forward, clenching his fists. He wanted to help Hannah, but didn't know how.

"Ramel, let go!" Benjamin shouted as he pried Liraz's fingers from his sister's wrist. "No good traitor!"

"It's Lucifer," Hannah whispered, and her chin trembled.

"I'm back," Liraz hissed.

Dismas shivered at the sound. The smell of rotting garbage filled the chariot as Liraz released Hannah. Dismas glared. But when Liraz's eyes changed from violet to blood red, he drew back in his seat.

Benjamin shook his head. "He's still Ramel, and he's tricking us. No way would God allow the devil in his special chariot."

"It's Lucifer all right." Gonael's yellow eagle eyes flashed as he flew closer to Liraz. "He's channeling."

"Well, if you must know," Lucifer's voice sneered through Liraz's mouth, "I gained access to Ramel's body per our contract. Honestly, I hate his pathetic human body, but your petty God refuses to let me go back in time to deliver the next riddle."

"You could have just sent a scroll," Jachniel said.

The creatures hovered around the chariot, glowering at the devil.

"This way is more enjoyable." Lucifer paused. "The Uncreated One's restrictions do not deter me. Humans' painful memories are my bridge to the past. All I have to do is remind them of their previous mistakes, failures, and dreadful situations, and I've gained a stronghold in their pitiful future. Wouldn't you agree, Dismas?"

Dismas flushed. It was not the first time he had experienced Lucifer dredging up his past. Instead of letting the enemy win, he searched for Jesus' promise: *Your past is forgotten.* But the words seemed far away.

"You piece of filth! You don't belong in this chariot." Padel zoomed closer to the devil. "Give them the riddle and get out."

Lucifer turned Liraz's chin toward Padel in defiance. "Go ahead, you two-legged cow. Hit me as hard as you can." He crossed Liraz's arms. "It won't hurt me a bit, but what about poor Liraz?"

Just like Barabbas—always causing trouble.

"Produce the riddle and go to hell," Dormel snarled, baring his lion teeth.

"I don't take orders from anyone." Lucifer scowled. "When I am ready, I will depart." He turned to the occupants of the chariot. "I heard you stumbled upon the first key piece. If by some miracle you fools solve this riddle, you're heading into a real dung storm."

"Stop the drama and deliver the riddle," squawked Gonael.

"Listen carefully. I will say it only once. Murder and strife forced one to settle for less while the other picked the best." Lucifer coughed and hit Liraz's chest. "Sorry. There's more."

Dismas frowned. *I believe he's sorry like I believe pigs fly. He's doing this on purpose.*

"Less ended up saving best not once but twice." Lucifer again broke into a coughing fit and coughed between each word,

"But—efforts—were—saving—land. After—play—fire."

"You're not making any sense. Stop with the infernal coughing," demanded Padel.

"I don't know what's wrong with me." Lucifer pounded on Liraz's chest, then continued in a gravelly, rushed voice, "You're bound to smell like smoke." He hacked some more. "So best—less—less—more." He grinned with darkness in his eyes.

"That's not fair!" Benjamin said. "You spoke so fast and skipped some words. Did you get the last part, Hannah?"

Hannah shook her head, threw her hands in the air, clearly frustrated by the devils tactics.

Dismas couldn't make sense of his words either. .

"I think best and less must represent two people," Hannah said. "But who?"

"Maybe Cain and Abel?" Dismas guessed. "They had strife, and Abel was murdered."

"No," Benjamin said harshly. "It's not them."

"One of my favorite days," Lucifer bragged. "I relished every moment of Cain killing his brother." His eyes narrowed fixing his evil glare on Dismas.

Dismas berated himself for opening his mouth. *Everyone must think I'm a fool.*

"A good guess, Dismas, but I think the fire is the crucial clue," Hannah said kindly. "It was impossible to hear with all that coughing though."

Think, Dismas, think. If he solved the riddle, he'd prove he belonged here.

"But less efforts were futile in saving this fertile land," Liraz's voice returned. "After all, when you play with fire, you're bound to smell like smoke. So best became less and less became more."

Lucifer's eyes flashed, and he covered Liraz's mouth. But

Liraz pried it away.

The four creatures broke out in laughter.

"Liraz is beating you at your own game, Lucifer!" Dormel chuckled. "His voice is coming through loud and clear."

Liraz's voice continued despite the wrestling match of the two hands in front of his lips. "After all, when you play with fire, you're bound to smell like smoke. So best became less and less became more." Delivering the last lines, both of Liraz's arms dropped to his sides. Then, he slapped himself in the face.

Dismas rubbed his forehead. *This Liraz-Lucifer thing is confusing.* "What place was once fertile and then became barren because of a fire?" he asked.

Hannah leaned forward and her eyes sparkled "Sodom and Gomorrah, it was like the garden of Eden before God destroyed the city with fire."

"And there was strife and murder between Abraham's and Lot's herdsmen, which caused them to separate," Dismas added, bracing his shoulders waiting for Benjamin' .

"They ended up dividing the land between them. Lot picked the best land, leaving his uncle Abraham with the lesser land," Benjamin agreed. "So, 'best' is Abraham, and 'less' would be his ungrateful nephew, Lot."

"Are you sure about that?" Lucifer challenged .

"Abraham saved Lot twice," Hannah said crisply.

"And Lot lost his wife and Abraham had a son," Dismas blurted. "He, too, experienced losses."

"So best became less, and less became more," the siblings said together triumphantly.

"Yeah, yeah, yeah. You answered correctly." Lucifer clenched his teeth.

"You're sending us to that horrid place?" Benjamin contorted his face in disgust.

For once, Dismas agreed with Benjamin.

"Oh, Benny boy, you got it all wrong. It was a magnificent place to live. The party was just getting started before the Uncreated One torched my four special cities. Padel, don't you think Sariel would agree?"

The veins in Padel's neck looked like they might pop.

Who or what is Sariel?

"Enough." Jachniel pointed at Liraz. "They solved the riddle, now leave."

Lucifer violently shook Liraz's head and shrieked "I'm not leaving, I miss my Sodom. I will continue using Liraz to channel through."

Jachniel placed his hand on Liraz's forehead. "In the name of Jesus Christ of Nazareth, leave Liraz's body and never return to it ever again."

Jesus' name and hometown? Peculiar, Dismas wondered.

Liraz's eyes returned to violet, though his shoulders sagged in exhaustion. The living creature's words proved effective, Lucifer parted like the Red sea. Dismas's chest expanded releasing all the tension in his shoulders, marveling at the power of that simple invocation.

"Are you all right?" Hannah stared at Liraz.

He waved her question away. "Leave me alone."

"Off to Sodom and Gomorrah, the night before the big blast," commanded Jachniel with a tinge of glee.

As the creatures took their positions under the chariot, the flames erupted, nearly burning Dismas' feet. He overheard one of them say something about making things right. *What do they mean?* The creatures hummed a happy tune in perfect harmony. *Peculiar.* Were the creatures looking forward to visiting Sodom?

The glorious tapestry of constellations stood out against the deep black sky. Whirling amid the vastness of the stars, Dismas felt small and alone. His gaze fixated on his thumb—overwhelming darkness still dominated, covering more than half, and they'd found only one piece. I'm just going to fail, Jesus ... why was I even born?

"I formed you in the womb. I am the Lord who makes all things, who stretched out the heavens."

Dismas looked around. "Did someone say something?"

"No," Hannah answered.

The others ignored him, offering no response.

"Why? What did you hear?" Hannah touched his arm.

Do strange voices speak to her, too? Dismas closed his eyes for a moment, struggling with the admitting he heard voices. No, he didn't want to appear weak. He gave a slight shake of his head and brushed her off.

Benjamin pointed to the right. "We are headed back through the blackhole for the next fragment."

Dismas braced himself.

The chariot veered into the gray area before the swirling blackhole. It sped up as it circled outside the blackhole, but they weren't pulled in this time. He hated the spinning feeling. It reminded him of the time Barabbas had taunted him into a drinking game. Barabbas claimed it would make him a man. Dismas still couldn't figure out how vomiting his guts had turned him into a man.

The chariot stopped for a moment, though Dismas felt like he was still twirling. With a violent force, the chariot flung forward, as though catapulted from an enormous slingshot. Hannah and Benjamin bumped heads. Dismas' cheek slammed into the side of the chariot, and Liraz crumpled on the glass floor. Quickly, the gray area transformed into blue sky. Dismas saw the top of a date palm grove below. As the chariot slowed, it clipped the top of a tree, spilling dates. *Must be our next location.* The flames extinguished and the chariot banged to the ground, screeching to a halt. The creatures slid out from the wheels, now covered in olive-green stains. Sometimes Dismas regretted witnessing the landings from the glass floor. His heart still raced.

"You look wretched, Ayin," Jachniel said, picking out thick grass blades stuck in a few of Ayin's eyes.

"What about us?" Benjamin said, rubbing the top of his head.

Dismas' cheek throbbed. *Perfect. My one good side.*

"I apologize for the rough ride," Dormel raked his fingers through his tangled mane. "Because Sodom was blown into oblivion, navigating through time to find its geographical location presents formidable challenges."

"What did those cities do to deserve being wiped out?" Liraz asked wearily.

Hannah's face pinched in concern, but Dismas scoffed. *Giving up his angel powers for love doomed him from the start.*

"God destroyed Sodom, Gomorrah, Admah, and Zeboiim for their lewd behavior," said Hannah.

She sounds like a schoolteacher. How does a mere woman know so much?

"You don't know the truth of what really transpired the night before God blew up these wicked places," Padel said.

"Haven't you read the Book of Jasher about how these people mistreated strangers?" asked Gonael.

A skeptical look crossed Hannah's face. "I'm not sure I believe that book. It says citizens of Sodom would chop off or forcibly stretch a stranger's legs to make them fit on the bed located in the town square."

"What town would have a bed in the middle of it? Seems like a fable," Benjamin said.

Rich boy doesn't know the evil that lurks around every corner.

Padel plucked one of Ayin's eyes. "Show them the wickedness of Sodom."

Another vision? Dismas sighed. *Can't we just retrieve the key piece and leave this awful place?*

A crowded, open-air market appeared. Between the stalls overflowing with food and goods stood an old, wrinkled man with at least thirty thick gold chains around his neck.

He could buy anything he wants with all that gold, Dismas thought.

"Water," the old man whispered from parched lips. His skin had the bluish-gray pallor of death.

No one responded. As if he didn't exist.

The man staggered to a table of red apples. He pulled gold coins from his pocket and handed them to a dark-haired young woman behind the stand. "I want to buy an apple. Please."

With all that gold, why is this man begging?

"You know your money's no good here," the pretty woman said nastily.

"Why are you doing this to me? I will give you all these gold coins for one measly apple."

"Don't bother. We'll take your coins and whatever else you have when you're a corpse," another woman said and grinned as she patted her pregnant belly.

A young boy placed his foot next to the old man's. "Close fit. I claim the sandals when he keels over."

These people are cruel. Dismas was a thief, but not like this.

"What is wrong with this town?" the old man asked weakly.

"We don't like strangers, and you might be a spy," bellowed a plump man as he shoved a fistful of grapes into his mouth. Purple juice ran down his chin like blood.

The old man left.

"Something's not right," said a man selling tents. "That old man should have died days ago."

"Someone must be helping him," the plump man said, pushing more grapes into his fat face. "I will follow him."

Barabbas would have fit in perfectly in this town.

Ayin blinked, and the scene changed to a barn where a young woman with kind, brown eyes and a yellow robe handed a cup of water and a piece of bread to the starving old man.

"Drink up," she urged. "You need to live until my husband returns—"

The barn doors flung open, and twenty townspeople rushed in. The woman flinched, dropping the cup of water. The old man quickly swallowed the piece of bread.

The grape-eating man pointed. "Paltith's been feeding him."

"Seize them both and take them to the king!" yelled the townspeople.

Four young men dragged the pair out of the barn and back through the marketplace. The crowd swelled by the time they reached the gate of Sodom. They shoved Paltith before a man wearing a gold crown sitting on a white marble throne.

"King of Sodom, I witnessed Paltith feeding this stranger," said the grape-eater, bowing.

"Paltith, you're fortunate I happened to be in town to hear your case," said the king with a cruel smile. "Otherwise, you'd be waiting in my dungeon. Where is the man she fed?"

Two young men pushed the old man to the ground in front of the king.

"Anyone who saw Paltith give the old man food, raise your hand."

Every person in the mob raised a hand.

"I declare Paltith guilty." The king flashed a crooked smile. "Since you're Lot's daughter, we'll show you mercy and kill you quickly by fire."

Paltith is Lot's daughter? But I thought his daughters survived Sodom's blast.

"Murdering me before my husband returns?" challenged Paltith. "This wretched town wouldn't exist if my great-uncle Abram hadn't rescued it during the War of the Nine Kings." Her body shook and tears streamed down her face.

"I'm the King of Sodom, and I fear no one. Burn her now."

A woman pulled a blanket off an object in the middle of the square.

It's the bed.

Paltith screamed as four men threw her on the bed and tied her hands and legs to the bedposts.

"Make sure the knots are tight," instructed the king.

The adults instructed children to gather straw for the bed. "It'll burn faster," they said.

Paltith closed her eyes and clamped her lips shut.

The children danced and shouted as they ran back and forth to the barn, gathering hay.

"You made your bed, now die in it," a pregnant woman yelled, holding a little girl's hand.

Dismas noticed almost every woman in the crowd was with child. *How is that Possible?*

A group of five men hauled the starving man next to the bed and forced him to watch. "This is your fault," they told him. "You killed the girl."

"No!" the man whispered before he fell to the ground dead. Several men and women pounced on him, ripping the gold necklaces from his neck. The young man who had claimed the old man's sandals snatched them and cackled triumphantly.

One man held a torch near the bed.

Dismas could almost smell the smoke.

"Lord, judge Sodom. Burn it all to the ground!" Paltith yelled.

Hannah covered her eyes. "Please, I can't take it anymore.

Ayin, make it stop. Those people are horrid."

Dismas' hands trembled, and sweat rolled down his back. He couldn't help but wonder, *Could I have been part of that crowd urging them on?* He'd stolen from a corpse, too. He had watched silently as Barabbas murdered Hannah and Benjamin's grandfather. Dismas had been just a child, but Barabbas had forced him to go through dead men's pockets. His first refusal had earned him the scar on his face. He touched it. *I'm sorry, Lord, for everything. Please forgive me.*

"I have seen this human behavior firsthand," Liraz said. "This is how things were during the days of Noah."

"Don't act so holy," Padel said, pointing his finger at Liraz. "Your actions had a direct consequence on Sodom blowing up."

"Were these my children?" asked Liraz.

"We don't have time for the blame game," Gonael said dismissively. "We must reach Sodom before nightfall when they close the gate. Please disembark."

Dismas lumbered down the stairs. As soon as his feet touched soft grass, the stairs transformed to a wheel once more.

Gonael patted the wheel and whispered, "Return."

Ayin's eyes spun around, causing the chariot to twist in a circle.

Dismas felt as confused as Ayin looked.

"Return, Ayin," Gonael repeated, raising his voice.

The chariot disappeared, but the creatures remained.

"Don't look so surprised, Dismas. We can't journey through Sodom with a golden chariot," Padel huffed.

"You're going with us?" Benjamin looked relieved.

"New clothes for all," commanded Dormel as he waved his hands.

Dismas' new clothes felt like the finest fabrics: a purple inner garment and a robe of gold and dark blue. His head scarf matched. A wide, black leather belt with a money pouch girded his waist. He opened the pouch. To his delight, it was bursting with gold and silver coins. So were his pockets. *So, this is what it feels like to be a wealthy man.* Dismas stood a little taller.

Hannah, Benjamin, and Liraz also wore extravagant clothes. But in the most stunning transformation, the living creatures were now men! Each had feet instead of hooves. They lost their brightness in favor of ordinary faces. Jachniel had changed the least since he already had a man's face. Gonael's hair was brown streaked with blond, resembling eagle feathers. His neck was thin, and his shoulders hunched forward. He still had piercing eyes. Padel was the tallest and bulkiest, muscles bulging under his robe. He had coarse, jet-black hair and a wide nose with flared nostrils. Dormel's curly blond hair and beard hung around his face like a mane and he had a toothy smile.

"With the four of you by our side, we will uncover the key as swiftly as the wind parted the Red Sea!" Hannah twirled, spilling coins from her pockets. She knelt to retrieve them and return them to her purple robe.

Dismas didn't feel the same enthusiasm. *If the creatures are accompanying us, something must be wrong.* He recalled Lucifer's statement about heading into a dung storm.

"What's with all the gold and silver?" Benjamin held up a gold nugget the size of a walnut.

"Bribes for us to enter Sodom," Jachniel said.

Dismas clutched the money in his pocket. No way was he giving up these coins. Not one.

16

*For their vine is from the vine of Sodom
and from the fields of Gomorrah.
Their grapes are poisonous;
their clusters are bitter.*

—Deuteronomy 32:32 (HCSB)

Sodom's palace, 1650 BC
The thirty-fifth hour in hell

Impatience surged within Mahway. How dare the kings make him wait under the watchful eye of twenty guards. Didn't they realize he could rip their throats before their protectors could intervene?

Tonight would be the rebirth of the Nephilim, though not to their former glory. Mahway didn't care about his new appearance—it was a joy to inhabit a body and indulge in earthly pleasures again. At least he'd escaped hell.

All his devious plans had brought him to this moment: a seat at the king's ebony table. Curved, solid silver chairs stood at attention around the table. On it, an assortment of lamb, deer, and cow meat overflowed gleaming silver platters.

They'd pay for making him wait.

Mahway shivered, moving closer to the stone fireplace to warm his flesh. Once a demon experienced hell's intense fires, everywhere else seemed freezing. In fact, every time he entered a room, the temperature dropped, and the humans got goosebumps.

The fireplace stood in the center of King Bera's strategy

room, which overlooked the courtroom filled with heavily armed guards. He harrumphed at their outrageous uniforms: short, brown linen skirts trimmed in royal red with matching short-sleeve shirts. Three white feathers poked out of their bronze helmets, a symbol of service in the king's elite guard. The windows were bolted closed to ensure no eavesdroppers. Spies lurked everywhere.

Mahway rubbed his right human hand against the top of his left furry paw. After his transformation, he avoided mirrors. In this room, however, there was no escape. He saw his reflection everywhere—in the polished silver covering the ceiling, the oversized rectangular candlesticks lining the mantle, and on the semicircular chair backs. He arched his back as he stared at his unusual reflection in the ceiling. Half-human and half-lion, split right down the middle with distinct features of each on his right and left sides respectively. His regal mane flowed seamlessly from lion fur to dirty-blond human hair, while his orange-yellow predatory eyes missed nothing. With a satisfied grin he opened his mouth and admired his full set of lion teeth. Mahway's annoying tail swished behind him despite how hard the Sodom tailors tried to hide it in his custom pants. He covered his animal side in a special cloak.

Tonight, he would unveil his new identity. Of course, he preferred his original, pre-flood body, but at least he had total control of this hybrid vessel, no longer having to possess a human to enjoy fleshly desires. A new era would begin as he welcomed more members of his race. He relished the idea of blending in after the others were birthed. But make no mistake, *he* was the king of this new hybrid race.

A horn blasted outside, announcing the two kings' arrival. Two guards rushed to the silver door and pushed it open. More guards spilled into the room, followed by two stooped, wrinkled judges. After them strolled King Birsha of Gomorrah in his blue flowing robe. The trumpeter blasted the horn again, and everyone took their seats at the table. Mahway abandoned the warmth of the fire and chose the seat to the left of the head of the table.

The old judges of Sodom openly gawked at him. He grinned, exposing his fangs.

King Bera appeared in the doorway, a gold ruby-encrusted crown resting on his thick black hair. He sauntered to the table, his royal red robe with long wings jiggling as he stood by his chair. A guard assisted him to his seat, while two more guards stood behind him, ensuring the wings didn't get caught in the back of his elevated chair.

He looks ridiculous, Only birds, insects, and angels have wings. Not humans.

"After tonight, no one will conquer us again. Our hybrid army will be invincible," proclaimed King Bera. The cupbearer poured the king's wine and tasted it. After a moment in which nothing happened, he returned the golden goblet to King Bera, who raised it to his thin lips. The king continued, "Without Mahway none of this would be possible. Stand." King Bera beckoned Mahway with his stubby, pudgy fingers. "I want our distinguished guests to see how you turned out."

Mahway fumed. He didn't want to be paraded in front of the wrinkled judges of Sodom. He forced himself to rise, deciding he wasn't taking orders from the king—he just needed to stretch his tail.

"Let me get this straight," began the vulture-like judge with sunken cheeks and a hooked nose. "There are going to be more of these half-lion, half-humans born tonight?"

Mahway noticed the man's bony hands shook. He fed off the fear and leaned over the table, staring at both judges.

"Yes," King Birsha announced. "The festival tonight will be pure madness. Everyone respects the judges of Sodom, so we need you to order the men to drink our special wine that will keep them away from the temple tonight where the birthing will happen."

He shouldn't be so forthcoming. Mahway crossed his arms. The fewer people who knew, the better. So much could go wrong.

"What about Lot? He's always been a problem," inquired the other judge, smoothing his slicked-back white hair while averting his eyes from Mahway.

"He never leaves his home during our festivals," King Bera answered. "And he keeps to himself ever since I sentenced his daughter to death."

"Will we be safe tonight? Can these things eat us?" asked the white-haired judge. His beady, narrow eyes fixated on Mahway's teeth.

Mahway sneered. *Maybe I should jump on the table and devour them.*

The white-haired judge scraped his chair back, away from Mahway.

"Sit down, Mahway," ordered King Bera.

He shrugged. *It would be nice to sit again anyway.*

King Bera sank to his throne and noisily slurped his drink.

Mahway mentally rehashed their scheme. *Right now, 666 pregnant women of Sodom are on their way to the fertility goddess's temple to drink a potion to induce labor. All the midwives will be in attendance, thinking they are delivering normal babies.* He chuckled inwardly. *Tonight, this town will get the shock of their lives when they see these special deliveries. Of course, none of the women will survive giving birth.* He sighed, almost feeling bad about it. *Oh well.*

Would Lucifer follow through on his promise to release the hell hounds? He'd better. Those dogs were essential to the entire operation. No one trusted Lucifer.

So many things could go wrong tonight.

"I've been promised two hundred hybrids to take back with me tonight," demanded King Birsha.

"Yes, they will be divided between the four cities. But not one hybrid will set foot in Zoar. They refused to participate." King Bera's eyes flashed in anger.

Mahway snatched a piece of lamb from the table and shoved it in his mouth, barely chewing. *Humans. How dare they think they have control of my hybrid army? Soon they'll learn who is really in charge.*

King Bera stretched his arms toward the feast. "Let's enjoy this meal while waiting for the festivities. Ah! Where are my manners? We forgot to include our guest of honor." King Bera pointed at two guards. "Go bring us the man who made all this possible."

The guards rushed from the room and within moments returned, dragging a man through the doorway, and shoving him into one of the silver chairs. Blood dripped from a fresh gash on the prisoner's forehead, and a black eye adorned his face.

Why are they bringing him here? The captive should stay in the dungeon where it's safe. Mahway's eyes darted to the windows. *The fools. Bolted windows can't keep out pesky angels.*

"Let's all drink tonight!" ordered King Bera.

The wrinkled judges nervously downed their chalices.

Mahway groaned. *Don't they know how important tonight is?*

The kings and the entire city of Sodom would use any excuse to get drunk. Mahway lifted his cup to his lion's side nostril and sniffed. *Not made from the tainted Sodom grapes. What a relief.*

"We all know your type doesn't drink," the king of Sodom sneered at the prisoner. "You live off the praises of your God."

"Force him," commanded the king of Gomorrah.

One guard pried open the captive's mouth while the other poured wine down his throat.

The prisoner gagged and spewed the crimson liquid like a venomous serpent spouting its poison all over the table.

"Obey your kings. Make him drink," instructed Mahway.

One guard tilted the bottle into the prisoner's mouth, then forced him to swallow by pinching his nose. The wine dribbled down the man's jaw.

"To victory," declared the King of Sodom.

The guards clapped while Mahway pretended to drink. He needed his mind alert tonight. He kept his eye on the window, expecting it to burst open at any moment. Then he cocked his ear toward the door. Someone on the other side was demanding to speak to King Bera. But far surpassing Mahway's excellent Nephilim hearing was his heightened smell, thanks to being part lion. The stench of the visitor's leather loincloth reached him. A watchtower archer. This was going to be one long, memorable night.

17

About this time the Sodomites grew proud, on account of their riches and great wealth; they became unjust towards men, and impious towards God, insomuch that they did not call to mind the advantages they received from him: they hated strangers and abused themselves with Sodomitical practices.

—Flavius Josephus, Antiquities of the Jews Book I

The forty-third hour in hell

"Sodom is this way," Gonael directed and walked east through the date palm grove. The four creatures walked side by side, Hannah, Benjamin, and Dismas following. Liraz kept his distance. Dismas fiddled with the gold coins in his pocket as he stepped over sticky dates.

Padel popped a handful of dates into his mouth and smacked his lips.

"Once you're done devouring the dates, you can *mooove* onto the grass," mocked Liraz.

Padel ignored him and kept munching. A branch snapped in the distance. Immediately, he dropped the dates and sprang into action, disappearing behind a boulder. The creatures sprinted after him. "You are safe now. I will not hurt you," Padel said in a gentle voice.

Dismas caught up and found Padel comforting a thin, wild-eyed man in his thirties, crouched on the grass, clutching a fist full of dates. Fifteen golden necklaces adorned his neck and his dingy robe dripped water.

"We're here to help you," said Jachniel soothingly.

"Please, don't take me back to Sodom," begged the man. "I just escaped, and all I want to do is go back home to Jericho and hug my wife and children."

"We have nothing to do with Sodom," Padel reassured him, pulling a leather satchel from behind his back. Dismas swore the satchel wasn't there a minute ago.

"Take this." Padel offered the bag. "It will provide you with nourishment. I promise nobody from Sodom will ever hurt you again, Oren."

"You know my name? Are you a prophet?" Bony fingers grasped the bag.

"Something of the sort." Padel flashed a warm smile. This unexpected kindness left Dismas touched and bewildered.

"How did you escape from Sodom?" questioned Benjamin, keeping his distance.

Dismas burned inside. *Rich boy assumes he's better than most people.*

"I was falsely accused of being a spy of King Chedorlaomer," Oren explained. "Then the Sodomites forced me to wear these gold necklaces so no one at the marketplace would sell me food." He ripped off the necklaces and flung them into the grass. They landed near Dismas' feet where they sank into the dirt.

Amid the gold, a cobra-shaped pendant with ruby eyes seemed to stare at Dismas. Something compelled him to pick it up. When no one was looking, he scooped it into his pocket. *We might need this to get into Sodom.*

"A kind-hearted young man took pity on me," Oren continued. "He showed me where the river is low so I could cross. I'd prayed someone would help me and he did."

"I'm thrilled your prayers to escape were answered," Jachniel said. "We must go if we are to arrive in Sodom by nightfall."

"You don't want to go there!" Oren glanced anxiously toward Sodom.

Gonael cocked his ear. "I think I hear soldiers. Oren, you'd better hurry and do not stop until you reach Jericho."

Oren swung the bag over his shoulder and raced across the palm field.

Soldiers? Dismas searched in all directions. He didn't hear anything. He rubbed the smooth ruby eyes of the snake pendant tucked in his pocket. *Oren is right. We are crazy to go into Sodom.*

"Sodom soldiers?" Hannah frowned and moved closer to Gonael.

"Relax, Hannah," he said. "I just needed Oren to stay away since Sodom will soon be razed and everything surrounding it."

Gonael spoke about Sodom's destruction as if it were nothing more than the weather or crops. *Angels and their words are as unpredictable as a tempest on Lake Galilee, appearing and vanishing without warning.*

Padel resumed the group's trek through the palm trees.

Liraz broke the silence, "Who is King Chedorlaomer?"

"He's the King of Elam. He fought against the King of Sodom in the Nine Kings War." Again, Hannah with that annoying teacher's voice. "It came to pass in the days of—"

"Boring," interrupted Benjamin. "Let me explain what happened." He held up four fingers. "On one side were these four evil kings. Some say King Tidal was the devil himself, and King Arioch was half-lion and half-man and ate human babies for breakfast."

"Dormel, one of your long-lost relatives?" asked Liraz.

The angel roared in disgust, shaking his golden mane.

"No roaring." Liraz wagged his finger. "Remember, you're trying to pass as a human."

Now Liraz is taunting Dormel? Dismas' brow furrowed. *Are they all part of this feud or is Lucifer invading Liraz again?*

"On the losing side were the five kings of Sodom, Gomorrah, Admah, Zeboiim, and Zoar." Benjamin held up five fingers on his other hand. "The four kings beat the five kings and, for twelve long years, cruelly ruled over them. The five kings, including Sodom and Gomorrah, had enough of being ruled and plotted to overthrow the four kings."

"Then the king of Sodom entered into an agreement with the seven tribes of the giants in the land," said Dismas. *Benjamin isn't the only one who knows this story.*

"Giants," exclaimed Padel. "Now that sounds like some of Liraz's long-lost relatives."

Liraz's face reddened like an overripe tomato.

Benjamin cleared his throat. "King Chedorlaomer had sent spies into the five cities and learned of the secret agreement between the five kings and the seven giant tribes. The four kings' vast armies conquered the giant tribes, one by one, and then resolved to kill the five rebel kings and enslave the people. The final battle happened in the Valley of Siddim. The armies of Sodom and Gomorrah were being massacred, so they retreated to the mountains, right into the tar pits."

"In the dark," Hannah took over, "the soldiers sank into the tar pits like quicksand. More soldiers perished in those tar pits than in the actual battle. The survivors claimed demons emerged out of the tar pits and dragged them straight to hell."

As a child, Barabbas had told Dismas that tar pit demons would drag him to hell if he wouldn't fall asleep fast enough.

"Woman, stop interrupting me," scolded Benjamin. "King Chedorlaomer's military stormed Sodom and seized treasure, women, and the remaining men, including Lot. When Abraham heard about his nephew's capture, he gathered 318 men. They destroyed the conquering forces and rescued all the citizens of Sodom."

"How did Abraham rescue the captives?" asked Liraz.

Jachniel pointed up. "Friends in high places."

A fishy smell wafted into Dismas' nostrils as he brushed past the last palm tree.

Hannah sneezed and held her hand over her mouth.

"You'll become accustomed to the smell," said Padel. "It's from the river that circles the city like a moat. God has blessed ungrateful Sodom with an overabundance of fish."

Dismas spotted the river but was captivated by the impressive city of Sodom. The red mud walls soared to the sky with at least six watchtowers at strategic intervals. Rectangles were cut into the top of the walls, giving the appearance of missing teeth. Archers stood in the gaps.

"The king's highway." Gonael pointed to the road that bridged the river, straight to the massive iron gates of Sodom. Countless footprints led into the dreadful city.

"With all those archers up there, Sodom looks like it expects to be attacked at any moment," Benjamin said, gawking.

Rich boy looks like a fool staring with his mouth hanging open. Like Beelzebub and his flies.

"The Sodomites built a fortress and vowed their city would never be captured again," said Jachniel. "And they suspected everyone of being spies."

"Typical humans," Padel huffed. "Putting up walls instead of trusting God."

Anger surged through Dismas. *Easy for an angel. He never had to scrounge for food or be knocked off his feet by Barabbas's fist.* Dismas clenched his jaw, tripping on a rut and stumbling into Hannah. *Move, woman!*

"The Sodomites truly are wicked," she said quietly.

Dismas followed her eyeline and gasped. Scattered throughout the field were pagan idol poles. Young women danced around naked, worshiping the fertility goddess, Asherah. Between the poles stood an altar for sacrifices—two rectangular stones holding up one larger flat stone. Dismas saw remnants of dried blood along the sides of the crude altar. Carved into the bottom stones were images of Baal dancing with half-naked

Asherah. Clearly, the people of Sodom overcame their fear of attack long enough to risk engaging in their drunken festivals and who knew what else. Even Barabbas wasn't involved in pagan worship.

"Keep your eyes straight ahead. Don't gaze to the right or the left," suggested Dormel.

Something whizzed past Dismas' ear and he froze. An arrow landed next to his feet. A succession of arrows pierced the ground all around them. Beside him, Hannah gasped.

Four guards emerged from under the bridge wearing loincloths, sleeveless blue tunics, and a blue feather in their bronze helmets, longswords tucked into their belts. Each clutched a bow and arrows.

"Don't move," shouted one guard, aiming at Dismas' head.

Dismas held his breath, obeying.

"State your business in Sodom," demanded another.

"We're headed to see Lot," responded Padel, puffing out his chest. "We have a message from his uncle Abram."

"Abram! Are any of you members of the 318?" asked the guard still holding the arrow poised at his scar.

A bead of sweat dripped off Dismas' nose.

"Four of us fought," Dormel said. The three other creatures nodded, and the guards slowly lowered their bows.

"How do we know they're not lying?" questioned a guard, his impenetrable eyes devoid of emotion. The weapons hanging off his thick leather belt clashed and gleamed—a double-headed ax and a sword with a blade extending beyond his muscled thigh.

"We're not like most men. We don't lie," Padel said, with his don't-defy-me look.

"Fine. We'll verify your story with Lot. If you're liars, you'll be locked up in the dungeon and beaten. It's four pieces of silver for each of you to cross." The guard licked his lips and held out a greedy hand.

"That's highway robbery!" exclaimed Dismas.

"You would know all about that," muttered Benjamin, handing four silver pieces to the guards.

Dismas fisted his coins in his pocket, while the others easily handed over their silver. No way he would pay to cross their stupid bridge when he could swim for free. He jumped into the choppy river feet first. The water felt like ice. He shivered and his muscles tensed. The strong current steered him like a whirlpool. Something bumped into his calf and he assumed it was a fish. He flailed his arms overhead, attempting to swim, but the current was too powerful and pulled him under. Everything turned black like hell. He swore he faintly smelled sulfur amid the stench of fish. Dismas' neck hair prickled. Just then, he spotted a set of red eyes by his leg.

"Loser, I'm dragging you back to hell," whispered a hoarse demon's voice.

Dismas was sinking like an anchor toward the glowing eyes. *The coins!* With horror he realized he had to empty his pockets. It was his only hope. He yanked his prizes from his pockets and let the current take them. The snake pendant wrapped around his wrist and then swept away. *If the demon dragged me back to hell, would Jesus still let me into Paradise? After I failed him?* He flapped his arms. No use. Something still weighed him down. *The belt!* It contained even more coins. He struggled to release it, but the leather was tough when wet and his fingers were numb. Dismas panicked as water whooshed up his nostrils. He clawed at the belt until, finally, it loosened and the water stole it away. He broke through the surface.

Somebody grabbed his shoulder and yanked him from the water. He coughed, throat burning.

The four guards swarmed him and dragged him onto the muddy riverbank.

"Now it's eight pieces of silver to cross," one of the guards said. His companions laughed.

Dismas heaved water from his lungs and nostrils. "I can't pay. I've lost all my silver in that wretched river." He continued to gag.

Hannah took coins from her pouch. "I'll pay for him."

Dismas wiped the offending liquid from his mouth and bowed his head. *A woman paying my way. The shame.*

"Usually, we would beat you as well, but since you are traveling with four of Abram's warriors, we'll let it slide today." A guard roughly pulled Dismas to his feet.

Dismas lagged behind the others as they crossed the bridge. Being beltless, he kept tripping over his long, soaked robe.

"What's wrong with you, Hannah?" Benjamin scolded. "He killed our grandfather and you're rewarding him. I should have insisted that the guards pummel him."

The way the rich boy emphasized the word 'he' sounded like a swear word. Dismas huffed.

"After seeing what happened to Paltith and Oren, haven't you learned about having compassion on the less fortunate?" said Hannah.

Less fortunate?! Dismas balled his fists.

Liraz changed the subject. "I thought you couldn't lie. You four were part of the 318? Did you parade as men to fight for Abram?"

"While the natural battle raged, we engaged in spiritual battle," Padel said. "When Abram rescued Lot, demons crawled out of the tar pits."

Finally, they reached Sodom. On top of the city gate loomed statues of Baal and Asherah casting ominous shadows in the sunset.

Gonael pointed at Dismas. "Dry."

Dismas pawed at his dry robe and nodded thanks. Even his skin felt warm, and he no longer stank of fish.

"Add belt."

A belt cinched around his waist. *What a relief.* He grinned in anticipation as he ripped open the pouch. *Empty. Punishment for jumping in the river.* His hands trembled in shame and nervousness.

They stopped at the gate in front of another guard. "Stay in front of us," ordered Padel.

"State your business in Sodom," the guard demanded.

The creatures remained silent.

"We have a message for Lot from his uncle Abram," Liraz said with authority.

Why are the creatures letting Liraz manage the gate?

"In that case, come in. But it will cost each of you four pieces of silver."

"We paid at the river," Dismas spat.

"It doesn't matter. Strangers must pay—and in so many unusual ways," the guard sneered, scrutinizing Dismas head to toe.

"I'm paying for the boy, the woman, and scar face," Liraz said, pulling silver coins from his belt. Under the guard's watchful eye, he counted sixteen pieces of silver and placed them in a small leather pouch. The guard licked his lips and held out his hand. Liraz winked at Dismas, then pretended to trip, sending the coins rolling in every direction. While the guard stooped to pick up the coins, they proceeded through the gate.

As Dismas passed the walls, he felt an icy draft, and shivered. The glimpse of a black shadow made him take a second look around. *Strange.* He turned to the creatures, but they had vanished.

"I can't believe they left us again," Benjamin moaned.

"Now how will we find Lot?" Hannah said, eyes downcast.

White marble chairs sat to the right of the town square, just like the vision Ayin had shown them. In front of the judges' seats was a blanket covering a square object. The infamous bed of Sodom. Dismas turned his attention to three men engaged in conversation on the other side of the square.

"No," muttered a short man, eyes concerned. "You can't wander around Sodom tonight. My name is Lot, come home as my guests."

Hannah whispered, "If that's Lot, the other two are angels."

"Thanks for your offer of hospitality," said the man with violet eyes, "but we can sleep on the bed in the square."

"I'd like to interact with the people of Sodom," said the other man. His belt appeared to be solid gold. The tops of his sandals were pure white, not a speck of dust.

"I insist," Lot grabbed an elbow of each man. "Both of you will be my honored guests. It's not safe to be out during the Asherah festival."

"Fine, we accept your hospitality. I am Malakh," said the man with violet eyes. "And my companion is Mishpat."

Mishpat bowed and then pointed to Dismas. "What about those four who just came in? Are the streets of Sodom safe for them tonight?"

Lot waved them over. "You have entered Sodom at the worst possible time. Please be my guests tonight as well."

The four companions hurried to join Lot and the angels.

"We would be honored to be your guests," said Liraz, offering a bow.

"Follow me, but keep a couple paces behind. I don't want the whole town knowing I have guests."

They turned down a brick red street—their soft clicking against the cobblestones sounded like haunting whispers in the empty street.

Too late. Dismas spotted archers along the upper wall, pointing at them and whispering. One guard stared at them and left his post.

Lot's house was not far from the square. He opened the gate

to a courtyard leading to a single-story, light-red mud brick home with a flat roof.

"Ado, we have an extra six for dinner tonight." Lot gave a nervous laugh as he pushed open the iron door.

"Oh, that's nice," answered a harsh woman's voice from the back of the house. "And on a night when all our servants have left to attend the celebration." Pots and pans clattered from the kitchen area.

Dismas washed the dust off his feet in the basin by the door. As they settled on soft purple cushions, two young women emerged from a back hallway. *Lot's daughters.* One girl had loose, fiery red hair. She placed a water jug on the low table. The brunette carried a large platter of figs, almonds, cut apples, and a mound of grapes. They wore multicolored robes cinched at their tiny waists. Each sister jangled and rattled from an excess of necklaces and bangles. Their eyes were lined in black and their cheeks were scarlet.

"Meet my dear daughter, Penina," said Lot.

Penina kissed the air with plump, blood-red lips.

Would a betrothed woman be so brazen? Dismas wondered, remembering the story.

"And my youngest, Puah," Lot continued.

Puah slammed the platter on the table. "You." She pointed a sharp nail at Hannah. "Women aren't allowed to sit at the table. You're helping us roll out the unleavened bread."

"That is not how you treat our guests," Lot said.

"We need more hands in the kitchen, and we can get to know our visitor better." Puah placed her hand on Hannah's shoulder.

Hannah swallowed hard but slowly rose from the overstuffed pillows and followed Lot's daughters out of the room. Dismas watched her every move, his unease growing with every step she took away from him. Anything could happen.

"Ado, come meet our guests for the night," Lot's voice carried a pleasant tone.

From the shadows came a tiny woman with salt-and-pepper hair, wiping her hands on a towel tucked in her belt. "Make yourselves welcome," Ado said through clenched teeth, glaring at her guests. "Where are you all from?"

"We've just come from Mamre," Mishpat replied, selecting a plump grape from the platter.

"Mamre? Do you know my uncle Abram?" Lot asked.

"Yes." Malakh eyes lit up. "We had a wonderful lunch with him while his wife prepared bread. Perhaps you do not know—Abram is now called Abraham, the father of many."

Ado huffed. "Oh, that's right. God promised Abram and Sarai a child." She scrunched her wrinkled face. "The lunatics! They are too old to have children."

Lot chuckled, attempting to placate his wife. "It does sound crazy, but no crazier than when Uncle Abram rescued us from King Chedorlaomer. God has been good to us."

"Where was your good God when our daughter was set on fire in the streets of Sodom?" scoffed Ado. She picked up Lot's glass to fill it. But her tense grip looked like she'd rather throw it.

Mishpat leaned forward and said in a compassionate voice, "I am sorry about your daughter. This town is wicked,"

Ado grunted, gripping the water jug.

"Why do you stay?" asked Benjamin.

"I wanted to leave Sodom, but then I wouldn't have met my lovely wife." Lot reached for Ado's free hand.

Lovely? Definitely not the right word. Complaining women like Ado were why Dismas never wanted to marry. Now Hannah was different, kind and encouraging—the opposite of Ado. *But a woman like Hannah, I'd never be able to afford her wedding gifts and her father wouldn't allow her to marry a thief like me.*

"Maybe if you would have chosen the lesser land, my daughter would be alive." Ado snatched her hand away, sloshing water all over him. Lot shrugged as Ado blotted his robe with a towel.

"Ado, asking 'what if' is a dangerous game," Mishpat said.

She froze.

Malakh added, "Ado, you can't live your life backward. Keep your eyes focused on what is ahead."

"Well, you aren't me." Ado whipped around and bumped into Hannah, who was carrying a tray of unleavened bread and honey.

Hannah placed the platter on the table. "Lord of the house, may I make a request? I hope you won't refuse your guest, especially one who helped make dinner."

Lot nodded.

Hannah held up the partial key.

I hope Lot has a fragment and we can just leave before all the trouble starts.

"Do you happen to have a key piece that matches this?" asked Hannah. Her hands shook slightly.

Dismas' hands also shook as he tore off a chunk of bread.

Before Lot could answer, the door flung open, and a young man burst into the room.

Everyone jolted. Hannah dropped the key, and it clanged on the table.

"They're coming! You're all in danger. We need to leave at once." The dark-haired stranger panted and fumbled to bolt the door.

The warm unleavened bread stuck in Dismas' throat. *It's happening—the men and boys of Sodom are headed this way.* Dismas' legs began to shake, and his heart raced.

18

The men of Sodom who acted arrogantly, who were notorious for their vices.

—3 Maccabees 2:5

[The men of Sodom] said: "You know well that we have no claim on your daughters; and you surely know well what we desire."

—Qur'an 11:79, Ali Unal translation

Lot's house
The forty-sixth hour in hell

Ado stood in the kitchen entryway with a hand on her hip and waved a tiny cutting knife. "Ziv, *we* are not in danger!" she shouted. "By now, the entire town knows *you* assisted Oren's escape."

"The man in the forest?" whispered Hannah.

Dismas' cheeks flushed as he remembered the snake pendant.

"I told you to never come here again," snarled Ado. "It's your fault Paltith is dead."

Ah, Dismas realized, *his black sackcloth means he's Paltith's widower.*

"That's enough, Ado," Lot said sharply as he joined Ziv at the door.

"Father," Ziv spoke in ragged gasps, "all the men in the town are headed to your house because they think your visitors are spies." He leaned his back against the door.

"Spies?" Mishpat spat.

"We are messengers of the Most High," proclaimed Malakh.

Lot's daughters' jewelry jangled as they entered the room.

"What trouble did you cause this time?" Penina asked.

Puah crossed her arms.

"None," Ziv said. "I was walking near the Asherah temple, and I heard a low, guttural growl. I spun around and found a snarling dog, black as night, the size of a horse with huge yellow eyes. It smelled like death."

Malakh grimaced. "The hell hound has arrived."

"Not just one. At least twenty more materialized and rushed toward the temple doors."

"Twenty demon dogs, that can't be good," said Mishpat. His lips twisted into a deep frown as he exchanged an uneasy glance with Malakh.

Ziv's eyes widened with fear. "The drunk men yelled at the dogs. One man poked his torch at one. The beast bared his fangs, then ripped his throat."

"You're always lying," Ado scoffed.

"Then, some of the women inside the temple started screaming in agony," Ziv continued. "Like no sound I've ever heard. Palace guards swarmed the temple and told the men Lot's guests are King Chedorlaomer's spies."

"Liar!" Ado's eyes glared a challenge.

"But Uncle Abram rescued the entire town," Lot said. "Why would these ungrateful pagans think I would harbor spies?"

"The guards incited the men into a frenzy by shouting, 'Seize the spies!' They forgot all about the dogs and screeching women. Their eyes turned glassy. I swear they were in a trance…" Ziv's voice trailed off.

Lot arched his eyebrow. "Sounds like they had a strong batch of Sodom wine. Did you indulge, too?"

"No!" Ziv exclaimed. "I swear."

"Do tell, how did you get away from the man-eating dogs?" asked Penina, twirling a strand of red hair.

"It doesn't matter," Ziv replied. "I told you everything I witnessed."

"Yes," mocked Ado, "*do* tell how the brave Ziv got away."

"Well, if you must know, I played dead. The hell hound sniffed me but left me alone."

Penina and Puah burst out laughing.

"Stop laughing. We need to leave at once," Ziv pleaded. "The mob is closing in."

"Thanks for the bedtime story," said Penina. "I'm going to sleep." She yawned and stretched her hands over her head.

"I smell torches." Hannah pinched her nose.

"And people are shouting," Dismas added. He tried to decipher the words. *Sounds like, "Rape the spies."* A shiver went down his spine.

Ado became very still.

"See? I speak truth," Ziv said.

The crowd grew louder by the second. Penina scurried to the window and threw back the animal hide curtain. "Ziv's right," her voice trembled.

Dismas strained to see out the window. A mass of men and boys filled the streets. *Now we're trapped.* Men began climbing over the wall and pushing through the gate, flooding into Lot's courtyard.

"Bring out the spies. We want to rape them!" the sea of men cried out.

"Penina, get away from the window!" Ado cried.

"They will have to go through me," said Lot, standing next to Ziv, pressing his body against the door. "It's my duty to protect our guests."

"Like you protected our daughter?" Ado taunted.

Fists banged on the door, and Dismas jumped. More angry knuckles pounded on the entryway and the walls of Lot's home. The frame around the door groaned as hairline cracks appeared in the mud bricks. *Oh Lord, let the door and walls hold under the weight,* he prayed.

"I need to reason with them." Lot gently moved Ziv away from the door.

"No, Daddy. No!" Puah sobbed.

"I have to defend my guests." Lot slid the bolt on the door.

"Wait!" Ado raced to her husband. She pecked him lightly on the cheek. "Tell them to stop wrecking my beautiful house and get out of my yard."

As Lot opened the door, Dismas could see approximately twenty intoxicated men swaying just outside the entryway. The nauseating, stale wine smell washed over them. *Disgusting. Just like Barabbas.*

Lot stepped outside and slammed the door behind him. The constant rapping on the door and walls stopped. Dismas and Benjamin moved toward the door.

"Go home, brothers," Lot said. "The men inside my home are my honored visitors, not spies."

"We want to rape the spies and send them back to King Chedorlaomer," a drunk said, words slurred. The mob whooped and hollered in agreement.

"Why are you so wicked? Don't you understand? I made a sacred vow to protect my guests. What would you have me do? Offer you my virgin daughters in their place?"

Lot's wife and daughters gasped.

Malakh eyes filled with compassion and pity in his eyes. "Your father wouldn't send you out to those men,"

"Keep your daughters and send out your male guests. Don't

you dare tell us what to do," yelled another furious voice.

"Sodom wouldn't exist if my uncle Abram didn't save this town!" Lot argued. "Leave us alone."

The mob grumbled in response and began to murmur. "We're tired of hearing about your uncle. Let's kill Lot and slaughter everyone inside, just like we killed Paltith."

Dismas heard a scuffle outside the door.

"Please don't cut my throat," pleaded Lot.

"You open the door," Ziv said pointing at Dismas. "And I'll grab Lot."

Ziv and Dismas worked together and pulled Lot inside the house. Then Dismas slammed the door shut as Liraz frantically slid the bolt. Lot's robe hung disheveled off his shoulder, and a gash above his left eye, oozed blood.

Ado ran to her husband. "Those filthy animals killed my Paltith and are ruining my home!"

Lot's daughters wept.

The men outside began kicking the door, causing the frame to crack. Rocks pelted through the window.

Mishpat rose from the table and commanded, "Strike blind."

A deafening crash of thunder followed a blinding flash as lightning struck Lot's roof. A bright light filled the night and the sharp smell of singed hair lingered in the air. The ground trembled beneath Dismas' feet. For a split second, the mob quieted, then began shouting again. Only this time, their words were different.

"My eyes!"

"I can't see!"

"I'm blind!"

Mishpat settled back on his cushion. "The blind men won't bother us for the rest of the night."

"Look!" Benjamin peered out the window. Dismas hurried to

join him.

The men of Sodom didn't look tough now—a few of them cried like babies over their blindness. Dismas smirked at the sight of grown men crawling around on all fours like lost dogs while others stood, feeling around with their hands. Some walked into walls while others bumped heads. Half-lit torches littered the ground. Dismas sighed in relief as his breathing returned to normal. Everyone inside the house shared relieved looks.

Hannah grabbed the partial key from the table and held it up for everyone to see. "We're looking for a key piece."

"Hey, I've seen something like that," Ziv said, excited.

Dismas smiled, encouraged. *I hope it's somewhere inside the house.*

Benjamin snatched the key from Hannah and placed it in his pocket.

"Where?" Liraz tinged with curiosity.

"Sometimes the king of Sodom wears a piece like that around his neck."

Dismas groaned inwardly. *Why does everything have to be so difficult?*

"How could we get near the king?" Hannah's, brow furrowed.

"I can sneak you into the palace," Ziv revealed. "I worked there as a gardener. There's a hidden passage between the palace and the temple."

"We could pay you in gold," offered Benjamin, pulling out a handful of coins.

Dismas' pockets were still empty.

Ziv shook his head. "I won't take your money. While the men are still blind, I will guide you to the palace and the king." He pushed open the door and sidestepped four men writhing on the ground, wailing about their lack of sight.

Liraz, Benjamin, and Hannah followed Ziv. As Dismas stepped out the front door, he overheard Malakh inform Lot's family to gather their loved ones. The angels were going to destroy Sodom in the morning. *We'd better hurry to get the key piece and escape Sodom.*

"We'll need this." Ziv picked up one of the abandoned torches.

Dismas grabbed another nearly extinguished torch and blew on it as he hurried through Lot's gate and out onto the street.

Ziv led them back to where they had started at the town square.

Hannah gasped. "Oh no!"

A group of ten blind men huddled together near the white marble judgment seats at Sodom's gate.

"They can't see us," Ziv reminded her. "We'll just walk by. We have to pass through the market. On the left will be Asherah's temple."

"Where are the hell hounds?" Benjamin frowned.

Dismas didn't want to tangle with a hell hound either. His neck hairs prickled as he smelled sulfur.

"What is that putrid smell?" Ziv coughed and covered his mouth.

A shadowy figure with red eyes blew past them and stopped at the group of Sodomite men fumbling around the gate. Goosebumps appeared on Dismas' arms.

"Demon on the right," murmured Liraz.

The demon whirled around the men's ears.

"Kill the spies!" chanted the blind men as they ran toward them, the red-eyed demon leading the way.

"Follow me," Ziv said barely above a breath. .

They ran through the narrow marketplace, but the blind men remained on their tail.

Dismas panted, hoping there wasn't much more to go. As he and his companions hurried, it seemed the blind men did as well. *Maybe the demon gave them supernatural speed.*

"They're catching up!" Benjamin said, high-pitched.

Dismas glanced back and, sure enough, the men were gaining on them, showing no signs of slowing. Hannah fell behind.

Ziv darted toward the nearest market stall and motioned for them to stop. "Let's move this table," he ordered, lifting one side.

Dismas grabbed the other side. Lemons rolled off the top as they dragged the table to the middle of the street. Liraz and Benjamin swiped another table and lined it up with the first, making a barrier against their sightless pursuers. With a firm grip, Dismas yanked Hannah's hand and pulled her around the tables. The men smacked into the obstacles and fell. The demon deserted the stumbling men, and flew in the direction of the temple. A chuckle escaped Ziv as additional men tripped over those crawling around their table barricade.

"Shh, they will hear you and kill you," chided Liraz.

They ran into a couple more stumbling blind men. Ziv danced wildly around them. Dismas suppressed a laugh.

"Put out your torches," Ziv whispered. "We don't want the guards to see us."

They turned the corner and there it was—Asherah's temple, a blood-red, rectangular stone structure. Bathed in torchlight, a colossal statue of the very pregnant goddess adorned with jewels peered down from the entrance. The sides of the building were decorated with smaller statues, aglow in the flickering torches. On the open porch, a guard leaned against a stone pillar resembling a palm tree. On the right, overlooking the temple, stood a three-story clay palace bathed in a deep, rich shade of mahogany that seemed to go on forever.

A shrill scream rose from the temple—the gut-wrenching sound continued for several moments.

Then silence.

A high-pitched newborn wail pierced the air, which quickly turned into a demanding snarl. The lone guard rushed to the rear of the building.

"That doesn't sound human," whispered Hannah.

Ziv elbowed Dismas and led them to the front entrance. Their soft footsteps would remain inaudible in the rising cacophony of newborn cries mixed with their mothers' tortured wails. Dismas' heart raced as he crept into the temple, the panicked shrieks echoing in his ears. What had caused such terror?

Inside, the full moon shone through the open ceiling, highlighting the Asherah carvings covering the walls. More palm tree columns held up the temple walls and a huge naked goddess sculpture had the tree of life growing out of her oversized belly, with twenty naked breasts poking out of her chest. *Hideous.* Dismas averted his eyes.

Ziv and Dismas hid behind a column to the right of the entryway. Liraz, Benjamin, and Hannah edged left toward another massive stone statue of Asherah with a lion on either side of the goddess's hips. Hannah and Benjamin crouched behind one lion while Liraz hid behind the other. Hundreds of shrieking women writhed on the marble floors in hard labor. Others were dead. Hell hounds sat at attention next to the midwives as they watched the women giving birth. The drooling dogs clicked their fangs as though waiting for fresh meat. About one hundred midwives held newborn babies at arm's length. A few hundred more swaddled fussing babies surrounding them on the floor.

Eyes wide and breath catching in his throat, Dismas squinted for a better look at the newborns, but instead saw only the midwives' faces twisted in revulsion.

In the middle of the room, a stone-faced midwife said, "Stop your screaming. You're giving me a nasty headache."

"One more push and the baby will be out," said another nurse. Under her breath, she added, "And you will be dead."

These uncompassionate people truly are wicked. No wonder they are being wiped off the face of the earth.

A sudden rush of icy air whipped across his face. Dismas tensed. Perched along the roof were at least one hundred shadow demons watching and waiting. His heart pounded. Thankfully, their hiding spots were not directly under the demons. *Lord, cover us with your feathers. Under your wings, we will find refuge.* Why would he pray that old psalm? Childish. They were just words. They couldn't help.

"Next," yelled a midwife.

A demon swooped, landing on the hound's back. Drool dripped from the hell hound's fangs, staring at the mother-to-be. The birthing woman let out one last blood-curdling scream and then fell silent. Immediately, the midwife snatched the baby from the floor and held it in front of the hell hound's snout.

Dismas gasped at the naked baby. On the infant's right side were human features from head to toe. But the left side was all lion—mane, snout, whiskers, paws, covered with brown-yellow fur. And it had a tiny tail.

"That's one messed up baby," murmured Ziv.

The hell hound bared its teeth before the baby's whimpering mouth, flailing both his paw and hand. "Da mihi vitam tuam," commanded the demon perched on top of the dog.

"Give me your life," translated Dismas, rubbing his head. *Is that correct?*

"Da mihi vitam tuam!"

The baby gurgled up shimmery black smoke. The hound opened its mouth over the baby's, sucking out the smoke. Then, the hound held the smoke in its mouth. The baby stopped moving, eyes closed. Dead?

"Good, Barghest. Thank you for making a clean vessel for me," the demon said to the hound. His shadowy figure jumped inside the lifeless newborn.

The baby opened its eyes. Red. Dismas gripped the column,

heart pounding.

"Revertere ad infernum," said the baby.

"Go back to hell," repeated Dismas.

Barghest disappeared.

This same scenario played throughout the room. Hounds sucked up black smoke and demons jumped into the babies. Hounds disappeared and reappeared.

What manner of sorcery is this?

Ziv tilted his head toward the group of midwives holding the demon hybrids. A midwife screamed, dropping one of the swaddled babies. The baby grew into a tall man-lion hybrid, continuing to grow at an alarming rate. The creature pounced on the woman's arm and tore into it with its fangs. Dismas' stomach churned. The nursemaids placed the babies on the floor and fled the temple. The hell hounds growled and leaned against the nurses assisting in births, trapping them.

"Let's go before we are lion food," Ziv urged and sprinted from the column to the tree of life carving. His hands darted over the apples dangling from the tree. After Ziv rubbed the last apple, Asherah's belly opened like a door into a dark passageway. Ziv grinned. "Into the belly of the beast, my friend." Then Ziv mimicked a woman's scream.

Hannah, Liraz, and Benjamin jolted to attention.

Dismas pointed to the open door. Hannah nodded and tiptoed across the room. Her face looked green around the edges, and she held her stomach. He couldn't blame her. What they had witnessed sickened Dismas to his core. He'd never be the same.

Ziv ran his hands along the walls inside the passageway and whispered, "I need to push the lever to close her belly. We don't want anyone or *anything* following us."

Dismas waved at the others to hurry.

Hannah slinked behind the column near them. Benjamin and Liraz crouched, making their way across the room.

Dismas tapped his foot, peering into the pitch-black tunnel. *We should've kept the torches.* Firm hands pressed into Dismas' shoulder as something sharp poked his side. He heard a familiar squeal. *Hannah.* Dismas turned. *No!*

Guards swarmed around them like bugs on a candle. Hannah, Liraz, and Benjamin's hands were being tied by guards wearing bronze helmets with red feathers. A burly guard knocked Ziv to the ground.

"Inform King Bera we have captured the spies," ordered one of the guards.

Dismas moaned in hopelessness. Why couldn't Mishpat have made everyone blind? *Because that would have been too easy.*

19

"All its soil will be a burning waste of sulfur and salt, unsown, producing nothing, with no plant growing on it, just like the fall of Sodom and Gomorrah, Admah and Zeboiim, which the Lord demolished in His fierce anger."

—Deuteronomy 29:23 (HCSB)

Dungeon of Sodom's palace
The forty-seventh hour in hell

Three guards shoved their fists into Dismas' back, prodding him along the twists and turns of the dark passageway. At the end of the corridor stood a faint outline of a door illuminated by the hesitant glow of a dying torch. Closer to the door, the stale air turned into a rusty, bloody smell, tinged with human waste. The pungent odor intensified with each footstep. Hannah gagged behind him.

The guards swung open the heavy metal door, revealing whips, knives, and chains dangling from blood-splattered walls. On the far back wall was a row of prison cells. Dismas froze. Two hands shoved him over the uneven threshold, throwing him off balance. He fell into a beady-eyed bald man. The man wore a stained, black leather skirt and an open shirt.

"Don't touch me, spy, or I will personally give you what you deserve," snapped the jailer. Keys rattled from his belt.

The guards dragged Dismas toward the wall of cells and hurled him into the center one. In the next cell, a person snored under a blanket, reeking of vomit. Dismas held his breath. Another guard tossed Liraz in with him. His companion's eyes darted around the cramped cell.

A palace guard licked his cracked lips and yanked Hannah by her tiny waist. "You're a pretty little thing."

She squirmed. "Let me go, pig!" She sounded tough, but Dismas saw terror in her eyes. He clenched his fists in frustration.

"You're not ordering me around, princess," said the guard. He tightened his grip and stroked her hair with grimy fingers.

Hannah winced.

"Leave my sister alone!" shouted Benjamin as he elbowed his guard.

The jailer tossed Benjamin into the next empty cell. "I give the orders here, not you."

"Is she worth King Bera's wrath?" said Ziv to Hannah's guard. Two guards dragged him across the dirty floor. "We all know how he enjoys being the first one to interrogate women."

"Mind your business, Ziv," replied the guard. He threw Hannah into the cell with her brother, slamming the door.

One guard stopped dragging Ziv and asked, "The gardener thief who stole vegetables from the king's supply to feed strangers abandoned to starve?"

"Yup." The jailer jangled his keys and puffed out his chest. He grabbed Ziv by the back of the neck and pulled him to his feet. He sniffed the air. "Any of you smell smoke?"

"No," responded the guards, shaking their heads, making the red feathers quiver on top of their helmets like crazed roosters.

"It reminds me of the day we burned your wife." He sneered at Ziv, with a tilt of his bald head.

"You son of a perverse and rebellious woman," Ziv hissed and landed his fist in the jailer's gut. The palace guards swarmed him and tossed him into Dismas and Liraz's cell. Ziv sprang from the ground and pressed his face against the bars. "May God show no mercy on you murderers!"

The jailer spat into the cell. "No mercy for *you*. I will enjoy watching you die, just like Paltith." The key clicked in the lock.

Dismas sympathized with a pat on Ziv's shoulder, but the man brushed him away.

The jailer and guards returned to the metal door. Most of the guards marched back through the passageway, while a handful stayed behind, whispering with the jailer, glaring at their prisoners, and still making perverse comments about Hannah.

His gaze landed on his thumb, where the advancing light crept closer to the halfway mark of his thumbnail. *We're running out of time.* He kicked the unyielding iron bar, frustration bubbling over as the guards snickered at him.

"Liraz, what were those babies?" Hannah's voice quivered.

Dismas whipped around toward his cellmates, memories of deceased mothers and their innocent babies flooding his mind.

"Hybrids," he answered. "A woman, an angel, and lion blood."

"And the black smoke the hounds inhaled?" asked Dismas.

"Since the souls are produced from an illegal union, they are vulnerable at birth. The hell hounds can steal them, spit them into the Lake of Fire, and destroy them, leaving an empty vessel for the Nephilim to dwell.

"Nephilim? Impossible" Ziv crossed his arm.

"The red-eyed demons in the temple and roaming the streets of Sodom," Benjamin explained.

"I saw a giant black bird with amber eyes," insisted Ziv.

Mysterious, Dismas mused silently. *Maybe he couldn't see them because he's still alive.* He changed the subject, "Ziv, when we locate the key piece, leave Sodom immediately. Something horrible is going to happen tomorrow at sunrise."

"Something horrible is happening now," announced a slurred voice in the next cell.

Footsteps pounded down the corridor outside the dungeon.

The drunk struggled to extricate himself from beneath the blanket. "They're on their way to kill you all."

New guards with white feathers in their helmets rushed into the dungeon and demanded the jailer unlock the prisoners. "The king desires to interrogate the spies."

Nausea washed over Dismas. *I can't believe one of us is going to have to get close enough to the king of Sodom to snatch the necklace from his neck. I may be a good thief, but this seems an impossible task.*

"Pity. I was looking forward to extracting the truth from you," the jailer leered at Dismas unlocking the cell.

Dismas' skin crawled; he balled his fists. *Steady. Don't react. Keep your wits about you.* He resisted the urge to raise his arms as the king's guards flooded the cell.

"They want their prized Sariel, too," said one of the palace guards.

Sariel? Lucifer mentioned that name to the creatures. One of the guards yanked Dismas' hands behind his back.

"You stink." The soldiers snatched the blanket off Sariel and doused him with water. Sariel flinched as a deep gash on his forehead began to ooze blood. His shoulder-length dirty blond hair was tangled. His eyes appeared the same purple as Mishpat's. It startled Dismas, like Pharaoh's daughter discovering baby Moses among the reeds.

Another guard ripped off his stained robe and shoved Sariel's arms into a white robe. "Now you're more presentable to the king." Once they had Sariel ready, the king's soldiers ushered them out of the dungeon.

With his hand behind his back, Dismas trudged up the narrow spiral stone steps. The scent of pork and oranges grew stronger at every turn, teasing his empty stomach. At the top the guards opened the oversized silver door and walked into a long corridor. Dismas caught a glimpse of his reflection in the framed silver mirrors lining the walls. Their ragtag group looked terrified. Liraz appeared unaffected.

"Spy, be on your best behavior in front of the king or we'll drag you back to the dungeon for a beating," Dismas' guard threatened in a whisper. He whacked Dismas on the back of the neck.

His neck stung, yet the stranger's neck punch seemed mild compared to Barabbas's knuckles. *Maybe hits from someone you know are extra powerful.*

The guards began brushing off their leather skirts and straightening the feathers on their helmets as they approached the polished entrance at the end of the hallway. A stationed sentry opened the door and the guards pushed them through. Dismas shuddered. Despite the raging fire in the middle of the room, the air felt chilly. He looked around.

Twenty hybrids occupied seats at the long table next to the fireplace. The monsters gorged themselves on roasted pig laid out on oversized shiny platters. Despite carving knives available, the beasts ripped apart the whole pigs and shoved the meat into their mouths. Their lips smacked in delight as grease dribbled down their chins. The hybrids had matured since Dismas last saw them a few hours ago. They even wore black pants. Blond tufts of human hair and curly fur covered their chests. A little mane covered the left side of their faces while facial hair sprouted on the right.

One lion-man didn't eat and appeared to be fully grown. He wore a custom-made black cloak and his orange predatory eyes bore into Dismas. He darted his eyes to the opposite side of the table where the two haughty kings of Sodom and Gomorrah sat, each wearing a gold crown. Dismas figured the king of Sodom sat on the elevated chair at the head of the table. He was flanked by two broad-shouldered men with gold feathers in their silver helmets. His heart skipped a beat. The king wore a gold chain around his neck. Dismas squinted to see if the key piece hung from the chain, but the bottom of the necklace was tucked behind the king's red-winged gown. *Stealing from unsuspecting people in a crowd is one thing, but a well-protected king?*

Would he still be welcomed in Paradise if he murdered the king for the key piece? Dismas reasoned the king was destined for death anyway.

"It's just not possible," roared the lion-man. "Ramel?" He leapt from his chair, black cloak fluttering behind him, and landed next to Liraz.

The smaller hybrids ceased chomping mid-chew, watching.

"Ramel? Isn't he in Tartarus?" came the child-like voice of a small hybrid.

Another hybrid sniffed. "It *is* Ramel! I can still smell his watcher scent after all these years."

Like spoiled children, the hybrids began chanting Ramel's name.

"It's me in the flesh. In this form, I am called Liraz." He gave a little bow.

The hybrids watched his every move.

"I recognized your voice, Mahway, but you've changed. Have you dyed your hair or lost weight?"

The hybrids hissed at Liraz's mocking tone.

"Guards, take them out and prepare to clothe them," Mahway instructed, nodding toward the hybrids. "In the next hour, they will bust out of those pants."

Nobody moved.

"Yes, take them out," ordered the king of Sodom.

The guards swarmed the hybrids, but they refused to budge, returning their attention to the meat. The guards grabbed the roasted pig platters, and the hybrids followed the food out the door.

Once the last hybrid left the room, Mahway turned back to Liraz. "How did you escape Tartarus?"

Liraz wrinkled his nose and stared Mahway up and down. "How did you transform from an unclean spirit to an overgrown man-cat?"

Mahway smacked Liraz on the left cheek.

Liraz didn't even wince.

"Why are you here?"

"Do you have the urge to crawl on all fours?"

"Enough with this game. You will answer my question one way or another." Mahway fisted his human hand.

"Is this any way to greet an old friend? After all, we go way back before the flood."

Mahway dropped his fist. "Never friends but destined to be enemies. Now quit stalling and tell me why you are here and how you got here."

"Mishpat and Malakh helped me," Liraz finally answered.

Mahway's lion half bristled and his man face froze in shock. "Why would *they* break you out of prison?"

Dismas held his breath. Would Liraz tell the truth about the key piece on the king's necklace?

"Mishpat and Malakh are staying with Lot. Go ask them yourself."

Impressive. Liraz wasn't telling the truth, yet he wasn't lying.

"Who are Mishpat and Malakh?" the king of Gomorrah asked.

"Probably the ones who struck most of your citizens blind," Mahway answered.

"Send my hybrid army to Lot's house to retrieve them," demanded the king of Sodom.

"No!" Mahway said sharply. "My hybrids need to stay here to protect Sariel so we can make more hybrids and expand our army."

Sariel groaned. "I should just throw myself out the window and end my miserable existence. Forcing me to mate with women. Keeping me drunk with that awful Sodom wine."

"How are you, the powerful Sariel, even under their control?" asked Liraz.

"Lucifer and the fallen angels tricked me by appearing as angels of light," Sariel answered. "Then they captured me and sewed one of those coins deep into my shoulder. Turned me into a man, rendering me useless."

"All the coins were destroyed in the flood," insisted Liraz.

"I found one!" replied the king of Sodom his cheeks flushed with excitement, matching the rubies in his crown.

"My firstborn son, Dekar, gave up his life for that coin. None of this would be happening if it weren't for him." King Birsha of Gomorrah straightened his sapphire crown and rose from his chair.

"Birsha, sit down!" commanded the king of Sodom. "All of you join us at my table and hear how our cities will never be destroyed again."

Dismas' hand twitched, longing to punch their arrogant royal faces. He bit his lip to keep from muttering, *You have a surprise coming when God flattens your cities.*

Sariel took a seat to the left of the King of Sodom. Mahway settled on Sariel's other side. The guards shoved Liraz and Dismas into adjacent chairs. Across from them sat King Birsha, Ziv, Benjamin, and Hannah.

"You all must be starving," said King Birsha, mimicking concern but his eyes held evil intent. "Well, too bad. Hunger pains are music to our ears." Both kings cackled like maniacs.

They are either wicked, insane, or both.

After the two kings stopped laughing, King Bera's face turned serious. "The coin was found by accident in the tar pits. It was a dark, moonless night. I couldn't see anything, but the air reeked of sulfur." He paused, adjusting his crown. "My soldiers perished quickly in the tar pits. That's when I saw the shadowy figures with crimson eyes dragging my men into the slimy pits. Screams sounded all around me. Something huge was chasing me and my son. It was Mahway over there."

Mahway smiled apologetically. "Sorry. You didn't know you had stumbled into one of the portals to hell. And I had orders from my boss to drag some souls away that day."

"Everything happened so quickly," the king of Sodom continued. "We were running from demons *and* our human enemies. A section of tar overflowed on the ground. And that's when we spotted something shiny. It twinkled like a star. King Birsha's son, Dekar, stooped to pick up the coin, but he slipped and tumbled into the tar pit. I tried pulling him out, but the force of the tar was overpowering. Dekar's hand slipped away and the tar pit swallowed him. Yet I held the coin in my hand." He shrugged half-heartedly. "So sad." His voice carried no trace of sorrow. But he noticed the coin in my hand. He promised not to kill me if I relinquished it. He also swore to make Sodom powerful again. So, we shook hands, and Mahway vanished with the coin."

"I showed the coin to Lucifer," Mahway picked up the story. "And we plotted to build our hybrid army. Places like Sodom and Gomorrah are special to Lucifer."

"Two years ago," the king said, "Mahway appeared in my bedchamber and revealed the plan to birth a hybrid army to ensure Sodom's dominance. All I had to do was supply the women, then Mahway and his friends would do the rest."

"We captured Sariel." Mahway puffed out his chest. "I was the firstborn."

"I don't understand. Why do they look like lions and not giants?" asked Benjamin weakly.

"I'm not a watcher angel," Sariel said.

Mawhay pointed at Sariel. "All we could catch was this fool, a low-ranking Malakim."

Sariel wagged his finger at the kings. "Now that Mishpat and Malakh have arrived, God is going to judge you and your wicked cities."

King Bera's face reddened and he slammed a fist on the table. "I do not fear Lot or Abram's God. Tomorrow, let's march our hybrid army to Abram's household. We will kill him, his wife, and his servants. I will never forget how Lot's uncle embarrassed me in front of King Melchizedek, refusing to take the spoils of war—not even a sandal strap."

Wait a minute, Dismas wondered, *did God destroy Sodom to protect Abraham? Without Abraham, there would be no Hebrews, no line of Judah, no Jesus.*

"Tomorrow night, I will lead the hybrid army to Abram," Mahway announced. "Seize Liraz. He will be added to our breeding program." The guards obeyed.

King Birsha rubbed his palms and grinned. "Oh, goody. We can expand our army and speed up our plans."

"Of course, you won't have Nava to mate with. She's long dead," Mahway sneered. He roared, and ten hybrids burst through the door clad in black cloaks, longswords, and bronze helmets with three hawk feathers.

"Check Liraz. Locate his coin," Mahway ordered.

The lion-men forced Liraz from his chair, rubbed their paws and hands along his arms and legs and pried open his mouth. Liraz bit a finger and the hybrid yelped. But they found nothing.

"Escort Sariel and Liraz back to the dungeon and then beat him until he gives us the coin," Mahway commanded. "And take the girl. We can use her for breeding, too."

As the palace guard yanked Hannah's arm, her chair tumbled to the floor.

"You're not taking my sister anywhere," Benjamin said, rising.

Rich boy has courage, but we're outnumbered.

One of King Bera's personal guards drew his sword, rushed to Benjamin, and pressed the blade against his throat.

"Mahway, you forget your place," King Bera said with

authority. "I give the orders here. Guards, take those three back to the dungeon. Kill the three remaining spies and feed their bodies to the hybrids."

Dismas swallowed hard. *This can't be happening.* A hybrid's hot breath steamed against his neck. He closed his eyes, waiting for it to rip his throat. He prayed, *Lord, protect me from these young lions. Trample them under my feet.*

Something crashed down on the table. Dismas opened his eyes. Stones fell around the room like hail. Seizing the distraction, he pivoted from his silver chair, hoisted it into the air, and brought it crashing down on the hybrid's head. The impact not only crushed its skull but also left an armrest protruding from the eye socket.

"Your fireplace!" shouted King Birsha.

King Bera's mouth hung open in disbelief. Stones continued to fly out of the massive double fireplace. The two kings, their palace guards, and the hybrids dove under the table. Dismas refused to hide. He'd take his chances out in the open.

A rock struck the guard holding Benjamin and he dropped to the floor with a thud. Another stone hit the hybrid holding Hannah. She scrambled free and grabbed for Benjamin. Dismas looked for a path to help the siblings through the flying rock, but then realized none of the stones hit him or his companions. Bewildered, Dismas felt like Rahab at Jericho, untouched by the debris.

Liraz and Sariel exchanged knowing glances.

"I'm getting that key piece," whispered Ziv. He dropped under the table.

Dismas debated if he should join Ziv to help take the necklace, but more hybrids began to race toward Hannah. Protecting her took priority. He grabbed a short hybrid by its lion mane and punched its human face, and the creature hit the floor. Another hybrid leapt on Dismas' back. The fireplace flashed a white light. It rumbled, and amid the rock dust on the hearth stood the four creatures brandishing blazing swords. As the four angels stormed the room, Dismas exhaled with relief. *Thank you!* The hybrid on Dismas' back fled, and he made his way to Hannah, stepping over the fireplace stones littering the floor. Another hybrid sprinted from under the table and leapt in front of Hannah and Benjamin. Padel charged, swinging his sword, and splitting the hybrid right down the middle, separating the human half from the lion half. Hannah scrunched her face in disgust as black vapor rose from the hybrid's mutated body. *A demon.*

The shadow demon jumped into Benjamin's gaping mouth. He gagged.

While Padel and Dormel chased the remaining guards and hybrids, Jachniel and Gonael circled Benjamin and held up their arms. "In the name of Jesus Christ of Nazareth, come out of Benjamin and return to hell," they commanded in unison.

The black vapor shot out of Benjamin's mouth and vanished. He bent over, coughing.

Hannah patted her brother on the back.

Dismas touched his scar and his chest tightened. *The living creatures evoked the name of Jesus and the demon fled Benjamin's body. They also used Jesus' name to force Lucifer to leave Liraz's body.*

In that moment, Mahway rushed from under the table and jumped toward the window. The wooden slats snapped like twigs under his weight.

Gonael flew to the window. "He landed on his paws! Coward won't even face us."

Ziv and King Bera rolled out from under the table just to the left of Dismas. "You murdered my wife!" Ziv grasped at King Bera's ankle.

"Guards!" shouted King Bera.

But no guards remained.

In the middle of the room stood Dismas, Hannah, Benjamin, Liraz, Sariel, and the living creatures.

"Let me go. I didn't set the bed on fire. Not me!" King Bera's voice sounded shrill.

"You sentenced my wife to death," countered Ziv.

King Bera kicked Ziv in the head with his free foot. Ziv lost his grip, and the king scrambled to his feet, fake wings flapping behind him. Ziv leapt up and pulled a carving knife from the table.

"He's not worth it, Ziv. Put down the knife," said Dismas. *Everyone in this wretched city will be dead in the morning anyway.*

"We should have burned you with her!" King Bera said.

Ziv lunged at King Bera, slashing the necklace from his neck. The pendant flew,.

Dismas snagged it. "Got it!" He stared at the gray piece.

"Why, you arrogant little jerk. You forget your place. Guards!" The king held his hand to his throat, holding back the blood flow from the new wound.

The group gathered by the window. In repayment for helping them, Dismas waved for Ziv to join them. *He was kind, not like his fellow citizens. He shouldn't have to die.*

But Ziv ignored him, stepped closer to King Bera, and drove the knife into his chest. King Bera dropped to the ground in a pool of blood. "For Paltith," he said.

A figure crept from under the table behind Ziv—King Birsha with a sword.

"Look out behind you!" yelled Dismas.

But the king of Gomorrah pounced, stabbing Ziv in the back of the neck.

Ziv dropped to the floor as thick blood poured from his head.

Dismas rushed over and kneeled by his side.

"Now I will join Paltith," Ziv said weakly. "It's all I ever wanted." His eyes went vacant, body lifeless.

Dismas shook with rage. He snatched another carving knife from the table, spun around, and saw King Birsha sprint out the door, calling for the guards. Dismas followed.

"Stop, Dismas. Drop that knife!" ordered Jachniel.

Despite his will to rebel, his hand obeyed the command, and the knife slipped from his grasp.

"God will avenge Ziv's death," said Padel.

"Can't you bring Ziv back to life?" Dismas pleaded.

"Ayin, come forth," called Dormel.

Golden light appeared outside the palace window. The chariot awaited.

"I can't go in our Lord's chariot like this," Sariel said. "Free me."

"Sorry, this is going to sting," Gonael murmured as he pecked twice at Sariel's shoulder.

The coin bounced to the floor. A flicker of light burst through the room. Sariel's facial features changed into a lion, a yellowish-brown mane framed his face, but his eyes stayed purple. Sariel stood tall, glimmering wings attached to his back. Golden limbs, hands, and hooves shone like brass. His white tunic flowed to his knees and was cinched with a silver belt.

"Thank you—the wretched coin is finally out," said Sariel with a sad smile.

The creatures commanded, "Burn in the Lake of Fire." The coin vanished.

Dismas huffed and crossed his arms. *The creatures can send a coin away and help Oren and Sariel, but they can't bring Ziv back to life.*

Benjamin held out a hand toward Dismas. "Hand over the piece."

Dismas dropped King Bera's skull pendant into the boy's hand.

Benjamin held out the larger key section, but the new piece pinged onto the floor. "It didn't supernaturally affix itself like at the ark," he said.

What did we miss? Ziv gave up his life for nothing.

"Repeat the rhyme again. Maybe you overlooked something," Jachniel suggested.

"Murder and strife forced one to settle for less, while the other picked the best. So best became less and less became more," recited Liraz.

Hannah's eyes sparkled. "Abraham has the key."

Benjamin's eyes turned down. "Obviously God's favor is on Abraham because he and Sarah conceive a child at their advanced ages of 90 and 100. Why would he have the piece? Lot is the one who survived Sodom."

"The king ordered the hybrids to kill Abraham and his family," Hannah said. "Maybe God's plan was to destroy the hybrids along with these wicked towns so Abraham and his family would survive, since their descendants birthed Jesus."

Benjamin kicked the skull key across the floor. "I'm glad the piece didn't fit. I don't want anything from Sodom."

It seemed like poor planning to Dismas. Evidently, God had used up all his favor on Abraham. *Ziv and Paltith died so young. And why was my father afflicted with leprosy? That only opened the door to Barabbas being in my life.*

"Everyone, into the chariot," said Jachniel. "The sun's about to rise."

Hannah, Benjamin, and Liraz climbed out the window, carefully avoiding the jagged wood slats broken during Mahway's escape. They slid onto the same seat. Dismas looked back at Ziv crumpled on the ground and leapt into the chariot. Sariel flew out the palace window and settled beside Dismas as the creatures took their positions under the chariot. The sun began rising over Sodom.

Benjamin pointed. "Look, four fireballs in the sky!"

Dismas watched as one ball of fire veered toward Sodom while the other three swerved west, southwest, and northwest to their targeted cities. The chariot launched into the sky in the opposite direction. The fireballs erupted, spreading into a massive ring of fire when it hit the palace. A forceful wind howled against the open chariot.

Over Sodom, everything turned to a thick white smoke, expanding into a mushroom cloud, complete with an ever-growing stem. Fiery yellow stones the size of lemons hailed down. *Brimstone.* Dismas couldn't see the city through the smoke, but he knew it was gone, along with everyone in it. In the western sky, an inferno exploded, adding more smoke to the air.

Boom!

The chariot shook. *Goodbye, Gomorrah.* The third fireball erupted southwest of Sodom. *There goes Admah.* The chariot rattled again. Finally, a flash of flames rose in the distant northwest. This time, Dismas felt a slight tremor. *Goodbye Zeboiim.* Everything destroyed in the blink of an eye. No second chances. Tears streamed down Hannah's face. Benjamin looked at his sandals. Liraz closed his eyes.

"None of you cry for these evil towns," Padel said gruffly from below the chariot. "It had to be done. Remember, not even ten righteous people lived there. And the hybrids had to be eliminated."

The chariot slowed and descended on a grassy section of a mountain. A man stood at the edge of the mountain looking down at the destruction of the cities. *Abraham?* Dismas wondered. His blue robe hung loose on him, as though he'd recently lost a substantial amount of weight. He had dark hair at his roots, but the rest was white. *Peculiar.* Dismas remembered Abraham hugging him in Paradise.

"My friends, is Lot still alive?" shouted Abraham as he raced to the chariot. The sight of the living creatures and Ayin didn't fluster him.

"Yes, Abraham," said Jachniel somberly. "Lot and his two

daughters made it out alive. Sadly, Ado turned back and perished. I'm sorry."

Tears slid down Abraham's face. "Our good Lord heard my petition and saved Lot and his girls," he said, bowing his head. "It's still tragic. All the people perished. The animals are gone and the land barren."

But God didn't save Lot's wife. Or Ziv. Yet Abraham still has faith.

"What happened?" Hannah asked, pointing to Abraham's upper arm.

Blood oozed through a bandage around his arm. "A miracle happened," he said. "I woke up today and felt fifty years younger, my hair at the roots is black. No aches and pains. My wife woke looking like my young bride. At first, I thought I was dreaming."

"But what happened to your arm?" repeated Hannah.

"I was walking to see if God would go through with his plan to destroy the four cities. I tripped over that boulder and ripped open my arm. I found this strange object." From his robe, he withdrew a sand-colored star shape, its center adorned with a captivating ruby.

Abraham does have the key piece!

"You found what we've been seeking," said Benjamin in a rush.

Abraham handed it to Benjamin. "By all means, take it."

"Thank you." He took the piece and handed it to Hannah.

Hannah tucked it in her robe pocket and Dismas heard it click into place. A look of relief washed over her as she gave a slight nod.

"I have to tell Sarah, Lot and his girls are alive," Abraham said. As he pivoted toward a worn path between two pine trees, he moved like a young man.

An ear-shattering lion's roar filled the air.

Benjamin slapped his hands over his ears. "Didn't all the hybrids die in the fire?"

"Mahway. He survived," answered Jachniel.

Sariel stood. "I will smite him now."

"No. We can't interfere. Mahway will be part of another story eight hundred years from now."

Dismas clenched his teeth. *Mahway gets to live another eight hundred years, but Ziv dies and then his body is blown apart. Barabbas walks free. How is any of this fair?* Dismas pointed an accusing finger at Sariel. "You saved him. You saved Mahway, but you couldn't lift a finger to help Ziv." Everyone stared at him, but for once, Dismas didn't care.

"Did you forget Jesus saved you at the cross?" Padel said in a crisp voice. "You'd be burning in hell right now instead of in God's chariot."

"That is true, but why did I have to die?"

Gonael flew out from under the wheel and hovered like a hummingbird in front of Dismas. "If you must know, originally, when Sodom was wiped out, Sariel did die as a man. Since we were sent back in time, we were granted the opportunity to rescue him. Sariel is outside of time, so saving him causes no ripple effect. We couldn't save Ziv, and we can't kill Mahway."

Dismas bit his lip to keep himself from shouting out what his mind screamed. *There were four living creatures in that room and not one of them saved Ziv. Barabbas was freed, and I died. None of it is fair.*

20

"On the day Lot left Sodom, fire and sulfur rained from heaven and destroyed them all."

—Luke 17:29 (HCSB)

The tunnel under Paradise
The forty-ninth hour in hell

A stream of sweat ran down Mahway's brow and back. Lucifer's plan of digging this tunnel to the Lake of Fire had to work. Mahway whacked at the large ebony stone, holding an axe in each hand. Besides excellent hearing, the mighty Nephilim were completely ambidextrous. Once Hahya and Ohya had stopped brawling and imitated Mahway's dual axe method, they made swift progress. Mahway estimated they had shifted ten thousand tons of stone. He debated summoning Lucifer and informing him of their progress, but Mahway didn't dare bother him.

Big drops of the gruesome twosome's perspiration hit Mahway's cheek. "Move back, fools," he seethed. "You two are like a couple of hell hounds slobbering all over me."

They ignored him and continued swinging their axes at the massive wall while whistling a mournful tune to drown out Jesus' annoying voice. "Wipe the dust of hell off your feet. The kingdom of God is near," Jesus droned on.

Wretched Nephilim ears. Mahway tried humming as well, but Jesus' voice still came through loud and clear.

"Remember what happened with Lot's wife," said Jesus.

Mahway froze. *Why in the devil's name is Jesus mentioning*

Lot? Hahya and Ohya stopped whistling, and tilted their ears. They heard it, too.

"Do not long for your past earthly existences or cleave to this meager life in Paradise," Jesus continued. "Whoever loses his life for my sake will find it. If you believe I am the Son of God, you will be raised up with me and spend eternity with my Father."

"What dung," Ohya muttered.

"The Creator murdered us twice—once in the flood and again at Sodom—and barred us from Paradise," said Hahya. His huge, piggish nostrils flared.

"Not all of us lost our hybrid bodies." Ohya glared at Mahway. "What made you so special?"

Mahway refused to answer. *It's not my fault my vessel lived and their vessels were destroyed.* He paused for a moment thinking of the endless, wasteful hours he had spent sifting through the ashes of Sodom's palace searching for the coin. Finally, Mahway had to accept the amulet had melted in the blast. The hybrids could never be recreated again, and the Nephilim whose vessels were destroyed in Sodom held that against him. At first, it bothered Mahway, the outcast treatment. But he had enjoyed being human again, even the little pleasures of feeling grass brushing between his toes. Roaming on earth in his new vessel had been pleasant. He had even found love. *Until Lucifer ruined everything like he always does.*

With a shout, Mahway struck the wall with both axes, using all his force. Large stones tumbled around his feet, and a gust of oppressive hot air rushed over his face. It had to be the Lake of Fire—the two tunnels would connect soon. He smiled. *I'm getting closer, Cecilia.*

Don't become idolaters as some of them were; as it is written, The people sat down to eat and drink, and got up to play.

—1 Corinthians 10:7 (HCSB)

Half past the fiftieth hour in hell

Deafening silence hung in the air as Hannah and her companions waited on the mountain for the next riddle. Dismas perched at the edge of his seat, jaw clenched, glaring at the billowy mushroom cloud that loomed over Sodom. Sariel stared straight ahead, his face pale in comparison to his brilliant white robe. The creatures huddled by the front wheels of the chariot, glancing at Sariel with concern. Hannah overheard them discussing something about the second heaven. She wanted to ask if anything was wrong but didn't dare bother them. She rubbed the key nervously, feeling its weight in her pocket, the cold metal a constant reminder of their dwindling time. Watching the cities be destroyed had unsettled her, coupled with the awkwardness of the creatures reprimanding Dismas for questioning Ziv's death.

Benjamin raised his thumb—the white had passed the halfway mark. He spoke dejectedly, "Woe to our misfortunes. Two mere pieces? If my estimations are correct, we're left with twelve or thirteen hours. We've squandered precious time."

"Behold, The top is complete." Hannah pulled the key from her pocket, revealing its current state. The skull handle was now encircled by a vibrant rainbow, forming the bow of the key. Abraham's sand-colored star filled the missing section completing the skull with a second ruby eye embedded within it. The two rubies gleamed an almost malevolent light, yet something about the key felt enthralling.

Dismas rubbed his temples, "Who knows how many pieces there are. Or how big the key is."

"Those two rubies remind me of Lucifer's evil eyes," Liraz said. "It's glaring at me."

Hannah agreed and shoved the key back in her pocket.

"Speaking of Lucifer, be alert," said Jachniel. "He could appear at any moment."

Ugh. What horrible place will Lucifer send us next? Hannah rubbed her temples. She needed a nap, not another word game with the devil.

As though reading Hannah's mind, Lucifer appeared, wedging himself between Dismas and Sariel on the chariot seat opposite her. Dismas flung himself beside her, plopping down next to Liraz. The creatures swarmed the chariot like angry wasps.

"Did you miss me?" Lucifer hissed, flicking his narrow serpent tongue over his blood-red lips.

Disgusting.

"Relax, it's just Lucifer's image," assured Liraz, stretching his hand through Lucifer's twisted horns. "Think of him like a reflection in a pond. He can't inflict any damage."

Hannah tensed her shoulders. Lucifer had a talent for making her feel inadequate.

"I sent my spirit here. The physical me is sitting on my throne in a trance back in the second heaven," Lucifer boasted.

"Deliver the riddle and depart," ordered Padel. His nostrils flared while his wings flapped.

Lucifer pointed at Sariel. "Where are you taking him? To Tartarus? To chain him up?"

They wouldn't save Sariel just to take him back to that terrible place. Would they?

"No," Jachniel said firmly. "He's going to heaven where he belongs."

"Home," Sariel said. He began to wheeze.

He looks sick, but how can that be? Angels don't get ill, do they?

"Are you so sure the Creator will take you back?" Lucifer said. "Don't you remember what you did in Sodom with all those women? You're destined for Tartarus. I heard Liraz's old cell is open—for now." He glared at Liraz.

Sariel trembled. His face and hands seemed dim, reminding Hannah of a flickering candle ready to die out.

"Sariel, don't listen to his lies," said Dormel. "Lucifer's livid all his wicked plans were blown to smithereens."

"Don't be so sure, pussycat," Lucifer said. "Throughout time, the mindless multitude will recall their God destroyed these cities because he's mean and spiteful. The true story of my demon hybrids is buried under the ashes." He cackled.

Padel snorted. "You're going to lose."

Lucifer's chilling laughter ceased and he narrowed malicious eyes. "No. I win. Every time I hear a human whining and blaming God for a tragedy I caused brings me immense pleasure. I erode humanity's faith in God one misfortune after another."

Lucifer certainly is devious. I'm sorry, God, for any time I blamed you when really Lucifer was the one behind it.

A voice surrounded her. *"What he meant for evil, I turn to good."*

Who said that?

"Why are you telling your secrets to us?" blurted Benjamin

Hannah poked her brother. What was he thinking, challenging Lucifer?

"He's not real," Benjamin told her.

"Oh, I'm real," Lucifer sneered. "I'm telling you these things because dead men don't tell tales, and you're a walking corpse, Benny boy. Dead, like your foolish sister and scar face. Haven't you fools figured it out yet? You have no chance of getting out of hell and going to heaven." He shrieked the last word like a curse.

A wave of doubt washed over Hannah.

"Don't fall for Lucifer's lies," Gonael told her. "The closer you are getting to completing the key, the angrier Lucifer becomes and the more he will try to deceive and confuse you."

"Stop stalling and give them the next clue," Jachniel insisted, his voice firm and his wing flitting in impatience.

Lucifer's image flickered from the depths of hell. "I have deadlines, too," his choppy image faded in and out. "I am working on something of utmost importance in hell right now."

"Making plans for all that extra space when the saints move to heaven?" asked Gonael.

"My captives aren't leaving," Lucifer growled.

"You have no voice in the matter. Now, pull yourself together, give the riddle and leave this chariot at once," bellowed Padel.

"A man after my heart, disobedient from the start." Lucifer shouted so loud Hannah feared her ears would burst. All she could catch was the word *disobedient.*

Adam? Lucifer's lips started moving again. *Pay attention.*

"God told him to stay, but he rode his own way. On the quest for riches and fame, his foot became lame." Lucifer's voice turned to a whisper. "His braying beast was to blame for his shame."

Hannah leaned in trying to hear. *Someone who owned an animal doesn't narrow it down. Everyone has a couple of beasts.*

"Mephibosheth? He was lame on both feet," guessed Benjamin.

Hannah gave a quick shake of her head.

Lucifer smirked, then returned to neutral. "Stop guessing until I'm finished. He failed once, twice, thrice to reverse God's blessed, this time his obedient mouth was to blame for his shame." As Lucifer spoke, his image shimmered in and out.

"Stop that right now," Liraz snapped and folded his arms across his chest.

"Sorry, astral projection can be so unreliable," Lucifer said, as his image continued wavering. "He devised a perverse plan to lead them astray, their straying flesh was to blame for their shame. Any guesses?"

Dismas groaned. "How can we make sense of this?"

"Just concentrate on the important parts of each sentence. Think what people did God favor?" suggested Gonael.

Lucifer's eyes flashed. "Shut your beak."

"Gonael doesn't take orders from a traitor," Padel said, flapping his wings and hovering next to Hannah.

"The Hebrews," said Hannah and Benjamin in unison.

When Lucifer pouted, she smiled in triumph.

"Reverse the blessing might be a curse," Dismas said hesitantly.

Hannah nodded.

"So far, we have the Hebrews and a curse, but the animal. I don't get it." Benjamin rubbed his forehead.

"You're doing well. Keep going," Padel said with a toothy grin. In that moment, he had a donkey-like appearance.

Wait. A donkey? That's it! "It's Balaam, the paid prophet!"

"Are you sure?" Lucifer, his voice dripping with skepticism.

"Yes. King Balak of Moab didn't want Moses's people invading Canaan, so he hired Balaam to curse the Hebrews. Balak believed Balaam's words had magical powers, and if Balaam spoke evil against Moses and his people, they would lose the inevitable war brewing between them."

"It fits." Benjamin face lit up. "The beast is Balaam's talking donkey, who tried to prevent Balaam from going with King Balak's men."

"A talking beast?" Liraz said, arching his eyebrow.

Hannah explained, "On the journey to curse the Hebrews, Balaam's donkey stopped in the middle of the road three times and crushed Balaam's foot. In anger, the prophet began beating his disobedient donkey. But God gave the donkey the ability to speak, and the animal told her master she stopped because an angel with a sword blocked their path."

"King Balak hired Balaam to curse the Hebrews," added Benjamin. "But whenever the prophet opened his mouth, he ended up blessing them, causing King Balak to fly into a rage."

Dismas muttered, "And Balaam didn't get any of the gold or silver the king promised him."

"Balaam lost, no one can curse what God has blessed," said Jachniel.

"Not true," shrieked Lucifer. "I still used Balaam to lead the Hebrews into sin. I appeared to Balaam while he rode back home after failing to curse the Israelites. I informed him how he could trick the Hebrews into sin and obtain the riches King Balak offered him. I caused the people of Moses to fall into sin!"

"How did you manage to persuade the Hebrew men to worship Baal-peor, the repulsive Canaanite deity, turning their backs on the Lord?" Hannah leaned on the edge of her seat.

"My three proven tactics—the lust of the flesh, the lust of the eyes, and the pride of life. I will show you." Lucifer waved his hand and an image of thousands of red tents appeared. They could smell mouthwatering scents of baked bread, onions, garlic, and roasting fish.

The smells stung Hannah's senses, reminding her of helping her mother make bread and laughing in the kitchen with their servants.

"No, Lucifer, you are not bringing those perverse images into this chariot or into their minds," said Jachniel sharply.

Dormel blew a gust of wind, sending the images and smells away.

Lucifer's lips curled in a deceptive smile and he said in a falsetto voice, "The information I am providing might assist them in finding the key in Balaam's time."

Hannah furrowed her brow. *The devil's trying to trick us. He has never assisted us.*

"Fine, but keep the details to a minimum," said Gonael.

"I told Balaam how to set a sin trap for the Israelites, which would infuriate their Creator. You know how unpredictable he is when you don't follow his rules. You've seen for yourself—he wiped out the earth, he blew up Sodom and Gomorrah, and I hoped he'd continue his killing spree and destroy all his chosen people." Lucifer's eyes flashed with glee.

"Stop with the theatrics and get on with your story," commanded Jachniel.

"I told Balaam to have the Midianites set up thousands of food tents near the Hebrews' camp. All the delectable smells from their former home in Egypt drifted through the air, bringing the men out in droves. We stationed grandmotherly type women outside the food tents to deceive the men into thinking everything was innocent. Once the men began eating, the wrinkled hags freely poured Ammonitish wine." Lucifer chuckled.

"What's Ammonitish wine?" asked Liraz.

"It's a variation of Sodomite wine. Lot's younger daughter, Puah, passed Sodom's seducing wine recipe to her son. Of course, she had to substitute Sodom's special grapes because your vindictive God blew them all up. But the Ammonitish wine is extremely effective in luring men to do what I want." Lucifer waved his claw hand dramatically. "No more questions, I'm getting to the best parts. The men became drunk, and we replaced the old hags with stunning, half-dressed Midianite women, paid by King Balak. They filled the men's glasses and petted their egos. In no time, the men succumbed to lust." Lucifer paused, eyes gleaming. "The next step was pure genius on my part. The women hid small Baal-peor statues between their breasts. If the men wanted to know the ladies, they would have to bow to the statue. The ones who refused to bow could relieve themselves on the statues." Lucifer winked. "Those foolish men didn't know that's how the Midianites worshiped Baal-peor. Once the men sobered, their revelry soured, and guilt reigned supreme. And how did they smother that gnawing shame? By enticing their friends into the pleasure tents."

He threw his head back, a dark, triumphant chuckle rolling from his throat. "Baal-peor worship spread like wildfire among God's chosen people."

"You forget all the men who did flee out of those tents, not taking your bait. Only four percent bowed their knee to Baal," said Padel.

Lucifer shrugged. "Whatever. I got the results I wanted, and the ringleaders had to be hanged. The Creator brought a plague that killed twenty-four thousand people in one day. Such chaos ensued. Fear, death, and grief spread throughout their camp. What a fun day."

Padel hovered near the chariot, his nostrils flaring and his eyes sharp a steely expression on his bovine face. "I've been waiting a long time to tell you this," his voice steady and resolute. "After all these years, haven't you figured it out? Our Father used you. He couldn't move his people into the promised land unless the previous generation died off due to their sin of unbelief in the wilderness. Your trap for killing God's people actually sped up their entrance into the promised land."

"What you meant for harm, God turned it all around for good," Jachniel said brightly.

"What?" Lucifer flew into a rage as his image exploded away.

"He hates being confronted with the truth," Dormel told the

others. "You better watch your backs. With this new revelation, there is no telling what Lucifer will do next."

In that moment, Sariel slipped off the seat and crumpled to the floor of the chariot. His skin looked dark, as though he'd just rolled in dirt. In a flash, Jachniel was propping him up in the seat opposite Hannah. Jachniel raised Sariel's eyelid. His eye had turned purplish black, like someone had hit him. Liraz sprang across the seat to help.

"What's wrong?" Hannah asked, her voice trembling.

"His light is almost out," Jachniel said in a grave tone. "Sariel has been away too long from God's light. We need to return him to heaven immediately so he can soak in God's presence, or he might never recover."

"But we need to get them back to the past to retrieve the key," Padel shifted his weight from one hoof to his other clearly conflicted "We have to do what we discussed earlier. We will force our way through the second heaven."

Liraz clenched his hands. "Do you think that is wise?"

Sariel moaned as the brownish color on his face and hands blackened like coal.

"We don't have a choice." Gonael squawked as the creatures rushed to their positions inside the wheels. Beating their wings and igniting the flames, the living creatures launched the chariot into the sky.

Hannah's stomach lurched in worry.

"Prepare for war!" commanded the creatures in unison.

War? I'm not ready for war.

The chariot's top transformed into a gilded cage, and golden shackles encircled the passengers' waists. Hannah shifted in her seat and peered at the sky.

"I feel like I'm back in prison," Dismas said.

Liraz stared at the sky. "Soon you will be thanking God you're strapped in."

As the chariot rose, the wind howled. The carriage bounced like a boat on the sea right before a tempest hit.

"Four in one," ordered the creatures.

The chariot swung and dropped at the same time. Through the crystal floor, a queasy Hannah watched as the four larger wheels formed one giant wheel. At the same time, the flames of the four smaller wheels merged into one raging fire. The four creatures disconnected their wings from each other and faced away from the large wheel. Their ankles were held to the wheel by golden shackles. Ayin's eyes gathered at the top of the rim, aimed at the sky. The air smelled damp. In the distance, Hannah saw a wall of dark clouds.

Benjamin squinted. "Did you see something move in the storm clouds?"

"That is why the second heaven is dangerous," Liraz's tone was ominous as the gathering clouds ahead. "Look closer," He pointed into the twisting formations.

Hannah squinted, from within the darkness, red eyes gleamed. Black hooded figures took shape. Hannah shivered.

These were not storm clouds—fallen angels headed straight for them.

In mere seconds, the forces of good and evil would collide, and she was powerless to prevent it.

22

The misfortunes of the Book of Balaam, son of Beor. A divine seer was he. The gods came to him at night.

—Deir 'Alla Inscription, translated by B. A. Levine

Almost the fifty-first hour in hell

The stench of sulfur flooded the air. Hannah wanted to pinch her nose, but the restraints prevented her hand from lifting.

Four fallen angels broke away from the approaching horde. The wind ripped off their hoods, revealing red bull faces—short, thick horns, and glowing crimson eyes surrounded by black rings. *They're like evil versions of Padel.* The monsters landed on the chariot's outer wheel. The chariot dipped until the living creatures adjusted for the trespassers' extra weight. Hannah held her breath, expecting the rest of the fallen angels to pounce on the chariot. But they didn't. The hoard kept pace above the chariot, flying in a threatening circular formation.

"Asmoday, you satanic filth, remove your treasonous talons and your unholy hooves from God's vessel," commanded Padel.

"Release Sariel and we will leave at once," bargained Asmoday.

Sariel thrashed upon hearing his name.

Another fallen angel scraped his stubby horns on the chariot's bars, making a horrible screeching sound sending shivers down Hannah's spine. Once the evil being captured the four living creatures' attention, he demanded in a low menacing voice "Turn over that lowlife angel to us. He deserves our realm, having tasted pleasure unfit—"

"Enough, Morax," Jachniel cut him off. "Remember the last time you dared to challenge me? I shortened your horns. If you continue down this path, I'll sever your head and cast it into the Lake of Fire."

"Leave, stubby, before we smite you all," Dormel threatened.

Hannah wondered, *Why don't they smite the evil angels now?*

"Don't waste your energy on us. Just hand over Sariel. He legally belongs to us since he originally perished in Sodom," Morax sneered. "It's the four of you who violated the laws of time."

"Lucifer has no legal rights to him since he violated Sariel's free will by capturing him and transforming him into a man. Leave our vessel at once," ordered Dormel.

"It looks like a cage to me, with five pet birds. Ayin imprisoned in the rims and the four of you chained inside the wheels."

"Morax is right." Asmoday's voice filled with persuasion. "You blindly obey orders, but deep down, don't you desire to embrace your true self, unburdened by the shackles of the Creator's design? You have the power to shape your own destiny, to rewrite the outcome of your existence. Turn over Sariel, then you will taste true freedom."

Hannah gasped. *They twist God's words to make him sound wicked!*

"Are those the lies Lucifer used to convince you to turn your back on our Father?" asked Dormel.

"The amazing part is one-third of you were foolish enough to fall for it," said Jachniel.

In retort, the evil angels let out a shrill yapping noise.

"Enough," screamed Asmoday.

The others fell silent.

"We rule this realm of the second heaven, and we are claiming Sariel one way or another," threatened Morax.

"Remove your claws from our vessel and go haunt someone

else," bellowed Padel.

A flaming sword appeared in the right hand of each of the living creatures, and they used them to flick bits of blazing embers at the evil beings. The fallen angels shrieked, releasing their holds, and flapping their wings, trying to extinguish the flames.

Fury burned in Asmoday's eyes as he hovered near Hannah. "Let my Sariel go!"

His companions repeated the phrase as Asmoday, Morax, and the two others hacked and coughed up something in their throats. Each puckered thin red lips and spat a red substance on the passengers. Hannah flinched. *Blood?* It stained her special sandals. Red stains also appeared on Benjamin's and Dismas' robes, while Sariel and Liraz got hit on their foreheads.

Liraz shook his head. "I'm going to drown you in the Lake of Fire when my powers return."

"The only place you'll return to is Tartarus," jeered Morax. The fallen angels rejoined the horde above. In their place came five green creatures with onyx staffs.

Liraz muttered, "Here come the Heqets."

Their green wart-covered faces reminded Hannah of enormous winged frogs.

The Heqets raised their staffs and commanded, "Ranas impetum."

"Frogs attack? Up here?" whispered Benjamin.

The Heqets chanted. On top of their staffs sat red rubies. Each ruby opened to reveal a frog. One jumped onto Hannah's head. She shook her head to and fro, eyes wide in fear. The webbed feet stuck to her hair. Hannah frantically shook her head and shrieked repeatedly, "Get it off!" Finally, the toad jumped into the growing pile of frogs on the chariot floor. She pulled up her feet to avoid the slimy creatures.

"Disappear, you miserable frogs," Padel shouted over the croaking.

The frogs vanished.

Hannah sighed in relief.

"See the ladder in the distance?" Jachniel said, his voice steady and reassuring despite the chaos around them. He pointed with his free hand under his wing.

Hannah squinted in the direction indicated.

"Once we reach it, the fallen angels will slither away."

With a bang, a fallen angel landed on the chariot, making Hannah jump. "Let Sariel go," he demanded. Black dust flew off his wings and blew into the chariot. Hannah held her breath. Another group of angels swooped down. Each took a deep breath and blew a black cloud into the chariot. Flies swarmed, covering Sariel in a moving blanket of blackness. Morax led a swarm of bull faced angels on the right, coughing up a cloud of brown which transformed into mosquitos. The pests bit Hannah's ankles. More Heqets flew in from the left and spit out a green substance. Locusts. They began to tear and chew Hannah's robe.

"Get these off me!" cried Dismas, shaking and flailing his arms in every direction.

A green dust settled on Hannah's hip. Locusts marched into her pocket. Hannah squirmed in her seat and wiggled her hips from side to side, despite the belt restraint. She let loose a yell loud enough that Grandmother Abigail could hear back in hell.

"Why aren't the living creatures commanding these bugs to go away?" shouted Benjamin, spitting out a mosquito.

A muffled sound came from below the chariot. The passengers looked through the clear floor and saw the insects swarming the living creatures. Their mouths were completely covered.

The fallen angels continued their chant, "Let Sariel go!"

Something about this seems familiar. Wait! Blood, frogs, mosquitos, dust, flies, locusts... Hannah pursed her lips and tried speaking with minimal movement. "The fallen angels are requesting the living creatures to let Sariel go, just like Moses asked Pharaoh to let his people go. When Pharaoh didn't release the Hebrews, God—through Moses—brought plagues into the land."

"What are you talking about?" asked Liraz through his teeth. Flies swarmed around his head like a halo.

"Abraham's grandson, Jacob, had twelve sons who became the twelve tribes of Israel," Hannah explained. "There was a famine, so Jacob's family relocated to Egypt. Eventually, the Hebrews became Egyptian slaves, and Moses helped free them through God's plagues against the Egyptians. The evil angels are mocking God."

Hannah swatted at some mosquitos with her foot and tried to shake off more locusts from her robe. "The first plague was turning the Nile River into blood. The second was an invasion of frogs. Third, gnats. Fourth was flies and the fifth was the death of livestock. We haven't seen that one yet." The skin above her lip started to burn and itch.

Above Liraz's eye, a festering boil appeared. Dismas and Benjamin had large red hives covering their faces.

"Sixth is boils," Benjamin said with disgust.

"Hail, the seventh plague?" Dismas said, unsure.

A crack of lighting exploded behind the chariot and shekel-sized hail fell between the bars and battered them. It felt like someone slapping Hannah's cheek but hurt worse because of the boils.

Benjamin continued, "The eighth is locusts, which have already appeared. The ninth plague is darkness."

As if on cue, a black fog enveloped the chariot.

Four red eyes appeared below the chariot, then flames erupted around Sariel's ankles. Through the darkness, forms took shape. The flames came from two dragons. Hannah screamed and a fly flew into her gaping mouth. Her scream ended in a gagged cough as she tried to clear her throat. Her legs burned from the fire. Hundreds of locusts crawled into her pocket. The key shifted. One of Sariel's shackles clattered to the floor. Two frog-faced fallen angels carrying chains flew to Sariel and began wrapping his freed legs.

"Help! Help! They're taking the key and Sariel!" Hannah shouted urgently. She flicked bugs away as she fought to reach her pocket. The locusts had already dragged the key halfway out.

The living creatures stilled their wings and turned their bodies to the right. The chariot twisted and plummeted. The key pinged to the floor. Hannah trapped it under her foot. The chariot righted itself and the bugs vacated. *What a relief!* But the darkness remained, suffocating them.

"The tenth plague killed all the firstborn sons," Benjamin said in a frenzied voice.

A wave of fear spread through Hannah.

"I'm a firstborn," whispered Dismas.

"I'm number 1,578," said Liraz.

Padel yelled from beneath the chariot, "Number 1,577."

Hannah squashed another bug. *So, Padel and Liraz are brothers. That's why they fight all the time.* But she shook her head. *No, that's silly. Angels aren't like humans.*

Shadowy figures circled the chariot like vultures. With each rotation, they drew nearer, wielding long, thin swords. The two dragons directed their fire on the chariot bars.

"Let Sariel go, or I will kill Dismas, the only first born son in this chariot," Asmoday hissed, raising his clawed hand threateningly.

The fallen angels flung themselves on the large wheel, slowing the chariot to a crawl. The living creatures furiously flapped their wings.

Wait. Out of the corner of Hannah's eye, she saw blue sky and an enormous ladder. She couldn't gauge the ladder's height since white fluffy clouds covered the top and bottom. Perched on each rung were angels of various sizes.

"At least a thousand angels on that ladder," Dismas said in awe, like the sky split and heaven poured out

"Jacob's ladder," uttered Hannah. Relief flooded her as the living creatures steered toward it.

"It's a portal between heaven and earth," said Liraz.

The dragons' fire breeched the chariot bars. Two fallen angels yanked Sariel's legs. The angelic beings along the ladder watched but none of them lifted a feather to help. They held burning swords. *Why won't they help us?*

A gentle voice spoke behind her, "You need to ask your heavenly Father for guidance and he chooses how to help you."

She obeyed the steady yet firm voice. *Dear Father, please command your angels to protect and defend us against the powers of darkness.* The angels didn't budge. Then, Hannah remembered how the creatures had cast out the demon from Benjamin. *In Jesus' name I pray.* Jacob's ladder swayed as all the angels flew toward them.

"Retreat! Retreat!" Asmoday screamed. The fallen angels vanished and took the darkness with them. The sweet aroma of roses replaced the stench of sulfur.

The angels created a path to the chariot. A gentle breeze blew. All the boils disappeared, the bug bites healed, and the blood washed away. The restraints released and the chariot bars disappeared. Hannah grabbed the key from under her sandal and put in back into her pocket. An angel with kind green eyes smiled as he picked up Sariel like a baby and flew him into the clouds covering the top of the ladder.

Now Hannah could see the ladder rungs looked like tree trunks. The army of angelic beings stood to the sides and stared at the chariot in anticipation.

"Reveal the ring which will take us back to the time of Moses," Padel ordered.

The ladder cracked and crunched. One side of a rung disconnected from the rail and swung toward them, exposing its circular pattern of tree rings.

Liraz kicked the glass floor to get the creatures' attention. "You can't be serious. Has anyone tried this?"

"Nope. We will be the first," Dormel said.

"The first?" Hannah asked.

"See the big red ring in the center of that tree stump?" Gonael spoke excitedly. "The theory is that the ring was created at the time of Moses, so it will take us to that time."

"We have an audience," Benjamin said, astonished.

Hundreds of angels flocked to the ladder, cheering and singing them on with a beautiful song.

"I don't desire to witness us crash into a tree." Liraz lowered his head.

Maybe he just can't face the angels he had betrayed.

"Brace yourself," Jachniel warned.

Hannah huffed. She was starting to hate those words, along with "collide" and "theory." The chariot once again accelerated.

Dismas closed his eyes. "We are going to be squashed."

"At least you three have a one-way ticket back to Paradise," said Liraz. "For me, it's back to my cell in Tartarus."

Hannah's eyes widened with dread as the chariot zoomed toward the red ring. As they blasted through, the scent of lumber filled the air, and everything turned a cherrywood color.

Their surroundings turned into a sapphire sky. Hannah spotted thousands of Israelite tents arranged in a cross formation. In the center of the cross billowed the smoke of a vertical cloud pillar. The living creatures steered straight into the flames.

23

And the lover being, as it were, taken in the net of her manifold and multiform snares, not being able to resist her beauty and seductive conversation, will become wholly subdued in his reason, and, like a miserable man, will obey all the commands which she lays upon him, and will enroiled as the salve of passion.

—The Works of Philo Judaeus Book 24,
translated by Charles Duke Yonge

The wilderness, 1451 BC
The fifty-second hour in hell

A blast of desert heat tinged with black smoke greeted Hannah. Squinting against the harsh sunlight, her heart pounded as the group neared a red tent covered in Baal images. Blood seeped from beneath the tent flap, soaking into the cracked earth.

"What is this place?" Liraz's eyes darted to one horrifying sight to another. asked as he looked around.

Everywhere, their landscape resembled a battlefield. Hannah averted her eyes from the corpses.

Dismas grabbed a stick and opened the tent's front flap, peering in. He paled and dropped the stick. "You don't want to go in there."

The angelic living creatures, their wing laboring, moved slowly from their four wheel-within-a-wheel positions, each surveying the grim situation.

"Awful, isn't it?" a loud voice boomed behind them. An old

man waved his staff as he approached. "Leave! Haven't you angels killed enough of us with the plague?"

Jachniel held out his hands. "I swear, Moses, we didn't harm your people."

"It's justified. Your people broke the law," Padel rumbled, his wings flaring slightly as he stomped a hoofed foot against the ground "They bowed the knee to Baal. They broke God's first commandment: You shall not have any other gods."

"And number six: You shall not commit adultery," added Dormel, sounding firm yet compassionate.

Gonael chimed in, "Sin carries a heavy price."

The prophet's brown eyes flashed. "Because of Balaam, twenty-four thousand are dead!"

Jachniel stepped closer and placed a reassuring hand on Moses' shoulder. "God will avenge what Balaam and the Midianites did to you," Jachniel said.

Moses leaned against his staff and sighed wearily. "Our God is fair and faithful."

Dismas snorted.

"I apologize for being rude," Moses faced her. "I know the living creatures, but I haven't met any of you." When Jachniel introduced them, Moses froze. "I've heard of you, but not Liraz. Are you searching for key pieces?"

"How did you know?" asked Hannah in a shaky voice. The nauseating smell of death filled her nostrils, making her sway. The sight of the lifeless bodies around her, combined with the weariness from the trials the rotten fallen angels had put them through, weighed heavy on her heart. Now, she couldn't grasp how the man who had led her people out of Egypt knew her, her companions, and their quest. She swiped her sweaty brow.

Moses gently grasped her elbow and signaled to someone behind the group. Three priests brought wooden chairs from a nearby tent and placed them in a half circle, offering a place for her companions to sit. Hannah sank into her seat, sending a grateful gaze to Moses. The living creatures rested on a flat rock to the right. A kind soul handed her a glass of refreshing water, which she accepted with a nod. The cool liquid quenched her parched throat.

"The Lord told me you would need rest when you arrived," Moses explained. "I'm familiar with the feeling of everything crashing on you all at once." Moses stared at them with such compassion while he brushed some sand off his robe and continued, "Five months ago, when we were gathering crops during the Festival of Booths, I had a vision. I was standing on a mountain with two strangers named Jesus and Elijah. Jesus shone like the sun and informed me of your quest for a key piece. Jachniel jarred my memory when he spoke your names."

"Impossible," muttered Benjamin.

"Do you have the piece?" asked Hannah. She held her breath. *It can't be this simple.*

Moses held up his hand. "Phineas."

A young man in a blood-splattered robe emerged from the red tent carrying at arm's length a partially covered Baal statue. Two priests followed Phineas, holding amulets, jars of bones, and ornate arrows.

Hannah wrinkled her nose. Items involved in divination, an abomination to God.

"Put this outside the camp," Phineas instructed the priests. "Bury it deep with the bones and other amulets. Toss the arrows in the fire, then we'll move the bodies and torch the tent. I never want to see it again." Phineas took a couple of hesitant steps toward them.

"His single action ended the plague," Moses said with pride.

"How?" Liraz tilted his head, his eyes wide with curiosity.

"Cozbi, a high priestess of the Midianites, had the audacity to set up her Baal shrine. Zimri, one of the princes of Israel, committed unspeakable acts with that harlot close to God's tabernacle." Moses pointed to the tent of God's dwelling place, where a pillar of cloud loomed, shifting and swirling as if alive, standing sentinel over the entrance.

Hannah's jaw dropped.

"Because of Zimri," Phineas spoke slowly, "God sent a plague. People started dying throughout the camp. I took my javelin, entered the pagan tent, and killed my best friend and that woman." Phineas looked at his feet.

"You did it in righteous anger," Moses said. "Once you killed them, the plague ended. What a waste, all this death." Moses slammed his staff on the ground.

Yes, far too much death. The flood, Sodom, and now this.

Everyone grew quiet.

Padel broke the silence. "Where is the key fragment?"

Phineas reached into his pocket and retrieved a dark gray, spear-shaped piece of iron about half the length of his palm. It was covered in dried blood. "After I killed them, I saw this on the ground."

Forgetting her weariness, Hannah rushed over and held out her hand.

Benjamin slapped her arm out of the way. "You can't touch that! It's unclean!"

"Maybe it doesn't apply to us since we are dea—" Hannah cut off. *If everyone knows we're dead, they'll think we're unclean, too.* She cleared her throat. "Since we've dealt with difficult situations."

Moses arched his eyebrow.

The key piece slipped from Phineas's hand to the dusty ground. He backed away.

Benjamin shook his head, "We don't want to take any chances."

"Phineas has touched unclean things and murdered people. If you handle it, you will now be defiled, too," said Dismas.

They didn't have time for the seven days' waiting period.

Moses pulled a small gold jar with a tiny hyssop branch attached to it out of his robe pocket. "To cleanse the key piece, let's wipe some bull's blood, and Dormel can pass the key piece over the fire. Then I will consider it purified."

They followed Moses's orders, and Dormel handed the clean spear-shaped portion to Hannah. She pulled out the key's handle and the piece leapt onto the bottom of the skull forming an elongated key shaft.

Moses rubbed his beard. "Are any of you descendants of the tribe of Levi?"

"I have a tiny bit of Levite blood," answered Dismas.

Moses held out the jar. "Take this with you."

Dismas carefully placed the sacred items in his pocket. "Thank you."

"Gird yourselves. I have a big revelation," Moses declared.

Hannah's heart quivered. What could be more surprising than parting the Red Sea and making water come out of a rock? She held her breath.

Moses reached into his inner tunic and held out two more key pieces: a lapis lazuli ring and a pinky-length, crimson auger seashell.

Hannah froze. "How did you get those?"

"In that vision, Jesus told me two odd stones I'd been keeping had significance, and I needed to start carrying them in my pocket."

Benjamin leaned forward. "Where did they come from?"

"Pharaoh ordered all the male Hebrew babies killed at birth. My mother couldn't fathom it, so she placed me in a wicker basket and floated me down the Nile River. Pharaoh's daughter spotted the basket, and when she lifted me up, the blue ring fell out. When I became older, she presented it to me. I discovered the seashell staff after the Red Sea parted. The Lord told me to pick it up as a reminder to fear not, stand firm, and see the salvation of the Lord. I have kept them secure all these years, even carried them out of Egypt on the first Passover."

"Thanks for your help," Hannah murmured with gratitude. When she raised the key, the ring sailed in the air and slid over the shaft to form the raised collar. The seashell staff followed and nestled under the ring, forming a pin under the collar that extended the key's shaft. Her heart soared with gratitude at finding three key pieces in such a short time. The outline of the key appeared completed, but Hannah's heart dropped when she glanced at her thumbnail. Two-thirds light, one-third darkness.

A priest rushed from the wilderness holding a gold necklace shaped like a snake with ruby eyes. "Moses, look what we dug up when we were burying the accursed items!"

"Another artifact of Sodom and Gomorrah," Moses said gruffly. "Rebury it, but go deeper this time."

"Sodom?" asked Dismas weakly. He averted his eyes.

Hannah frowned at him. *That looked like one of Oren's necklaces. Maybe it reminds him of Ziv.*

"Part of this desert is the original location of Sodom. Nobody would want to live here on purpose. After our disobedience, God had us camp in this wilderness wasteland for forty years, training the younger generation to trust him and to learn to fight our enemies so they would be ready when the unbelieving generation died. The Lord kept us safe, providing food and water."

"Time to depart, we are on a tight schedule." Padel said gruffly, yet he hugged Moses.

The show of affection surprised Hannah. *Maybe he knows Moses will die soon.* That part of the story had always bothered her. Moses made one mistake by not listening to God, so he was not permitted to enter the promised land. *Lord, help me not mess anything up.* Hannah approached the chariot and steeled herself. *Next up is Lucifer with another riddle.*

"Stop," Moses ordered. "In the vision on Mount Tabor, Jesus mentioned that the devil violated your game rules when he attacked you with the imitation plagues. So he gave me the names of the next two locations: Goliath's skull." Moses paused, tapping his chin in thought. "And the other place had a man's name."

Benjamin reached his seat in the chariot. "Well, that narrows it down."

Moses drummed his fingers against his forehead. "I recall something about a gallows, and a man's name ... Haman, a descendant of Agag, the king of the Amalekites." Moses spat. "I loathe those cowards. When we fled Egypt, they attacked us like wolves picking off the weak stragglers."

Hannah's ancestors in the tribe of Benjamin had warred with the Amalekites for generations. But her heart leapt at the possibility of meeting Queen Esther.

Distant voices called for Moses.

"Coming," Moses sighed. "It's always something. Remember, when you are close to victory, the devil will douse you with doubt and disbelief. Don't fall for it. Pray. And keep advancing, no matter the cost." The calls for Moses became urgent. "Turning chaos into calmness once again," muttered Moses as he headed in the direction of the voices.

"He's an extraordinary man. The greatest prophet in all of Israel," Benjamin remarked.. "It's a shame he never reached the promised land."

"Moses went somewhere better than the promised land," Jachniel said. "You didn't see him in Paradise because God took him straight up to the third heaven, like Elijah. And that's why Elijah and Moses were able to meet with Jesus on the mountain of transfiguration."

"God buried him," Benjamin insisted.

"You're right. God did bury Moses." Dormel confirmed. "But remember, the archangel Michael and Lucifer fought over his body. Michael won and brought Moses's corpse to our Father, his Holy Spirit, and Jesus. Together, they raised Moses from the dead."

"Why the secrecy?"

"Liraz, you know how humans are prone to idol worship. God didn't want the Hebrews to idolize Moses," Padel explained.

"If Moses, Lazarus, and others rose from the dead, what is so special about Jesus returning to the land of the living?" Benjamin asked, shrugging.

The living beings gasped. Padel stuck his bull face an inch from Benjamin's and snorted at him.

Hannah sighed. *Someday, my brother will learn to keep quiet.*

"Leave him alone, Padel," said Jachniel. "He does not know what he's talking about."

Padel's nostrils flared, his eyes sparking with disdain, as he took a swift sidestep away from her brother.

"Jesus is fully God and fully man. Those previously raised from the dead were mere mortals," Jachniel explained.

"Sorry, I don't understand," Benjamin said in a small voice.

"What is the strongest shape in the universe?" asked Gonael.

"A triangle," ventured Benjamin.

Gonael nodded. "Now picture the strongest force acting as one—the Father, Holy Spirit, and Son—as a triangle. But then, one side is gone. What happens to that triangle when one side is missing?"

"It collapses," answered Hannah.

"Not one human was brought back to life without the full force of the Holy Trinity," Jachniel said. "Some angels don't think it is even possible that Jesus will rise to life without the three of them working in unison."

"Shut your mouth, Jachniel," snapped Padel. "Just because you look like a man doesn't mean you can speak your unbelief out loud."

Ignoring Padel, Jachniel continued. "Some angels think Jesus needs the completed key of hell to bring his believers from hell to heaven."

"It's all speculation. Our Father doesn't reveal everything to us," Gonael said wisely.

"Can Jesus raise the dead without the key?" asked Dismas wearily. He slumped and held up his thumb—only a small dark section left. The unspoken question hung in the air. Could they locate the remaining fragments in time?

"Don't worry. We will find the pieces. We have ten hours left," Liraz said unconvincingly.

Her stomach twisted, like a vine caught in an unexpected gust of wind. Could they outsmart Lucifer in this desperate race against time?

"With God, all things are possible. But just in case, let's dig up Goliath's skull," suggested Jachniel.

"Positions!" Dormel commanded.

The living creatures slid into the wheels and blasted off. Hannah looked at the sky, searching for fallen angels. She touched the key in her pocket and vowed she'd keep it safe.

24

"And they do not lie with the mighty, the fallen from among the uncircumcised, who went down to Sheol with their weapons of war, whose swords were laid under their heads, and whose iniquities are upon their bones; for the terror of the mighty men was in the land of the living."

—Ezekiel 32:27 (ESV)

The tunnel under Paradise
The fifty-third hour in hell

Making headway moving the boulders, Mahway whistled a mournful tune, anything to blot out Jesus. But his voice still buzzed like a mosquito.

"My death has fulfilled the law of Moses," Mahway heard Jesus say. "My death paid the price for your sin. Our Father will no longer hold sin against you."

The Paradise prisoners collectively gasped.

Mahway clamped his lips and strained to listen.

"The Ten Commandments are holy and excellent, but impossible for anyone to keep. The age of the law is dead, and when I rise from hell, the age of grace will begin."

What is this? No sin held over the humans? Mahway's brain raced with the implications. No wonder Lucifer needed to throw Jesus into the Lake of Fire. Lucifer adored the Ten Commandments, along with the countless other laws the Pharisees decreed. These laws proved to be effective strategies for making humans feel guilt, condemnation, and shame, opening the door wide for demonic activity in their lives. They had harassed humans before the law, but after the Ten Commandments, Mahway had legal access to their lives. He rather enjoyed nailing the humans with lengthy lists of violations.

Jesus continued, "Through my death and resurrection, you will be in right standing with my Father and have access to him whenever you want. This gift of grace will make you a new creature. I will live in each one of you who accepts me. This goes for your relatives in the land of the living."

The Paradise prisoners applauded and cheered, singing praises.

What? Jesus living inside a human? How is that going to work? Can I possess a person if Jesus is living inside? Grace sounds like an abomination. There won't be any for Nephilim. I despise it. Mahway's body shook with rage, and he punched a rock. *The cornerstone. Oh, dung.*

The boulders tumbled like an avalanche, pelting him. Dust filled his lungs. Mahway tried wiggling his fingers, but he couldn't move. He lay trapped under the weight of the boulders. Those Paradise fools still shouted for joy, concealing Mahway's predicament from Ohya and Hahya. Or maybe the twins were laughing at him. He willed himself to calm down.

After a few moments, Mahway tried regaining his strength. *Grrr ...* He strained, pushed, and tried lifting the boulders like an Olympian. *Grrrrr ...* But even with all his efforts, only a pebble rolled off his foot. *Who is going to save me now?*

"Jesus, Jesus," roared the exuberant crowd above.

Mahway released a bitter laugh. The Creator did have a twisted sense of humor. Mahway chanted Lucifer's name in the hopes he'd help free him. Should he tell Lucifer the latest information about Jesus planning to live in people who believed in him? Maybe he should keep this to himself—for now.

25

> ***Then [David] cut off [Goliath's] head ... David took Goliath's head and brought it to Jerusalem.***
>
> —1 Samuel 17:51, 54 (HCSB)

The fifty-fourth hour in hell

The chariot settled with a thump, jolting Dismas awake. *No, it can't be.* Beads of sweat slid down his back as he saw the waning moon shining on three crosses. Jesus' body and his were no longer displayed on Golgotha, but Gestas's corpse still hung on the cross. *Where's my wounded body?*

"Wake up," Padel nudged Hannah.

"The Skull? The place we died trying to get to?" Hannah rubbed her eyes.

Something flew out of the skull's eye. *Demon?* The hair stood up on Dismas' arms. *No, just a bat.*

"Something's wrong," Benjamin stood. "Shouldn't we be meeting Esther or on the battlefield watching David kill Goliath with a slingshot?"

Despite his heart pounding and his ears ringing, Dismas forced himself to ask, "Why did you bring me here?"

Jachniel tucked his wings as he leapt from the wheel. "Everyone, calm down. Remember, David buried Goliath's head in Jerusalem right here on this hill."

"The land formation resembles a dead human's head," Liraz remarked as he studied the rocky hill beyond the three crosses.

Padel pointed to the three crosses. "Goliath's skull is buried beneath the middle cross. David's one-man victory over Goliath caused the Philistines to surrender to Israel. Just like Jesus' victory over death will free humanity from the clutches of Lucifer."

Dismas' brow wrinkled. *I wasn't freed from anything. I died a horrible death, and God allowed Barabbas to live.*

Dormel, Jachniel, and Gonael disappeared.

In a hushed tone, Hannah asked Padel, "Where did they go?"

"These three days, while Jesus is in Paradise, are perilous. Judas hanged himself, feeling condemned after betraying Jesus to the Sanhedrin. Many other disciples are guilt-ridden, having abandoned Jesus. Lucifer's forces are swarming them, trying to spread despair and hopelessness. Since your quest intersected with this timeline, Jachniel, Gonael, and Dormel are helping our angelic forces strengthen Jesus' followers and fight off hordes of demons. I was selected to protect you while you dig up Goliath."

"Dig with what—our hands?" asked Benjamin.

Padel moved toward them, twirling his hand. Now, they clutched shovels. Padel led the way to Jesus' cross. As they reached the cross, Padel bowed so low his ox horns grazed the ground. He brushed away some stones. "Dig deep right here. But do not trample on Jesus' blood." He pointed out the areas.

"I am not going near there," Hannah averted her gaze from Gestas's crumpled body.

"Don't look, Hannah," advised Benjamin, thrusting his shovel into the stony dirt.

A boulder fell from the top of the hill, crashing into Gestas's cross, knocking it over, and covering his battered body.

"Padel, you sure have a flair for the dramatic," said Liraz.

"Not from me. This entire area is unstable after the earthquake. Dig faster. I estimate five cubits more."

Dismas felt like his feet were stuck in quicksand as he stared at his empty cross. Why did he have to die while Barabbas still roamed the earth? Anger rose like lava. "Why don't you help or, better yet, use your magic?" he blurted.

"It's not magic," Padel answered. "It's the power of the living God. Angels guide, protect, and give messages. We're not allowed to do your work or violate your free will."

"Free will," Dismas snorted. "What choice did I have?" He threw down his shovel in disgust and started walking toward the bushes.

Liraz threw a shovelful of dirt to the side of the cross. "What's with him?"

Hannah shoveled a smaller pile onto the growing mound of dirt. "Maybe because this is where he just died a gruesome death."

"I will collect Dismas," Padel offered. "Don't stop digging—be quick. Romans and demons are lurking about, and a few rocks are teetering on the hill. One strong gust of wind, and… splat."Liraz called after him, "When did you start caring about humans?"

"When they don't look like you," Padel called back. "Less talking and more digging."

Dismas walked until he couldn't hear the others talking about him. Now he felt guilty leaving them to dig for themselves.

Padel's warm fingers lightly touched his shoulder. "It's not safe to be on your own, Dismas. Besides, they need your muscle power. Liraz is such a weakling."

Nobody needs you. Dismas heard Barabbas's voice in his mind. *You're nothing but a useless burden.* The mental image of Barabbas raised his fist. *Shut up, fool. It's all his fault I'm dead.*

"Seeing your cross upset you. Would you like to see what happened to your body?" Padel's voice held a soft, inviting tone.

Dismas nodded.

Padel plucked a feather from his wing and brushed it over Dismas' eyes.

His knees crumpled. The next thing he knew, Dismas stood inside a simple stucco house. There was something familiar about the cracked brick walls, beaten earthen floors, and little windows with grills over them like a prison. *Barabbas's house!* His mother materialized into his dream.

"You are a liar! My son is not dead." His mother wept.

"It's the honest-to-God truth," Barabbas said, towering over her. "The Romans planned to crucify me, but Pontius Pilate freed me and crucified Jesus in my place."

"You should have demanded to change places with my son!"

"Mara, you don't understand. I deserve to be set free."

"It's always about you." She wiped her tears and turned toward the wardrobe with a crooked door.

Barabbas clenched his jaw. "Let's not argue. You have to hurry and buy spices before the market closes and bury Dismas before nightfall. I refuse to return to the Skull, but I will send some of my men to help you."

Of course, Barabbas would refuse to help bury me, afraid that Pontius Pilate would change his mind.

Mara wrapped a few of her clothes in a blanket. "I don't need your help."

Barabbas blocked her from leaving and reached for his belt.

She cowered.

"Easy, Mara," he said in a soft voice, "I'm not going to hurt you." Barabbas reached into his pouch and pulled out some coins.

"I am leaving tonight for good," Mara said, standing tall. "You may be alive, but you are dead to me." She opened the door. Rays of sun streamed on her as she walked out.

Keep going, Mother. Don't look back.

Barabbas glanced at the ceiling. "Bring her back, God," he muttered. "But you won't. Seeing now we're finally even. You finally paid your debt to me."

Absurd. How could God owe him anything? Barabbas has to be drunk.

Again, Dismas felt a feather touch his eyelashes. The images shifted back to Golgotha, where Dismas observed his lifeless body dangling like a puppet on the cross. A man tugged his hammer's claw at the last nail on Dismas' right wrist. The nail came free, and Dismas' body fell against the man's shoulder, causing him to stagger. The man struggled to guide Dismas onto a blanket spread on the ground.

"What are you doing to my son?" Mara rushed up and knelt beside her son's battered body, stroking his hair.

"Mara?" The man dropped the hammer. "Mara, is it really you?"

Dismas' heart raced as he watched.

"How do you know my name?" Mara demanded.

"It's me, Nathan. Your husband."

She shook her head. "You can't be. Nathan has leprosy and is probably dead by now."

Dismas' father kneeled beside her. "It's me, Mara."

"How can this be?" Mara peered at his face. "I don't understand. How were you healed? Impossible."

"I have a lifetime to explain." Nathan tried to touch her cheek, but Mara moved away.

"I'm sorry for everything that has happened. Dismas died, and it's all my fault." Mara's shoulders shook as she sobbed.

Dismas shrugged half-heartedly, he took no pleasure in his mother's confession.

"I forgive you, Mara." Nathan's eyes also filled with tears. "You had no choice. I heard how cruelly my family treated you. I saw them this morning, and they told me you were dead, and that I'd find Dismas here. We will place our son in my family's tomb whether they like it or not. You can help me carry his body to the cart." Nathan held out his hand.

Mara took it and clung to him. "After we take care of our son, we're leaving Jerusalem—forever."

The images faded. Dismas felt woozy. Padel grabbed his arm and assisted him to his feet. "Did my parents actually reunite?"

Padel nodded. "All that you saw truly happened."

"If I was still alive, the three of us could have been together."

"Not so. Your death acted as a bridge. If you hadn't died, your mother and father would have never found each other." Padel paused. "Even from tragic circumstances, God manages to make something good happen."

Dismas couldn't comprehend these revelations. For years, he'd prayed for his father to be healed and return home. But he never imagined he would be excluded from the reunion.

Hannah screamed.

Padel flew toward the cross. Dismas followed but then froze. Benjamin clutched Goliath's enormous skull while Asmoday tugged on the opposite end. Flanking Benjamin were Hannah and Liraz. Then, the fallen angel shrieked and vanished.

"How did you banish Asmoday?" asked Padel, joining the others.

"He stepped in the blood of Jesus," Hannah said in disbelief.

Dismas rejoined the group and asked, "Did that fiend manage to take the key?"

"Asmoday didn't steal it," said Benjamin. He lifted Goliath's skull above his head like a prize. Something rattled inside the hollow skull. Benjamin shook it again, and an ivory rectangle key piece fell out, landing in a pool of Jesus' blood. Benjamin and Hannah exchanged horrified looks.

Dismas hurried to the key piece and pulled out the jar Moses had given him. He respectfully cleaned the jar with the bottom of his robe and then scooped the key into the jar. He used the hyssop branch to fish out the key and brush off the remaining specks of blood.

"Look, it has a cross engraved on it." Dismas handed the clean key piece to Hannah and returned the jar and branch to his pocket.

They watched the ivory piece leap and position itself onto the red pin just under the collar, forming the bit portion responsible for turning the bolt. How many bits remained?

A bright flash lit the sky. Dismas leapt back as a blast of wind rose. The heavens filled with an angelic host led by Jachniel, Dormel, and Gonael. Once Padel joined them in the sky, the angels started singing in unison, "You were born for such a time as this."

Their words reminded Dismas of his mother. She used to hum the words said to Queen Esther, and they made her feel brave. After she had met Barabbas, Dismas had never heard her hum again.

As the angels sang and descended, he tried to remember what his mother had told him about Esther's time. A Persian king had married Esther, unaware of her Jewish roots. The king's advisor, Haman, plotted to kill the Jewish citizens and seize their goods. Esther's uncle advised her to go before her husband and plead for her people. But because she was uninvited by the king, he could have sentenced her to death. And that's when her uncle had said she was born for a time like this.

The rest of the story faded from memory as Dismas' attention was captured by the brilliance and beauty of the angels swooping closer and encircling them while singing, "You were born for such a time as this." They spun faster, their movements creating a whirlwind, whipping at his face and hands. He felt dizzy and nauseated. The three crosses seemed to multiply and swirl around him. He closed his eyes and fell to his knees. And then he blacked out.

26

And Benaiah … slew two lion like men of Moab.

—2 Samuel 23:20 (KJV)

The tunnel under Paradise
The fifty-sixth hour in hell

While Mahway waited for Lucifer to appear, he wiggled, and the rocks around his left ear gave way.

Now Jesus' voice came in loud and clear. "Who wants to hear from King David, the man after God's heart?"

The applause from Paradise was incredible.

Mahway groaned. Raged boiled within him every time he heard David's name. He tried balling his fist, but all he could do was rake the earth with his six fingers. *I will jump in the Lake of Fire if David sings one of those fool songs or relives his glory days when he single-handedly slew Goliath.*

"We are now in the era I've described in my songs," Mahway heard David say. "'Blessed are those whose sins will be forgiven.' Jesus is the one who can forgive our sins because he is the only one to arrive in Paradise sinless. He is paying the ultimate price for all of us."

"On the third day, when I rise back to life," Jesus explained, "all you will be made righteous in God's eyes. But only if you believe in your hearts and confess with your mouths that I am God's Son, who died for you. Only then will you be eligible to leave hell and be transferred to heaven, where you will stand in my Father's presence."

David started singing in his deep, annoying, perfect baritone,

"The Lord has made known his salvation. He has revealed his righteousness. Blessed is the one whose transgression is forgiven, whose sin is covered. Be glad in the Lord and rejoice, righteous ones, and shout for joy."

Enough! Mahway gnashed his teeth. After Sodom exploded, he had prowled the earth as a man-lion for eight hundred years. Mahway discovered something new during his second life on earth—love. Until he lost everything because of David.

He replayed the conversation in his mind:

"Your next assignment," Lucifer had told him, "is to assassinate King David."

Why didn't I say no, take Cecilia, and flee? But there is no escaping Lucifer.

"It won't be like the others I've killed for you over the years," Mahway had said. "This will be difficult. David never goes anywhere without his band of mighty men."

"Aren't you up for a challenge? By now, it must be a bore living with Cecilia. Or perhaps the excitement of living a lie keeps you going?" Lucifer had flashed a devilish grin. "Lying is fun, isn't it? Is she dumb as well as blind? Of course, she can't see the real you, but can't she feel all your hair and fangs? Cecilia does touch you, doesn't she?" Lucifer had winked.

Mahway should have punched him right there. After all these years, Lucifer's insults about his wife still hurt. Yes, his wife was blind, but not unintelligent. He had stumbled upon her in the forest. She had been wandering alone and helpless. In all the years they were together, she hadn't wanted to talk about her past, and he had never asked because he didn't want to reveal anything about his prior life. Mahway had lived twice but finally experienced what it felt to be alive when he met Cecilia. They settled in a cave near Moab and were content until the day Lucifer intruded on their peaceful existence.

He remembered Lucifer had tried tempting him. "You must be running out of gold by now. For murdering David, I will give you double our usual deal. I'd offer you fame, but with your looks, the last thing you need is people noticing you. How many times have the villagers hunted you?" Lucifer guffawed.

Mahway should have pointed out that Lucifer's looks were terrifying when he displayed his true form. It wasn't fair that Lucifer could masquerade as an angel of light or disguise himself as a human and prance around freely. Instead, he stated simply, "I don't care about money."

"Fine," growled Lucifer. "Let's talk about the people you do care about, your blind wife and your freak son. You know the world is a dangerous place. Accidents happen all the time. Tragedies lurk behind every corner, and a helpless blind woman can fall off a cliff." He had snatched a tiny lizard scurrying down a branch. He tossed the creature into his mouth like a grape. The lizard's tail dangled from Lucifer's lips as he chomped.

At that moment, Mahway had known he'd do anything to save his wife. Cecilia would be heartbroken if something happened to Ariel. He tried to redirect the conversation. "Why are you targeting David?"

"David is a man after the Creator's heart, so I'm stealing his destiny," Lucifer answered. "And you're correct. It won't be easy to kill David. But Ariel has agreed to help you. It's a double miracle you and Cecilia were able to conceive, and she survived the birth."

Ariel. He couldn't remember the last time he'd seen his son. Cecilia had given him the name meaning "lion" since she had thought his infant cries sounded like tiny roars. But his son hadn't wanted to pretend to be human and continue lying to his mother. Mahway was thrilled when Ariel ran away from home. His son had taken too much of his wife's time. With him gone, he had Cecilia all to himself.

"My spies have discovered a place where David is alone," Lucifer said. "After a battle, he cleanses himself in the waterfall at En Gedi, rinsing away the blood of his enemies. And that's where you and Ariel will pounce on him."

The plan sounded simple, but the execution was anything but easy.

Mahway recalled the mossy smell of the slippery rocks lining En Gedi's waterfall. His stomach clenched when he caught the faint stench of sulfur blowing from the Dead Sea, reminding him of hell. Just as Lucifer had predicted, David stood on a rock platform, under the frothy white falling water. He scrubbed his enemies' blood from his fingernails. Green vines like thick curtains draped behind him, giving the cascading water an emerald sheen. He was alone.

Then, Mahway smelled smoke through the damp air. He guessed David's elite guards were lighting a fire in the cave. Getting into position, Mahway had crouched behind four slimy boulders. Ariel crept along a natural rock ledge to the left of David, spear in hand. His dark golden fur and tan skin blended in with the smooth, glistening rocks. Ariel nodded to Mahway as he approached the waterfall. David tilted his head back and ran his fingers through his wet hair, oblivious that death lurked. Ariel bent his arm, ready to thrust the spear into David's back. Mahway dug his toes into the jagged underwater rock formation, preparing to soar through the air and attack David's throat.

The vines behind David parted. A muscular man wearing a short tunic emerged, stabbing Ariel in the heart sending him flying off the platform and into the water. He had sunk like an anchor. Mahway, desperate to flee, attempted to dive under the water to escape. But he couldn't move. *My foot.* Trapped in a crevice.

"Benaiah, kill the second beast in one stroke. If you succeed, you will be my captain," David called as he moved away from the water spray and looked at Mahway with disgust.

The mighty warrior snatched up Ariel's spear and dove into the water. Mahway cursed. Acting quickly, he kicked the boulder off his stuck foot while reaching for the knife strapped to his calf.

Too late.

Benaiah hurled the spear. Cold steel pierced his skull. Images of Cecilia's long flowing hair and trusting eyes flashed in front of him before he fell into the water. Everything went dark. Then, a wave of heat scorched his face, and he woke in hell.

Mahway couldn't bear the thought of Cecilia stumbling alone in the world without him. He debated possessing her, but couldn't bring himself to control her body. He assumed they'd be reunited in hell. Lucifer and the other demons even agreed not to torture her. Cecilia loved the heat of the summer. Maybe eventually, she'd get used to hell's intense heat, too.

To get his desired outcome, Mahway had possessed a man and shoved Cecilia off a cliff. Once he had killed Cecilia, Mahway persuaded his wife's killer to leap off the same ledge. After all, the man deserved to die for murdering his wife. *Surprise, surprise.* Cecilia had ended up in Paradise. Maybe the Creator had given her a pass since she had unknowingly married a demon, or he had showed mercy since she was blind.

The memory ended as rocks began to fly away from Mahway's eyes and head.

Lucifer hovered over him, crimson eyes glowing with excitement. "Did you miss me?

"What took you so long?" Mahway grumbled. "I've been summoning you."

"Getting you some help." Lucifer waved his hand toward Ohya and Hahya who were flinging rocks off his body. But Lucifer had brought a third man.

Freed from the boulders, Mahway sat up, rubbing his eyes. "Ariel? It's been so long," he murmured. A maelstrom of emotions sloshed in his stomach—Ariel had avoided Mahway for nearly a thousand years after the incident at En Gedi. But now he could breathe new life into Cecilia's memory, unearthing a magical time that had been buried under layers of sorrow and regret.

"Don't get all sentimental on me," Ariel snarled. "The only reason I've agreed to this plan is so I can rescue Mother and drag her back to hell where she belongs." Ariel flipped his mane back.

Mahway leapt off the ground. Grabbing his axes and bursting over the treacherous avalanche of boulders, he surged ahead to the next barricade.

He didn't need Ariel's help. The last time they had worked together had been a catastrophe.

27

> **"The LORD will be at war with Amalek from generation to generation."**
>
> —Exodus 17:16 (HCSB)

Susa, Persia, Adar 14, 473 BC
The fifty-seventh hour in hell

The angels' soothing singing had stopped.

Where am I? Hannah realized she lay on her side in a courtyard, her knees tucked close to her chest, her left cheek pressed into the rocky ground. She looked up and gasped—ten men had been impaled on poles, blood trickling from their throats.

She scooted away and managed to stand on wobbly legs. There was an eleventh pole higher than the others, and from it hung a skeleton with a black bag covering its head. *That must be Haman, and the others are his sons.* Hannah remembered there was an eight-month delay between Haman's execution and when Esther pronounced the death sentence over his wicked sons. Hannah's stomach twisted as she looked at the corpses. *They are just Amalekites.* The enemy of her people. And because of Esther's bravery, the Amalekites had vanished from the world.

Liraz, Dismas, and her brother scrambled to their feet, also gaping at the bodies.

"What happened here?" Liraz looked at the long poles with revulsion.

"Haman and his sons," Hannah answered. "Once King

Xerxes realized Haman had tricked him into killing all the Jewish people, including Esther, the king executed him on the spot. Although the king couldn't repeal his first order, he issued a second order, declaring the Jews may defend themselves against anyone attacking them. It looks like Haman's ten sons tried assaulting the Jews, but it didn't end well for them. I'm guessing the angels sent us back to the second day of the purge."

Hannah turned her attention to a nearby yellow house with boarded-up windows, similar in size to her parents' home. She had hoped to see Queen Esther in the palace, since she adored the woman's unlikely story of transformation from orphan to queen by winning the favor of a pagan king. Hannah even modeled Esther's prayer life. When her family had discovered Seth missing, Hannah had prayed and fasted for three days. Unlike Esther, Hannah's prayers had gone unanswered.

Benjamin pointed. "I see it. The key piece is tied to the wood beam under Haman's feet." A glass rectangle fragment glistened in the blistering sun.

Dismas lifted his head, "It's a long way up,"

"I'm an expert at climbing trees." Benjamin began shimmying up the pole. "Look, there are even little knots in the tree trunk."

Hannah had knots in her stomach watching her brother climb. "Be careful."

"As opposed to being dangerous?" Benjamin smirked. He grabbed the key piece and placed it in his pocket. Then he froze, concern spreading across his face. He scurried down.

Dismas stood on his tiptoes "What's going on?"

"A battle is headed this way," said Benjamin, his voice frantic as he slipped.

Hannah prayed silently, *Lord, make his feet like a deer's hind feet. In Jesus' name.*

In the distance, swords clanged and people screamed.

Through a small crumbling section of the courtyard wall, Hannah spied neighing Persian horses sprinted down the street, their braided manes and tails flailing. Riders on their backs released a torrent of arrows with precision. Anguished cries followed and the thuds of bodies hitting the road.

"Hurry," whispered Hannah.

While Benjamin remained an easy target, Dismas and Liraz crouched and crept on the ground.

An arrow whizzed by, striking Benjamin's arm. He fell and landed hard on his back. Hannah raced to her brother and knelt beside him. Benjamin moaned and his eyelids fluttered. *He's wounded. But if he dies... again, my brother will be sent back to hell.* Hannah's heart pounded.

The courtyard door burst open, and a woman strode in. Her face streaked with tears, she wore a black pleated skirt down to her calves, short leather boots with leopard cuffs, a purple cloak, and a leather headpiece with brown circular patches and five vultures perched on top. "The arrow that struck him has been poisoned by the deadly orange and black beetles," the strange woman said, the phony vultures bobbing with each word. "Quick, take him inside where we can find a knife to cut out the poison."

Poison. She refused to let Benjamin die again. "Do what she says," ordered Hannah.

Liraz and Dismas gently carried Benjamin toward the house.

"Hurry," the woman urged. "It's not safe for Jews wandering the streets. The palace cavalry might pass through again and shoot us all."

Odd. How did she recognize us as Jews? It must be our simple robes.

Benjamin winced, face as white as lamb's wool. When they reached the door, Hannah hesitated. A pagan carving of a winged man hung above the entry. Benjamin moaned and she raced after the men. As she stepped across the threshold, the pungent smell of incense reached her.

The woman pointed to an open door. "Right in there is the knife and strips of cloth to wrap the wound. I'll bring some salt water."

Liraz and Dismas entered and gingerly placed Benjamin on two oversized purple cushions in the center of the room. Hannah stood at the doorway, watching. Then, nails dug into her back and shoved her into the room. Behind her, the door slammed and a key clicked in the lock.

Hannah's heart dropped as dark clouds shifted across a window cut into the roof, casting a haunting glow. Baal appeared in paintings on the ceiling around the skylight and in statues along the walls. Before her, a low wooden table was adorned with figures of the pagan god and a purple satchel next to the glowing incense burner. An ornate floor-length mirror leaned against fiery-red walls, reflecting the numerous cow faces of Baal. The woman had trapped them in a Baal worship room.

Hannah banged on the door. "Let us out!"

The woman cackled, then exclaimed in a shrill voice, "I've caught four Jews, and now it will give me immense pleasure to watch you die. An eye for an eye, the four of you for my ten sons and husband. I'm going to get Haman's brothers and bring them back to torture and kill all of you. If I don't return, you'll perish from hunger. Either way, I'll get my revenge."

"Open this door! We had nothing to do with the death of your family," Hannah pleaded, jiggling the handle. "Please help my brother."

"It was all a trap, foolish girl. The boy isn't poisoned, but soon he will die by the sword. I and my brothers-in-law will chop and slice you into little pieces and offer them to Baal." The woman's boots clacked on the tiles as she ran out of the house and slammed the front door.

"Who is that horrid woman?" demanded Liraz

"Haman's wife, the wicked Zeresh." Hannah shook her head. "I can't believe I fell for it. Now I remember, Haman had the gallows built at his house to kill Esther's uncle. The entire family is evil." She kicked the door and then turned her attention to her brother.

"We can't wait until the living creatures turn up." Liraz yanked the arrow out of Benjamin's arm.

Benjamin bit his lip, trying not to cry out.

Dismas ripped the hem of his robe and wrapped it around Benjamin's arm. "See, the bleeding stopped." He finished dressing the wound.

Hannah exhaled—Benjamin's face was no longer pale.

"The old hag had me believing I was poisoned," Benjamin snapped. He sat up and reached into his robe pocket, handing Hannah the glass key piece.

Dismas squinted "That's a diamond, with another cutout of a cross."

"Odd," Hannah reached into her pocket and held up the key. The diamond piece soared to the red post under the ivory bit. "It's another bit piece. Those are the parts that turn in the lock." Hannah slid the key back into her pocket. Relief washed over her. *This will be over soon and Benjamin is fine.*

Liraz glanced around the room. "We need to get out before Zeresh returns."

Dismas slid the table under the skylight. "I'll hoist myself to the roof and see if there is a way to pull everyone up, too."

As Liraz helped Benjamin stand out of the way, Dismas climbed onto the table, causing the purple satchel to tumble to the floor. White stones tumbled on the tile. Carved into the individual stones were months and numbers.

Hannah stared at the pouch, her voice tight with disgust. "That's the bag Haman used to draw lots and decide which day to kill the Jews," "This entire room is ghastly. The sky window is for the practice of astrology and all the statues are for idol worship. I don't want to know what Haman did with this oversized mirror."

Just then, a word appeared on the mirror. Hannah gasped, catching the others' attention.

Benjamin rubbed his eyes. "Now what trickery is afoot?"

Dismas' jaw dropped and Liraz's eyes narrowed as they watched more words form.

They read in unison, "The one you seek has a sad sort of tale. In the morning, this male became like a camel crying in the desert. Around lunch he was like a whale diving underwater. For an after-dinner dance, his head was severed, and served like a fish on a silver platter. Fools, can you guess who I am? From your adversary, Lucifer."

Hannah's mind went blank. All she could focus on was how the words had appeared.

"Impossible," shouted Benjamin.

Dismas tilted the mirror forward and looked behind it, "Someone is tricking us,"

"Demons and fallen angels use mirrors like portals between the physical and spiritual worlds," explained Liraz. "Haman must have summoned Lucifer himself to help him plot against the Jews."

"Maybe if we answer the riddle, the living creatures will come," Hannah said hopefully. She returned her attention to the words on the mirror.

"Jonah, he was in a whale," guessed Benjamin.

"The main clues," said Dismas, "are camel, underwater, head, and platter."

But how do these four things connect? "It's John the Baptist," Hannah murmured.

Immediately, the sentences disappeared.

"It was the talk of the town when King Herod cut off John's head and served it on a silver platter," said Benjamin.

"What do the camel and the whale have to do with John?" asked Liraz.

"John wore clothes made of camel's hair and he told people to repent because the kingdom of God was coming. John baptized me in the river Jordan." Tears came to Hannah's eyes thinking of her mother standing by her in the river.

"I've trapped them in Baal's room," Zeresh's voice came from outside the courtyard.

A man yelled, "Let's kill them and throw their bodies to the dogs."

Footsteps pounded like drumbeats down the hall toward them.

"We answered the riddle," Hannah said, voice rising in panic, "but still no living creatures. We're stuck!"

"Hold hands, everyone," ordered Liraz as he reached for Hannah. Then, he raised their clasped hands at the mirror and commanded, "Aperi speculo."

Open the mirror. Hannah speculated the meaning as Benjamin squeezed her hand with his good arm. Dismas held his other hand. The door handle jiggled. Hannah's heart raced.

The glass portion of the mirror began swirling like metal waves. Wind whipped around the room. The Baal statues and the table toppled. Liraz tugged her hand and leapt into the mirror, pulling her behind him. She clung to her brother's and Liraz's hands.

Now she stood on a tarnished silver bridge surrounded in gray fog. Hannah glanced back at the mirror and saw Zeresh charging through the door. Two of Haman's brothers followed, brandishing swords. The madwoman froze for an instant and then frantically kicked the pillows. Haman's brothers shook their fists at their sister-in-law and screamed she had wasted their time.

"I'm shutting down the portal." Liraz twisted his body toward the mirror and shouted, "Speculum confractus."

Break the mirror, which sounded perfect to Hannah. Instantly, the mirror fell forward and shattered into pieces before the portal closed. She marveled at Liraz's act. *I thought the living creatures had removed his powers.*

"Whatever you do, don't let go," warned Liraz. He added another command, "Accipe nos ad iohannem baptistam." *Take us to John the Baptist* sounded like a great idea to Hannah.

They had taken only a few steps when a figure emerged from the mist … Seth.

My husband.

28

For Haman son of Hammedatha the Agagite, the enemy of all the Jews, had plotted against the Jews to destroy them. He cast the Pur (that is, the lot) to crush and destroy them.

—Esther 9:24 (HCSB)

The tunnel under Paradise
The fifty-eighth hour in hell

Mahway still couldn't believe Ariel had volunteered to help free his mother from Paradise. Maybe Ariel's human side had kicked in. Or maybe Mahway had done something right in raising the boy. Before he patted himself on the back, he'd hear Lucifer's offer to Ariel on this fool's mission of diverting the Lake of Fire on top of Paradise.

Jesus started to speak again. "Remember how Haman issued the first decree to kill all Jews?"

Lucifer will not like this. Maybe he won't be able to hear him.

Lucifer's muscles tightened, his face contorting through a spectrum of shadowy reds, with bulging eyes primed to explode, glowing like molten lava, his spiked tail thrashing with violent fury. The air around them turned constricting like a python tightening its grip. Mahway and Hahya and Ohya took a couple giant steps away from this unpredictable spectacle

"You can hear Jesus down here?" Lucifer snarled, kicking a boulder with such force it cracked. "Can he hear us?"

"No," Ariel answered quickly. "He must still have limited hearing since he's confined to a human body."

"If he knew about our plot to kill their souls with the Lake of Fire, wouldn't he intervene to stop it?" reasoned Hahya.

Or Jesus knows the plan will not work, so he doesn't have to stop it. But Mahway didn't have the nerve to say that part out loud.

Hahya's words seem to placate Lucifer until Jesus continued speaking. "Lucifer's scheme to imprison you in hell will fail, just as Haman's plot failed. In this war between me and Lucifer, your souls are my reward, and I will escort all of you to heaven in my victory."

The people of Paradise erupted into joyous cheers and thunderous applause. Mahway's head throbbed from both their deafening volume and the magnitude of this dreadful information.

"You are wrong, Jesus." Lucifer stomped his hoof, the ground splintering beneath. "This is nothing like Persia. The people on earth have lost all hope in you. No one is praying or fasting. They are all weeping. Right now, those fools running around collecting hell's key pieces are walking right into my trap I set for them using the mirror portal." Lucifer turned his attention to the others. "Get back to work." And then he vanished.

Mahway paced, trying to concentrate on the fastest way to move the boulders as he recalled that, in an unforeseen reversal, Haman had died on his own device.

29

And anyone not found written in the book of life was thrown into the lake of fire.

—Revelation 20:15 (HCSB)

The fifty-ninth hour in hell

Hannah's body quivered as she stared at Seth.

He waded through the fog in a ghost-white hooded robe, his plump red lips parted in a bewitching smile, and his soft eyes flickered seductively. "Hannah, come to me. We can be together for all eternity."

"Seth, how is this possible?" She hesitated. Alarm bells rang through her mind. *Why wasn't he in Paradise?*

"Let go of their hands and run to me. I'll tell you every detail of the tragedy that kept me from my beautiful bride." Seth held out strong arms, ready to snatch her.

Hannah tried squirming and twisting away from Liraz and Benjamin.

Liraz dug his nails into her palm. "Don't listen to him. He's a fallen angel mimicking Seth. He'll drag you back to hell and steal the key."

"Liraz doesn't know the demons kidnapped me and are holding me hostage. If you give them the key, they will release me, and we can live in Paradise together forever."

Beelzebub and Baal emerged from the fog and dug their claws into Seth's upper arms. "We will drag him into the abyss and toss him back in a cell if you don't turn it over," threatened

Baal, baring his teeth.

"They did trap Sariel." Hannah leaned forward but Liraz yanked her arm.

"Jesus told us Seth wasn't in hell." Dismas stuck out his chin in defiance.

"I recognize that scar." Seth pointed to Dismas. "You, robbed me, and killed me on my way to bring my beautiful bride home. It's all your fault we aren't together."

"Dismas?" uttered Hannah. Her body went limp. If Liraz and her brother weren't holding her up, she would have crumpled like the walls of Jericho.

"Liar! Don't listen to him, Hannah." Dismas tried lunging forward.

Liraz grabbed his arm and said in a stern tone, "Seth will drag you back to hell."

Beelzebub said in sing-song, "Dismas is a murderer." His flies danced around his shoulder.

"Release me!" Hannah struggled to be free of her brother.

"Don't let go!" pleaded Benjamin, grasping her fingers. "Think Hannah. Did Dismas play a part in Grandfather's death *and* Seth's?" he challenged. "Someone's lying and it's not Grandfather."

"Hannah, Jesus said Seth wasn't in Paradise," reasoned Dismas. "If that's the case, then this person isn't Seth. He must be evil."

Baal pushed Seth closer to Hannah. "Give us the key and he's all yours."

Her body ached, longing for him to hold her again.

"Toss the key, now," Seth demanded with a slight growl, his brown eye's flickering with a speck of crimson.

Hannah's body trembled as if submerged in frigid waters. She clung to the memory of Seth's kind voice and compassionate eyes, torn between desperately wanting to believe it was her

Seth and not willing to be fooled.

Another white hooded figure emerged behind Seth.

"Father?" Benjamin asked cautiously.

Hannah tore her eyes from Seth and examined her father—his brown eyes appeared lifeless.

"Yes, son, it's me," he said in a stiff tone. "Hannah, toss the key to me and I will forgive you for stating you hate me. I love you, daughter."

Hannah couldn't move her lips, so she shook her head. How she had longed to hear those words from her earthly father, but this being had coldness in his voice and no life in his eyes.

"Benjamin, my heir and my son in whom I'm well pleased, seize the key from Hannah. We can find the rest of the key pieces together."

"Yes Father." Benjamin took a step forward but both Hannah and Dismas yanked him back.

"It's not him. When has Father ever been pleased with anyone or anything?" challenged Hannah. She glared at the fallen angel pretending to be her father. "I forgive you, Father, for your part in killing Jesus."

At the mention of Jesus, her father's eyes turned to obsidian, while Seth's now resembled smoldering crimson embers. Pure evil. Hannah could play games, too, and she'd won this round.

Twenty black-robed evil angels descended to the bridge like a pack of vultures landing one by one, ready to devour them. Hannah's heart raced. She stepped to the edge of the bridge. *Trapped again.*

"I couldn't fathom being married to you for five minutes," Seth hissed. "You're an insufferable, stupid, pathetic, ugly woman."

It's not Seth, Hannah kept reminding herself, yet each accusation felt like a slap. She blinked and swallowed, trying to hold back hot tears.

"Seth, you forgot to add 'disobedient daughter' to Hannah's list of sins," her father said. "She broke the fifth commandment: You shall honor your father and mother. How many times have you murmured your hatred of me, your loving father?"

Hot shame surged in her cheeks. *How does this evil being know I'd disrespected my father?*

The thing resembling her father licked his lips, leapt in the air, and dropped with a thud in front of Hannah. Seth and the other fallen angels, half running on their legs and half flapping their wings, sped toward them. Hannah took a step back, tottering on the edge of the bridge. As the evil beings descended upon them, she saw their sharp teeth and claws ready to strike.

Hannah whispered, "Liraz, can't you say some Latin words to make them disappear or get us off this bridge?"

"I've got nothing." Liraz stood his ground. "The living creatures will have to rescue us."

The demons stretched out their claws.

Hannah took a half step backward—her heels teetered over the edge.

"Remember what Moses said at the Red Sea?" Benjamin's voice was uncertain. "Fear not, stand firm, and see the salvation of the Lord."

Hannah grasped her brother's hand, and he winced. She whispered, "Sorry, my faith is not the type to stand still and do nothing." In her other hand, she squeezed Liraz's hand and then thrust her body back, leaping off the bridge causing them to plummet like crippled birds.

Her hands slipped from Liraz and her brother, and she was free-falling.

Alone.

Her stomach flipped as she bent her legs to her chest and clasped her knees. Hannah became totally immersed in a dense, white fog. She couldn't tell what direction she tumbled—north, south, east, or west. The screeching from the sinister fallen angels faded.

Then, a burst of brilliant light blinded her. She stopped plummeting, and the sound of flapping wings gave her the sense of being carried. She touched the fabric around her. *Am I in a sack?* After several seconds, light filtered through, and she pressed her forehead against the gold, silky material. An enormous angel clutched the top of her bag like a sack of vegetables. The angel had a long, white, elegantly curved neck like a giant stork. She spotted three identical angelic beings bearing similar sacks. *I hope those are Benjamin, Dismas, and Liraz.* Hannah trembled. *But are these angels good or evil?*

"You're safe now. You're very safe. I'm an angel of reassurance. My name is Samuel." Through the gossamer bag, Hannah saw the angel's smile, gray eyes sparkling. Coupled with his soothing voice, Hannah's body relaxed.

Something tickled her foot. She reached down and picked up a bird feather. Inside the bag were assorted sizes and colors of delicate plumes.

"They are symbols of reassurance," explained Samuel.

"I don't understand." *All feathers do is help birds fly.*

"Have you ever asked God if you should follow a certain path? And at that precise moment you glance down and find a special feather in your path. Doesn't it encourage you? Sometimes it's the discovery of a coin, or a butterfly landing, or a stunning rainbow in the sky. All these items bring hope or reassurance to those who need it or are looking for divine guidance. One just needs to open one's eyes."

"The day I received the news of Seth's disappearance," Hannah said, her voice growing excitement, "I found a dove feather, stumbled upon a shekel, watched purple butterflies flit around me, and later, a rainbow arched across the sky. All those signs had filled me with hope."

"That was us. Look to your right, Dismas is secured in the coin bag, Benjamin is bouncing around in the butterfly bag, and Liraz is nestled in the rainbow sack." Gazing through the fabric, her eyes widened in awe. The trio of angels, with their glistening white wings, soared nearby. These celestial beings held her companions in their satchels, clutched close as if cradling precious gems. She strained to catch the faint sound of Dismas' voice.

He harrumphed in his bag. "I think these angels have indulged in strong drink. I've never been reassured by a found coin, feather, or a rainbow."

A blush crept over Hannah's face, embarrassed for believing a Seth-lookalike fallen angel over Dismas. But seeing Seth's likeness had stirred her. She had to ask Samuel, "Is Seth still alive?" Hope surged. *But if he's alive, and I'm dead, what does it matter?*

"Can't answer. I'm assigned to deliver feathers to reassure humans,"

"I'd be reassured knowing what happened to Seth. Every day, the not knowing has been torture for me." Hannah gulped and forced down her tears.

"Our Father sees your pain and hears your prayers. We hardly come by this way when we happened upon you dropping from the sky. The evil ones scattered like the wind when they saw us." Samuel's wings slowed and he began to glide. "Be prepared. I'm dropping you off at your destination. Benjamin, Dismas, and Liraz are already waiting for you. Hurry, time is of the essence." Hannah's heart raced as she held up her thumb—a small, stubborn remnant of darkness persisted—she estimated four hours left.

Hannah peered through the bag again and spied the men standing inside a shimmering, arched, gold doorway. The gold bricks of the entire building glistened. Next to the door were floor to ceiling windows. The structure stretched far into the sky and appeared to have no end. A bright green canopy of trees lined the golden path, leading to the building and through the gardens. A sweet rose fragrance filled her nostrils.

"What is this place?" asked Hannah.

"It's the Book of Life Library. Everyone has a story." Samuel shook his head in dismay. "Except some humans' books never arrive inside."

Hannah hoped she had a book in there.

"No need to worry. Your story has volumes." Then, Samuel grew serious. "There's not much time. You need to locate John the Baptist's book. Open it and you will find the key piece."

"The place is enormous. How will we find it?" asked Hannah.

Samuel didn't answer but tossed her sack into the open door. She tumbled out onto the mahogany floor next to her brother. Hannah sprang to her feet and plucked feathers from her robe. Samuel gave her a reassuring smile and flew away with the other angels.

Hannah glanced around the room. A cozy, wood-burning, white stone fireplace, two oversized purple chairs, and a chestnut brown table with a stack of books. But Hannah didn't recognize the writing. Candles flickered on the wall. *Maybe this is a reading room.* She hugged her brother and gave a weak smile to Liraz. "I can't believe you pushed us through the mirror."

Dismas stared at her with newfound respect. "Hannah, when you shoved us off the bridge, I thought I was going to die and end up back in Paradise before the angel caught me in that coin sack."

Hannah winced at the reminder of Seth and her father and their accusations against her.

Benjamin crossed his arms. "I thought the living creatures removed your powers, Liraz. How did you open the mirror?"

"I may look like a man, but underneath this form I must still carry some angelic essence. The words of angels hold power, which is one of reasons why the Lord put us to sleep in Tartarus. My words combined with the mirror Haman probably used to communicate with fallen angels and demons enabled me to open the portal." Liraz shifted his feet and changed the subject.

"Did anyone's angel reveal why they brought us here? Mine refused to converse with me."

"The Book of John the Baptist," Benjamin and Dismas said in unison.

"I think we're in a reading room," Hannah said. "Let's go to the hall."

Their footsteps echoed down the endless corridor. Dismas stepped into the first room to the right. It held a white marble fireplace at the rear. Three worn, oversized leather chairs with matching footstools arranged in a half circle sat in front of floor to ceiling windows overlooking a brick terrace with more gardens. Suspended from the ceiling, flickering white candles hung in clusters of diamonds. Bookshelves lined three of the walls.

Liraz whispered, "See, the spine of the book has the name. *This one says The Life and Times of Adam.*"

The design of the book reminded Hannah of tree bark. Wait, is it hissing at us? She leaned in for a closer look.

"*Eve: The Mother of All Who Live.*" Benjamin tugged on an apple-red book. It wouldn't budge.

"Smells like apples." Dismas sniffed. "How can we find one specific book? This place looks like a maze and goes on forever."

Hannah remembered the angel's advice about praying. She bowed her head and said a silent prayer to find the right book. When she looked up again, there was movement in the grand entrance. They rushed to the doorway and saw feathers floating down the hall.

Hannah nudged Benjamin. "We need to follow them." The four sprinted after the feathers, their footsteps echoing in the never-ending corridor, where ancient doors stood like sentinels. Framed pictures of people from countless time periods adorned the walls—a tapestry of humanity. The feathers led them to a room with a gold plaque above the solid silver door reading "Hall of Prophets." More feathers floated into the room and stopped at a large shelf of oversized books. A feather disappeared inside a book almost as tall as Hannah.

"This is it!" Hannah pointed to a blue book. Etched in simple silver lettering on the spine was *The Life of John the Baptizer, Son of Zechariah and Elizabeth.*

Benjamin tugged at the book with both hands. "I need help."

Liraz clutched the top half of the book and grunted. "A little more help?"

Dismas grabbed the bottom of the book. They counted to three and yanked. Finally, the book slid off its shelf.

"Can't hold on …" Benjamin lost his grip.

The book wobbled.

Dismas tried guiding the book out of the shelf, but it slipped from his hands and fell to the floor with a thump. It looked like a door rather than a book. Engraved into the front cover were drawings of people.

Hannah peered at the cover. "The pictures reveal John's story. There's John's father, a priest burning incense in front of a massive angel."

Liraz pointed at the angel. "Gabriel is one of the highest-ranking angels in the army of God. John must have been in trouble."

Hannah leaned forward, relishing the chance to explain, "Gabriel informed Zechariah he would have a son who would grow into a great prophet and announce Jesus' coming. Zechariah refused to believe, since he and his wife were old. Gabriel made him mute until John was born."

Liraz snickered. "Humans don't understand the power of life and death is in the tongue. You are snared by the words of your mouth."

Hannah willed herself not to roll her eyes. Had Liraz whispered promises in his wife's ear that she'd survive Leviathan's attack before she drowned? Every time she professed her conviction that Seth would eventually return, her family and friends would exchange pitying glances, inquire if she needed to rest, or discreetly murmur that she was a fool behind her back.

Dismas pointed to a man with wild hair down to his elbows. "Is that John?"

Benjamin snorted. "A lunatic. He ate only locusts and wild honey and wore a tunic made of itchy camel hair."

A locust flew out from the pages and water dripped on Hannah's toes. "The book seems like it's alive," she said. "Well, what are we waiting for? Dismas, open the book!" She sure hoped the key piece was inside.

Dismas opened the cover and water rushed out like a river.

Hannah jerked back. *The water is headed straight for the other books!* But a glance over her shoulder revealed the library walls had disappeared. Her feet became stuck in mud and the smell of salt water filled the air. Hannah knew where they were, and her heart ached for home and familiar surroundings.

30

[Herod] gave orders to massacre all the male children in and around Bethlehem who were two years old and under.

—Matthew 2:16 (HCSB)

Jordan River, AD 2
Half past the fifty-ninth hour in hell

Dismas found himself waist deep in murky, chilly water and John the Baptist's hand pressed against his forehead. Hannah leaned in and whispered in his ear, "You're next in line to get baptized by him."

Behind John on the riverbank, the adults sang psalms of deliverance while others wept. The Pharisees, arms crossed, looked down on the celebrations.

"Repent, for the kingdom of heaven is at hand." John placed his other hand firmly on Dismas' back.

He saw an encouraging smile from Hannah as John tilted him back and immersed him beneath the murky water. Besides theft, what additional things did he need to repent of? Dismas squirmed. Time seemed to stand still below the water. He needed air. Muscular arms pinned him under the water. Dismas couldn't breathe. *Maybe the Baptizer is killing me for my crimes.* He kicked and flayed his arms. Finally, John released him.

As he broke through the surface, Dismas heard a whisper. *"Bitterness and unforgiveness are blocking your heart and hurting your soul."*

His fist balled, ready to punch John, but Dismas stood alone on the riverbank. *What's happening.*

"Hannah?" he breathed, his voice strained with desperation.

A frog croaked in response.

Farther down the riverbank, Dismas spotted two boys playing, leaping over and around the intricate roots of the aged oaks. The roots twisted and gnarled like skeletal fingers, reaching toward the water's edge as if thirsting for the cool embrace of the murmuring river. The older boy, about ten, began making a green reed into a whistle. Raising the crafted whistle to his lips, he emitted a series of sharp notes. The infectious giggles of the younger child, barely two, made Dismas smile.

The rays of the fading sun left red streaks on the river, like blood. Dismas' chest tightened. John had baptized him in the middle of the day. *Where is everyone? Could this be another trick from Lucifer?*

A gray-haired woman staggered toward the boys. The toddler on her hip peeked out from under a blue-and-white prayer shawl, revealing blond ringlets. She gently set the toddler on the ground next to the other boys and said through labored breaths, "Mother needs to rest."

Dismas noticed the two children appeared almost identical in age and features.

She looked over her shoulder. "I hope I lost them." She bit her lip as tears streamed down her face.

"Who?" the older boy narrowed his eyes.

"Herod's men. They seek to kill my son."

Is this Elizabeth and John? Dismas wondered.

"Why would anyone want to kill him?"

Elizabeth wiped her eyes and steadied her breathing. "Haven't you heard King Herod's decree that any baby boy under two shall be killed? You shouldn't be in the open with him."

"You're mistaken,The murders are in Bethlehem. It's safe here." He pointed to his brother. "Nepheg is safe."

The two little ones grasped the prayer shawl and tugged it back and forth, covering their faces with it.

"There is no such thing as a safe infant right now," Elizabeth's, lip quivered. "This morning, those brutal Romans murdered my husband right in the temple since he refused to reveal the locations of my son or my nephew. A priest slipped out of the temple and warned me of the search. I picked up John and fled. The soldiers have been trailing me all day. Somehow, I've managed to elude them, but they are still close. We need to take the boys and hide in those caves."

"Woman, I am not going anywhere. My parents forbid me to leave this area."

John snatched the prayer shawl from Nepheg's head. "Mine," he said wrapping himself in it from head to toe

The thunder of horses' hooves rolled toward them and Dismas spotted the soldiers brandishing torches.

Elizabeth grimaced as she whispered, "Hide in the reeds before they spot us."

In a panic, the older boy snatched the small boy closest to him and bolted toward the reeds. Elizabeth grabbed the other child and tried following, but her foot snagged on a tree root at the riverbank. The toddler wailed as she stumbled. Elizabeth placed a hand over his mouth, but it was too late. The riders raced toward them.

Dismas debated if he should help them, but he remembered the living creatures had warned them not to interfere with the timeline. Besides, he knew John lived into adulthood.

Ten soldiers dismounted and surrounded Elizabeth like a pack of wolves.

"How dare you defy King Herod by fleeing with this child," the commander demanded..

"You can't take him." Elizabeth held the boy against her chest. "My living God is watching over John."

One of the soldiers waved his torch and scoffed. "Today, our mighty Zeus guided us to you."

"Seize the baby," the commander told another soldier.

Elizabeth clutched John closer and held up her free arm to block the soldier. But the Roman grabbed him from her. John howled in protest as the soldier lifted him to one of the cavalry officers.

"We will spare you the agony of seeing your child perish," said the commander as he kicked his horse's sides and departed. The rest of his men followed. The cries faded as the horses vanished into the night.

Elizabeth crumpled and wept uncontrollably under the oblivious shine of the moon and stars.

The reeds parted and the boy, little brother tangled in the prayer shawl in tow, walked to Elizabeth. Her sobs came in a hiccupping rhythm. The boy placed his hand on Elizabeth's trembling shoulder and murmured, "Sorry."

Under the shawl, a chubby hand reached for Elizabeth. "Mama?"

Elizabeth sprang to her feet. "John?" She whipped off the shawl. "That's my child!"

"No!" The boy held up the baby and gasped in disbelief.

Elizabeth gently took her son. "The Romans came so quickly. Your brother and John were playing with my shawl. You were brave to protect your brother, but the darkness must have concealed their identities." Elizabeth released a guttural sob. "You're not to blame."

"My stepfather will never forgive me. It's all your fault for coming here!"

"What is your name?" Elizabeth placed a trembling hand on his shoulder.

"Barabbas." He swatted her hand away.

The world stopped. From his hiding place, Dismas studied the boy. Same wide-set brown eyes, same thin lips, and the right age.

"I picked up the wrong child, and now Nepheg is dead." Tears flowed down the boy's face.

"Barabbas, it's not your fault. You are not to blame. It's that cruel Herod and those ruthless Roman soldiers. How could they kill an innocent baby?" Elizabeth sobbed out the last words. Her shoulders sagged and she looked like she had aged another fifteen years.

"It's all your fault. If you hadn't come here, my brother would be alive."

"Barabbas, you are right to blame me. I should have never stopped here." Still holding her baby, Elizabeth fell on her knees. "Oh Lord, help Barabbas and his family."

"God. I want nothing to do with your God. Before Nepheg's birth, my stepfather beat me. But afterwards, he did not. I figured the love my stepfather had for Nepheg held his hatred for me at bay. Now Nepheg's gone, and it's all my fault. The beatings will start again, but this time, I deserve it."

"Come with us," Elizabeth pleaded. "We are going to live among the Essenes. A few of their members are meeting us in the cave. They will protect you, and I will raise you as my own child."

"I will never be holy enough to be accepted by the Essenes. Besides, woman, have you looked in the mirror?" Barabbas gave a spiteful chuckle. "You're old. I must tell my parents about the fate of Nepheg."

"I will go with you to your—"

But Barabbas fled across the riverbank.

"No, don't go without me." Elizabeth attempted to run after Barabbas while balancing John on her hip, she stumbled on an uneven stone, twisting her ankle. With determination and a tight grip on John, she regained her composure, straightened her back and planted a kiss on his forehead. "I'll never find him. I'm too slow. We need to pray for Barabbas every single day of our lives." She held John close and took measured, limping steps in the direction of the caves nestled in Elijah's Hill.

As Dismas mulled over Barabbas's tragic past, he caught a glimpse of a pearlescent rectangle key piece bearing the imprint of the cross lying in a soldier's sandal print on the riverbank. He rushed over and touched it.

Immediately, he was transported back to the library. *The Life of John the Baptizer book was closed.*

Hannah rushed toward him. "Where have you been? After John baptized us, we returned here."

He couldn't bring himself to tell them what had happened. He still couldn't even believe it. Dismas held up the pearl rectangle. "I found what we needed."

"You're pale, like you've seen a ghost." Hannah accepted the piece from him. She held it to the key and the pearl bit snapped into place under the two others.

Liraz squinted. "Looks like another bit or an ornate gem covering the key's tip. I think we need only one more piece."

"And there's only a sliver of darkness remaining." Benjamin held up his thumb. "Don't let our guard down. Lucifer will be lurking about."

Dismas focused on helping Liraz and Benjamin heave the book back onto the shelf. "Why did King Herod kill little boys?" he asked.

Liraz arched an eyebrow. "He must have been a vile beast or Lucifer whispered in his ear."

Hannah answered, "I heard one disciple tell a story about the night Jesus was born and an unusual star appeared. Three wise men from Persia thought it indicated the birth of the Jewish Messiah, so they journeyed to where the star shone down. On their quest, they met King Herod, who asked them to reveal the child's location under the pretense of wanting to worship him. When the wise men didn't return, King Herod decreed all babies around the age of Jesus be killed. But why do you ask?"

Benjamin interjected, "If the wise men were so learned, why did they even stop at Herod's in the first place?"

Dismas couldn't hold back a belly laugh.

Hannah giggled. "That's the first time I've heard you laugh." She leaned toward the door.

Another feather floated past.

The angels of reassurance!" Benjamin called out, tagging Dismas with a grin. "Last one there's a snail!"

Laughing, they chased the feather down the hall toward the front door. Blinding yellow light flooded in as Dismas pulled it open, forcing him to squint. Through the glare, he could barely make out four figures, each clutching open bags.

"Hurry, jump in the sacks and we will take you to the living creatures," one said with a croak.

Dismas hesitated. The voice didn't reassure him, but he stepped into the coin bag. His angel tightened his grip on the satchel and flew. Dismas shifted inside the sack and an undeniable sulfur odor wafted up his nostrils.

31

"For if you forgive people their wrongdoing, your heavenly Father will forgive you as well. But if you don't forgive people, your Father will not forgive your wrongdoing."

—Matthew 6:14–15 (HSCB

The tunnel under Paradise
The sixtieth hour in hell

Mahway breathed a sigh of relief. The stone trench running through the tunnel was complete. A demon crew had finished applying pitch along the trench and stone structures supporting it to contain the fire. Lucifer rationalized the pitch had held the ark together, so the sticky tar should prevent the flames from jumping the trench or melting the stones and spreading through hell. The Lake of Fire couldn't burn the pitch, but it melted iron. Mahway's eyes darted to exit routes in case he had to prepare for a swift departure.

He ran through the plan: Once they destroyed Jesus' soul, any Paradise prisoners not consumed by the flames would be dragged back to hell by the demons and tormented. During the chaos, he'd grab Cecilia.

Mahway gripped a chisel and hammer and chipped away at the red circular line in the black hardened lava, marking the Lake of Fire's point of entry. He stood shoulder to shoulder with five other demons. They had to remain vigilant constantly—not wanting to alert the captives to their position, they could strike only when the Paradise losers cheered or applauded.

Currently, Jesus spoke about the nearness of the kingdom of God and suggested it was time to forgive others and love those who had hurt them. A hush fell over the crowd.

Mahway could feel a rush of anger surge in his body. *Forgiveness*. Why would Jesus speak about this miserable topic? No one rejoiced in forgiving others. Fallen angels and demons held on to grudges, both small and huge, for all eternity.

He stole a quick look at Naphil and imagined him in the Lake of Fire. Mahway justified his vengeance this demon had killed the man Mahway had enjoyed possessing the most. The memory was still clear. Mahway had warned Naphil to stop frightening their host or risk giving the man a heart attack. Predictably, that's exactly what happened, leaving Mahway to endure a long and frustrating search for a new suitable host.

His own son had been invited to Pergamon dozens of times when Mahway had been there only twice. Envy washed over him as he glared at Ariel. *No thanks. I'll hold on to my bitterness and let it grow into something stunning—even weeds fester into flowers.*

Jesus continued, "When I rise from the grave, there will be an enormous burst of energy, and some of you standing here might wake up in a tomb and find yourselves alive again. Go home and find your friends and family. This will be a wonderful opportunity to make amends with your loved ones. All the men and women who return to the land of the living, remember to share what you have witnessed down here and spread the good news to bring my flock into my Father's kingdom."

Mahway seethed. *That's the plan?* Some humans would return to earth, and when they died for a second time, they would arrive in heaven. And none of the ones rising from hell included the mighty Nephilim.

Upon hearing the information, the Paradise prisoners erupted into applause. Mahway and the demons used the cover of noise to strike the molten rock with a renewed fury. The Nephilim ceased when the cheers waned.

"Remember to forgive those who have hurt you," Jesus said. "Sometimes it's best to say it out loud."

Paradise filled with words of apologies being given and accepted.

Again, there was ample opportunity to continue chipping away at the cliff to weaken the wall.

Success. Mahway had made a tiny hole, completing his part for the next phase.

A man bellowed, "I forgive Salome for asking for my head on a platter."

Fool. Taking your head is an unforgivable offence. This Salome sounds fun. After this is over, I'll ask Lucifer if she's available to possess.

Through the ruckus a familiar soft voice said, "Lord, I forgive Mahway for all he's done to me. I release the pain from my husband's lies."

Mahway almost dropped his chisel and peered through the tiny break. He gasped. There stood his wife, and she could see.

32

> *"If you ever wish to punish some man … shut him up within the bull and lay a fire beneath it; by his groanings the bull will be thought to bellow and his cries of pain will give you pleasure as they come through the pipes in the nostrils."*
> —Perilaus, as quoted in Diodorus Siculus: Library of History, Volume IV

The sixty-first hour in hell

Dismas stared through the scratchy white-gray bag as Asmoday materialized through the dwindling light. *No. I'm such a fool.* Sariel had warned them—fallen angels disguise themselves as light beings. Dismas couldn't understand how they could appear in heaven's library but not penetrate Paradise's bars. Asmoday's crimson eyes bore into him as he beat his powerful wings and clutched the bag with his talons.

Dismas clenched his teeth. "Where are you taking us?"

"For the thrill of your life." Asmoday chortled and released the sack.

Dismas gripped the cloth over his head to keep himself in the bag and prayed for God's help to end this miserable ride. Then came the swoosh of wings and his freefall stopped.

Asmoday swung the satchel. "Master desires your presence in his throne room."

"In hell?" *We can't return without the key.*

"No, fool, in the second heaven. Look down."

A white stone temple appeared, resembling a long, thin flattened horseshoe with straight sides and curved middle. A broad staircase in the center led to a raised platform. Like ants, black-robed angels gathered on the steps and flat roof. As Asmoday drew near, Dismas heard faint singing.

The deceptively beautiful voices sang terrifying words. "Evil, evil, evil is the lord Lucifer almighty. The whole earth is filled with his wickedness. You are worthy, O Lucifer, our god, to receive glory, honor, and power. For you corrupt all things and do what you please."

The sentries stationed on the roof had sinister, crow-like faces, beady red eyes, and swords in their belts. They snarled and bared sharp teeth at Dismas as Asmoday continued to drift down. Along the edges of the open building stood massive carved pillars etched with scenes depicting Lucifer and the fallen angels beheading humans and other unspeakable things. Sculpted serpents wrapped around the top of each column, holding torches in their predatory mouths.

"See the bronze bulls at both ends with smoke coming out of their nostrils?" Asmoday said. "That is where we roast disobedient humans."

Dismas gulped.

Asmoday dropped the sack behind the bull, and Dismas scrambled out. Despite the creepy place, relief rushed over him as he saw Hannah and Benjamin emerging from their bags unhurt. Dismas tensed as eight more fallen angels swarmed them. He moved closer to the siblings and looked around. Lucifer sat in the center of the platform, puffed up on the worship music. That old devil tapped his claws on the golden arms of his throne, which were molded into snakes sinking fangs into apples. His spiked tail draped lazily over the side of the throne, flicking in time with the dark melody. He seemed oblivious to their arrival. To Lucifer's right sat Beelzebub and Dagon, on his left, Baal and Moloch, each seated in smaller silver thrones.

Morax flew toward them and tossed a sack.

Liraz wobbled out and rubbed his back. "Morax, did you

forget how to land?" he shouted louder than the fallen angels' fiendish chorus.

Lucifer's eyes darted their way. "Bring my guests to me."

"Not guests. Prisoners, like everyone else," countered Liraz.

"Silence watcher-man, or I'll crush your tiny, fragile human head," Morax muttered.

The circle of fallen angels shoved Dismas, Hannah, Benjamin, and Liraz until they stood on the platform in front of Lucifer and his court. The singing ceased. Hannah pulled her brother closer and crept her way toward Dismas. Asmoday and Morax flanked Liraz and elbowed his ribs.

"Don't be timid. I will not bite." Lucifer leaned back on his throne, a sinister spreading across his ugly red face. His eyes danced in dark delight. His tail extended and pointed toward the audience. His grin widened, revealing sharp teeth that glinted in the dim light, "But some of my friends might."

The fallen angels erupted in maniacal laughter.

The beings were everywhere. Those on the bone-white steps had black circular wings over their heads resembling hooded cobras, ready to strike. Menacing faces of pigs, horses, eagles, lions, bulls, goats, and humans all had glowing red eyes. Dismas caught glimpses of fangs, horns, snouts, and beaks. He caught Hannah's gaze, who looked as terrified as he felt.

"Thanks for dropping by Pergamon, where I rule the principalities of the air in the second heaven." Lucifer gestured to a stone apple on the back of his throne. "The glorious, original apple, minus two bites, to commemorate the day I tricked Adam into eating from the tree of the knowledge of good and evil and stole the keys to hell."

Beelzebub, Dagon, Baal, and Moloch chanted in unison, "You are worthy, O Lucifer, our god, to receive glory, honor, and power." The fallen angels repeated as if in a trance.

"We have heard your origin story," Liraz shouted to be heard above the din. "Didn't you bring us here to give us a riddle?"

The fallen angels began growling.

Lucifer snarled. "Helping the enemy? I knew you'd betray me. I only picked you because you represent failure. Jesus couldn't save his good friend, the once perfect watcher angel Ramel, from being condemned to Tartarus, and he can't save the Paradise prisoners either."

"I think Jesus can do anything he wants," Liraz said, crossing his arms.

Lucifer flew out of his seat, picked Liraz off the ground, and shook him like a dirty carpet. Dismas heard bones cracking but showed no emotion. Lucifer grinned.

Hannah dangled the key to hell for all to see. "It's almost complete."

Instantly, Lucifer released Liraz and extended his claw. "Let me hold it one last time."

Liraz lay on the ground where two fallen angels picked him up and forced him to stand next to Dismas.

"Maybe if you give us the riddle." Hannah's hand shook as she placed the key back into her pocket.

Lucifer returned to his throne, straightened his crown, and thundered, "I am the second and the first. I have no voice. My blood speaks for me. Who am I?"

Benjamin looked at his shoes, and Hannah shrugged in defeat.

Beelzebub said, "They will never figure this one out." Even his flies snickered.

"Abel," Dismas said assuredly. He remembered his father had taught how Abel's blood cried out to God after Cain killed him. During the beatings Dismas endured from Barabbas, he prayed God would hear his blood spilling on the ground and strike down his stepfather.

"You're right," agreed Benjamin. "Abel was the second person to be born, but the first person to be murdered."

"Best day ever when Cain killed his brother," exclaimed Lucifer, eyes gleaming. "And the worst day was when that woman gave birth, a potential threat to me."

"How dare the Creator say her seed should bruise our heads," said Dagon defiantly.

"Those horrid newborn cries pierced our ears and drove Lucifer to break the first key piece," said Moloch.

"Time is running out," Lucifer spat as he rose, pointing furiously at them. "Hand over my key, *now*!"

"Don't do it," whispered Liraz. "Lucifer will kill us all."

Baal charged out of his chair and punched Liraz in the mouth with such force, Dismas heard his teeth shatter.

Bright red blood spewed from Liraz's lips as Lucifer said, "Shut your treasonous mouth."

"I will never give you the key," said Hannah in a quiet, even voice.

Moloch growled. "If you don't comply, we will send the demons of depression to torment your grieving parents."

Benjamin lunged at Moloch. Asmoday whacked him to the unforgiving stone floor. Hannah gasped. But her brother rose and planted his feet in a wide stance, balling his fists.

"Return the key to me, and I will stop the attack on your family," bargained Lucifer.

Hannah stood firm, her jaw tightening as she stared defiantly at Lucifer.

"Give it to me!" Lucifer flew out of his chair and towered over her. With one of his sharp talons, he touched Hannah's pocket, tracing the outline of the key. "I can make you a goddess in my kingdom."

"I don't want to be a goddess. I serve the Lord." Hannah swiped Lucifer's hand away and stepped back. "You're not getting the key."

Lucifer flinched, eyes blazing with hatred. "I tried to play nice, but you leave me with no choice. Dagon, Moloch, feed her to our bull. From her charred body, I will seize the key."

Moloch and Dagon leapt from their seats and clutched Hannah's arms, dragging her toward the bull.

Benjamin spat in Lucifer's face.

Lucifer flinched as he brushed away the spittle with his claw. "Benjamin will get a front row seat and watch you die a horrible death. Then I'll roast Liraz and Dismas."

Liraz struggled against the guards, while two more black robed fallen angels seized Benjamin and yanked him behind his sister.

Asmoday lit the hay hanging out of the bull's open mouth and the wood pile below the beast's belly. Smoke billowed from the bull's ears and sparks flew from its nostrils. Asmoday swung open the metal door in the beast's side with a clang. Hannah continued struggling against Moloch and Dagon as they forced her to bend her knees and pushed her head toward the opening. She screamed, the sound carrying through the bull's interior metal pipes and magnifying through the horns like trumpets. The fallen angels beamed, soaking up her cries. Hannah bit her lips and stopped screaming. Tears rolled down Benjamin's taut face.

Dismas' heart ached. *No. It can't end like this.* The pain of being burned alive would fade when they reentered Paradise, but failing to retrieve the key would stay with them for all eternity.

"Get the fire nice and toasty before you push her in," Lucifer goaded.

Dismas itched to punch Lucifer but shoved his fist in his pocket instead. He felt the smooth container Moses had gifted him. *The blood of Jesus! There must be a few drops in the jar from when I brushed them off the key piece back at the cross.* The blood would make the fallen angels flee. He discreetly twisted the lid, dipped the tiny hyssop branch into the container, and soaked up Jesus' blood. Then he sprinkled it toward Hannah.

Dagon and Moloch collapsed, writhing in pain. The bull broke apart and fell onto the wood, extinguishing the fire. Relief sprayed across Hannah's face as she stood atop the broken bronze bull. Her eyes widened when she saw the items in his hands.

Dismas shook the branch, splattering the red droplets everywhere. *Miraculous, Like Elisha's oil filling up the vessels,* the more he shook, the more blood there seemed to be. Blood landed on Benjamin's guards, and they fell to the ground, shrieking. Benjamin stepped over them and joined his sister.

The whole building trembled. The massive pillars toppled, causing the roof to cave in, trapping the evil beings under the wreckage. Their twisted horns and goat hooves stuck out from the carnage, and they cried in pain. The fallen angels not trapped under the rubble flew away.

Liraz rubbed his jaw. "Once the blood touched my mouth, my teeth grew back." He shook his head in disbelief.

Then came a familiar voice, "Your ride awaits!"

Relief spread through Dismas. The glorious chariot appeared to the right of the platform next to the toppled bull. Jachniel flew from under the chariot hovering at the side of the temple.

"The prince of the power of the air, pinned under his fake throne." Liraz pointed at Lucifer as Dismas helped him to the chariot.

Dismas smirked at Lucifer's crown crushed under a pillar and his prized apple broken in two.

Lucifer ordered in Latin, "Columna movere!" The pillar rolled off him. He rose shaking off the dust and debris with a growl of irritation.

Hannah leapt into the chariot as she wiped dust from her face and robe. Her eyes never left her brother as he jumped over the demolished bull, dodged the dazed fallen angels pinned under the collapsed pillars, stepped onto the chariot. The siblings embraced. Liraz and Dismas slid onto their seats. Dismas couldn't believe Jesus' blood had this effect on the fallen angels. No wonder they hated Jesus.

"In less than an hour every one of you will bow to Jesus," shouted Padel.

The fallen angels didn't respond as some still clawed their way out from the wreckage while others dug out their comrades.

Dormel chuckled. "Now there is something you don't see very often—fallen angels helping one another."

"They are living in desperate times," remarked Gonael from inside the wheel.

In a burst of flames, the chariot soared from the ruins of Pergamon and hurled toward a swirling blackhole looming ahead. Ash from the wreckage trailed behind them followed by a sea of black-robed fallen angels who stopped mid-flight and gathered in a multitude of circles, clasping their claws together. They began a collective incantation, summoning dark forces, churning Pergamon's dust into thousands of spiraling white whirlwinds now barreling toward the chariot.

Hannah squeezed her eyes shut, while Benjamin's outer robe whipped about furiously. Liraz's elbow banged against the armrest. The chariot spun out of control into the blackhole with the fallen angels' cackling laughter in the background. Darkness settled around them with only a few flickering embers remaining within the four inner wheels. Dismas clenched his jaw so tightly that his teeth ached while a tight belt cinched his waist. *What did those evil monsters do?*

33

*"Behold, I have refined you, but not as silver;
I have tried you in the furnace of affliction."*

—Isaiah 48:10 (ESV)

Mount Carmel, 863 BC
The sixty-second hour in hell

The carriage careened down the abyss. Liraz rubbed his tingling elbow and squinted, struggling to see anything. The limitations of his human form made him berate the choices he'd made. *If only...* his constant refrain.

From the bleak darkness, Jachniel's concerned voice came, "Those rebels sprang a trap, extinguishing the flames. Few embers remain—"

"Not enough power for us to travel to Adam's time," Dormel interjected, his breath ragged.

Benjamin groaned and Hannah let out a heavy sigh. Dismas stomped. Liraz's legs quivered, knowing the angels could return him to his cell at any moment.

Gonael's authoritative voice broke the tension as the chariot continued whirling widely, "Mount Carmel?"

"Brilliant," agreed Padel. "When God's fire falls, we can borrow some flames to ignite our wheels to travel back to the realm of Adam and Eve. The challenge lies in arriving on time and finding a way to seize the fire"

"The peril would be in touching the fire." Dormel roared, his voice low and ominous. A heavy cloak of doom seemed to drape over the chariot, casting a shadow on all who were aboard.

Liraz could not discern what they meant—he knew only the historical events from before he'd fallen.

"Pray," advised Jachniel.

Hannah cried out for God's intervention while Dismas and Benjamin recited rapid prayers.

Liraz pressed his lips together, declining to pray to a God he had betrayed. Ayin's eyes glimmered brightly, spinning around the wheels as if weaving their prayers into a single strand, uniting them with a shared purpose, leaving Liraz out.

Padel commanded, "Now fan your inner wheel's cinders toward Dormel." The chariot surged with renewed energy as the glowing embers sputtered. In an instant, they burst through the dark, entering a radiant beam of light emerging into a dusty blue sky.

The chariot descended on a mountaintop. Liraz's eyes widened at a multitude gathered around two altars. Among them, the Baal priests stood out—adorned in purple and red robes, with amulets of lightning bolts and bulls' heads. Blood trickled down their foreheads, staining their fervent and devoted faces as they cut themselves to move their god. Liraz shook his head. Nothing had changed since the flood.

Dried-out evergreens concealed the chariot a safe distance from the commotion. Then, a man wearing a coarse animal hair robe, leather belt, and an intense look in his eyes placed a cut up bull on the second stone altar. Modestly dressed men poured buckets of water on the sacrifice, causing an overflow into a trench at the base.

Liraz's thoughts scattered in all directions like the destruction of the tower of Babel. "What's going on?"

Hannah leaned forward. "Elijah, our Lord's prophet, challenged the Israelites to choose whom they would serve, the Lord or Baal. The prophet and the Baal priests each sacrificed a bull, awaiting the one true God's heavenly fire."

The living creatures flew out from the wheels, scattering pine needles on the ground as they hovered beside the chariot.

"Israel worshiped Baal, and because of their disobedience, the Lord caused no rain to fall for three and a half years," Padel said. "Now, it is decision time." His gaze bore into Liraz.

Liraz avoided Padel's scrutiny and shifted his attention to the valley bearing its scars, withered plants, leafless trees, and animal carcasses on the cracked ground—a mosaic of despair.

Gonael peered into the blue still sky, "It's almost three o'clock, time for fire to fall from heaven."

Dismas tilted his head. "How will you bring the fire?"

"Now is the part of the plan I despise." Padel swished his hand like a tail. "Liraz must collect a few flames."

Liraz crossed his arms. "Me? What's wrong with my companions?"

"They might burn up. The altar's going to explode, even the stones. Despite your human appearance, the coin can't hide your angelic nature. You shouldn't be harmed."

"You're all angels, too. Why don't one of you go?" fumed Liraz. *This obstinate bull intends to kill me to avoid escorting me back to Tartarus.*

"Archangel Michael ordered all of us not to interfere with this moment," informed Jachniel.

Dormel added sternly, "We don't want to distract Elijah from his task. He'll recognize us."

Hannah held up her thumb, her nail now almost bathed in white, the journey from night to day almost complete. "We must retrieve the last key piece in time," she implored, doe eyes fixed on Liraz.

Memories of Nava flashed through his mind.

Liraz stood. "I'll go." He disembarked.

Dismas peered over the side of the chariot. "How will you transport the flames back to the chariot?"

Jachniel pulled a red iron staff from his robe and turned the top, revealing a hollow interior. "It's dipped in pitch and should hold the flames."

Should? Sweat rolled down Liraz's back.

Gonael chimed in, "Be sure you're standing near the altar when Elijah says, 'O Lord God of Abraham, Isaac, and Israel.'"

"Then," Dormel continued the instructions, "dip the staff in the trench when Elijah states, 'O Lord, answer me, that this people may know that you, O Lord, are God.'"

"When everyone bows their heads, that will signal you to return to the chariot." instructed Dormel.

"Be swift. You will be in danger if you're mistaken for a prophet of Baal," warned Padel.

What have I done, volunteering for this fool's mission? He'd be burned by fire on his way back to Tartarus. *I should have stayed asleep in my cell.*

Liraz brushed his way through the evergreens, navigating through the edge of the crowd. To his left stood the Baal worshipers, freshly wounded from trying to summon their deity and disappointment etched on their faces. On the right, Israelites, with pained expressions and stooped shoulders, watched Elijah and shuffled their feet. Liraz refused to judge their divided hearts, for he himself had fallen victim to Nava's seduction and Lucifer's lies. Idolatry held a seductive allure.

A lump formed in Liraz's throat. The dusty air suffocated him, his chest tightening with each step. *I should have trusted you with Nava. Her path was destined for Paradise. I didn't save her, you did. Instead, I brought monsters into the world. Why didn't you stop me from myself?* He paused and leaned on the staff. *Forgive me, Lord, for my selfishness.*

Liraz elbowed his way into the front row, eyes fixed on the prophet who raised his hands in fervent prayer. The air crackled with anticipation, and Liraz waited for Elijah's statement, sweaty fingers grasping the rod. A crinkling fireball appeared in the cloudless sky, hurtling straight toward the altar.

"Move back," Elijah commanded, fierce determination in his eyes.

Liraz surged forward. A rush of heat hit his face, hands trembling as he seized the open end of the stick and plunged it into the watery trench. The fireball crashed into the altar, devouring the sacrifice, stones, and wood, and soaking up the water. In an instant, flames curled into the hollow staff, knocking Liraz off his feet. He clutched the hot, glowing stick, despite it scorching his hand.

The multitude fell on their faces and repeated, "The Lord, he is God."

As he soared through the air, a radiant light assaulted Liraz's eyes, and then it dimmed as a figure took shape. *Jesus.* Kneeling with hands clasped in prayer, he raised his voice, resonant with compassion, "Father, I pray you'll consider removing Ramel from his watcher position. He's blinded by lust. Lucifer set a trap to sift him like wheat. Father, forgive him. He doesn't know what he's doing."

The scene shifted to a multitude of angels gathered in solemn assembly, faces lined with sorrow. Among the weeping angels, Padel's figure came into focus, his eyes filled with tears of grief and his voice choked with emotion. "My brother Ramel is gone," he sobbed, finding solace with the three other living creatures.

Liraz landed on the ground with a thud, the impact jarring his senses. Padel stood over him, prying the staff from his fingers. The burning sensation subsided. Padel tilted the rod, releasing the flames over the four inner wheels, one by one. The chariot roared to life as Ayin rolled the wheels back and forth.

Raindrops fell on Liraz's face, refreshing him and the land. Jachniel scooped him up and flew him into the chariot, placing him on the seat with a grateful nod. Hannah's face bore concern, eyes reflecting her worries. He mustered a weak smile and released his breath.

Jesus had tried to save him, and his angel friends had grieved for him despite his betrayal. Something to reflect on during his return to Tartarus.

With a mighty roar, the chariot blasted off. They spun around in a whirlwind, leaving Liraz momentarily disoriented. However, his focus gradually sharpened with renewed purpose as a brown stone house came into view.

34

Now Adam knew Eve his wife, and she conceived and bore Cain, saying, "I have gotten a man with the help of the Lord." And again, she bore his brother Abel.

—Genesis 4:1–2 (ESV)

Adam and Eve's house, 4000 BC
Half past the sixty-second hour in hell

Hannah inhaled the fresh, pre-flood air intwined with the sweet, heady fragrance helped chase away. The lingering stench of her burnt hair and steadied her nerves after almost being roasted alive, then witnessing God's fire fall from heaven.

Nestled in the middle of tall, weedy grass sat a small, one-story stone house adorned with white, red, and yellow lilies bursting forth like dawn. Animal skins covered part of the roof and draped over the door. A couple of missing stones made tiny windows offering glimpses of a darkened interior. Nearby, a rough-hewn barn stood, filled with the sounds of braying animals.

The living creatures emerged from under the chariot. Hannah could both kick and hug the angels for leaving and then rescuing them.

"We are proud of each one of you," squawked Gonael as the stairs rolled out. Ayin's eyes darting across each step, reminding Hannah of her first ascent into God's chariot."Hannah floated down the steps, standing tall in their praise. The thick grass tickled her ankles .

"I commend your gallant effort in retrieving the flames,"

Padel's voice carried a note of respect as he tilted his chin.

Hannah's attention turned to Liraz, noticing tears welling in his violet eyes. A surge of sorrow washed over her. *These might be our last moments together before Liraz returns to Tartarus.*

"Pure genius using Jesus' blood to destroy Pergamon." Jachniel patted Dismas on the back.

Dismas' eyes widened. "It seemed there were only a few drops, but when I sprayed Jesus' blood around, it multiplied."

"Jesus' blood brought down the seat of Lucifer," Dormel bowed his head in reverence.

Benjamin leaned forward, gripping the edge of his seat."Where were you? We almost died," he called out, his voice tight with frustration

"You're alive."Padel murmured. "Keep your voice down, we don't—"

"Now you show up," Adam huffed from behind them emerging from the barn carrying a cradle. "I don't need you after I delivered two boys all by myself."

"Twins?" Jachniel's eyes widen in surprise

Adam held up the cradle and nodded with a hint of pride in his voice. "My first attempt. A little lopsided. I used it to feed the animals some seed. But now we need it for our second child." His expression hardened. "I'm glad Eve birthed two boys. When they're older, they can help me crush that devious serpent's head."

"That's why we've come," Padel stepped forward. "The devil has hidden something here, and our friends need to retrieve it." Padel waved his hand toward Hannah, Benjamin, Dismas, and Liraz.

"We think a piece of hell's key might have materialized inside your home when Eve delivered the babies," Jachniel added.

"Only the woman can enter my home. The rest of you stay

outside. Eve is exhausted. She's been up for two days and endured so much pain."

Adam lifted the leopard skin door and strolled through. Hannah followed. In the corner, Eve slept on a pile of animal skins, a cooing baby under each arm. Adam brushed his lips over her forehead. "Sleep, Mother." He gently took one newborn and whispered, "Cain, let your mother rest. He has a slight bruise on his forehead. I hope it fades." He placed him in the imperfect cradle and covered him with a soft lamb blanket.

"Aww, Cain is so handsome," Hannah said in a quiet voice, but she didn't mean a word of it. She stared at Cain's tiny fists, the ones he would use to murder his brother one day.

Adam rocked a fussy Abel. "I'm going to show my son to the living creatures. They have never seen a human baby before." The new father carried his baby in strong, muscular arms back outside.

Hannah began her search for the key piece, lifting a basket of cherries on a small log table. Cain coughed. She ignored him and sifted through a pile of animal furs stacked on one of the chairs at the table. A mother-of-pearl teardrop-shaped piece slipped to the dirt floor with a soft thud. *The key piece.* Hannah's heart leapt.

Cain's coughing became a high-pitched noise. *Something's wrong.* Neglecting the piece, Hannah stood over the cradle. *Oh no!* Cain's face and lips had turned a pale blue. She reached to turn him over, but froze.

She glanced at Eve, still asleep. Hannah's chest tightened. Should she let Cain die? Everything would be different. A dead Cain couldn't kill Abel. The repercussions would be no Cain's blood to make those wretched coins. No Nephilim, flood, demon spirits, or hybrids. Human Liraz would still be watcher angel Ramel.

During Hannah's indecision, Cain fell silent, and his chest no longer moved—he became white like a ghost. *Seize the key piece and go!* But Hannah saw the infant's pleading eyes and quickly flipped him onto his stomach, smacking him several times with her cupped hand. After a few terrifying moments, a seed shot out of Cain's mouth, and he started to cry. His cheeks returned to a pink hue. Hannah's body shook at what she had almost done.

"What are you doing to my baby?" Eve said sharply, sitting up and glaring at Hannah.

With shaky hands, Hannah handed Cain to Eve. "Your child is fine. He choked on a seed and I got it out."

"Thank you. A seed? I told Adam I didn't want that second cradle in here after he used it to feed the animals." Eve looked around. "Where is my other son, and who are you?"

"Adam has Abel outside. I'm with Padel and—"

"Oh, what a relief. You're with the living creatures. At first, I thought you might be the devil disguised as a woman to murder my twins. Lucifer tried to kill me when I became pregnant. I guess he won't ever leave us alone." Eve began to nurse Cain.

Now Hannah felt like an intruder. Her heart ached for the family she had imagined having with Seth. Averting her eyes, she explained, "I'm also fighting Lucifer. I need that item to defeat him." She pointed to the piece.

"Take it," Eve said in a strong voice. She stared at Cain in amazement and love.

Hannah picked up the shimmery mother-of-pearl piece, placing it in her pocket. The smaller piece locked into position at the bottom of the post with a satisfying click. *It's finally finished.* Checking her thumb, only a tiny speck remained on her nail bed. Soon every trace of black would be obliterated like the triumphant sun erasing the night. She wanted to rush and show the others, but she couldn't move. Her legs felt like anchors. The stone hut of Adam and Eve faded.

She was back in Paradise, staring into Jesus' warm brown eyes.

35

***For you will not abandon my soul to Sheol,
or let your holy one see corruption.***

—Psalm 16:10 (ESV)

The sixty-third hour in hell

Mahway gawked at his wife through the tiny opening in the weakened wall. Her eyes were bright brown, no longer milky white. *Perfect, I won't have to drag her around hell since she can see now.* Cecilia must still care about him since she had publicly proclaimed her forgiveness.

A smidgen of happiness crept over him. *Keep your head in the game.* This next phase of the plan proved tricky. The weight of the liquid fire had to break through this section of the compromised wall to pour directly over Jesus. Mahway's lip curled at the continued preaching. Enough of this nonsense. His arms ached to seize Cecilia.

Jesus' voice droned on. "The robes covering each of you are not suitable for meeting my Father. I need to cleanse you of your sins once and forever—" Jesus tilted his head, listening to something beyond even Mahway's superior hearing.

Instantly, the woman, her brother, the traitor, and the thief materialized in front of Jesus. The men looked confused, but the woman's face beamed as she reached into her pocket.

Jesus gestured for the woman to wait.

Mahway figured she possessed the key, and he mimed the actions to Ariel to snatch the key from her when the Lake of Fire broke through the wall.

Ariel acknowledged with a nod.

Outside the gates of Paradise, Lucifer appeared and plunked down with a thud. He beat his wings with fury and his face twisted in rage. "Jesus, I'm going to destroy you."

Jesus laughed.

Lucifer held up his claws. "Forces of evil, arise!"

Behind Lucifer, Beelzebub, Moloch, Dagon, and Baal along with myriad fallen angels with gleaming ruby eyes entered hell's sky. Their wings kicked up ashes and caused sporadic gusts of hot wind in all directions. The Nephilim rushed across the bridge and stomped onto the shores of Paradise. Mahway heard soft footsteps behind him as more giants sneaked into the tunnels, ready to pounce through the wall. Mahway flashed a malevolent smile. Evil beings filled hell's every nook and cranny. The crowd surged toward Jesus, and Cecilia vanished from his view through the tiny peephole.

Lucifer's twisted horns bobbed as he snarled at Jesus. "Your blood has no legal right to topple my throne and temple."

What? Has Pergamon fallen? Mahway groaned inwardly. He didn't want to rebuild that monstrosity.

"Watch what else my powerful blood can do." Jesus held up his wounded wrists and looked up with a victorious smile. "Behold, I take away Adam's sin and all the sins of the world."

The ground shook and the black spots on the prisoners' garments leapt onto Jesus' robe. The Paradise prisoners looked over their dazzling white clothes in awe. No black marks remained.

If Jesus took on Cecilia's sins, it might prevent her from entering hell. If it turned out he couldn't have Cecilia, neither would heaven. Mahway clicked his teeth together in anticipation. With his sixth finger, he widened his vantage point so he could watch the impending explosion. He covered his ears and licked his lips. The big bang should happen any second.

Boom!

Lucifer, the ultimate showman, roared just as the top of the volcano exploded. The volcano peak flew east and landed at the prearranged spot on the mountain with precision, thanks to the Nephilim's construction knowledge. Then, the dirt swallowed the peak. Now, it would fall 1,045 cubits through the caverns, straight into the Lake of Fire, causing the flames to spill into the trench. The channel would carry the soul-destroying liquid through the tunnel, spill out against this wall, and dump over Jesus' head. Poof. No more Jesus. *This must work.*

While the volcano spewed lava into the Sea of Despair, the white-robed fools remained focused on Jesus' every word as he explained some garbage about finding peace only in him.

Mahway continued to peer through the opening, trying to locate his wife, but couldn't find her. The pains in his stomach felt like a swarm of stinging bees. If the plan didn't work, he'd be the outcast of hell, like Sodom all over again.

The roar echoed through the tunnel. Mahway flattened himself against the wall, desperate to avoid any contact with the Lake of Fire. The other demons mirrored his actions. Their scarlet eyes burned with eagerness.

Ariel's voice cut through the chaos like a blade, "It's almost here." His son flung his curly mane back, preventing it from being singed as the fiery flames rushed through the last bit of trench.

Mahway's hands shook as the red-hot river surged through their pre-weakened wall. *Success.* The wall easily collapsed against the weight and the lake flowed into Paradise. The bars of Paradise melted as liquid death gushed toward Jesus. *We have won!*

Jesus held up his hand. "Now, Hannah."

The girl tossed the multicolored completed key. The moment it touched Jesus' fingers, the key transformed into bright gold, the top shaped like a crown with glistening pearls. Jesus appeared to be on fire, but the flames did not consume him. Continuous waves from the Lake of Fire struck Jesus, but he absorbed it all like a sponge.

Impossible! Mahway's mind reeled at Jesus' appearance within the burning inferno. His hair was pure white, and his eyes burned like flames. With one hand, he held up the gold key, and the other held back the flames from reaching anyone else in Paradise. *Even the flames obey him.*

"I hold the keys to death and hell." His voice sounded like rushing water. Jesus reached into his pocket, withdrawing a second ornate key. As his fingers cradled it, the gold flecks adorning its surface stirred, swirling like stardust. Radiance flowed from the key's core, flooding its surface until the entire key transformed, developing into a solid, luminous, gold-flecked masterpiece.

"Behold, I am he who lives. I was dead and now I will be alive. Lucifer, you can never destroy me. I am the first and last, the beginning and the end."

Lucifer pointed to the widening hole where the Lake of Fire had melted the bars. "Breach the gap. We can still drag them into hell."

No fallen angel or demon dared to move a muscle since the flames burned bright around the opening. Lucifer's eyes pierced Mahway's as he stood at the edge of the tunnel opening. *It's over. No way am I going anywhere near those fires.*

"You've lost all authority. You can't snatch any of my Paradise saints from my hand," Jesus said within the flames.

Lucifer screeched, "Breach the gap!"

Beelzebub, Moloch, Dagon, and Baal flapped their wings, but their hooves remained on the ground. Asmoday and Morax flew through the gap, closing their wings at the last minute to avoid the flames. They flew high above Paradise and swooped toward a few prisoners.

Jesus gripped the keys and commanded, "Return." The flames left his body, and a few shot into the air as the fire river retreated into the tunnel.

Asmoday swiftly peeled to the left, and Morax maneuvered

right. A wayward flame shot up and hit one of Morax's wings. The wing vanished, and he plunged headfirst into the widening stream of liquid fire. His body evaporated as the flames consumed him. The evil beings howled in horror.

Now, the retreating flames approached the trench. Mahway skittered out of the way, but the flames rushed through the opening. Without hesitation, Mahway grabbed Ariel like a shield against the oncoming fire. In the blink of an eye, Ariel evaporated, along with his own right hand. *Oh, dung.* In shock, he tumbled on the ash-streaked floor as the inferno poured back into the trench and returned to its origin. All the demons scattered.

Alone, Mahway stood at the jagged opening, peering into Paradise. He hoped to see Cecilia and witness her ascent into the realm he was barred from.

Jesus threw the golden key of hell like a knife into Paradise's lock. A violent tremor shook the ground. The iron bars surrounding Paradise turned vivid gold, then blew into the Sea of Despair. The vines around the sides fell away and the grass became a vibrant green as if the land had healed. Trees, flowers, and all manner of greenery bloomed, filling the air with a sweet fragrance. For once, Mahway didn't smell sulfur. The people praised Jesus and sang one of David's annoying psalms.

The ground trembled again, and that awful gold chariot materialized beside Jesus. A pure white cloud covered the vehicle and the fires within the inner wheels burned fiercely. Mahway squinted. No sign of those annoying living creatures. He couldn't see Ayin's eyes on the wheels through the bright white swirling cloud.

"Behold," a voice boomed from the cloud like thunder, "this is my beloved Son, in whom I am well pleased."

The cloud swept over Jesus. The four fires within the inner wheels burst into a single white flame shaped like a dove and leapt into Jesus.

A light exploded, and the ground rocked and tottered. The

intensity of the light made Mahway dizzy. His chest pounded. An invisible force lifted him off the ground and shoved him to his knees. Mahway shivered in fear as a horrible realization came to him—Jesus *is* Lord of all. His lips even confessed it. Mahway gagged. He fought the urge to vomit. This explosion reminded him of Sodom, but much worse.

Finally, the bright light disappeared, and Mahway regained his sight. He stared into the scorched abyss that had been Paradise. He clenched his teeth as a lone tear slid down his face. He tried wiping it away, but his hand was gone—just like Paradise and all its prisoners. Including Cecilia.

36

And they came out of the tombs after His resurrection, entered the holy city, and appeared to many.

—Matthew 27:53 (HCSB)

Hannah fought to breathe through the tight fabric over her mouth. The material squeezed her chest, waist, and legs. The woody, spicy scent of spikenard couldn't mask the musty odor. She couldn't see anything through the material either. *Where am I? What happened to that brilliant, comforting light?*

Something shattered behind her, and pounding footsteps raced toward her. Jesus? Hannah hoped. Her body tensed, afraid Lucifer's claw would swipe at her. She struggled against her bound wrists and ankles.

"Take it easy," advised a voice that sounded like Grandfather Ebenezer.

She flinched as a hand lifted her head and another unwrapped the shroud around her face. "Grandfather?" Hannah blinked several times. Sunlight filtered through an opening in the surrounding rock. *The family tomb?* Goosebumps prickled on her arms. Had Jesus raised her and her grandfather from the dead? She lifted her arms. All her wounds from the Roman chariot accident were healed.

"It's me," reassured Grandfather.

Hannah stared in disbelief. His forehead and hands had deep wrinkles, his hair white. He no longer looked young like he had in Paradise. They both wore white robes, but no shoes. A muffled scream startled Hannah. She turned and saw movement on the bench on the other side of the tomb. "Benjamin!"

"His soul has just returned," her grandfather beamed with joy.

"We will set you free," promised Hannah, stepping off the ledge and onto damp dirt. While she unwrapped her brother, Hannah noticed only one broken ossuary in the inner chamber of the crypt. She had been just a child when her family had placed Grandfather's bones there thirteen years ago. Another miracle! The prophet Ezekiel's words came to life through her grandfather: "I will lay sinews upon you, and will cause flesh to come upon you, and cover you with skin, and put breath in you; and you shall live, and you shall know that I am the Lord."

Benjamin leaped off the bench and exclaimed in an excited voice. "The power of Jesus' resurrection saved us, Jesus triumphed over the devil, and we witnessed it!"

Hannah beamed at her brother. *Thank you, God, for raising us and giving my brother faith to believe in You.*

The three of them embraced, overwhelmed by the miracle. Grandfather wiped his eyes and said in a tight voice, "Jesus said that when he ascended, some of us would return to earth to make peace with those we have hurt."

Am I supposed to make amends with Father? Hannah searched her heart—she had already forgiven her father. Why did Jesus bring her back? Hannah didn't know but she couldn't wait to reveal this extraordinary gift to her parents. The three of them linked arms as they emerged from the tomb. *Wait.* Who had rolled away the rock sealing their family's crypt? Maybe the earthquakes? The living creatures? Maybe even Jesus? Hannah spotted three more people in white robes walking out of a different tomb. She wondered how many others Jesus had brought back to life.

A woman muttering to herself walked right into Hannah.

"Mary?" Hannah recognized her as the one from whom Jesus had cast out demons.

Mary stopped. "Aren't you Reuben and Susanna's children who were killed by a chariot a few days ago?"

"Yes," Hannah said. "We were trapped in hell, until Jesus brought us back."

The woman's face brightened. "I just saw Jesus alive outside his tomb. I wanted to hug him, but he wouldn't let me touch him. He told me he had to ascend to his Father."

"Jesus prevailed over the devil and took the Paradise prisoners to our Father. Jesus even took away our sins," Grandfather Ebenezer said.

"Oh, please tell me every detail!" Mary's eyes sparkled in anticipation.

Hannah's mind whirled. Tears flooded her eyes. She didn't get to say farewell to Dismas or Liraz. She hoped to see Dismas on the journey back to Jerusalem, or maybe he was in heaven and they'd meet again there. But Liraz—she'd never see him again. Hannah held back a sob.

37

"When he ascended on high he led a host of captives, and he gave gifts to men."

—Ephesians 4:8 (ESV)

The searing white light temporarily blinded Dismas. A mighty blast of wind wrapped around him like a father's embrace. As his eyes slowly adjusted, he saw Jesus, his face radiant and his hands glistening like fresh snow. The Son of God wore a billowing white linen robe and golden sandals. A simple gold crown rested on his head, a sash of gold fabric wrapped around his chest, and the keys of death and hell swayed from his golden belt. A magnificent golden lampstand with seven flames stood between Jesus and the throne covered in a white cloud. Jesus bowed his head and acknowledged both the swirling cloud and the seven flames.

Dismas' mouth hung open—for once, he was speechless.

On each side of the cloud-covered throne, two huge cherubim knelt, facing each other. Their enormous gold-dipped wings stretched over the top of the throne, like a palm tree canopy. In perfect harmony, the cherubim sang, "Holy, holy, holy, Lord God Almighty, the Lord who lives."

The throne room had no walls. A rainbow hovered above the cherubim's wings against a sapphire sky. The four living creatures flew in circular orbit beyond the rainbow. All of Ayin's gleaming eyes peered out from the four living creatures' feathers. Padel glanced at Dismas and flashed a reassuring smile. More and more angels filled the skies. Their feathers glittered like diamonds as they joined the chorus of cherubim worshiping Jesus. As the glorious voices continued to lift praises, an exquisite incense filled the air. Dismas inhaled the unfamiliar scent and saw colors more vibrant than anything he'd ever seen before. Excitement and warmth spread through his body.

Jesus glided through the blazing golden lampstand unscathed and into the cloud that hid God's throne. *Impossible!* Dismas' hands dropped to his sides, openly staring. *Only a ghost can traverse solid matter, yet Jesus seems to be a flesh and blood human.*

Jesus stretched his arm over the honey brown seat. The angels fell still and silent.

It struck Dismas that *this* was the holiest place, not the empty holy of holiest room in the temple he'd visited after his death.

As a droplet of blood oozed from Jesus' wrist and splattered across the mercy seat, time seemed to halt. For a brief moment, everything turned crimson. Jesus poured out his blood drop by drop. "Father, I hereby offer my sacrificial blood, for now and eternity, to pay the ransom for Adam's sin and for your forgiveness of all humanity—past, present, and future. All those who receive me are holy and can dwell in your presence now and forever on earth and in heaven."

When Jesus withdrew his hand from the mercy seat, thunder and lightning reverberated through the chamber. The cloud over the throne turned a deep, fiery red, but its interior remained pure white.

Dismas' eyes watered as he peered into the fire and saw a man sitting on the throne. He could only make out the outline of the figure's golden hands and feet clad in golden sandals. Dismas gasped and trembled. *Father God!*

"My beloved and worthy Son, Jesus," Father God said. "I give you power over all things on earth and in heaven."

A second golden throne appeared next to the Father's. Jesus sat. A long gold scepter, shaped like a sheaf of barley, materialized in Jesus' hand as he declared, "I now give the gift of the Holy Spirit to the Paradise saints."

In response to Jesus' command, embers disbursed from the seven flames in the lampstand. Some of the glittery sparks landed on Dismas' face and feet. They burned as they absorbed into his body, yet it didn't hurt. Instead, he felt a burst of energy. His entire body was ablaze. An aura of light obscured his body and white robe. Dismas' mind felt clear, peaceful, and sound. His cheek itched, and Dismas touched the scar. That mark he hated had disappeared! In awe, he dropped to his knees. Below him, the floor was a sea of glass. Refreshing red and white foamy waves lapped at his knees and feet, yet he didn't sink—he floated on the smooth surface.

Peculiar.

"What's so peculiar, my beloved son?" Dismas recognized the voice that had encouraged him on the key quest. The same voice that had comforted him as a child. "I have been with you your entire life. I am your Everlasting Father, Wonderful Counselor, Prince of Peace. You can hear me now because you carry my glory inside you, and it makes you shine. But I can still see doubt in your eyes. Dismas, why don't you test me? Stand up and look at my throne. I will wave to you."

Dismas obeyed. The Father waved. Jesus grinned and also waved. The seven flames on the lampstand looked like seven waving hands. Dismas waved both hands back at the Father, the Son, and the Holy Spirit. "My body shines just like Jesus' does," marveled Dismas.

"Not quite like Jesus," the voice said gently. "There is only one person like him. But when it's the end of the age of grace, you will receive a glorified body, one I can converse with face to face. Until then, Jesus will teach you how to use your improved body. You have all eternity to learn."

"But I'm not worthy because of my past," Dismas protested.

"You accepted Christ, and your sins were forgiven," the Creator explained. "We will never condemn you, so avoid condemning yourself."

A deep peace Dismas had never experienced flooded his mind.

"I know it's a lot to understand. Do you have any other questions before we begin our feast?"

The smell of fresh bread filled the air, along with other smells Dismas didn't recognize.

"What happened to everyone else?"

"Look to your right."

He did and tears of happiness welled at the sight of Ziv, Paltith, Lot and his wife and daughters. Each carried a glow of light around them as well.

Ziv flashed a radiant smile. "Friend, we've made it to heaven." Dismas heard Ziv's voice, but his lips hadn't moved. *Is this how we communicate now? Strange.*

When the two men embraced, images of Ziv's life flooded into Dismas' mind. He saw Ziv burying his parents, how he cared for his brothers, when he fell in love with Paltith, and Lot informing him of his wife's death. In an instant, Dismas knew everything about Ziv, yet he felt no judgement in what he had observed. He felt only brotherly love.

In the same way, he assumed his own life must have flashed into Ziv's mind because he sensed a new level of compassion from him. Lot and his family hugged Dismas, and the same thing occurred. He felt sorry for judging them when they had first met. *How overwhelming to know so much about others.*

"Dismas, your mind has been cleansed," a voice echoed within him. "Reversed from the curse of the tree of the knowledge of good and evil. Because of my Son's work on the cross, you now carry a piece of my heart inside of you. Now you see my children for who they are without your faulty human judgement. In heaven, you can see others with no false illusions or from a tainted heart."

Dismas cracked a wide smile. *I wonder what marvelous visions await when I get to see Liraz.* Immediately, a wave of sadness hit him. *He's been sent back to Tartarus.*

"Turn around," the voice insisted.

Dismas did. There stood Liraz in his human form.

"Don't touch me. You already know too much about my past," ordered Liraz as he held out his shiny hands and grinned.

Dismas gasped and took a step backward, unable to form one thought.

Liraz's thoughts came to Dismas. "You can close your mouth now, Dismas. I can't believe it myself! When the powerful light entered Jesus, I felt the coin piece explode throughout my body. Every trace of angel essence left me, and I transformed into a true man."

Dismas still couldn't gather his thoughts, astonished.

"Now Ramel is an actual man," Dismas heard God say. "I have shown him mercy. Jesus died for men, and therefore Ramel, being a man and believing Jesus is my Son, is permitted to enter heaven. I will be gracious to whom I will be gracious, and I will have compassion on whom I will have compassion."

What about Hannah and Benjamin?

"They aren't here. Both of them have much work to do back on earth."

Dismas heard Jesus, "Your action of accepting me on the cross will be known throughout time. Knowing I snatched you from the clutches of hell helped me endure unbearable pain."

Dismas trembled at the thought of a thief like him helping Jesus in his critical hour. He heard three distinct voices bleed into one, "No longer a thief, you're a new creation."

Father God, still obscured in his cloud, stood with Jesus. "Come, my sons and daughters! It's time for our celebration feast where I will give each of you a white tile with your new name and a special song written just for you. Then your angels will escort you to your mansions in heaven." Father God, Jesus, and a whirlwind of fire from the lampstand headed toward the banquet hall.

Dismas danced into the celebration, grateful to start his new life.

38

The reason the Son of God appeared was to destroy the works of the devil.

—1 John 3:8 (ESV)

Mahway's back stiffened against the ebony chair in Lucifer's strategy room. "You're replacing me with Ohya and Hahya?" he bellowed. "I've lost everything—my wife, son, hand, and now my job."

Lucifer growled. "Stop your whining. All my Paradise prisoners are gone."

"Mahway, your string of failures is insignificant compared with what has happened to hell," Beelzebub said angrily. "Thousands of souls entered heaven as a result of listening to Jesus for those three days and nights. Not only our Paradise captives, but those souls we'd locked in cells now reside in heaven. And each is beyond our power to torment again." Two of Beelzebub's pet flies emerged from his flared nostrils.

Mahway fumed. Jesus' diabolical sixty-three-hour preaching plan had been to try to clear out hell.

"I'm horrified," Moloch said, flapping his wings and toppling his chair. "Along with the rest of you, I knelt before Jesus." His feathers shook.

"Whoever speaks of this unfortunate incident," Lucifer said through gritted teeth, "I will throw them into the Lake of Fire. Besides, none of us bowed. The earthquake just toppled us over, and we landed on our knees by chance."

Mahway fought back a bitter laugh. *Lucifer's revisionist history at its best.*

"Jesus resurrected some of the dead," Beelzebub announced, "and now they're telling how they escaped hell."

Everyone fell silent.

Baal drummed his sharp claws on the table. "There's also a problem with Liraz—"

A murderous look crossed Lucifer's face, and his eyes darkened with rage. "Never speak that name again. I witnessed him burn in the Lake of Fire."

I heard the Creator had allowed that piece of garbage into heaven.

"Enough with all this terrible news," Lucifer's voice dripped with contempt. "I will visit the throne room and report to the Creator everything that is wrong with his humans. I'll start with Dismas. It will provide me much pleasure." Lucifer vanished but reemerged in an instant. His bottom lip quivered, and he rambled something about Jesus' blood.

"What happened to you?" Beelzebub leaned in, his voice low and sharp. A couple of his flies spewed out and dropped dead on the table

"I couldn't enter the throne room. Jesus' blood sacrifice bars me from the third heaven." Lucifer stomped his hoof, veins popped on his neck.

"What—wait, that means we can't break into the Book of Life Library and thwart God's plans for his people." Baal spat. "Not to mention all the enjoyment we had creeping around heaven and coming up with ways to vex those perfect angels."

Mahway tried to hide his gloating with his remaining hand. *Now these haughty demons are no different from me.*

"Oh, it gets much worse." Dagon's claws shook as he flipped through the ancient book of God's words and stopped at a passage. "The Uncreated One revealed he would give a piece of his Spirit to men. I believe this moment has arrived."

Mahway swallowed hard. *Will I be able to possess a man if God's Spirit is in him?*

"When I eavesdropped on the Last Supper," Beelzebub's voice carried a sharp edge, "Jesus stated the Holy Spirit would dwell inside those who believe him. And all those foolish followers would perform amazing feats because Jesus would run home to his Daddy." He laughed nervously.

Lucifer's smile broadened, a dangerous gleam ignited his eyes. "Every time we hurt a human would be like a knife wound to the heart of the Uncreated One, especially those who carry his Spirit within them. He leaned in closer, his voice dropping to a low conspiratorial tone, while his spiked scale scraped the floor with every word. Let's plot our revenge. Ideas?"

Beelzebub's features twisted in a dark smirk, his pet files swirling around his head like a sinister halo. "Well, we can rile up the high priest and the Roman emperor to kill anyone who follows Jesus," Beelzebub

Dagon rubbed his scaly forehead. "Let's make people think they are lunatics if they hear God's voice."

"We can whisper in their ears that they are unworthy, unloved, and unusable by God," Baal recommended. "Let's put snares and obstacles in front of them every step of the way. Those humans won't discover they carry the power of the Holy Spirit inside of them."

Moloch rubbed his bull horns. "We could tempt them with every imaginable sin."

"God is no longer holding their sins against them. We can't guilt people with the Ten Commandments anymore," Lucifer said. Lucifer growled as he stood up, pacing back and forth. His massive antlers accidentally struck one of Moloch's curved horns, producing a loud clank as they collided.

"Watch it, Lucifer... I mean, forgive me."

Lucifer shot him a glare. "You're not forgiven, Moloch."

Moloch's scowl twisted into a grin. "You're on to something,

Lucifer! The people don't know God has forgiven them—we can exploit that," he flexed his clawed fingers looking pleased at himself.

"Send out our spirits of infirmity," suggested Mahway. "We can give people many diseases, and they'll blame it all on God."

Beelzebub rolled his eyes. "We've already been doing that."

"Since you're useless to us with one hand," Lucifer pointed toward the door, "you can go back to earth and try to possess those who claim they have the Holy Spirit. On your way out, send in your replacements."

Mahway rose from the table. Maybe losing his hand was his ticket out of hell and away from Lucifer.

39

I will greatly rejoice in the Lord; my soul shall exult in my God, for he has clothed me with the garments of salvation; he has covered me with the robe of righteousness, as a bridegroom decks himself like a priest with a beautiful headdress, and as a bride adorns herself with her jewels.

—Isaiah 61:10 (ESV)

Hannah knelt in her room as the morning light filtered through the shutters. Hot tears streamed down her cheeks as she gave thanks to God. The past few days had been a whirlwind. When Father spied her, Benjamin, and Grandfather from the rooftop, he had taken the stairs two at a time to greet them. Father had caressed Hannah's cheek and looked at her with such love, all the hurt he had caused her melted away.

Since that day, her grandfather and father seemed inseparable. Her once irate father had transformed into a peaceful man. Their home, had changed, too. Instead of Father's constant yelling, threats, and mean looks, he spoke kind words, smiled more, and even resigned from the Sanhedrin court.

Jesus had been appearing in various places all over Jerusalem. Hannah, Benjamin, and Father planned to visit the places where the resurrected Jesus had materialized. She prayed fervently to see him today. She had a multitude of questions.

In that moment, the wall became bright, and Jesus walked through. He wore a brilliant white gown that covered his feet. Hannah's lips trembled, and she froze. She couldn't even formulate a single thought.

"Don't look so shocked, Haven't you ever seen a man walk through a wall?" Jesus guided her gently supporting her with a strength both tender and divine. He gestured for her to sit on her favorite chair. She noticed his nail wounds remained, a constant reminder of his sacrifice. "I heard you have some questions for me." Jesus eased into another chair across from, Jesus eyes filled with compassion.

"I …" she paused, uncertain. "I don't understand why you brought me back."

"I have chosen you to help spread the story of my resurrection. And I also need you to pray for your uncle Saul. He's about to receive the shock of his life."

"I will do both," Hannah agreed but was now worried and confused for her uncle.

"Also, do you remember when you stood in front of Cain, choosing if he lived or died?" Jesus asked in a gentle tone.

Hannah's stomach twisted as she nodded, horrified at what she had almost chosen to do.

"There's no need to be anxious, my daughter. I'm pleased you made the wisest decision, and the one that brought more people to heaven. If you had let Cain suffocate, the key piece would have vanished since you would have altered the timeline. A few souls would have been trapped in hell because they wouldn't have believed in me without seeing the completed key."

"I'm grateful I did the right thing," Hannah murmured, "but I still don't understand why you picked me."

Jesus chuckled the merriment shining in his brown eyes. "Did you have somewhere else to be? It's our Father's will for you to have gone on this quest, even delaying your marriage to Seth so your children wouldn't suffer. Seth needed to do some growing up before he married you."

Hannah gasped, mind spinning. *God delayed my marriage? Seth needed to change? Children?*

A trumpet blast interrupted her thoughts. Every second, the horn grew louder and more persistent. Soon, singing and shouting accompanied the trumpets. The uproar sounded like the entire quarter of Jerusalem had erupted in celebration. Hannah assumed another groom was taking his bride home, and for once, she didn't feel sorry for herself. She glanced at Jesus. He tapped his foot to the music, but she felt annoyed by the disturbance. Hannah leaned toward Jesus to ask another question.

Before she could speak, the front door opened downstairs and her father yelled, "Seth's alive!"

Her jaw dropped.

Jesus nodded.

Hannah's heart thumped as she raced to the window and slid back the shutter. She recognized Seth walking through the gate. He wore a blue robe with a gold crown and an ecstatic grin. Seth's relatives, and hers, surrounded him and continued to sing and dance. Women shook tambourines, waved scarves, and yelled for her to come down.

Hannah turned back to Jesus. "How is this possible?"

"Roman thieves captured Seth and sold him as a slave. The exact moment you rose from the dead, Seth gained his freedom and journeyed back home to you."

A stream of unanswered questions ran through Hannah's thoughts—why is Seth here now? Could she trust her husband? How would she share Jesus with others when she's married?

Jesus stood and said, "Seth is part of our Father's plan for your life. The moment you've been dreaming of is finally here—it's time to look like the beautiful bride you are."

"I've aged and changed. My groom won't recognize me."

"Hannah, like my church, a bride never ages." Jesus' eyes shone with love. "Be prepared you won't know the date or time when I'll return."

Hannah's mind whirled. *Seth has come for me.* Excitement rushed through every inch of her. Her fingers trembled as pulled on the knob of her old wardrobe. She froze. Her wedding dress had yellowed, covered in layers of dust and tears. A faint mildew smell overwhelmed her nostrils. Her eyes stung, trying to hold back hot tears. How could Seth find her lovely in this wrinkled, soiled garment?

Jesus approached the cabinet and softly exhaled on the garment. An exquisite scent of roses filled the air.

Hannah's eyes widened in astonishment watching the stained fabric restore to its original pristine condition.

"You are beautiful Hannah. There is no flaw in you," whispered Jesus and then he kissed her cheek. He placed a gold, pearl-encrusted crown on her head. Her gold ring—the one that had caused her death as she tried to get it back from Benjamin—appeared on her hand. "My wedding gifts to my precious daughter." And then he vanished in a flash of light, blinding Hannah for an instant.

Her mother burst in, crying. "Hannah, your groom awaits."

She trembled as her mother helped her prepare for the procession to Seth's house. Hannah straightened her crown, took a deep breath, and welcomed her new life waiting to unfold.

AUTHOR'S NOTE

Hello Reader,

As the last echoes of 63 Hours in Hell linger in your thoughts, I hope this journey has stirred your spirit and ignited your soul. This book has been a labor of love, crafted through years of diligent research, countless late-night Scripture searches, and many hours of dedicated work—steeped in tears, fraught with fears, and adorned with cheers as every element finally fell into place.

If this book stirred your heart or sparked a smile, could you share your thoughts in a review? Your feedback, whether it's about a comforting message or a reflective moment, means the world to me and can help others find this book.

And if this tale didn't strike a chord in your heart, please know I value your perspective. All feedback, whether positive or constructive, is both welcomed and appreciated. It's the diverse symphony of thoughts that makes our world an enchanting place. And we can still be friends—I promise!

Thank you for your time invested in 63 Hours in Hell and with me. If you're drawn to delve deeper into the teachings of Jesus, explore free resources, or simply stay in touch, I invite you to continue your journey—**discover free tools and exclusive gifts** at susanldavis.com/63-hours-resource-hub or use your phone's camera to scan the QR code below and find your VIP resources.

May blessings abound in your life!
Susan L. Davis

Resource Hub

APPENDIX A

Why a Thursday Crucifixion?

In Matthew 12:40, Jesus states, "For just as Jonah was three days and three nights in the belly of the great fish, so will the Son of Man be three days and three nights in the heart of the earth." A popular belief is Jesus died on Friday. But if that's true, he'd only be in the grave for two nights. In the above Scripture, Jesus clearly states he'd be in the heart of earth (Hell) for three nights.

Three Days Explained

The book of Genesis reveals the meaning of three days: "And evening passed, and the morning came, marking the first day" (Genesis 1:5b NLT).

"And evening passed, and the morning came, marking the second day" (Genesis 1:8b NLT).

"And evening passed, and morning came, marking the third day" (Genesis 1:13 NLT).

The death of Jesus on Thursday fulfills the Genesis account of what three days entails.

Jesus informs his disciples in Luke 9:22, saying, "The Son of Man must suffer many things and be rejected by the elders and chief priests and scribes, and be killed, and on the third day be raised" (ESV, emphasis added).

Friday Crucifixion Timeline

Friday evening to Saturday morning: First Day

Saturday evening to Sunday morning: Second Day

The Bible states Jesus died Friday at 3:00 p.m., and let's assume he rose from the grave on Sunday at 6:00 a.m. — thirty-nine hours. Not even two full days!

Thursday Crucifixion Timeline

Thursday evening to Friday morning: First Day

Friday evening to Saturday morning: Second Day

Saturday evening to Sunday morning: Third Day

Changing Jesus' death to Thursday at 3:00 p.m. and his resurrection to Sunday at 6:00 a.m. means sixty-three hours.

If Jesus died on a Thursday, fulfilling both Scriptures that said he would be dead for three nights, and the Genesis meaning of what constitutes the third day, this makes sense.

Of course, the day Jesus died and rose from the dead doesn't matter. What's important is that he died for our sins.

APPENDIX B

Archaeology and the Bible Intersect

Caiaphas

In the article "The Short List: The New Testament Figures Known to History," Steven Feldman and Nancy Roth write of construction workers in 1990 who uncovered the Caiaphas family tomb's burial vault. An ossuary had been found with the remains of six people. One set of bones was identified as a sixty-year-old man believed to be Caiaphas, the high priest responsible for Jesus' crucifixion.

The Pilate Stone

In Steven Notley's article on Pontius Pilate, he describes a fragment of limestone discovered in Caesarea in 1961 with an imprint of the name "Pontius Pilate." The inscription reads as follows: "[Po]ntius Pilate, [pref]ect of Jud[e]a, [made and d]e[dicated] Tiberieum to the [divine August]us." This is the same Pontius Pilate who presided over Jesus' trial.

The name of Pontius Pilate has been discovered on coins, and his exploits are chronicled in the writings of Josephus, Tacitus, and Philo.

The Flood

The story of God sending a flood to the world due to wickedness, but saving one man and his family is found in countless cultures and time periods with at least five hundred variations. Although Noah's ark has not been discovered, there is physical evidence of a flood across the world.

Fossil Evidence

Fish fossils discovered on the peaks of the Himalayas suggest a disastrous geological event, which is consistent with what we would expect from Noah's flood.

In 1880, fossils of dragonflies two feet wide were discovered in France. These oversized dragonflies are believed to represent that, at one time, there might have been a higher proportion of oxygen on the planet. Scientists have recently raised dragonflies in an oxygen-rich environment and found that they grew to a larger size.

Out-of-Place Artifacts

There are other relics that don't fit the traditional scientific narrative and have therefore been labeled as out-of-place artifacts. Many of these out-of-place artifacts suggest a high-tech prehistoric civilization.

In Columbia, tiny relics appearing to be modern airplanes were discovered. These objects are known as the gold Quimbaya airplanes. Similar wooden airplane figures were unearthed in Saqqara, Egypt. These small, bird-like artifacts looked like airplanes or gliders. Both the wooden and golden airplanes have origins ranging from 200 to 2000 BC. However, the period is not conclusive, and these items possibly could have been pre-flood.

In recent history, odd items have been found in pieces of coal. In June 1891, in Morrisonville, Illinois, a resident found a solid, ten-inch, eight-carat gold chain embedded in a chuck of coal. A drill bit was discovered in a piece of coal in Glasgow in the 1850s. In 1944, in West Virginia, a brass bell was found in a lump of coal. It has been theorized that, during Noah's flood, these objects became buried in the swampy plant debris and rapidly transformed into coal. It's an interesting notion. Therefore, I added ferns and a floating tree island as a backdrop for my characters.

In the 2017 film, *Is Genesis History?*, scientists explain how the global flood event is hidden within geological rock layers and how Mount St. Helens illustrates how a geologic catastrophe can cause rapid change in the environment.

Baalbek

Baalbek in Lebanon was a temple where Baal was worshiped. It is where the largest manmade stones are located. These large rectangular stones are 64 feet long, 19.6 feet wide, 18 feet thick, and weigh around 1,600 tons. Arabic tradition believes Adam's son Cain built Baalbek, and the deluge ruined this fortress. Others believe after the flood, Nimrod rebuilt this city with help from giants. Later, the Romans built their temples on the foundation of Baalbek.

Giants/Nephilim

Although findings of giant skeletons have been reported throughout history, these giants have not been confirmed with scientific evidence. Since the Bible mentions the Nephilim and giants, one must lean on faith to believe they existed without confirmation of physical evidence.

Sodom and Gomorrah

According to scientists, an asteroid exploded in the sky above Siberia's Tunguska River in 1908, resulting in a rain of fire. This calamity killed three people and destroyed 830 square kilometers of forest. This blast was equivalent to a fifteen megaton TNT explosion, which was around a thousand times greater than the nuclear weapon dropped on Hiroshima.

Is it possible that, like the event in Siberia, an asteroid exploded and caused it to rain fire and brimstone over Sodom and Gomorrah? We might never know, but the Planisphere, an ancient tablet found in Nineveh, suggests there may have been an asteroid impact at the time of Sodom and Gomorrah.

Planisphere Tablet

The Planisphere Tablet is a Babylonian replica of a previous Sumerian stone depicting the night sky following an asteroid strike on earth, which Sir Austen Henry Layard discovered in 1849 in an archeology excavation in the Assyrian royal library in Nineveh.

The Planisphere Tablet's mathematical figure and constellation alignments were computer analyzed by rocket engineers Alan Bond and Mark Hempsell. As a result of this data, they discovered a mile-long asteroid had hit the earth just before dawn on June 29, 3123 BC.

"The rough modeling of the plume suggests the reentry would be over the Levant, Sinai, and Northern Egypt ... It is probable many more people died under the plume than died in the Alps due to primary impact," they state.

This plume theory supports Abraham's eyewitness account of the blast, "the smoke of the land went up like the smoke of a furnace" (Genesis 19:28 ESV).

The Planisphere Tablet has its own set of critics. Some academics believe that this is not an eyewitness account but rather a fictional event, comparable to a contemporary cartoon.

Sodom's Possible Location

There is evidence to suggest that Sodom is actually in Tall el-Hammam, the northeastern section of the Dead Sea. After carefully studying the Bible, Dr. Steven Collins found Tall el-Hammam. Upon excavation, he found a layer of ash and charred human remains, which suggests fire destroyed this city.

Tall el-Hammam's soil and sand were analyzed, "These samples give evidence of a high-heat event that was hot enough to turn desert sand into 'desert glass,' a phenomenon more associated with lightning, airburst or atomic explosion in the deserts of New Mexico than the one fertile Jordan River valley." As they dug deeper into Tall el-Hammam, Dr. Steven Collins's group discovered that this city was surrounded by huge walls more than fifty feet long and seventeen feet broad.

Sodom and Gomorrah Repeated in the Bible

In Judges 19, we see a similar occurrence to what occurred in Sodom. One man invited a traveler into his home for the night. The men of the city surrounded the home with the intent to sexually assault the male visitor.

"Behold, the men of the city, worthless fellows, surrounded the house, beating on the door. And they said to the old man, the master of the house, "Bring out the man who came into your house, that we may know him" (Judges 19:22 ESV).

Another parallel between the Lot narrative and the Judges 19:16–30 narrative is the homeowner pleads with the townspeople not to do such a horrible thing, even offering his daughter and concubine to appease the men. The concubine was tossed out of the door and killed as a result of the men's maltreatment. This sequence of events did lead to war, but God didn't wreak havoc on the entire town as he did with Sodom.

Balaam

In 1967, in Deir Alla, fragments from the Book of Balaam were found. A portion of the book states, "Balaam son of Beor, he was a divine seer, and the God came to him at night."

These fragments confirm the existence of Balaam, a prophet mentioned in the Bible. Although Moses is not mentioned in these fragments, we know from Numbers 22–24 that Balaam lived during the time of Moses.

Moses

Although Moses's name hasn't been found in any archaeological excavations, there is plenty of evidence to support the events surrounding his life.

The following are a few findings that add support to the biblical Moses.

- Discovery of the Egyptian document called "The Admonitions of an Egyptian Sage" about the ten plagues written by Ipuwer, a scribe.
- Egyptian words show up in Exodus 2:3 regarding Moses's origin story.
- The Rehkmire tomb painting shows Hebrew slaves making bricks.
- The Merneptah Stele is an ancient Egyptian stone dating back to 1213 BC. The stele references the Israelites, the earliest known archaeological reference to Israel outside of the Bible.

King David

In 1993, an inscribed ancient stone tablet was discovered in Tel Dan, providing the first historical evidence of King David from the Bible. This inscription discusses a king of Aramea's victory over two southern foes: the "king of Israel" and the "king of the House of David." This confirms the royal line of the "House of David" existed.

Esther

So far, there's no concrete evidence of Queen Esther's existence. Even though her name hasn't been found through archaeological digs, there is plenty of circumstantial evidence.

The Shushan palace is where these events occurred. Jean Perrot, a French archaeologist, devoted years to the Shushan palace archaeology site and stated the following.

"One today rereads with renewed interest the book of Esther, whose detailed description of the interior disposition of the palace of Xerxes is now in excellent with archaeological reality."

The Bible mentions Esther's husband, King Ahasuerus—yet no historical record of him exists. However, there is proof King Xerxes existed, and many believe these two kings are the same person: Ahasuerus being the Hebrew name for Xerxes.

The account of Ahasuerus in the Bible matches the facts known about King Xerxes from history, and the timeline found in Scripture coincides with events in Xerxes's life.

The annual Purim celebration, which is described in the book of Esther, is perhaps the most compelling argument for Esther's existence. Purim is a holiday with Persian origins. The word Purim means "lots," and Haman selected lots to determine the date when he had planned to exterminate the Hebrews.

Garden of Eden

Chinese is the world's oldest written language, and it consists of picture symbols which can be strung together to make words. The saying "every picture tells a story" is true in the

Chinese language. Steven Rudd and Dr. Don Patton describe how several Genesis stories match the individual characters.

The Chinese word for "ship" contains one of the characters included in the number eight. This number may be a reference to the eight survivors on Noah's ark.

Two characters for "garden" seem to have an origin from the Garden of Eden. The first symbol, tián, resembles a cross and may be interpreted as the four rivers of Eden. "A river flowed out of Eden to water the garden, and there it divided and became four rivers" (Genesis 2:10 ESV). The second character, yuán, contains two symbols within a square. The first symbol represents dust, and the second symbol represents breath and two people. This may be a reference to Adam and Eve being created from dust and breath in the Garden of Eden. Surrounding these two symbols is a square representing enclosure. This could signify that Adam and Eve were concealed within the garden.

Hannah's Agunah Situation

Hannah found herself in a distressing situation: Her husband had vanished with no proof of his death, leaving her unable to enter a new marriage. This is called "agunah" in Hebrew culture, meaning an "anchored or chained woman." In contemporary society, if a husband goes missing with no evidence of his death or if he refuses to grant a "gett," a religious divorce, a woman faces significant challenges. Both situations leave her unable to remarry, thus "chained" to a marriage she cannot escape. The challenges posed by agunah have deep historical origins and continue to fuel discussions on tradition, gender, and modernity.

Hannah waited for her husband Seth to return in the same way the church anticipates the return of Jesus.

The Cast, Real and Imagined, of *63 Hours in Hell*

Actual Biblical People
Jesus, Adam, Eve, Lamech, Cain, Noah, Shem, Ham, Lot, King Birsha, King Bera, Abraham, Balaam, Moses, Phineas, David, Benaiah, Goliath, Haman, Zeresh, Elizabeth, Barabbas, Elijah, John the Baptist

Main Characters
Hannah
Dismas
Mahway
Ramel
Benjamin

Unnamed Biblical People Named in Story
Addo (Lot's Wife)
Petunia & Puha (Lot's Daughters)
Naamach (Noah's Wife)

Nephilim
Mahway
Ohya
Hahya
Ariel

Fictional Figures (Not in the Bible)

Hannah's Family
Benjamin (Brother)
Seth (Missing Husband)
Reuben (Father)
Susanna (Mother)
Ebenezer (Grandfather)
Abigail (Grandmother)

Dismas' Family
Nathan (Father)
Mara (Mother)

Other Fictional Figures
Nava (Noah's daughter
Paltith (Lot's daughter)
Ziv (Paltith's husband)
Cecilia
Nepheg

Fallen Angels
Lucifer, Ramel, Beelzebub, Dagon, Moloch, Baal, Samyaza, Asmoday, Morax, The Hequests

Angels of God
Padel, Jachniel, Dormel, Gonael, Ayin, Malakh, Mishpat, Sariel, Samuel

DISCUSSION QUESTIONS

1) Ramel became human Liraz for love. Have you ever made an unexpected decision driven by love? Were you satisfied with Liraz's outcome at the end of the book?

2) Dismas' journey of forgiveness toward Barabbas takes an unexpected twist. Would you have forgiven Barabbas? Have you ever misjudged someone and later discovered their true story?

3) The group's journey takes us through various biblical eras, marked by distinct societal norms and challenges. How would you handle the challenges faced by women in Hannah's time? Where do you envision yourself fitting in or standing out?

4) Hannah's experiences led her to grapple with trust and abandonment issues, especially regarding the men in her life. How do you perceive these struggles influenced her relationship with God? At what point did you notice a significant shift in Hannah's faith journey?

5) Imagine a knock at your door and finding a character from the book on the other side. Which character would make you pretend you're not home? On the flip side, which one would make you eagerly open the door, and perhaps invite them in for a meal and a heart-to-heart chat? Why?

6) Which teachings of Jesus to the trapped souls in Paradise resonated with you? As the story reveals Jesus' origin story, how did it alter or enhance your perspective of his sacrifice? Were there any biblical characters or locations that stood out, or that you saw in a new light?

7) Mahway, though a demon, displayed qualities and emotions that made him relatable and even sympathetic. Were you surprised to empathize with him? Do you believe he had the capacity to love Cecilia?

8) A recurring theme in the book is God's power to turn evil into good. Do you believe all things work together for the good of those who love God? (Romans 8:28) Can you think of a time when a challenging situation became an unexpected blessing?

ACKNOWLEDGEMENTS

Dear reader, join me on a journey of gratitude. I raise my steaming latte, reflecting the warmth in my heart, to celebrate and express my sincere appreciation to those who helped shape 63 Hours in Hell.

At the core of this endeavor, my gratitude extends to Teresa Janzen and Jenn Dafoe-Turner and their vision for Abundance Books. Thank you both for making my dreams come true with your friendships and support.

To Pastor Jenn Dafoe-Turner, the skilled hands behind the cover design, your artistry stands as the visual centerpiece of our celebration.

To Esther LoPresto, an unsung hero within this tale, your perceptive eye and gentle touch brought a radiant shine to each sentence. Your "red pens of wisdom" and "pearls of wisdom" have meticulously refined and enriched every facet of the manuscript.

A special thank you to my former editors, Leilani Squires and Jeanette Windle. Leilani, your firm deadline motivated me to complete my book, and your skilled hands chiseled each chapter. Jeanette, your honest critique transformed my half-finished, messy manuscript into a cohesive substance.

Special honor to Ginger Kolbaba, my first editor, who showed me how to write. Her wisdom and memory are not just embedded here—they're its spark.

To my Chicago writing group, your critiques, positive comments, prayers, and shared passion for storytelling have been my compass in navigating the world of publishing.

A grateful nod to my beta readers—your feedback forged this story to its finest brilliance.

To all the coaches and mentors who have stood by me, both personally and professionally, your expertise has been the guiding light propelling me towards growth and many accomplishments.

To my email subscribers, you've been my digital pen pals.

To my Facebook friends, Pinterest, YouTube and Instagram followers, your likes, shares, and comments, a have been the confetti to this celebration.

To my cherished friends, whether sharing a face-to-face moment or connecting via text, your prayers have consistently been the wind beneath my wings. During periods of uncertainty and frustration, your encouragement have helped me through challenging times.

In the middle of the daily grind, my friendly dog park companions—both human and canine—provided laughter and sunshine, proving there's beauty in simple moments.

To my Page Turners book club, your friendships, food, and fun have added delight to my life.

Amid the joy of this celebration, a solemn pause is needed to remember Charlie O'Halloran. It was at his funeral, where his wife Judy initiated an altar call for salvation—I raised my hand to accept Jesus, setting me on the path to writing 63 Hours in Hell.

In this reflective moment, my heart aches to share this book with my parents, Bob and Sylvia. My mother's strong devotion to books—a passion she inspired in me—burns even brighter as her daughter becomes an author. My father wrestled with spelling, and I embraced the mantle of his personal wordsmith. Their unconditional love, infused with their unique humor, has shaped my life, and their presence are whispers within the pages of this story.

To my siblings, both bound by blood and joined through marriage, your love and support have served as the secret ingredients in this literary feast. Each of you has brought a special and enriching touch to this adventure, and I'm fortunate to have all of you in my life.

To my steadfast husband, this journey has mirrored birthing a third child, one that I labored over for a decade. While this novel doesn't bear your genetic imprint, your unwavering support and selfless sacrifices have been its lifeblood. Thank you for holding my hand and reminding me to breathe through this remarkable adventure amid the plotlines, blank stares, and burnt steaks.

To my extraordinary son and incredible daughter, I extend my heartfelt apologies for the many times my "just five more minutes to tweak this sentence" turned into a much longer pursuit. I appreciate the patience and understanding as you two graciously shared your mother with her literary offspring. My love for both of you knows no bounds.

To the Trinity—Father God, Jesus, and the Holy Spirit—with tears of gratitude in my eyes, I offer my deepest thanks for orchestrating this grand symphony. Through your divine guidance, you brought hearts and hands together to craft this story for your glory. I humbly recognize that this journey would have been impossible without your constant presence.

Now, reader thank you from the bottom of my heart for picking up this book, I thank you for your investment and time.

God Bless!

ABOUT THE AUTHOR

Susan L. Davis is a novelist and storyteller. Her transformative journey from skepticism to faith has kindled a passion for weaving narratives that resonate with audiences spanning various beliefs.

Equipped with a marketing degree from Northern Illinois University and minors in history and psychology, Susan combines academic knowledge with natural curiosity in her storytelling. She delves into the Bible and seeks archaeological evidence to breathe new life into age-old tales. Her passion for uncovering truth culminated in her debut novel, 63 Hours in Hell, a gripping narrative that vividly portrays the time between Jesus' death and resurrection.

Susan remains dedicated to her craft through participation in writing classes, workshops, and conferences. She is a respected member of both the Jerry B. Jenkins Writers Guild and the Kingdom Bloggers community. Beyond her blog, Susan is a contributor to the devotional Extinguishing the Spirit of Fear: 30 Devotions to Battle Fear and Anxiety.

Besides her literary pursuits, Susan cherishes her role as a dedicated wife and mother. She and her husband have raised a son and a daughter. They have also attained an extraordinary talent for dog training, handling everything from their six-pound Japanese Chin to one of the nation's fastest German Shepherds. Completing their family is Susan's mischievous wolf-like dog, a charming troublemaker who excels at stealing hearts and anything left unattended. These four- and two-legged companions create an energetic and heartwarming home in a quaint suburb west of Chicago.

In her signature talk, Susan reminds her audience, "When fear grips tight, let your faith burn bright." This sentiment embodies her journey of faith and her unwavering commitment to inspiring others to discover their unique talents and overcome their fear.

Connect with Susan L. Davis at susanldavis.com and embark on a quest of faith, prayer, and inspiration.